Betting
the
Scot

HIGHLANDERS
OF
BALFORSS

Betting
the
Scot

HIGHLANDERS
OF
BALFORSS

JENNIFER
TRETHEWEY

Entangled Publishing, LLC
2614 South Timberline Road
Suite 105, PMB 159
Fort Collins, CO 80525
Visit our website at www.entangledpublishing.com.

Amara is an imprint of Entangled Publishing, LLC.

Edited by Erin Molta
Cover design by Erin Dameron-Hill
Cover art from Period Images and Shutterstock

Manufactured in the United States of America

First Edition April 2018

This book is dedicated to my husband, Richard, my one true love.

Prologue

Samhain. Declan Sinclair's favorite time of year. The time when Caithness turned a patchwork of color, the time when the veil between the living and the dead grew thin, and the time when his dreams of the future were most vivid.

Declan wove his way through the forested path, whistling to himself, a brace of red grouse slung over his shoulder, his other hand tucked into the waist of his breeks. Each year, the coming of Samhain marked a magical change in everything—the land, the air, the sea, all that was precious to him. But this year—this Samhain—was different. This Samhain marked a change in Declan's future, a change in his whole life, a change for the better, to be sure.

He reached his old cottage, the one in which his older sister Margaret and brother-in-law Hamish now lived, and sniffed the air. Good. He hadn't missed supper. Declan had argued with Margaret last week and she hadn't spoken two words to him since. At first, he'd welcomed not having to engage with his fractious sibling, but hers was a loud silence filled with groans, and huffs, and sighs. Though he couldn't remember what the argument had been about, he thought he should apologize and have done with it. After all, he had big news to tell, and he wasn't certain how she would react. He hoped a gift of the grouse might smooth the way for him.

Declan knocked on the door and called out, "Margaret, it's me."

Margaret swept open the door and a rich, oniony aroma hit him squarely. Rabbit stew. His favorite.

"It's yourself," she said without enthusiasm. She wiped her hands on her apron before giving him a brisk kiss on the cheek.

Lifting the grouse like a trophy, he announced, "These are for you."

"Aren't you the clever one," she said, taking the birds. "These will do nice for tomorrow's supper." Margaret ducked into the pantry to hang the birds.

"I come to say sorry and to tell you something."

Margaret stepped back out, folded her arms, and stood stone-faced like a sentry awaiting his apology.

"I'm sorry for...arguing."

Her head quirked as if to say, *And?*

"For arguing about..." *Christ, what had they argued about?*

She unfolded her arms and stared at him incredulously. "You dinnae even remember, do you?"

"I do," he said, not liking to be challenged. Then added, "Sort of." His mind scrambled for purchase until it caught on something safe. "I was rude and insensitive and I took you for granted."

Her chin lifted, again indicating that he hadn't finished to her satisfaction.

"But I want you to know that I appreciate you and

everything you do for me, Sister."

Margaret lowered her head and leaned forward.

Jesus, what else do you want, woman?

"Och, aye!" he remembered, "and I love you dearly."

At last, Margaret strode across the kitchen floor and embraced him. All was forgiven. Now he could tell her what he truly came to say.

"Where's Hamish?" he asked.

"He went to Thurso to have the horse shod. He'll be back in time for supper. Why?"

Declan rubbed his belly and ventured a look into the pot over the fire. "Will it be soon? I'm famished."

Margaret shooed him away from the hearth. "If you found yourself a wife, you'd be home right now eating *her* food instead of pestering me."

"That's what I come to tell you." He had planned on a longer preamble, but he couldn't contain the news for another second. "I'm getting married."

A look he couldn't interpret came over her. She staggered sideways with her eyes wide, but she didn't speak.

"Did you hear what I said, Margaret?" He beamed at her and waited. Still, she made no sound.

"Margaret?"

Why isn't she saying anything?

At last she shut her eyes and clasped her hands together. "Thank the heavens." She threw her arms open, and he stepped into her fierce embrace. "Good Lord, I thought the day would never come."

When he stepped back, she was, as he had expected, weeping a bit.

"I thought you'd never find a wife." Margaret dabbed away the tears with the hem of her apron and sniffed. "Well then." She smiled up at him. "Who's it to be?"

"What?"

She laughed. "Ye loon. Who's the lucky lassie you'll be marrying? Is it Tessa Maclaren? She's a pretty one and clever, forbye."

He had to think hard. He couldn't remember who Tessa Maclaren was. "Does Tessa have yellow hair?"

"No."

"Then, nae. It's no' her. Mine's got yellow hair."

"Yellow hair, ye say?" Margaret blinked twice. "Declan," she said as though talking to a horse that might bolt. "What's the lassie's name?"

He looked at the table, the hearth, the floor—anywhere but at her. "I dinnae ken."

Her eyes closed, and she tilted her head back. "Oh Lord give me strength." She found a kitchen stool and sat down hard, then leveled a look of resignation at him. "You've been having those fool dreams again, I suppose."

Chapter One

Declan Sinclair would have called to his wife, but he didn't know her name. They hadn't met. Not yet. Nevertheless, the pretty blonde seated on the far side of the tavern *was* his wife. Or *would* be. Soon. She was the wife in his dreams, and his dreams never lied.

A steady stream of people seeking shelter from the spring storm poured into the Crown Tavern. Declan and his two cousins had stopped here for the night before heading home to Balforss. Boisterous shouts of welcome and calls for whisky echoed through the hall. The place smelled of peat smoke, wet wool, and roasted meat. He should eat his lamb stew before it got cold, but all he wanted to do was marvel at the lass seated across the room.

In his dream, his wife was surrounded by gowans, the flowers the English called daisies. Her long yellow hair hung loose down her back, and her arms spread wide to touch the tops of the white petals circling her body. Each time, the dream would end the moment before she turned to reveal her face. Now, wide awake on a rain-drenched night in this crowded tavern, he was positive the lass seated at the corner table was the same woman in his dreams, his wife.

Declan jabbed his cousin Magnus in the arm. "That's her." He chucked his chin at the object of his affection.

Magnus twisted his massive torso around in his chair. "Where?"

"The lass sittin' in the corner. The one with the yellow hair and the green frock."

"Oh, aye. What about her?"

"She's the one I dreamed. The one I'm to marry." His heart stumbled when he said the word "marry."

"Go an' boil your head," Magnus said. "You never seen that woman before in your life."

"I have in my dream. It's her. I know it."

Cousin Alex flopped into a chair next to Magnus, his fat head blocking Declan's view.

"Move, move. You're in the way." Declan flapped his hand sideways.

Rather than move, Alex looked over his shoulder. "Why? What's amiss?"

"The numpty thinks he's spotted his bride." Magnus rolled his eyes and returned to his stew.

"What? Yon bitty lass in the corner?" Alex asked.

"I said move aside. I cannae see." Declan kicked Alex under the table.

Alex feigned an unnecessary show of injury before he scooted his chair sideways. "There. Better?"

Much better. He could see her again. She wasn't a dream. She was real. Declan consumed every detail of her face—the curve of her cheek, the fullness of her lips, the freckles sprinkled on her nose. How fortunate that he should have such a bonnie wee wife.

"Why do you think she's the one?" Alex asked.

"He dreamed her," Magnus said without looking up from his bowl.

Alex turned back to the lass. "Oh. I see."

They scoffed, but Alex and Magnus believed in Declan's dreams, even if they pretended not to. He had saved their lives more than once during their time in the army. His dreams foretold future events with accuracy. Like at Salamanca. The 42nd Foot might have been outflanked by the French that day in July, but Declan had dreamed of the battle the night before, and they were ready for the enemy.

No. His dreams never lied.

Declan leaned forward with interest. His future wife's brow had crinkled with concern. What was the trouble? A woman shouldn't be left alone without a companion, without a guardian. He should go to her and offer his help, but what would he say?

He'd made two attempts at romance in the past—the kitchen maid at the Latheron Inn, and the butcher's daughter, Gertie MacDonald—but they hadn't been for him. He had all but resigned himself to being a bachelor when one night three years ago, right around the time Alex had met and wed Lucy, he'd dreamed of his wife-to-be, and everything had changed.

Declan had prepared for married life straight away by building his own whisky distillery. He'd also built a house for his future wife—not a cottage, a big house—one she would be proud of. In fact, he'd come to Wick to collect a lady's bathing tub he'd purchased from a trader who dealt in goods imported from France by way of the Netherlands.

The increased frequency of his dream had signaled their meeting was fast approaching, so it was no shock to find her sitting across the tavern from him this evening. What *did* have his heart beating in his throat was her bonnie face. He hadn't expected one so pretty and so dainty. He could tuck her inside his coat and carry her home like a kitten.

As he considered the best way of conveying his new bride back to Balforss, she turned her head his way and their gazes locked. His chest seized, and his heart forgot how to beat. But she didn't turn away. Neither could he. To his delight, there was no reproach or indifference in her blue eyes. Quite the opposite. She continued to look upon him with equal interest as if *she* had expected to discover *him* here at the Crown. Had she dreamed of him as well? Did she recognize him just as he recognized her?

She looked away for a moment. Should he call to her? Win her attention again? Then her eyes flickered back in his direction. His heart stuttered back to life, and he smiled. The ghost of a smile formed on her lips, her pretty pink lips.

A man carrying two bowls of stew approached the lassie and shattered Declan's trance. He tensed, an overwhelming sense of possessiveness taking hold of him. The man set the bowls down and took a seat at her table. Declan got his legs under him, ready to spring, but Alex laid a hand on his forearm.

"Easy, man. Bide awhile. Looks like the lass is taken."

Alex's low rumble carried with it sincere regret. Declan didn't like hearing his cousin's words. He didn't want to believe that, having finally found his bride, he'd lost her. Then, after watching the exchange between his wife and the stranger, Declan eased back into his chair.

True. To see the man and woman together, their familiar way, one might assume they were a couple. But he knew better. His dreams never lied. Hadn't his vision of his own whisky business come true? And hadn't he been right when he dreamed Alex and Lucy would have a girl child?

"That's no' her husband," he announced.

"How do you ken that?" Alex asked.

"Because *I'm* her husband," he said with newfound

certainty.

"Excuse me for pointing out the obvious, man," Magnus said. "But dinnae ye have to meet the lass first?"

• • •

Every time the tavern door opened, another blast of cold wet air swept over Caya Pendarvis. She clutched her reticule closer. It held six shillings, all she and her brother Jack had left to their names. If Mr. O'Malley didn't meet them tomorrow as planned, they might not have the means for another day's room and board.

She wished Jack would return to the table. The tavern was loud, and there were three men who kept looking at her. One dark-haired man in particular had been staring ever since she sat down. His intense gaze made something flutter inside her stomach. Didn't he know it was ungentlemanly to stare at a lady? Though she knew it was unwise for her to return his look, she found it difficult not to stare back at him.

Her heart beating at a frightening tempo, Caya tore her gaze away and searched for a glimpse of Jack's blond hair. Wherever he was, she hoped the food he purchased from the tavern maid would be edible. She was hungry. They'd been nine long days aboard the ship from Cornwall to Wick Harbour. Like most passengers, she hadn't been able to keep anything down because of rough seas. When she had mustered the courage to eat, the food had been unidentifiable.

She spotted her brother and exhaled her disquietude. "There you are."

"Lamb stew." Jack plunked two steaming bowls on the table. "Doesn't smell too bad." He pulled spoons from his coat pocket, handed one to Caya, and tucked in.

She polished her spoon on her sleeve—Lord only knew what else lived in Jack's pocket—and cast a furtive sideways glance across the room at the dark-haired man. "I'm not sure I like this tavern. Are you certain this is the one Mr. O'Malley recommended?"

Jack shoveled a large chunk of meat into his mouth, then huffed and waved a hand to cool it. Twenty-two years old and he still forgot to test his food first. The silly incident would no doubt sour his mood.

He blinked back tears of pain. "What the devil's wrong with this place? I checked the rooms like you asked. They're clean. The food's good."

She ignored his petulance and leaned in. "Don't turn around now, but there's a man at the table over there who keeps looking at me. I said, don't—"

Jack looked anyway. She winced. What if the man mistook Jack's glance as an invitation to come over to their table and chat? She didn't like talking to strangers. And everyone in Scotland was a stranger.

Eyes dull and mouth twisted, Jack said, "What would you have me do? Demand they stop looking at you?"

"No."

"Do you want me to start a fight with one of them?" Jack jerked his chin at the three Scots. "They look like ruffians. I'd probably get my teeth kicked in. Would you like that?"

"Of course not." Caya felt her own temper rise. Jack was tired and hungry. Well, so was she. There was no reason for him to take his frustration out on her. "Forget I said anything," she said, putting an end to the conversation. She knew what he was like. Arguing in the middle of this crowded tavern in front of those suspicious-looking men would be unwise.

After a silence, she prodded Jack with an innocent enough question. "Tell me again what Mr. O'Malley is like."

Jack lifted his head as if it took great effort. "I only know what the solicitor who arranged the marriage contract told me," he said wearily. "O'Malley's a herring merchant. Out at sea most of the year."

"But did the solicitor say anything about his nature? Is he a kind man?"

"Why?"

"Because I'm to marry him, of course." She reined in her frustration and added calmly, "I appreciate that you've found a suitable arrangement for me. I do. But what if, when we meet him tomorrow, he's nothing like what the solicitor said? I can still decide against the union, can't I?"

"No." Jack dug his spoon into the stew. "The contract is signed and money has exchanged hands."

"But you told me—"

"I told you what you needed to know and no more. I received half your marriage payment upon signing and I'll receive the other half tomorrow."

"I see." Caya's appetite ebbed. Somehow, everything had happened so fast, it was hard to believe it was real. She'd agreed to marry O'Malley at a time when Jack was desperate for money. When Jack's creditors had threatened him with debtors' prison, he'd used the last thing of value he had left: her. He'd met a solicitor who, for a small fee, arranged marriages. The solicitor knew a man named Sean O'Malley, a herring merchant, who would settle Jack's debts in exchange for a wife. All Jack needed to do was deliver Caya to O'Malley in Wick Harbour, Scotland, by the first week in May, and their problems would be solved.

She'd swallowed her anger and asked him, "Why? Why should I do this for you after what you've done?"

"Marry him, Caya, and I promise on Mother's grave, I will never gamble again."

She had wanted to tell him damn it and to hell, but of course he would remind her of the promise she'd made to their mother to take care of him. This was her brother, her only family. She loved him. How could she let him go to prison?

What choice did she have?

"I'm doing this because Mother and Father would wish it, and because I love you. But if you break your promise to stop gambling, we're quits, Jack. Do you understand?"

Despite her fear of traveling so far from home, despite her aversion to marrying someone she'd never met, Caya had agreed to the union. So, here she was, three weeks later, sitting in a crowded pub surrounded by rowdy Scots, waiting to meet and marry a stranger named O'Malley.

Caya felt an emptiness in her heart, a wanting for something different, something more than home and family. Was it comfort, security, love? Or something she dared not name? She glanced across the room at the man with the black hair. He was still staring. There was no hint of menace in those dark eyes, nor did he make any rude overtures. Yet, he held her captive with his unwavering gaze, so warm, so familiar, and so…full of longing. Was he yearning for the same thing as she? Her heart tripped an irregular beat inside her chest. She should turn her back, ignore the stranger. But she couldn't look away.

· · ·

Jack used the tip of his little fingernail to tease a few stray bits of lamb from his teeth. He let his gaze roam around the room. Dock workers, fishermen, farmers, and merchants, the peasantry of Scotland. He was not likely to find his own kind in this establishment. His sister clapped a hand to her heart and gasped. What had frightened her this time? She'd been on edge the entire voyage, jumping at every sound.

"What's the matter now?"

"That man. He's still staring."

"Perhaps if you stop returning his look, he'll stop staring

at you."

"I can't help it. He looks at me as if he knows me, yet I'm sure I've never met him." She tore her eyes away from the stranger. "Do you recognize him?"

Jack stole another glance at the dark Scot who was troubling his sister. Given the size of the fellow and the intensity of his gaze, he understood her concern. "Never met him before in my life. I can tell by his dress he's a man of no consequence, a Highlander of lower stock. Pay him no mind." That should assuage his sister's fears. He needed her calm when they met O'Malley in the morning. He didn't want the flighty girl spoiling the deal he had with the man.

Caya's brow loosened. "It's late. I think we should get some sleep."

"Give us a coin and go on ahead without me. I'll have a brandy before my bed."

She narrowed her eyes at him.

Devil take her. Why had he agreed to let her hold the money? "You have a few coppers left. One brandy, Caya. I'm restless."

"You promised."

He knew damn well what he'd promised. He'd promised to find her a suitable husband, but did she thank him? No. Criticism was his only compensation for all his efforts.

"One damned brandy." If he ground his teeth any harder, they might crack.

She tossed two coins on the table. "There. Enjoy yourself." Her words sounded as if she'd snipped them off her lips with garden shears.

Caya shot to her feet, triggering a sudden chain reaction. Chairs scraped and clattered as patrons rose and tensed. In an instant, the entire tavern fell deadly still like a herd of cattle sensing danger. All focused on the three Scots standing like towers of stone, hands on the hilts of their knives, glaring at Jack. What? More accusations?

A room full of wary eyes darted from Jack to the tall trio, back to Jack. He assured himself no one would dare harm a man of his station. No cause for alarm. He rose cautiously and turned to his sister, frozen in place like a rabbit. "Good night, my dear." He brushed a kiss on her cheek.

The hum of the tavern patrons resumed, the one kiss having altered the atmosphere. He waited until Caya disappeared up the stairs, then approached the monoliths. After all, one must constantly remind the lower class of their place.

"How do you do, gentlemen?" He gave the slightest bow. "My name is Jack Pendarvis. As you probably deduced, my sister and I are new to Wick."

All three giants relaxed the grip on their knives. An odd exchange took place between the redhead and the black-haired one who had been staring at Caya.

"I'm Alex Sinclair," the red-haired one said and added, "These are my cousins, Magnus and Declan Sinclair."

The one introduced as Declan said, "Pleased to meet you, Mr. Pendarvis."

Of course, he was. Commoners were always pleased when gentry like himself took an interest in them. A glimmer of an idea formed in the forefront of his mind. "Jack. Please call me Jack. I was about to order a brandy. May I join you?"

"Thanks. We'll have a wee dram," the one named Alex said.

It was cheeky of the bastard to assume Jack had offered to pay, but he had to admire the man's gall. Alex was the tallest of the three and, as he acted the spokesman, perhaps the most astute. Magnus, the fellow who resembled a bear, looked like a dimwit. Though sharp-eyed, the one called Declan was likely a simpleton as well. He'd been warned most Highlanders inherently lacked intelligence.

Jack signaled the barmaid and ordered a brandy and three whiskies. All four sat at once.

The simpleton, Declan, grinned at him like a fool. "Where ye frae?"

Was the dullard incapable of speaking proper English? "I beg your pardon?"

"Where are you from?" Alex interpreted.

"Ah. Cornwall. I've brought my sister to Wick to be married."

The simpleton's smile faded. Jack sighed. Mingling with the rabble was a mistake. He should finish his drink as soon as possible and excuse himself from their company, but the promise of easy money was too much for him.

"Who's the lucky man?" Alex asked.

"A herring merchant named O'Malley. Have you made his acquaintance?"

The three Scots shook their heads. No surprise. O'Malley was a man of worth. These fellows were most likely sheep farmers. But they did have the well-fed look of men with money—money that would be better off in Jack's pocket.

The barmaid brought their drinks, and Jack raised his glass. "Cheers."

The others raised theirs and toasted in unison. "*Slainte.*"

Jack swallowed his brandy whole. The familiar warmth settled in his belly, and a sense of satisfaction coursed through his veins. He broke into his most charming smile.

"Gentlemen, are you familiar with a card game called Napoleon?"

Several hours later, Jack had amassed a sizable stack of coins. He'd judged the Scots to be rubes, and he'd been right. It seemed that all three men, no matter how hard they tried, could not master the strategy the game required. Yet, they happily placed their bets round after round. He was careful to lose once in a while, just to maintain their interest.

The tavern room was empty but for the four of them and one sleepy barmaid leaning an elbow on the bar, her cheek sliding off her fist. He supposed he should pocket his silver and say his good nights, but the hand Magnus had just dealt him was an excellent one. His luck was running rich, so he wagered every farthing on the table.

And lost.

He couldn't believe it. He checked his cards again. An accident. A fluke. Dumb luck. Sweat broke out across his forehead. Declan, the simpleton, had won. The idiot Scot sat across from him, smiling, his eyes black as onyx. The shit actually thought he'd outsmarted him. Anger rolled up Jack's spine like the incoming tide.

"Sorry, man," Declan said, still grinning. "Looks like the game is over. You're out of coin."

"Not quite." Jack stood, finished his fifth or sixth brandy—he'd lost count—and signaled for another. "Excuse me for a minute, gentlemen." He bounded up the stairs, borrowed a candle from the hallway sconce, and slipped into the room he shared with Caya, careful not to wake her. He shook the remaining coins from her purse into his palm. Not enough. It would take him hours to get his money back with only four coppers. He needed something of greater value. He could be whole again in two, maybe three, good hands.

The bedclothes rustled, and he froze in place without breathing until he was certain Caya didn't wake. Then he opened her traveling bag and rummaged through her few belongings until he found the small wooden box with ivory inlay. Inside, their mother's jade ring, Caya's treasure. The only thing of value he hadn't already…

He tasted sour bile in his mouth and swallowed. Hell. She'd been his mother, too. The ring was half his. He had every right to use it as he pleased. Besides, he didn't intend to lose it. He'd use the glittering bauble to dazzle the Scots and win back his money. Then he'd replace the ring afterward, and Caya wouldn't be the wiser.

An hour later, blood pounded in Jack's head. He had lost both coin and ring. The tavern had become suffocating. He tore at his stock, feeling like he couldn't catch his breath. His anger at the brainless Scots drove him like a fever.

The idiot Declan leered at him again. "Thanks for the ring, man."

"One more hand," Jack growled.

"Ye dinnae have any blunt left."

"One more, damn you. All or nothing."

"What will you wager?"

He met the Scot's shaded eyes and held his gaze. A wave of uncertainty washed over Jack. He dismissed the sensation, shoving it to a dark corner of his mind. The Scot thought this game was about risk. There was no risk. There wasn't even luck involved. Napoleon was a game of skill and intelligence. The Scot possessed neither.

"I wager my sister."

That wiped the grin off the idiot's face. Magnus groaned and fell back in his chair, shaking his head.

Alex asked, "What about the man she is to marry? O'Malley?"

"Makes no difference to her. She's never met the man," Jack said. "Besides, she'll do what I tell her to do."

Magnus tilted his head. "You sure you want to wager your sister?"

"Is that even legal?" asked Alex.

"I'm her guardian. I decide whom she weds. If Declan wins, he gives me his word he'll wed my sister. If I win, I take everything. The money, the ring, *and* that distillery you mentioned."

"Dinnae do it, cousin," Magnus said.

Declan stared without blinking. Gone was the idiotic

grin he'd worn all evening, replaced with a stony countenance that Jack found unsettling. The man seemed larger, more intimidating, his eyes darker, threatening. Then the Scot nodded to the deck.

Jack drew the cards together, shuffled, and dealt. When he fanned the tattered cards with his fingers, a glorious rush of excitement coursed through his body. A winning hand. He'd known he'd win big tonight. He was unable to suppress a smile. Declan, on the other hand, looked as grim as death. Most likely, the simpleton guessed he'd already lost his whisky business. He had him where he wanted him. Scared and stupid.

"Afraid you might lose?" Jack tossed out a card. A throwaway card. A lure.

Declan won the first trick and led the second hand, just as Jack had planned.

Jack won that and the next four tricks. A tiny thrill tickled the back of his neck each time he scooped up the cards, tapped them together, and piled them in his winning stack. He was planning what he would do with his takings when he reached for the next trick and a large hand swept the cards away.

"My trick," Declan said.

Chapter Two

Declan had a split-second choice to make. He could take the next trick, play out his winning hand, and walk away with his wife. Or he could throw the game and lose. Lose his money, his whisky business, and the woman he was supposed to marry. But which was the right thing to do? Obey his conscience or follow his dream?

He tossed the seven of spades on the table. Jack reached for the cards, but Declan swept them up. "My trick."

"Wait." The cocksure Cornishy man didn't believe him, thought he'd drawn all the trump cards from Declan's hand. Big mistake.

He spread the cards for Jack to examine, then watched a sick awareness cross the man's face. Pendarvis had made a fatal miscalculation.

Declan won the next trick.

And the next.

And the next.

Magnus and Alex tossed their cards in with sounds of resignation.

"I'm out," Magnus said.

"Me, too," Alex sighed.

Declan laid down his last three cards and, in a flat voice, said, "I have all the rest."

He sat motionless during what seemed like a long silent minute, wondering why he wasn't happy. He'd won. He should be elated, and yet he got no satisfaction from the man's defeat. Declan rose on shaky legs, utterly exhausted. The stench of the sodding fool's reeking body reached him from across the table. He needed fresh air. He also needed to leave the tavern before he did physical harm to the man. What kind of sick bastard would gamble away his own sister? Then again, what kind of sick bastard would gamble for his wife?

Jack Pendarvis held his head in both his hands. He made no move, simply stared at the pile of cards lying on the table.

"I suggest you take yourself to bed," Declan said, barely controlling his rage. "You'll have some explaining to do when your sister wakes."

When he made to leave, Jack shouted to his back, "You cheated me, you filthy Scot."

Declan half turned. "Nae. You're just a very poor player."

Jack started to rise, but Declan shot him a deadly look, one that made most men think twice, and Jack dropped back into his chair.

Declan stepped into the night and breathed in the blend of smells unique to Wick Harbour: the North Sea, cured herring, baking bread, burning peat. The rain had stopped, and nighttime sounds were gradually fading in anticipation of the dawn. The streets were quiet. A faintly putrid whiff of the slaughterhouse reached him, and he swallowed hard.

What had he done? He'd won a woman—his wife—in a game of chance. Well, not so much chance as calculation. He and his cousins hadn't fleeced someone so thoroughly since their days in the army, when they'd worked their game on any soldier doaty enough to try them.

They didn't cheat. Not exactly. Ever since he was a child, Declan had had a habit of counting things—cows, sheep, fence posts. He found it kept his busy mind occupied. Later, he'd discovered that his counting, though annoying to some, came in very handy when playing cards. Just like on the battlefield, he and his cousins were an unbeatable team. Declan would keep track of the deck and discreetly signal to his cousins when to bet. Alex and Magnus had only to play the role of frustrated losers. Running their game had always been great fun.

Not so tonight. No joy in winning tonight. Tonight, he may have done something bad.

From behind him, he heard Alex's footsteps. "What's wrong?" His cousin clapped him on the back. "You should be celebrating. You've got your wife."

"Aye, but not this way. I shouldnae take her this way." Did he sound as miserable as he felt?

"How was it in your dream?"

"I dinnae ken. She was already my wife."

Magnus lumbered out of the tavern to join them. "The reekin' stoater's gone off to bed. Ye ken he and the lass will try and run for it before morning?"

"Aye, and we'll be waiting. They'll not get far," Alex said.

Declan rubbed his forehead. A pain centered behind his eyes sparked white flashes in his brain. "Jesus. She's going to be heartbroken when she finds out what her ass of a brother's done." He looked to Alex. His cousin always knew what to do in bad situations. "She'll hate me. I cannae marry her if she hates me. Shall I give her back?"

"To that bastard? Never." Alex's tone lowered to a deadly growl. "He doesnae deserve to be her brother. It's obvious he cares nothing for the lass. She needs someone to see to her safety. You're the man for her." Alex placed a hand on

Declan's shoulder and gripped hard. "If she doesnae see that right away, she will. Give her time." He released him and chuckled. "Remember how long it took Lucy to see the good in me?"

"I wouldnae use your marriage as a comfort," Magnus rumbled. "It's been three years, and Lucy still wonders why the hell she married you."

Leave it to Magnus to make Declan smile at the worst of times, but another concern killed his humor almost immediately. "What about the man she was supposed to marry? The herring merchant?"

"O'Malley? An Irishman? *Pah*." Alex waved off Declan's question. "Pendarvis said she'd never met the man and wasnae keen to marry him."

"Nae, but what if he comes looking for the lass?" Magnus asked.

"The choice is hers," Declan said. "If she wants the Irishman, I'll not stand in the way. But if it's me she chooses, I'll no' let anyone take her."

"Dinnae fash, cousin," Alex said. "You're the best man for the lass. You know it. I know it." Alex took a deep breath and looked up to a second-floor window, where lamplight flickered. "Soon enough, Miss Pendarvis will ken it, as well."

Declan did his best to shake the cloud of doubt obscuring his future. He believed in his dreams. They'd never let him down. Yet—was he doing the right thing?

Declan sighed, preparing himself for what was to come. "Magnus, will you bring the dray around? They'll be leaving the tavern soon."

"I'll cover the back door," Alex said, and disappeared into the shadows.

Alone for the moment, Declan lifted his face to the pink and yellow predawn sky. "Lord, you ken me for a sinner, and I wouldnae ask you for my sake. But for the sake of the lass, dinnae let her heart break when she finds out what Jack's done."

• • •

Caya rubbed her eyes and blinked. Her brother, fully dressed in his overcoat and beaver hat, was packing his belongings at a furious rate. "Jack? What are you doing?"

"Get up. Get your things together. We're leaving."

She sensed an urgency in her brother's clipped words. Very unlike him. She sat up in bed. "It's not even light out. What's your hurry?"

Jack stopped what he was doing. In the dim light of the oil lamp, she saw the features of his face pulled into a grimace. "Get dressed. Now." He jerked his head toward the door. "And be quiet about it."

"Is Mr. O'Malley here? Has something happened? You have to tell me why—"

He reached down and yanked her from the bed. Eyes wild and teeth bared, he shook her violently by the shoulders. "I said get dressed now."

Breathless and rattled from Jack's rough treatment, Caya found her gown and went behind the dressing screen. She tied the closures of her gown with shaking hands and stepped into her boots. Something bad had happened. She thought back on last night and her argument with Jack. They'd quarreled about his drinking. God, no. She reached for her reticule and emptied the contents onto the bed. Her breath came in short, desperate gasps. No coin. He'd taken the last of their money. Nothing. They had nothing.

"Jack, what have you *done*?"

He stood at the open chamber door, holding her cloak in one hand and his bag in the other. Guilt swept across his face and then vanished. "You were right about those men."

His voice sounded brittle. "I overheard them talking. They planned to kidnap you. I used the money in your purse to purchase our safe escape. Now come. Quickly." He held out her cloak.

How could she have been so stupid? Those men, those Scots, the man with the dark eyes—he had planned to kidnap her, and she'd returned his look. Dear Lord, she had encouraged his evil plan.

"Hurry," Jack rasped.

Caya swirled her cloak around her shoulders and collected her bag, her mind in a muddle of panic and confusion.

Jack crept down the stairs and peeked into the tavern room. She hesitated at the top of the stairs. Doubt prickled the back of her neck. The past four years had taught her to believe only half of what her brother told her. Was he lying to her now?

He motioned impatiently. "The louts must still be abed."

What should she do? He looked frightened. Concern for her brother warred with her common sense. Yes, Jack was a liar and a scoundrel, but he would never risk her life. They were the only family the other had. What else *could* she do but follow? She tiptoed down the stairs to her brother's side.

He gave her a reassuring pat on the shoulder. "Follow me."

A dim gray light streamed through the slats in the window shutter. Other than the curled form of a girl sleeping by the smoldering hearth, the tavern room looked empty. Jack wove through the scattered tables and chairs. Finding it hard to see, she held on to his coattails for guidance. His pace quickened, and she scurried to keep up with him.

He opened the front door a crack and peered out.

"Do you see anyone?" she whispered.

"No. It looks safe. Stay close." He threw open the door and pulled her into the chilly predawn, then halted. Her forward momentum sent her thumping into his rigid back.

"What is it?" She clutched at her brother's arm for support.

The figure of a tall man stepped in front of them and crossed his arms. She could just make out his features. The dark-haired one from last night. Then the red-haired man stepped out from behind the building and joined his fellow Scot.

Too late. They were caught. These men would take her, kidnap her. And her brother—oh God. Would they kill Jack? She tried to scream but couldn't catch her breath.

"Stay back or I'll call for help," Jack said. She recognized her brother's attempt to sound in command. She also detected the fear and uncertainty in his tone. Had the Scots heard it, too?

"Did you tell her?" the dark one asked.

Jack said nothing at first, then whispered, "Get back inside, Caya."

"Did you tell your sister what you did?" he asked again. The rangy Scot didn't look dangerous so much as he looked angry.

An uneasiness crept into Caya's consciousness. She searched her brother's face. "What's he talking about, Jack?"

He tried to push her back into the tavern. "Don't listen to him. He means to trick you. Get back inside."

The dark one shouted, "Tell her, you coward, or I will."

The light had grown brighter in the few agonizing minutes they'd been standing in the yard. She detected a rare emotion on her brother's face—shame.

"Jack?" she said, her voice a soft tremolo. "Tell me what you've done."

His face crumpled.

Dread settled on her shoulders. "Have you gambled away the last of our coin?"

He nodded.

She opened her travel bag and searched. "Give them Mother's ring and tell them to leave us alone." She paused when her brother said nothing and asked in disbelief, "You lost Mother's ring, too?"

Jack didn't move. Fear, like a dark bird of prey, dug its talons into the flesh on her back. She glanced at the two Scots. By the looks on their faces, Jack had done something much worse than lose their valuables.

She dropped her bag. "What happened?" she demanded, taking a few challenging steps toward the dark Scot.

He unfolded his arms and let his shoulders fall. He had a plaintive look in his eyes as though he was about to tell her someone had died.

"Lass, I'm sorry." His voice was gentle. If she weren't so terrified, she might like the sound. "Your brother wagered your hand and lost."

Wagered her? Had she heard him right? "No." She shook her head and backed away. The man was playing a cruel joke. "No, he wouldn't."

The Scot's brow buckled as if pity for her caused him pain.

She opened her mouth to scream, but only weak huffing sounds came out. She turned back to Jack, her brother, her blood, her only family. Oh God, she would be sick. A groan escaped her that sounded more animal than human. Caya staggered toward Jack and swung a fist, striking him in the head as hard as she could. Again and again and again. The pent-up rage at her brother's selfish ways exploded in a pinwheel of violent blows.

He covered his head. "It was a joke. I never meant it. Stop. You're hurting me."

"A joke? A joke?" she screamed.

Strong arms wrapped around her from behind and lifted

her away from Jack, as if she weighed nothing.

"Here now," the man attached to the arms rumbled. "You'll hurt yourself."

She struggled. "Let me go." She eased free of his arms, almost regretting the loss of their surprising warmth.

"Catch your breath," he said.

The other man, the red-haired Scot, held out a silver flask. "Take a sip. It'll help calm you."

She snatched it away, took a greedy gulp, wheezed from the force of the spirits, and returned the flask. Whatever she'd swallowed had the intended effect. She was remarkably revived. Caya eyed the dark Scot. She could tell he didn't think this was a joke. He seemed more troubled by her situation than her damned brother. Jack's indifference was almost worse than the deed that had sealed her fate. As usual, her brother cared more about himself than what he'd done to her.

She dashed away tears and straightened. "You won the wager?" she asked the tall Scot.

"Aye." His response sounded like an apology.

"I'm your—" She searched for the right word. "Prize?"

The man was speechless for a moment.

"I'm your property now? What, your cook, your housekeeper? Or will you have me work the field?"

"No," he said, his voice almost a whisper. "I've won the honor of marrying you." His Adam's apple rolled up and down his corded neck. Caught off guard, his emotions played across his open face for her to read. Unmistakable longing.

She examined his words one at a time. *The honor of marrying you.* Caya's world went still. Last night, lying in her bed, thoughts of the mysterious dark Scot had led to guilty fantasies. She had imagined him touching her, holding her, kissing her. She had even gone so far as to picture what it would be like to lie next to him, naked. Feel his breath in her ear. Feel the weight of his body cover hers. Her fantasies had grown so passionate they'd frightened her. She'd locked them safely away in her mind because she knew if she dared peer inside, her desire might escape, run wild, and ruin her. Did she wake this morning to discover her fantasies about this man were destined to play out? Was this punishment for her sinful thoughts?

Or was this man offering her a *choice*? A real choice between Jack's dubious bargain with O'Malley or his folly with this man, this Highlander.

The sound of a horse and wagon rattling toward them caught her attention. The giant bearded Scot drove the rig to the front of the tavern and stopped. A large wooden crate secured by ropes lay in the open bed of the dray like an oversized coffin.

She addressed the dark Scot again. "Wh-what's your name?"

"Declan Sinclair of Balforss."

Without thinking, she made the reflexive response, "How do you do?" and bobbed him a shaky curtsy. "Do you have a house?"

"Oh, aye," he said, his face lighting up with a genuine smile.

"And will I be mistress of the house?"

"Of course."

Perhaps it was the spirits, but Caya nearly laughed at the absurdity of the moment. She was supposed to meet and marry a stranger today. What was the difference between this stranger and the next? She fought back mounting hysteria and swung around to her brother.

Jack's look was one of utter incredulity. "You can't leave me."

For a moment, she saw the brother she'd once loved and cared for—the sweet, dirty-faced boy with angelic curls who would cling to her when he was afraid—and she was tugged in his direction. Then the Scot spoke in his low silky burr, the words rolling off his tongue. "You have my word, we will marry, and you need nae be frightened ever again."

Mr. Sinclair's gaze didn't waver. There was no shift in his brown eyes to indicate a lie. The man reached out an open hand, large and powerful—not a demand—a gentle, beseeching gesture.

"You don't have to marry this man, Caya. He can't make you," Jack protested.

Caught between them, she sensed a tension inside her body, a tightening of the thread that connected her to her brother, a pulling in both directions. Jack needing her. This stranger *wanting* her.

Mr. Sinclair tilted his head toward Jack. "You can stay here with a brother who cares so little for you he'd gamble with your life. Or you can come with me, and I will see you treated with all the respect due a lady and a wife. It's your choice, lass."

Choice. When had she ever been given a choice? One or two spoons of sugar in her tea? The blue or the green gown? Never a meaningful choice. Never a real choice about her future. Her father had made those, and then her brother. But now, standing here, in this instant, she had to make a decision that would change her life forever. A choice between brother or stranger. The wastrel who would gamble her life away or the big Scot who looked as though he might perish if she didn't take his hand. The devil she knew or…the devil?

"Come awa' wi' me, lass." The sweet longing in Mr. Sinclair's voice was too much to resist.

"Goodbye, Jack. Good luck."

"No!" Jack shouted. "I forbid it."

Caya found the steely edge of her nerve. "Brother, you broke your promise. You gambled with my life and lost.

Perhaps you have no honor left, but I do."

"What about Mr. O'Malley?"

"O'Malley is your problem," she said. "You and I are quits."

He charged toward her, and when Sinclair stepped in his way, her heart jumped. How absurdly tragic that a stranger had to protect her from her own brother.

"Caya," Jack wailed. "O'Malley will come today. If you're not here, he'll kill me."

Humiliating. Why couldn't he act like a man just this once? "I thought there was no way for you to hurt me more than you already had. I was wrong." Grief struck her, sudden and sharp. "I'm done cleaning up your messes. This is the last debt I will ever pay for you." Her voice broke, and yet she didn't cry. She had no tears left for Jack.

Jack got to his knees. "Please, Caya."

"Stand up, ye silly wee man," Mr. Sinclair said. "Say farewell to your sister."

He stood, wiped his face on his sleeve, then straightened his jacket. His upper lip curled into a nasty sneer. "You'll regret this. All of you will live to regret this."

Mr. Sinclair's right hand shot out and grabbed Jack by the throat, toppling his ridiculous beaver hat to the ground. She flinched at the Scot's brutal reaction. Was he going to break her brother's neck?

The Sinclair man growled in Jack's ear. "Say goodbye to your sister." Then he released him as though he were casting away something offensive. The man was a complete stranger to her, yet he insisted on a civil parting, in spite of her brother's behavior.

Jack approached her, rubbing his neck. "Goodbye, sister." He hugged her, not an affectionate embrace, but an angry squeeze. He let his arms drop and said, "Sorry." By the tone of his voice, he didn't mean it.

Mr. Sinclair collected her bag and placed it in the wagon. As though cradling something precious, he lifted her into the seat next to the huge bearded man. "This is Magnus. He looks dangerous, but he'll no' bite."

A set of gleaming white teeth flashed through Mr. Magnus's burly beard. He draped a carpet over her lap. "To keep you warm, miss." One snap of the reins and the wagon rolled forward.

It all happened so fast, so very fast. There was no time to doubt herself or be afraid, no time to ask where they were headed or what awaited her when they arrived. Her life had changed with the turn of a card. One day the daughter of a Cornish landowner. The next, affianced to an Irish merchant. The next, lost in a card game to a Scot. Tears rolled down her cheeks. Not for the loss of Jack, but for the loss of who she was, who she would never be again. As they drove away, she glanced back at her brother, the last touchstone to her old life.

Dear Lord, have I made the right choice?

• • •

Jack spat on the ground. Ruined. That idiot Scot had ruined him. And his sister, the trollop, had run off with the criminal, leaving him with nothing. *Nothing.* He snatched his crumpled hat from the ground and knocked it back into shape.

"Filthy Scot."

He should have known. He should have suspected something was up between those two the way they were ogling each other last night. Caya had a face as plain as a plate. No surprise she would follow the first man who showed interest.

"Ungrateful bitch."

He had been robbed, cheated. What was he to do now? Alert the magistrate? To accuse those Scots of cheating at cards without a witness would gain him nothing but skeptical looks, perhaps even the humiliation of having his word doubted. And what would O'Malley do when he arrived and found his betrothed missing? He'd ask him to return his money—money Jack did not have.

He needed to think, and to do that, he needed a drink. Back inside the tavern, he removed the mop cap covering the sleeping barmaid's face and swatted her with it until she woke.

"Get me a brandy."

The girl staggered to her feet. "Wha—"

"Are you deaf? I said get me a brandy. Now."

The stale, yeasty smell hanging in the air only sharpened his need for a drink. He watched as the barmaid went behind the bar and retrieved a half-empty bottle of brandy. He took the proffered spirits without a word, collected his traveling bag, and returned to his sleeping chamber above stairs.

The first swallow felt like a lover's embrace, soothing his nerves, loosening his muscles, easing the pain in his head. The second swig brought him perfect clarity. He saw in the dark glass bottle the reflection of a selfish, deceitful, shame-filled man. It took the rest of the bottle to stamp out lucidity and allow him blessed sleep.

Chapter Three

Declan kept his horse, Gullfaxi, to an easy walk down the narrow highway toward Balforss. He twisted in his saddle to check on the lass seated next to Magnus in the dray.

"Will you cease your footerin'," Alex said, riding alongside Declan. "That's the dozenth time you've turned to look at her in the last hour. The lass is safe with Magnus. She'll no' disappear."

"I'm not fashed about that," he snapped. A sleepless night had frayed his patience. "What'll happen when we tell your mam and Lucy we won her playing cards?"

Alex groaned. "Oh. Aye. Lucy'll be furious I was gambling. She'll skin me alive."

Declan wanted to throttle his cousin. "I couldnae care less about your skin, man. What about Miss Pendarvis?" He winced. "I ken she's a proud woman. She'll be humiliated."

His cousin looked momentarily chagrined. Then, by way of apology, he offered, "Lucy and my ma will be kind to her. They'll understand. I'm sure of it."

"Aye, but I fear the lass will feel the sting of it even so."

He rubbed his eyes. The unreal events of last night were having a belated effect on his reason. "Alex. Be honest with me. Did I do the right thing? I was going to let Jack win back the ring. But when he wagered his sister, I got angry. I took her out of spite. Was that wrong?"

"When he wagered his sister, he showed himself for a bastard. She's better off. Even she kens it. The lass left with you willingly."

"It's no' turning out like I thought."

"What do you mean?" Alex asked.

"I thought my wife would be happy to see me when we found each other. I thought maybe she dreamed of me, too, but she didnae seem to know me. And now I ken she's afraid of me."

"You've got to give her time. She'll come 'round," Alex assured him.

"Aye, but look at her. She's miserable. I cannae stand to see her unhappy."

Alex leaned back and examined him critically, one eyebrow cocked up, the other arrowed down. Then his jackass cousin laughed like a loon.

"What's so funny?"

Alex chuckled, "You love her."

He opened his mouth to object, but the words died on his tongue. Love? Not possible. Want, yes. Need, yes. Desire, most definitely. But love?

Alex pointed at him. "If Lucy were here, she'd tell you to close your mouth lest you swallow flies."

He made a few skeptical sputters. "*Pah*. It's impossible to love someone so soon. I met her only hours ago."

Alex shook his head. "Nae. It takes less than that to fall for a woman. I should know."

A few minutes passed without conversation. The creak of the wheels and rattle of the crate on the flat wagon bed drowned out birdsong and bleating sheep. Alex yawned so wide his jaw cracked, and then he scratched his armpit contemplatively. How did his cousin fail to share the urgency of his situation?

Declan considered his own appearance for a moment. Dust-covered trousers, rumpled coat, a stained and frayed shirt without a stock. He swiped a hand down the bristles on his cheek. He needed a wash and a shave, too. Ah, well. It could be worse. It could rain.

As if in answer to his thought, a dark cloud boomed an angry portent in the distance. He cast a resentful glance at the heavens.

"*Tàirneanach*," he grumbled. Thunder. Damn.

"Do you think God wants aught to do with you and Miss Pendarvis?"

"Aye. He taunts me this day. Winning her was too easy. He means to make the task harder for me."

Alex leaned toward him, his face shining with good humor. "Try not to take the thunder personally, man. The storm might just as easily be meant for some other poor sod."

His stiff, cold cheeks creased with a smile for Alex. With any luck, the rain would hold until after they reached Balforss. He twisted in his saddle and glanced back at his intended. No change.

"Caya," Declan said reverently.

"What?"

"Her brother called her Caya. You ever heard that name before?"

"Nae." Alex shrugged.

"Must be a Cornishy name. Sounds pretty. Caya. I wonder what it means."

Alex released a long sigh and then uttered a disgusted, "That's it." He held up a hand and stopped his horse. Magnus pulled the dray's draft horse to a halt as well.

"Why are we stopping?" Declan cast a worried look Caya's way.

"Trade places with Magnus," Alex ordered.

"What? No." He had asked Magnus to ride with Caya for a reason. Magnus was kind and didn't have difficulty making polite conversation with women. Declan wouldn't know what to say to her, and he certainly wouldn't know what to do about her unhappiness.

"There's another three hours before we reach Balforss. Best you speak with the lass before we see my ma and da."

"But she's upset." Declan kept his voice to a low rasp.

"Of course, she is. She's probably scairt to death." Alex matched his volume but didn't hide his disgust. "You havenae told her anything. Nae doubt she's wondering what's to happen and imagining the worst."

His cousin was right. He'd been a coward not to talk to her.

Alex called out to Magnus, "We'll stop here and water the horses." They dismounted, and Alex pulled him aside. "Mind you, give her an opportunity to take care of her personal needs."

He stepped back, shocked and embarrassed. "How do I ken if she needs to…erm?"

Alex huffed and shifted his weight to the other foot. "Do *you* have to piss?"

"Aye."

"That's your cue," Alex said, jabbing a finger into the middle of Declan's brow on each word. Then Alex led their horses to a stream a few yards away, leaving him standing alone in the road, rubbing his forehead.

Magnus jumped down off the dray and grabbed a water bucket from the back.

As he passed him, he asked in a low voice, "Has she said anything?"

"Not a word." Magnus continued on toward the burn without stopping.

Declan approached the dray slowly, gathering his courage along the way. How the hell was he going to ask her if she needed to piss? When he reached her side, she brushed the hood of her cloak away. Between the sunlight in her hair and the blue of her eyes, he was transfixed for a moment, pinned to the earth and speechless.

At last, he said, "Are you well, Miss Pendarvis?"

"Yes, thank you, Mr. Sinclair."

He felt himself flush from his boots to the roots of his hair when she spoke to him. He reached both hands up, an offer to help her down.

She slipped into his embrace easily, his big hands circling her waist. She weighed less than a full sack of barley. He would have to be careful not to injure her.

"Erm. If you come this way, I'll show you a spot where you can have your privacy."

"Thank you." She made a pretty curtsy.

He bowed awkwardly and turned his head away, worried she might see how uncomfortable he was. Once Miss Pendarvis was tucked behind a patch of raspberry bushes, he walked back toward the road and waited.

When she returned, he asked, "Would you mind if I rode with you a while?"

She gave a slight shake of her head. Not an enthusiastic welcome but neither did she seem averse to his company.

After the horses drank their fill and everyone had a turn behind the raspberry bushes, Magnus and Alex mounted up, and Declan helped her aboard the dray. He snapped the reins, and the brawny draft horse clomped forward. Each time the wagon jolted and rocked, her wee body bumped against his, a sensation that both pleased and disconcerted him.

He chanced a keek at Caya. How had her bottom lip

become stained red? Ah, yes. She'd eaten a few of the newly-ripened raspberries from the bush. That must be why she smelled so sweet. His mouth watered. He swallowed and looked down. The lassie clasped her hands so tightly her knuckles had turned white. She was scared. Knowing she was afraid caused him physical pain, a sharp pang just below his left ribs. He had to ease her worry, if not for her, for his own comfort.

"There's naught to be afraid of, lass. You'll stay at Balforss. It's a fine house. The other ladies there will like you. I know they will."

She said nothing, kept her gaze on the road, back straight, hands twisting in her lap.

He plowed on, desperate to assuage her fear. "I'm building another house. It's almost finished. Almost ready. I even made a special room for you. A room of your own. To do what ladies do in private. I ken ladies like a bathing tub." He turned and motioned behind them to where the wooden crate took up most of the room on the wagon bed. "That's a bathing tub I bought for the house while I was in Wick." His eyes darted sideways to see what effect his words had.

She stared straight ahead in concentration.

"It's imported. From France. It's called a lady's boudoir bathing tub. Made out of zinc and painted a pretty green with flower designs—"

"Stop the wagon. Stop the wagon now," she shouted.

"Did I—"

"Stop the wagon or I'll jump."

He pulled the dray to a creaking halt. Alex and Magnus turned back, their heads cocked at a questioning angle. He shrugged helplessly.

She reached for her traveling bag, tossed it on the ground, and attempted to leap from the dray.

"Wait. Let me help you."

She hit the ground and crumpled to her knees. He scrambled out after her and tried to help her to her feet, but she shook him off. In a huff, she collected her bag and walked back in the direction of Wick. What had he said to trigger her anger?

"Did I say something wrong?"

No answer.

Declan followed at her heels. "Does the bathing tub not please you?"

Still, no answer.

"Is it the O'Malley man? The one you're promised to? Do you want me to take you to him?"

"Is something amiss, Declan?" Alex called.

He waved his meddling cousin off, then hurried to catch up with his Cornishy fiancée. "I'm sorry. Whatever I've done or said, I'm sorry, but you cannae go off on your own. It's no' safe. At least let me take you—"

Miss Pendarvis whirled around, her eyes flashing. "You lied to me, Mr. Sinclair. I would rather scrub floors than lower myself to work in a house of…of…of that nature."

"What nature?" he asked, baffled by her angry outburst.

"A house of…fallen women." She lifted her chin, spun, and continued her march.

He hurried to her side again. "Why would you think a thing like that?"

She kept her angry pace, spitting out her words with each step. "All you've talked about is houses with private rooms and French ladies and bathing tubs. What else am I to think?"

Realization dawned, and Declan paused in the middle of the road, mortified. His legs had stopped working. Words backed up in his throat. She thought he ran a bawdy house. He could kick himself for not explaining things better. He had to set her straight, but all that came out were half-finished words. Her assumptions about his moral fabric had rankled him so completely he was speechless. Finally, he forced a complete word out of his mouth in a shout.

"Stop!"

She ignored him and walked on, back stiff, head held high. Jesus, she was proud.

"I said stop," he shouted with authority.

Most grown men would have hesitated at the sound of his voice, but the wee bizzum kept moving.

Finally, he hollered, "I've never even seen the inside of a brothel. My sister would kill me!"

Alex and Magnus laughed. He would murder them later. At the moment, all he cared about was making things right with Caya.

She slowed her march until she came to a stop.

He took several steps toward her, so he needn't shout. "I built the house for you. You and me. No one else," he said in a voice he used to gentle horses.

She faced him. Her eyes narrowed, seeming to search his for the truth. "That's ridiculous. You just met me. How could you build a house for me?"

"For my wife. We are to marry. I gave my word." A long silence passed. Still she made no move. He ached to close the distance between them but didn't dare make any sudden movement. "I was trying to tell you before...you'll live at Balforss with the laird's family until the wedding. You'll be well cared for. Treated like the lady you are. If, after we reach the house, you change your mind, I'll take you back to your brother. But for now"—he straightened—"you're coming with me."

She made a *pssht* sound. Then she turned her chin away and lowered her gaze. He'd seen his sister Margaret do that when she was miffed about something but didn't want to admit she was wrong. He held his breath. She kicked a stone with the toe of her dainty boot. Some of the tension seemed to leave her body.

He wiped beads of sweat from his brow with the back of his hand. It shouldn't be this complicated. Collecting his wife should be a simple matter of taking her home with him, wedding her, and bedding her. Why was it proving so difficult?

He moved toward her, one careful step at a time, like stalking a deer, so as not to frighten her into running again. He took the bag from her small, pale hand. She didn't resist. Then he walked back toward the wagon, praying to God she would follow.

. . .

Caya turned his words over in her head. *I built the house for you. You and me. No one else.* He was so earnest, so in need of her understanding. But what did he mean?

"You just met me. How could you build a house for me?"

"For my wife," he'd said. "We are to marry. I gave my word."

His words scorched the back of her neck. *My wife. We are to marry.* For an instant, the kiss, the one she'd imagined last night, came back to her, the memory of it, soft and searing. The box containing her most wicked fantasies threatened to pop open and she quickly sat on the lid.

Who was this man?

Sinclair. His name was Sinclair. And he was not, thank God, a trader in flesh. He stood before her, still talking, saying things, things that seemed important to him, but the words held no meaning for her. His voice soothed her, and just like last night, his soft brown eyes looked directly into hers as if they'd met before.

"You're coming with me," he said.

Although his tone was kind, she didn't like the demand.

He moved closer to her. Slowly. Carefully. He was tall. Very, very tall. She noticed the great weight of her traveling bag only after he took it from her. She half expected him to capture her hand and pull her to the wagon. Instead, Mr. Sinclair returned to the wagon and waited for her.

Had she misunderstood his words because *she* was guilty of thinking wicked thoughts? Because, if she was honest with herself, choosing the dark and dangerous Scot had answered her most secret fantasy: to be desired by a powerful man, a man of strength and intelligence who could protect her from all the ills in the world. Caya set aside those thoughts to examine them when she could be alone.

"I'm coming," she said, moving toward the wagon. "But not because you ordered me to."

When she reached him, he asked, "Are you coming because you want to?"

"Because I choose to," she snapped back. She also chose to ignore the pleased look on his face.

For the third time, he helped her aboard the wagon. For the third time, she breathed in his scent. Not an acrid sweat like her brother nor the unwashed stink of the sailors. Mr. Sinclair smelled like saddle leather and road dust—earthy. Was he a farmer, then? Like her father? She would like to marry a farmer.

He was nothing short of decorous, his touch light and polite. Even so, she felt the man's strength. She had seen him come close to violence. He could have snapped her brother's neck with one hand. Yet, Mr. Sinclair had also been kind, soft-spoken, even gentlemanly. As he was being right now.

He motioned to the other Sinclair men. "Ride on. We'll catch you up." Then he climbed onto the wagon beside her. He fixed his gaze on the reins in his hand. "I need to know… do you want me to take you to O'Malley? If you have your heart set on the man, I'll understand. I dinnae want to marry someone who prefers another."

Her heart? Was he making fun of her? She'd never even met Mr. O'Malley. Her brother had made the arrangements, a small payment up front, the balance upon delivery, like a load of goods. She had been suspicious of her brother's bargain all along. Jack's business negotiations had all been failures. Why would the one with O'Malley be any different? And what kind of man would purchase a wife sight unseen?

"I ken you're sad," Mr. Sinclair said. "I'd do anything to change the way things happened."

His kind words left her breathless. She managed to say, "I appreciate your concern, but I don't wish to marry Mr. O'Malley."

He smiled at her. Again. A heartbreakingly sweet smile. One she couldn't ignore. She smiled back at him as if she had no power to resist.

"Och, I nearly forgot." He reached inside a pocket of his coat and pulled out her mother's jade ring. "This belongs to you."

She stopped herself from snatching the ring from his hand. "No. It's yours. You won it."

"Aye. I did. And now it's mine to give to you." He placed the ring in her hand and closed her fingers around it. "There now," he said, the tone of his voice and the two words conveying the understanding that everything was settled and she had nothing more to worry about, ever.

He cleared his throat and arranged his face into its earlier sober condition. "Erm…My family will want to ken how you came to be with us. They'll accept you no matter what I tell them. But I dinnae want to cause you any more pain. So, I leave it to you. What would you have me say?"

Again, Caya was momentarily stunned by Mr. Sinclair's offer. The consideration he afforded her was beyond anything she'd ever witnessed between men and women.

"There's no point in making up a story," she said. "I doubt any other explanation would suffice."

He smiled again, this time with an exhale of relief. "As you wish."

Without thinking, she barked out the question that had plagued her for miles. "Why did you do it?"

Mr. Sinclair tilted his head. "Do what?"

"Why did you accept my brother's wager? Why did you gamble for me?" Her body shook with suspicion and anger. She needed to understand why any man would do such a thing.

"I wanted you, of course." He seemed confused by her question.

"What did you wager in return?"

His soft brown eyes never wavered from her gaze. As if his answer should have been plain from the start, he said, "Everything."

She didn't know how she expected him to respond, but it certainly wasn't that. So used to Jack's lies, she'd almost forgotten what truth sounded like. Did Mr. Sinclair speak the truth? Did he really want her?

He dipped his head. With a sharp whistle and a snap of the reins, the wagon rattled forward.

. . .

Jack woke, brutal hands dragging him half-conscious from his bed and out into the hallway.

"Release me at once." He yanked himself free. "How dare you—"

"Get going." The fearsome-looking man shoved at his back repeatedly. Jack tripped down the stairs, stumbled through the tavern room, and lurched out of the tavern into the daylight. His tormentor gave him one final push that sent him sprawling facedown in the dirt. He got to his knees and squinted through the sunshine at a man, a ruffian, with a musket cradled in his arm. Standing to his right, a slightly better dressed man stared down at him with a malicious grin.

"Who are you?" Jack asked, bringing a hand up to shield his eyes. "What is the meaning of this?"

From behind him, Jack's assailant grabbed him by the back of his stock, making it difficult for him to breathe.

"You'll be owing me a wife, Mr. Pendarvis," the gentleman said with an Irish lilt. He gestured to the man holding his collar. "Mr. Boyle here says she's not within. Where is she?"

Shit. O'Malley. Though Jack had only a vague recollection of his exchange with O'Malley's solicitor—it had been late at night, he'd had much to drink, and he'd lost quite a bit of money at cards—this man appeared nothing like the gentleman described. Sean O'Malley looked more like a highwayman than a herring merchant.

Mr. Boyle struck him on the side of his head. "Answer the man."

Jack rubbed at the searing pain in his right ear. "She's—" He coughed and made a motion indicating he was choking to death.

O'Malley signaled Mr. Boyle to release Jack's collar. When he did, Jack fell forward on all fours. Mr. Boyle and the man with the musket laughed.

He moved his tongue around the inside of his cotton-lined mouth, seeking a drop of saliva with which to lie. "She's run off with three Scotsmen."

"Is that what you say?" O'Malley's tone implied he didn't believe him. "And who might these Scotsmen be?"

He got to his feet and brushed himself off. How dare the man not believe his lie? "They were Sinclairs."

This time all three laughed uproariously. The audacity. If Jack were not at such a financial disadvantage, if he were at home among his equals, instead of here in this disreputable country, he'd have these men placed in irons with a snap of his fingers.

O'Malley wiped his eyes and recovered himself. "Ya don't even know where ya are, do ya? This is Sinclair land, fool. Half the people living in this part of Scotland bear the name Sinclair."

"They were Sinclair of...of...of—" Jack searched his foggy mind. What had the red one said? I'm Alex Sinclair of—damn. "One was named Alex Sinclair."

"I'll ask ya to shut your filthy hole and quit your lyin'. The lass inside told us ya lost the woman in a game of cards, and I'm not about to chase all over the countryside after those billy boys. I'll settle for a return of my money."

Jack cursed under his breath. He'd wring the barmaid's skinny neck the next chance he got, the slattern. But first, he would deal with his most immediate threat, O'Malley. Best to stall for time. Get the man in a better mood, and maybe he could find his way out of this.

"Perhaps you'd like to join me inside, and we can discuss our business over breakfast."

"It's afternoon, Pendarvis." O'Malley gave him a derogatory shake of the head.

Insufferable. The man had no right to treat a gentleman of his standing with contempt. He chastised himself for his own poor judgment. Absolute foolishness on his part for dealing with an Irishman. Everyone knew the Irish lied and cheated whenever possible.

"Luncheon then. They serve a delicious lamb stew."

"If you don't have the woman, and you don't have the five quid I advanced ya, I'll take you instead. I lost a member of my crew to typhoid last month. I need a new hand." O'Malley signaled Boyle. "Take him. Jiggity-jig. Make it quick."

Jesus. He'd rather go to debtors' prison than spend a

lifetime pressed into service aboard a ship. Before Boyle could grab him by the collar again, he shouted, "Wait. I have the money. I have it hidden in my room."

O'Malley signaled his man to stop and said with complete civility, "Mr. Boyle, accompany Mr. Pendarvis above stairs and retrieve my five quid."

Boyle followed Jack up the stairs so closely he felt the man's hot breath on the back of his neck. In less than a minute, he would discover his deception. Jack's mind raced through ways to escape his predicament. He had nothing with which to bribe the man, and there was little chance he could overtake or outrun him. He could risk jumping out the nearest window, but those long, muscled arms would catch him before he got the damn thing open.

"Just in here," Jack said, opening his bedchamber door.

A light fragrance lingered. It was that of his sister. For an instant, he regretted having lost her. Shame at his behavior last night threatened to get the better of him. Just as quickly, rage fired his determination to escape this bloody mess, find his sister, and punish her for deserting him. It was her fault he was in this position.

Jack glanced around the room. "Ah. Yes. I've hidden the money behind a loose brick."

Boyle grunted an acknowledgment.

Jack reached into the fireplace and fumbled around up inside the flue, pretending to search while Boyle watched him, dull-eyed. "It's here. Somewhere. Ah. The damn thing is stuck." He pointed to his bag lying on the floor behind Boyle. "Hand me that dumfuzzle."

Boyle cocked his head. "Eh?"

"The dumfuzzle," Jack said, encouraged by the man's confusion. "The *dumfuzzle*," he repeated, still pretending to fumble with the brick inside the chimney.

Boyle turned to look in the direction in which Jack

pointed. "Where?"

"Right there. The silver thing—no, not there. Inside the bag."

When Boyle stooped to search the bag, Jack snatched up the fireplace iron with two hands and brought it down on the man's bald head. The hooked point of the poker sank into his polished skull with a wet *squelch* and stuck. Boyle dropped face-first into Jack's traveling bag, blood soaking the garments inside.

From outside below the window, O'Malley called up, "Jiggity-jig, Mr. Pendarvis. Jiggity-jig."

• • •

The black talons of fear that had dug deep into Caya's flesh that morning relaxed their grip. Although not at ease, she stopped shaking, and the knot in her stomach loosened. The Scot who won her was not a savage. He seemed to be an honorable man. He also wanted her, a fact that warmed her shoulders and neck, a not altogether unpleasant sensation.

The men in her village used to tell tales about the barbarians to the north. Whenever anyone spoke of Highlanders they had referred to them as uneducated savages who worshipped pagan gods and despoiled women. But Mr. Sinclair—all the Sinclair men—had demonstrated the good manners expected of civilized men, even if their clothing fell short of what befitted gentlemen. Caya had, on occasion, seen rude paintings depicting Highlanders, bare-legged, kilted men chasing down deer with bow and arrow. She glanced at Mr. Sinclair's long legs hidden inside gray trousers. Did he chase deer—with bare legs?

She shooed away the wicked notion of Mr. Sinclair wearing a kilt, more fodder for her box of guilty imaginings. Dark clouds on the western horizon forewarned an evening storm, but for now, the sky above was crisp and clear. She took a moment to breathe in the Scottish countryside, green and fragrant. She'd been terrified when she and Jack arrived in Scotland yesterday. Wick Harbour had been so crowded, and everyone a stranger. But out here in the country, the familiar-looking landscape calmed her—a vast expanse of rolling pastures, barley fields, and patches of forest not unlike Cornwall. Even the cliff-lined coasts of Wick reminded her of her home in Penzance. They seemed to be traveling away from the sea, though. How far away? The thought unsettled her. The sea had always been as much a part of her life as the sun and the moon.

"What's that over there?" She pointed north toward what looked like a large body of water.

"Loch Watten. We'll be passing through Watten soon. Are you hungry?"

"Famished, actually." Aside from the few berries she'd eaten, she hadn't breakfasted.

"There's a woman there that sells meat pies almost as good as my sister's."

Mr. Sinclair was what most women would call handsome. His rough-hewn features, so angular and masculine, appealed to her. He had a lean, attractive profile with high cheekbones and a strong jaw. It looked as though his nose may have been broken once or twice. Like most Scotsmen she'd seen thus far, he wore his hair long, tied back with a strip of rawhide. A few gleaming black curls escaped and floated around his forehead in the breeze. She rather liked his tall, lank physique. He had warm hands, too. She had felt their heat when he lifted her into the wagon.

"I saw you weeping earlier. Is it your brother?" he asked. "Are you sorry to leave him?"

His mention of Jack made her stomach churn. No point trying to hide what he already knew to be true. Her brother was a wastrel.

"The tears were for me." She owed Mr. Sinclair nothing. He'd implied as much. But she wanted to make clear to him she didn't cry for Jack. "I couldn't save him, you see. Jack had so much promise when he was younger. When the drink got hold of him, I tried to help. It was like watching someone drown. You swim into the deep waters to save them, but each time you reach out they grab at you and take you down until you're exhausted. You must make the choice: drown with them, or save yourself." She thought, but did not say, *I chose to save myself.*

"I'll remember that, should I ever find myself in deep water."

How odd. A man so large and capable as Mr. Sinclair not knowing how to swim. "Are you afraid of drowning?"

"It's no' the drowning I fear." He made an impish grin. "I'm afraid of falling in."

She appreciated his attempt to lighten her mood with his humor, but found it too difficult to laugh.

After a quiet moment, he said, "Dinnae berate yourself. I ken you did everything a loving sister could do." Mr. Sinclair fidgeted. She barely heard what he said next. "If you're weary, you can lean on me until your strength returns." His offer was intimate. Far too intimate. He must have known because pink patches appeared on his cheeks. Again, he was speaking directly to her deepest desire, to have someone large and strong to rely on. Did he know? Could he tell by looking at her how much he affected her?

"What are you?" she asked. "I mean, what do you do?"

"I was a soldier once. Now I make *uisge-beatha*, the water of life." Mr. Sinclair's eyebrows popped up and down. "Whisky." His voice had turned husky, and he seemed very pleased with himself.

"Whisky is a spirit?"

"Aye."

"You make it for the purpose of drinking?"

"Aye. I built a distillery."

A soldier. A man of violence who made spirits. She disapproved of both professions. The idea of a distillery concerned her, too. Strong drink had contributed to Jack's demise. She disapproved of drinking spirits and gambling. Mr. Sinclair and his friends were guilty of both. Had she left one bad situation only to step into another?

A more horrifying thing occurred to her, and her breath hitched. "Are you a Catholic?" she blurted, her black opinion of the faith undisguised.

Mr. Sinclair glared at her with his dark eyebrows buckled together. "I am not."

She'd offended him.

He turned his eyes back to the road. "I'm not a bloody papist," he muttered, then shot a look back at her. "And before ye ask, I'm no' a heathen, either." Mr. Sinclair focused on the road ahead again.

"Lutheran?" she asked, trying to sound less accusatory.

"Anglican," he corrected. "Episcopal Church of Scotland."

"Oh," Caya breathed out. "Good. That's good."

Mr. Sinclair gave her a sidelong glance. The corner of his mouth twitched. Was he laughing at her? "I suppose you and God are on good terms, then," he said.

"Do you mock me, sir?"

He smiled broadly. "Nae, lass. I can see he has favored you."

"And God does not favor you?"

"Let's just say, we dinnae often agree."

He was teasing her again, and she almost asked him to explain what he meant by not agreeing with the Lord, when someone called out. She spotted the other men up ahead.

The two sat side by side on a stone fence, eating while their horses grazed on the opposite side of the road. Apparently, they had already visited the woman who sold meat pies.

"Are they your brothers?"

"Nae. Cousins."

When Mr. Sinclair pulled the wagon to a stop, the huge one with the beard walked to her side and handed up a tied cloth package. "Mrs. Gunn's meat pies."

"Thank you." Caya opened the warm bundle. Two standing short-crust pies, each about the size of her fist. She held the pies out to her wagon companion. He chose one and took a big bite.

"*Mmm-mm.*" Mr. Sinclair talked around the food in his mouth. "Good. Pork pie. Try it."

She pinched off a piece of her crust and nibbled. Tasty, but not as light as the pastry she made. She forbore telling him so. Pride was a sin.

He withdrew a small black knife from his boot, wiped it on his sleeve, and handed it to her hilt-first. His eating knife, no doubt. Yet again, the man anticipated her needs.

"Thank you, Mr. Sinclair."

"We're not so formal in the Highlands. When we get to Balforss, the servants will call you 'miss.' Everyone else will want to call you Caya."

"I understand."

"Will you call me Declan?"

She hadn't addressed a member of the opposite sex outside her family by his Christian name since she was a child. Where she came from, in public, even wives referred to their husbands by their surnames. Mr. Sinclair's request shocked her, but if he was the man she would marry, she might as well get used to using his Christian name.

"If you like...Declan." Saying his name seemed too familiar, particularly when Mr. Sinclair—Declan—looked so very pleased upon hearing her say it. He even stared at her lips.

He pointed to the other two. "The big one is Magnus. The ugly one is Alex."

She suppressed a smile. The red-haired man was the exact opposite of ugly, and Mr. Sincl—Declan knew it. But, no. She couldn't bring herself to call his cousins by their first names. That would be far too—

"Caya. It's a pretty name."

She flushed. He liked her name. He even spoke her name as if it was pretty. Flattery. Yes. Pure flattery. She would not be taken in by such frivolous things. Vanity was no less a sin than pride.

"Sorry." Declan looked at her as if to gauge whether it was safe to tell her something. He glanced down when he spoke. "I'm no' so good with talking to pretty women." Caya stopped breathing and went very still. She sensed this moment was important. He had shared something of great value, something more precious than a mere compliment. He had revealed his uncertainty.

He lifted his eyes and met hers. It took courage to look at her after what he'd just admitted. Whatever Declan Sinclair was, he was not a coward. He waited for her to acknowledge his gift, to say something, anything.

"I think you're doing fine," she said.

He smiled at her again. That pleasing sweet, dimpled smile. He held her gaze a few seconds longer than was acceptable between strangers before they both looked away. He popped the last bite of his meat pie into his mouth and snapped the reins.

The wagon jounced and joggled down the road. She continued to eat Mrs. Gunn's meat pie. Minced pork and onion baked in a short crust. Good, but a shingle would taste good she was so hungry. She was tempted again to mention that her Cornish pasties were better, but she would wait until she had an opportunity to demonstrate her skill. Then she'd allow Declan to judge the difference for himself.

Another hour passed. They spoke very little. Occasionally, Declan would ask if she would like to stop and rest. She declined each time. She tried to calm her mind, not think about the past, about Jack's betrayal, about her father's farm and all their belongings auctioned off to strangers, about the life she might have had if her childhood sweetheart hadn't died. She didn't want to ponder the future, either. Everything seemed so uncertain.

Instead, she concentrated on the horizon. Each mile they covered carried her farther from her old life and closer to her new beginning. The distance between Wick and Balforss seemed like a kind of limbo. A space where her life remained suspended, her future placed in abeyance, her body numb to pain or pleasure.

Late in the afternoon, they crested a hill, and Declan pulled the wagon to a stop. He pointed to a house nestled within a dense stand of trees at the bend in the river about a mile and a half away.

"Balforss," he said.

The air around her changed. A salty breeze swept over her. The sea was close. She inhaled the briny scent and held it in, let it permeate her body, acclimating to her new world from the inside out. "It's magnificent," she said, and meant it.

"My distillery is hidden on the other side of the river. And my old cottage lies farther on, closer to the sea. My sister Margaret and her husband Hamish live there now. It's called Cleaver Cottage." He pointed to a hill another two miles or more east of Balforss. "And way to the right, just over that brae is our house, Taldale Farm."

The way he said "Taldale Farm" with such pride made her turn and look at him. His gaze, like a fist, shot through her chest, grabbed her heart, and squeezed hard. This man, this Highlander, this Scot, was now her life. She felt herself fall from limbo into the present—the all too immediate present. The man next to her, the home before her, the countryside all around her, became vibrant with color.

The talons of fear tightened again. This all seemed awfully quick, awfully easy, the way she'd fallen into this matrimonial arrangement. Had she cheated somehow? Broken rules? Would she be made to pay for abandoning her brother and running off with a stranger whose dark brown eyes had invaded her thoughts last night in a sinfully personal way?

Too late. Too late to change her mind. This was real. This was happening to her. This was her choice.

• • •

As the dray clattered down the last two miles of road toward Balforss, Declan inhaled the spring air and let his shoulder muscles relax. True, they'd experienced a false start, a big misunderstanding, but he'd cleared things up for Caya. They were to be married. He reminded himself that he'd had three years to get used to the idea. This was all new to the lass. It might take time, but eventually she'd come to see what Declan already knew to be true—they were meant to be together. His dreams told him so.

The meat pie helped improve his mood. He always felt better with a full belly. He stole a sideways glance at Caya. The meat pie must have altered her disposition, too. She seemed more at ease than before. Her brow had smoothed— no trace of the earlier creases. He took in her pretty profile, the delicate eyebrows arched over sky-blue eyes fringed with blonde, almost white lashes. And that dusting of freckles across the bridge of her wee nose. His heart squeezed whenever he looked at them. How very lucky to have such a bonnie bride.

He had told her he liked her pretty name. At first, he'd thought she didn't care for the compliment. When he'd explained his awkwardness, she'd said, "I think you're doing fine," which had made him feel quite good. In fact, everything about Caya, since the moment he'd first seen her, made him feel like he was more than he had been. Taller, stronger, smarter, braver—just…better.

His dream was coming true. Granted, winning one's wife in a card game was highly unconventional, but no one could deny he'd found his wife just as he had envisaged. Naturally, it would take time to adjust to each other. Things would be different for both of them. Caya would have to get used to the Highland way of life, and he would have to become accustomed to sharing his bed.

Declan felt a stirring below his belt and set aside that last thought for another time.

The banns. He should post the banns of marriage on the church door right away. Tomorrow was Sunday. He'd do it then. They would have to wait at least three Sundays for the banns to be called out in kirk. That meant they could marry in a month, enough time to start this season's whisky and finish the house before the wedding.

Caya would like the house. He'd built it with his bride in mind, consulted with his sisters Margaret and Lizzie, as well as Cousin Lucy and Auntie Flora. Declan had even asked Alex what a wife wanted most in a home. If all went according to plan, a month from now, his dream wife would become his real wife.

Wife. He shifted on the hard, wooden seat of the dray. An issue of a more personal nature pecked at his liver. His father had died when he was too young to remember, leaving him the only male in a house full of women—his mother and two older sisters. He understood the female mind better than most men, but he'd never actually *had* a woman. Romantically speaking, that is.

Oh, he'd kissed a few in his time. Gertie had let him fondle her breasts once or twice. He liked breasts. A lot. And the kitchen maid at the Latheron Inn had showed him more than one way to pleasure a woman. What would it be like to please Caya? To see her naked and open to him, to explore her body, pluck at her taut nipples, slip his fingers into her slick and complicated parts, to stroke and pet her until she—

Jesus, man. It's broad daylight.

He stared ahead at Balforss and swallowed hard. Only one more hurdle, his uncle, Laird John. He was certain his uncle would agree to host Caya until their wedding. And he knew Lucy and Flora would make her welcome, but would Uncle John bless their union? Or might he object to the way in which Declan had found his wife? He didn't need his uncle's consent to marry, but he wanted it.

He took an unsteady breath and gave the reins another snap. The draft horse kept a steady clop. No mind. Uncle John was a reasonable man. Once he explained the circumstances, made clear the reason it was necessary to remove Caya from the hands of her careless brother, his uncle would see his actions were justified.

He glanced at the beauty seated beside him. Hopefully, Uncle John would understand, because he would not surrender Caya no matter what his uncle said. Not now. Not after having heard her voice and smelled her hair. Not after having felt the weight of her small self in his hands. No. He wouldn't let her go. Not ever.

Chapter Four

Caya flinched when Declan snapped the reins. Her nerves were back, and she fought for control of her fear. The draft horse quickened its pace to a trot. Home was within sight, and the beast was probably eager for its reward—sweet grass, oats, and rest. She took a deep breath and prepared to meet her future.

As their party neared, she assessed the estate with an experienced eye, the eye of a farmer's daughter, noting a number of shaggy red cattle looking well-fed, a large field of winter wheat near to harvest, a collection of outbuildings in good repair, and, from the chimney smoke, people hard at work within them.

They turned down a tree-lined lane, and the familiar blend of farm smells and sounds reached her. The clang of the smithy rang in the air. Horses sauntered toward the fence rail, whinnying welcomes, and nanny goats scolded their babies. The wagon rattled past a pen of squealing pink and black pigs, and a few frantic chickens scurried out of their path at the last second.

She spotted the kailyard, a well-tended vegetable garden of an enviable size, showing a wealth of spring promise. Her father's farm had looked like this once—busy and prosperous—before it had died a slow death from years of neglect.

She turned toward shouts from robust laborers waving hellos, and the Sinclair men shouted back greetings in another tongue. Was it Gaelic? It sounded much like Kernewek, the Cornish language the simple folk of her village spoke. Three hounds raced to meet them and skidded to a stop. Their warning barks changed to excited whines of recognition.

Caya remained in the wagon, feeling uneasy while she watched Declan and Alex have a huddled conversation with three people standing in front of the house, two ladies and an older man who was clearly a person of authority. The younger woman would be the wife of Alex. She was one of the most beautiful women Caya had ever seen. Dark, almost raven colored hair, clear complexion, and delicate features. She held a little girl no more than a year old. The child had been blessed with a riot of red ringlets that glowed in the afternoon sun. Alex took the child in his arms, and the family of three embraced. Theirs was the behavior of people in love. Something tightened inside her chest. A twinge of envy, perhaps? To be jealous of another person's happiness was wrong. Yet, she longed for that kind of love, real love.

The older woman, strikingly attractive in her own right, also greeted Alex with affection. Alex's mother, more than likely. And the dark-haired gentleman equal in height to Declan was surely his uncle, Alex's father, the Laird of Balforss. As Declan continued to speak, his uncle's smiling face darkened. Caya shivered. The laird was not happy. That could not be good for her.

Magnus rode up beside the wagon and paused. "Dinnae fash, lass," he said, his voice low and gentle. "You will be well-received. It'll just take the laird a moment to…adjust."

"Thank you, Mr. Sinclair…Magnus."

The big man smiled back at her.

Declan broke from the group and walked toward her. His face, unreadable, gave no clue as to how things stood. Would she be turned away, in spite of Magnus's certainty? She resolved not to make a fuss. Whatever her fate, she would accept it. Yet, even though she barely knew him, she was certain Declan would not let her come to harm. He had, after all, given his word, and she believed he was a man of honor.

When Declan reached the wagon, he smiled up at her. Not his usual sunny smile. The smile looked more like one used to hide pain or worry. "Come," he said reaching out to help her down. "They are eager to meet you."

Again, she floated to the ground in Declan's arms. Once she was stable on her feet, he took her hand and patted it—a gesture far too familiar for the length and depth of their acquaintance. She liked the warm reassuring feel of her hand in his and wanted to cling to him—cling to anything to steady herself—but for propriety's sake she withdrew her hand.

On the slow walk toward these new people of Balforss, Declan informed her, "I've only told them we found you in danger and took you under our protection."

What? Was he leaving her to tell the whole story? He said he would explain. Caya was not prepared. She balked for a moment, but it was too late.

Declan made introductions. "My auntie Flora and Alex's wife, Lucy."

Flora and Lucy bobbed polite curtsies, their faces shining with interest.

"This is my daughter, Jemima," Alex said, pride oozing from his pores. "We call her Jemma." He pulled the little girl's finger from her mouth. Jemma looked at Caya dispassionately, stuck the finger back in her mouth, and then buried her face in her father's neck.

"And this." She heard Declan swallow audibly. "This is my uncle, Laird John."

She kept her eyes focused on the laird's boots and bobbed a curtsy, hoping that as she bent her knees, she wouldn't collapse altogether. She forced herself to meet his eyes. The laird's face softened.

"My dear Miss Pendarvis," he said. "Welcome to Balforss."

He was close enough she could smell the drip of pine sap pearled on the shoulder of his coat. The laird took her hand and clasped it between his rough, warm palms. At his touch, a surge of strength coursed up her arm. He reminded her of her father, Adam Pendarvis, a man who had generated power from within, then shared it freely with those he touched. Caya had an immediate liking for the patriarch of Balforss.

Flora and Lucy swept her inside the house before she realized she hadn't thanked the laird properly for his hospitality. She took in the soaring ceiling, wide center staircase, and dark paneled walls lined with family portraits. This was a grand house.

"Lucy, show Caya my parlor above stairs," Flora said. "I'll see Jemma down for her nap. Haddie will bring refreshments along soon."

Lucy slipped an arm through Caya's. "You must be tired and hungry from the journey. Lucky the rain held, or you might have caught your death of cold."

Upon hearing Lucy speak, Caya turned a surprised look on her young hostess.

"You're—"

"English. Yes. You and I are terribly outnumbered here, you know. I'm so glad to have a fellow countryman under our roof. Cornwall is not at all far from Maidstone Hall, my home in England."

"Maidstone Hall?"

"Didn't Alex tell you? The Duke of Chatham is my father."

"But…" She stopped herself from asking outright *what is the daughter of a duke doing married to a Scot and living way up here in Caithness?* That would have been rude.

"Don't worry." Lucy laughed lightly. "We'll have plenty of time to tell each other our stories."

When they reached the top of the stairs, she heard the laird bellow from below, "You three. In my study. Now." Magnus, Alex, and Declan ducked past Laird John and slipped into a room off the entry hall, all of them looking like condemned men. She was a little sorry for them. Her presence at Balforss wasn't entirely their doing.

A small animal with big floppy ears bounded down the hall toward her, making barking sounds. Lucy scooped the squirming bundle of brown and white fur into her arms. "This is my darling Hercules, my dearest companion."

Sweet Hercules looked up at Caya with round, soulful eyes. "He's so tiny."

"Would you like to hold him? He's always a comfort to me when I'm lonely." Lucy transferred the spaniel into Caya's arms.

She was immediately smitten. The dog's surprising warmth, the almost insignificant weight of him, alive and shifting in her arms like a fussy baby, pleased her. At last, the beastly raptor released its talons. Instead of flying away, though, it remained perched in the corner of her fear.

• • •

Declan didn't like the color in his uncle's face. It had been a long time since he'd provoked the man who, for the last fifteen years, had been like a father to him. Not since he and his cousins were lads had he been the cause of the laird's ire. Perhaps the last time was when he had dropped a handful of caterpillars into the pocket of cousin Maggie's apron, causing her to spill the pail of goat's milk and trample the clean laundry. He had tried to tell Uncle John the caterpillars had been a gift. He'd thought Maggie would like the green wigglers as much as he did. Declan still remembered the sting of his uncle's belt on his bare ass. He did not, however, remember his uncle looking as angry as he did at this moment.

The three cousins, Declan, Alex, and Magnus, stood at silent attention in the center of the library, arms at their sides, eyes staring straight ahead at the line of books on the shelves behind the laird's desk. The man paced in front of them, hands clasped at his back, head down, jaw muscle flexing—a bad sign. At last, his uncle paused and asked in a frighteningly calm voice, "Would one of you three gomerils like to tell me how Caya Pendarvis came to be under your protection?"

Declan's mouth went dry. "Erm...we...I mean...*I* won her." His voice broke like it had when he was fourteen. Alex and Magnus snickered.

Uncle John's eyes closed for a moment. His face remained unreadable save for the fact that he was clearly on the verge of unleashing his temper. "You *what*?"

Working hard to gather enough spit to continue, Declan glanced at Magnus to his right. Magnus gave him a shrug as if to say *this is your show. I'm just a spectator.*

"A man named Jack Pendarvis invited us to play a game of Napoleon—"

"Invited you?" Uncle John asked.

"Oh, aye. The game was his idea." He realized his statement sounded childish, the adult version of "he started it." Nevertheless, he plowed on, hoping to make a good case for himself. "And, well, he wasnae such a good player, ken."

"You mean he never suspected you three for swindlers?"

Alex spoke up. "He was so cocksure of himself, Da. He needed taking down a peg or two."

"Shut up," John snapped.

Alex drew his head back like a turtle into his shell.

"I was going to let him win his money back, Uncle," Declan pleaded. "Truly I was. But then..." The disgust he had felt last night for Jack Pendarvis threatened to rush up the back of his throat. He swallowed the sour taste in his mouth. "Well, he wagered his *sister,* and it made me mad." He searched his uncle's face for mercy, sympathy, some sign that he understood the impossible situation Pendarvis had put him in. He got nothing in return. "I ken it was wrong to win a lass in a game of chance, but it was even wronger to use her as a wager. Was it not?"

"I told him not to do it," Magnus added.

"Were you gambling, too?" John asked, already knowing the answer.

Magnus dropped his eyes to the floor and mumbled, "Aye."

"Then hold your *wheesht.*" Uncle John squinted his eyes shut and massaged the middle of his forehead with the heel of his palm.

Declan moved on with the hope that by describing the outcome of the evening he might defuse his uncle's anger. "Miss Pendarvis—Caya—was devastated when she came to find out what her brother had done. And understandably so. I gave her the choice: come with us or stay with him. She chose me—I mean us."

Uncle John swiped his hand down his face and let his palm remain over his mouth as if holding in whatever words were straining to be released. He looked at Declan for a long moment, his bottom lids drawn down, and his eyes looking bloodshot and tired.

Alex mumbled, "She's better off without that bastard

brother of hers."

Uncle John exploded. "Have you completely lost your minds? Are the three of you that daft?"

Declan's shoulders crept up around his ears.

"Ye cannae win someone in a game of cards, ye numpties!"

The air seemed to crackle with the laird's rage.

Declan raised his head. "I willnae give her back."

"Listen to yourself." His uncle turned an even darker shade of red, looking dangerously close to having an apoplexy. "You didnae win her. She's no' yours to give or take. She's her own person." He paced to the fireplace and back, apparently trying to calm himself.

His uncle's tirade hit a note of truth. He had thought of Caya as his own even before the card game. That he'd won her had only served to cement that notion in his mind.

"Did any of you stop to think that her brother might be at the magistrate's office right now, reporting you kidnapped her?" John looked each one of them in the eye. "You've compromised the reputation of the lass, yourselves, and the whole of Balforss."

Tempting fate and bodily harm, Alex spoke when Declan thought he probably should keep quiet. "Caya will vouch for us, Da. She's his wife."

"What?" Uncle John shook his head at his son like a dog shaking off water.

"He recognized the lass from his dreams and kenned she was his wife."

Uncle John's deadly gaze shifted to Declan, one unsettling eyebrow cocked higher than the other. "Explain."

Declan's stomach started to rebel. "I dreamed of the lass who was my wife—or will be," he said. "When I saw Caya Pendarvis in the tavern last night, I knew she was the one in my dream."

The laird turned his back as if it were too painful to look at him.

Magnus and Alex exchanged wary glances with him.

Uncle John released a long sigh of disgust and pointed to his cousins. "You two, leave. See to the horses before your dinner."

Magnus and Alex hastened from the room, a little too relieved and eager to leave him to his fate. *Traitors.*

"Sit down." His uncle pointed to a chair, then walked around the massive desk and practically fell into his own.

Declan moved the seat closer to the desk but far enough away to be out of striking distance.

His uncle rested his elbows on the desk, clasped his hands, and gave him a tired look. "I take it you harbor a belief that Caya Pendarvis is destined to be your wife?"

"I do, sir. I dreamed her."

"Listen to me carefully, nephew. Dreams and card games be damned. Caya is not yours."

He wanted to protest, to tell his uncle he was dead wrong. She *was* his.

"If you pressure her in any way to the contrary, I will take you to task. Am I clear?"

"But, I promised her—"

"I dinnae care what you promised, you cannae win your wife in a game of cards. And for God's sake, man, dinnae tell her about your daft dreams."

He bolted to his feet. "I gave my word. She's mine, Uncle. I willnae give her up." His voice faltered along with his courage. "I want Caya for my wife. She *is* my wife."

"That is not for you to decide," his uncle said, with finality. "From here on, I consider the lass my ward. I will make decisions that will serve her best interest. She is my responsibility until I say differently. Am I clear?"

Declan's entire body shook. Had anyone else attempted

to block his way to Caya, he would have taken them down, but this was his uncle, his laird, a man to whom he'd sworn his obedience. After a moment, he got his temper under control and let his fists uncurl.

"Aye, sir."

"Good. Now, sit down and listen."

. . .

Caya hoped her boots weren't tracking mud on Flora's fine carpet. She was grimy from travel and far too underdressed to be dining with ladies. "Where is my bag?"

"Haddie brought it to your room, dear." Flora took her cloak and motioned to a pink and green striped upholstered chair. "Sit down and have something to eat." After draping her cloak on the back of the settee, Flora poured Caya a steaming cup of tea and added two spoons of sugar. "The laird will want a word with you after he's finished talking to the men. Then you can rest until supper."

Caya took the teacup from Flora, and it rattled in its dish, all but announcing her nervousness.

"Och, lass. There's nae need to fret. It's just us women, after all."

She lifted the cup to her lips, more to hide her embarrassment than because she needed a sip of tea.

Lucy held out a small plate with a slice of cake and said, "Try this one. It's my favorite."

She dutifully took a bite of the spice cake—moist, sweet, and fragrant—and made a reflexive "*mm*" sound. Flora and Lucy laughed. Discomposed by her unmannerly slip, Caya swallowed quickly, swiped a crumb from the corner of her mouth with her little finger, and whispered, "Do pardon me."

"Dinnae fash, dear. That happens to everyone the first time they taste Mrs. Swenson's molasses cake."

"It's true," Lucy said, as she shared one of her treats with Hercules. "Mother Flora fed me Mrs. Swenson's molasses cake on my first day at Balforss, and I made the same sound exactly." She popped the last bite of a gooseberry tart into her mouth and closed her eyes in ecstasy. Hercules's tail thumped lightly on the carpet. "No more for you, you little beggar."

"If you don't mind my asking," Caya said, "how is it that you are here?" Goodness. Was that a rude thing to ask? "I mean, I'm surprised. I mean, not surprised, but confused—"

Lucy tossed her head back and laughed, a pleasing sound. She flapped a hand and said, "Trust me, when Papa promised me to Alex, I was outraged. By all rights, I should be married to an earl, or a baron at the very least. Am I right?" She laughed again and sighed. "Lucky for me, my father had other plans. You've seen how handsome Alex is…"

Caya stammered for a second, not knowing if it was good manners to comment on Alex's looks.

"Well, as handsome as he is, he's an even better husband. I am very happy here at Balforss. Scotland is my home now." Lucy reached toward Flora, and they clasped hands briefly. These two had a strong bond between them. Envy nipped at her conscience again. When was the last time she'd shared a friendship with another woman?

"I'm glad for you," she said and dropped her eyes to her teacup.

She was seated comfortably in front of a peat fire with Lucy and Flora, as her hostess insisted she call them. It would take some getting used to, all this use of Christian names, as if they were family. Yet, that's the way Flora and Lucy were treating her. Like family.

The parlor was as lovely as its mistress; a rich Persian carpet covered the wood floor, embroidered draperies flanked the glazed windows, and golden afternoon sunlight gave the room an otherworldly glow. In fact, she *had* stepped outside her life into another world. Her future had changed forever when Jack had gambled with her life and lost, breaking his promise and severing their familial bond.

Declan Sinclair had offered her a choice. She could have waited for the arrival of Mr. O'Malley, the man Jack had "sold" her to. Instead, she had chosen Declan, a man who wanted her and, if she was honest with herself, a man *she* wanted. She'd chosen Declan, and all that came with him— his family, his country, his house—for better or for worse.

Poor Declan. The laird had looked angry. She hoped he wouldn't be too hard on him. She felt relaxed enough to chance another sip of tea. It was strong and sweet. A very good leaf. A light rapping sound caught her attention, and they all three turned toward the parlor door.

"Come in," Flora called.

Declan stepped into the room, his face flushed and bothered as if he bore some unhappy news. "The laird would have a word with you and Caya, Auntie." His eyes darted a quick look at Caya. His distress made her heart falter. Would the Laird of Balforss turn her out? Had he forbidden the marriage? She searched Declan's face for some kind of answer. He pressed his lips together and shook his head slightly.

Flora extended a hand to her. "Come along, dear."

Declan led the way downstairs. When they reached the library, he said, "I'll wait out here," and made a feeble attempt at a smile.

She balked at the doorway, not wanting to meet whatever destiny lay within.

"Dinnae fash, *a nighean*," Flora said. "The laird isnae an ogre." She whispered, "He tries hard to sound like one, but he's really as sweet as a lamb."

In the low rumble Caya had come to like, Declan said, "It'll be all right, lass." The jagged edges of her fear softened.

Odd how this strange man could have such a calming effect on her.

The laird sat behind the largest carved oak desk she had ever seen. In a brusque, business-like manner, he rose and motioned for her and Flora to sit. She had an attack of the collywobbles and pressed a hand to her stomach, wishing she hadn't eaten the cake. Vomiting on the floor of the laird's library would not make a good impression.

"Declan has informed me of the circumstances that brought you to us," he said, his words clipped and terse. "I apologize for the actions of my son and nephews—"

She witnessed an odd exchange take place between Flora and the laird. Silent, but something definitely passed between the two. The laird's shoulders relaxed and his voice took on a lighter tone.

"Miss Pendarvis...Caya, it was wrong of Declan to remove you from your brother's care. If you wish it, I will see you returned and your brother compensated for his trouble."

Returned? To Jack? No. "I—I—" She stammered in a voice too small for the room. "I can't."

Flora put a hand on hers. "Is it that you're afraid to go back or that you dinnae wish to go back?"

"I do not wish to go back," she said as forcefully as possible.

"Your brother would be within his rights to complain to the magistrate," the laird said. He looked expectantly at her.

"I'm sorry." She made herself speak louder. "I don't mean to cause you trouble."

"John." Flora aimed a pointed look at her husband and exchanged another silent communication Caya wished she could decipher.

He nodded to Flora, then said in a rolling burr, "There's nae need for worry, lass. You are here through no fault of your own. But, I want to make this clear: no one can..." He struggled for a moment, and his face went slightly red. "No one can win another person in a game of cards or any such contest." He gave Flora a sidelong glance. "Regardless of the outcome of the aforementioned card game, you are under no obligation to marry anyone. Do you understand?"

But if she wasn't to marry Declan, then what would become of her? "Mr. Sinclair—Declan—he promised my brother—"

"A promise that holds no meaning in light of the events which led you to our door."

Panic tightened her chest, and she fought for breath. She rose from her chair without thinking. Where was Declan? Why wasn't he here to tell the laird that he'd promised? "But, he gave me his word."

The library door opened, and she turned to see Declan's worried face.

"Out!" the laird shouted.

Declan stepped back outside and closed the door.

Tears she hadn't expected collected and threatened to spill down her cheeks. She whispered her plea. "Declan gave me the choice. He said it was my choice. Mine."

The laird lifted his palms as if to signal her back to a state of calm. "*Wheesht* now, lass. I didnae mean to upset you. As of this moment, I consider you my ward, and like every person living under my roof, you are my responsibility." He rose and came around to her side of the desk, reaching for her hands. "No one can lay claim to you, no one can own you, and no one can pressure you to marry because of some damn—" Flora's sharp intake of breath gave him pause. "Because of some daft card game. Do you understand, lass?"

She nodded, still dazed by this turn of events. A man had given her a choice. Another man had taken her choice away. She was a fool to assume it would be otherwise. She had spent all day adjusting to the idea of marrying the tall Scot, and now she was on unsteady ground again.

"Yes, sir."

Laird John released her hands, and she dashed away her tears with a sniff.

"Declan," he shouted toward the door.

The library door opened immediately, and Declan poked his head in again, eyes wide with apprehension or expectation, Caya couldn't tell which. Had she ever been so relieved to see someone?

"Come," the laird said, crooking a finger at him.

Declan crossed the room and stood at her side, facing his uncle.

"Today's events have placed you, Caya, and everyone at Balforss in an awkward position. For the well-being of all involved, I have made her my ward. She will remain under my protection for as long as she resides under my roof. I insist you set aside thoughts of marriage or courtship or any such notion until you both can calm down and see things rationally. Have I made myself clear?"

"Yes, sir," Declan said. His voice sounded hollow, emotionless.

She was heartsick, but she supposed she was being ridiculous. How could she be disappointed about not marrying Declan Sinclair when she'd known him less than a day?

"After a reasonable passage of time," the laird continued, "if you are inclined *and* if Caya is agreeable, I will reconsider."

A smile spread across Declan's face. "Thank y—"

"After a reasonable passage of time," the laird said, cutting him off.

Declan brushed her hand with his little finger. His touch ignited a flame inside her breast that warmed her whole body, filled her with hope.

The laird cleared his throat, and Declan snatched his

hand away.

Obviously struggling to maintain his patience, the patriarch continued, "In the meantime, you will observe all the polite rules of society. You two are never to be alone. To do so would compromise the lass's reputation."

"Yes, sir." Declan smiled down at her, his sweetest smile. She bit her lip, suppressing her own. What had just happened? There seemed to be more unsaid than said between Laird John and Declan.

"You can go now, nephew."

Declan backed toward the door, never taking his eyes off Caya. He said to her, "I'll see you tomorrow, then."

"Goodbye, Declan." Laird John crossed his arms and dipped his head.

"At kirk," Declan said. "My sister will be there. I'll introduce you to her."

"Declan," his uncle warned. Declan was probably pressing his luck by testing his uncle's patience.

"G'night then, Caya." He turned without looking and crashed into the closed library door. "Och. Sorry." He fumbled with the handle before slipping out of the room, making more mumbled apologies.

The laird shook his head. "Dinnae ken what's got into the loon. You'd think he'd lost all his good sense."

"Bonnets," Flora exclaimed. "You know very well what's got into him, John Sinclair. Shame on you for torturing the poor lad."

Flora ushered Caya out of the library and up to a guest room, where she left her to rest awhile before supper. The upstairs maid, Haddie, a cheerful young woman with a beautiful smile, her most appealing feature, brought hot water for Caya's use.

"Miss Lucy says you're from England, too," Haddie said, emptying the water into a basin.

"Yes. Cornwall, actually." Caya's curiosity about Lucy got the better of her. "It's quite remarkable, isn't it? That the Duke of Chatham's daughter lives here? At Balforss?"

Haddie nodded and smiled. "Oh, aye." The young maid added more chunks of peat to the fire. "Laird John and the duke are old friends from when they served in the army. It was them that arranged the marriage."

"And Miss Lucy agreed to leave England and come here?"

"Well, she wasnae so happy about it at first, but Balforss has its own special magic, ken? The longer you're here, the more you'll come to love it. You'll see."

"And Mr. Alex? Did it take Miss Lucy a long time to get used to him?"

"Och. They didnae like each other at all. But after a while, Mr. Alex sort of grew on her." She picked up the bucket, then straightened. "Will ye need anything else, miss?"

"Thank you, no."

Haddie quit the room, and she was alone for the first time that day. The maid had said Balforss had its own magic. She didn't believe in magic, but she understood what Haddie meant. She sensed something warm and strong and alive about the house. Protective. Its walls, like strong arms, seemed to envelop its occupants in love, sheltering them from the outside world. Exactly the kind of house she would have one day. Exactly the kind of house she hoped Declan would give her. After all, he had promised. Or had Laird John canceled that promise?

She closed her eyes and tried to make sense of the day. The onslaught of dramatic life choices had come at her so fast and furiously, she hardly had time to weigh every decision properly. In one day, she'd accepted the marriage proposal of a complete stranger, left the company of her brother, traveled for eight hours, and been embraced by a new family, only to have her engagement broken by day's end. What did it all mean?

Laird John had seemed very angry about the card game, about the wager. He'd probably convinced Declan his decision to marry was unwise. Any reasonable person would be appalled to hear that their nephew had won a bride in a game of chance. Even more shocking, that the bride had willingly left her brother to marry the nephew. Perhaps Declan regretted his offer of marriage. Suddenly, her dream of a house and children were out of her reach again.

After a good wash, she stretched out atop the bed, luxuriating in clean sheets and feather bedding. This was her new bed, her new family, her new life. She supposed she should count herself lucky.

Luck.

Caya sat up abruptly. She didn't trust luck. Luck was a trickster meant to tempt weak people like Jack. Good things did not happen because of luck. Good things came to people who worked hard. People who performed acts of charity. People who were virtuous. If she was to deserve this new life and get her own house, she needed to work for the privilege.

On the way to her bedchamber, Flora had said, "You will live here as a valued member of our family. Like everyone else, you'll find your place. I'm certain you have much to contribute."

What could she contribute to this household? She crossed to the peat fire and stirred the embers with the poker, encouraging more warmth. She pulled a small hassock with pink roses done in needlepoint in front of the hearth, then sat and extended her bare feet toward the heat.

Flora and Lucy made candles and honey for the household. The laird and Alex ran the farm. They had staff for the kitchen and for managing the house. What would she have to offer Balforss? Where would she fit in?

Caya wiggled her toes, enjoying the warmth of the fire. Tomorrow was Sunday, a perfect time to start anew. Perhaps then, after she spoke to God, it would come to her—the thing she possessed that would be of value to Balforss.

The entire Sinclair household would be attending church or, as Flora called it, kirk. That's what Declan had meant. He had said he would see her at kirk tomorrow and introduce her to his sister. The idea pleased her, gave her something to look forward to, a concrete tomorrow after an ever-shifting today.

Declan. She had been disappointed when Laird John had taken away her choice. As much as she had worried about marrying a stranger, she wanted very much to be settled, to begin making her house a home. Those plans had been put on hold by the laird until he saw fit to allow Declan to court her.

Was courting different in the Highlands? She would have to ask Lucy. Truth be told, she didn't know what it was like in Cornwall. She'd never been courted before. There had been Hugo, of course. Hugo Killigrew. She smiled at the memory of him. His father had owned a tin mine. He had hair bleached white by the sun and a chipped front tooth he sometimes worried with his tongue. He had loved teasing her, and Caya had loved him like only a fifteen-year-old girl could love a fifteen-year-old boy. They had been too young to court, but everyone had said she and Hugo would marry one day.

Then Hugo had drowned.

There were drownings every year in Penzance. It was a fishing town. Peoples' lives and deaths were intricately woven with the sea. They had been children, playing among the dangerous sea coves used by the pirates in the last century, daring one another to venture deeper into the caves that pocked the cliffs at the water's edge. Hugo had been a good swimmer. But that day, he had ventured too far and had been trapped.

She could still hear his mother's cries as they'd pulled him from the water. Still remembered his father desperately trying to revive his son. The sea had taken the boy. The beautiful, terrible sea.

Declan didn't know how to swim. Everyone should know how to swim. Just in case.

Declan.

She had placed her brother, Jack, completely out of her mind, yet she couldn't stop thinking about Declan—tall, dark, and lanky Declan. Absurd, really. He was a complete stranger. Even more puzzling, she'd been upset when Laird John had dissolved their plans to marry. At the time, she hadn't thought about the loss of the house Declan had promised her. Something else had disturbed her more.

To her shame, she knew the answer. She was attracted to the towering Scot, had fantasized about what it would be like to be held by him, kissed by him, loved by him. *Oh dear Lord, to be loved by a man like him.* It was wrong to have those thoughts. Sinful, even. She should set those thoughts aside *right now*. But it was difficult to do when the image of his handsome face and beautiful eyes stubbornly refused to leave her head.

Released from his promise to Jack, Declan should be relieved not to have to marry a plain and dowerless Cornish woman. Yet she thought he had been a little pleased when his uncle suggested he might court her "after a reasonable passage of time." The spot on the back of her hand where he had trailed his little finger still burned. Were she and Declan equal in their desire to marry?

"I've won the honor of marrying you," he had said when she questioned him this morning.

Honor. That must be it. The tiny spark of happiness burning in her chest died. For Declan, marrying her was the honorable thing to do. No doubt he was one of those men to whom honor was everything. Not a bad quality, but sometimes the dogged adherence to the "code of honor" ran contrary to what was practical.

She had, for just a little while, believed that Declan *wanted* to marry her. But, no. Declan, gentle and honorable man that he was, felt compelled to marry her. That was all. Once again, Caya stuffed her sinful notions into the box and turned the key. She would atone for her transgressions tomorrow.

• • •

Declan called down to Magnus, "Hold." The task of hauling the bathing tub to the second-floor bedroom proved more daunting than he had anticipated. He regretted declining Alex's offer of help. The first eight treads hadn't been that difficult for him and Magnus, but the turn in the staircase had been an exhausting feat of mental and physical engineering that required shifting the tub on end. As a result, the second half of the ascent nearly broke the two Scots.

"Only one more step to clear. Ready, man?" he called down.

"Aye." Magnus had worked up a sweat and was blowing like a hard-ridden horse.

"You all right, cousin?"

Magnus gave him a sharp nod. "On three. One. Two. Threeee-ah!" They set the tub on the top landing. *Thu-thunk.* Magnus arched his back, and his spine made a series of popping sounds. "The damn thing must be made of stone."

"Nae. Zinc. I didnae ken zinc was so heavy when I bought it." Declan wiped the sweat off his forehead with the front of his shirt. "Have you got it in you to get this to Caya's room?"

"You calling it Caya's room now? Has she agreed to marry you?"

"She will."

"But Uncle John said you had to wait to court her."

"No need for courting. She's mine."

Magnus tilted his head to the side. "Awfy confident for a man what kens nothing aboot women."

"I've told you a thousand times, I ken plenty aboot women. I have two sisters." He held up two fingers, palm out, then turned his hand around, and gave Magnus a rude hand gesture. Magnus loved to taunt him about his lack of experience with women. The subject vexed him, not because he was embarrassed, but because it was none of Magnus's bloody business.

"Do you think a bathing tub is going to make Caya want to marry you?"

"Nae. But did you ken a hot bath always improves a woman's disposition?" He cocked a challenging eyebrow at his cousin.

Magnus's face went blank.

"Ha! See. I ken women fine," he said, thoroughly vindicated. "Now, help me move this bloody thing."

The bathing tub in place, they paused for a pull of whisky from his flask.

"Why'd you build a separate room for your wife? Will she no' be sharing your bed?"

Declan smiled at the idea of sharing his bed with Caya. "Oh, aye. We'll share. This is her room for bathing and some such. Lucy told me women like to have their own room. And it's not separate. See?" He showed his cousin the door connecting Caya's room with the next bedchamber. "She can come and go through here."

Magnus examined the workmanship on the doorframe and nodded his approval, then walked into the master bedchamber. He unlatched one of the shutters.

The view from the front was a source of pride for Declan. He had chosen the location carefully. His house faced east for the morning light. Emerald green pasture stretched as far as the horizon, and one could just make out a patch of blue-green sea over the treetops to the north.

"Will you be glazing these windows?"

"That will be the last thing. I've yet to finish the kitchen and build the washhouse."

"But you're living here now?"

"Aye. I let my sister Margaret and her husband Hamish move into Cleaver Cottage. She makes my meals and does my laundry in exchange. Hamish helps with the building when he's not working at the distillery with me."

"Fair trade." Magnus slapped a big paw on his back. "It's a fine house, man. You've done well."

"Do you think she'll like it?"

Magnus flashed a broad smile. "Dinnae ask me. You're the one what kens women."

Chapter Five

Declan didn't like church services and only attended when his mother had made him. His mother had passed nearly two years ago, now, and he reckoned her funeral was the last time he'd been to a Sunday service. This morning, though, he arrived at kirk in Thurso on his own accord, it being the perfect excuse to see Caya again. He had washed, plaited his hair in a neat queue, and wore a clean shirt and trousers. Perhaps, with a tidier semblance, he would make a better impression than he had yesterday.

He spotted Margaret on the road and waved. When she met up with him, she pulled a face and batted a hand at the loose ties of his stock. "What's the occasion, brother? Did someone die?"

"Nae."

Margaret was seven years older than Declan and had taken on their mother's role of bossing him around. Jesus, he hoped Margaret wouldn't embarrass him when he introduced Caya to her.

"Where's Hamish?"

"He's visiting with his mam. She's feeling poorly so I'm bringing her beef broth." Margaret held up a covered kettle wrapped in a tea towel.

"She all right?"

"She's healthy as a coo. Probably just wants attention. Want to come?"

"I'm to kirk. Will you give her my best?"

"Oh, aye. Enjoy kirk, you heathen."

He watched Margaret stroll away and felt somewhat relieved. His sister was the kindest and most generous person he knew. She could also be prickly and unpredictable. As much as he wanted Caya to meet Margaret and Hamish, introductions could wait until things between him and the lass were more settled.

The Sinclair women of Balforss milled about with other families outside the kirk door. He approached them, hoping to sit next to Caya, determined to speak to her. The women, all bonneted for kirk, looked like a pen full of hens with their heads bobbing and turning to and fro. How could he find Caya without her beacon of yellow hair?

Then, he saw her.

She smiled while Lucy introduced her to several women from town. Caya had hidden her hair under a starched bonnet. She wore a blue frock, cornflower blue like the color of her eyes. He watched her for a moment. Then those blue eyes met his and his breath caught with an audible *huck*.

A small figure stepped in his path—Mrs. Swenson, the Balforss cook. "Och, laddie. Did you never learn to tie your stock properly?" Before he could object, Mrs. Swenson reached up and untied his stock, making a general female fuss over him. He wouldn't have minded had she not chosen that very moment in front of God, Caya, and all of Episcopal Thurso.

"I didnae have a looking glass," he said as Mrs. Swenson

jerked and pulled at his neck. He darted a look over her shoulder at Caya approaching, her lips pursed and pulled to the side as if trying to keep herself from laughing. He must appear ridiculous.

"There," Mrs. Swenson said, patting his chest before stepping back to admire her work. "You look a proper gentleman."

A proper gentleman about to choke to death. He thanked her, and she toddled off toward the church steps.

Caya curtsied. Would she do that every time they met? "Good morning, Declan."

Again, the sound of her voice speaking his name made the tops of his ears burn. He dipped his head in return. "Morning, Caya. Are you well?"

"Yes, thank you. Is your sister with you?"

"Ah, no. Her husband's mam is feeling a wee bit peely-wally—erm, ill—and she's looking after her."

"I am sorry. I hope she recovers soon."

"Thanks."

People were beginning to wander into the church. Caya turned toward the flow, and he followed with the single-minded purpose of occupying the spot directly beside her.

"Are you happy at Balforss?"

"Oh yes."

"Good. Good. I kenned you'd like the—" A large hand clapped his shoulder. *What now?*

"Give us a hand, nephew," Uncle John said, hooking a thumb over his shoulder at Granny Murray in her wheely chair. She would need someone to lift her up the steps. Declan could hardly say no.

He dutifully followed his uncle to where Granny sat in the sun, her bonnet shading a face that looked like a dried apple. One gnarled hand fluttered to her cheek, and she grinned a gummy grin.

"Am I not the lucky one to have two strapping lads like yourselves escorting me into kirk?"

In the time it took him to roll her wheely chair to the front of the pews, the remainder of his family members were seated. Caya was wedged so tightly between Auntie Flora and Cousin Lucy he saw no way to muscle into a space by her side. Instead, he slipped into the pew behind. Bloody hell. A man should be able to sit next to his own wife in kirk, should he not? He edged past Uncle Fergus and Aunt Agnes, then kicked Magnus's foot to get his attention.

"Move."

Magnus grunted and slid sideways to make room. Once seated, Declan discovered he had a perfect view of the back of Caya's bonnet. Clearly a strategical miscalculation. He debated the risk of provoking Magnus with another request to shift when Alex arrived at the end of the pew carrying wee Jemma. The four of them were obliged to scoot down to make room for Alex.

He sighed back into his seat. Much better. Though the brim of her bonnet hid her eyes and the freckles on her nose, the lower part of Caya's left cheek and chin, as well as her lips, were exposed for his reverent contemplation. As soon as he had embarked on this holy endeavor, the processional began, and the assembled rose as one.

The Anglican congregation in this part of Caithness was so small they hardly warranted a church. For as long as he remembered, the old Reverend Makepeace Culpepper had serviced all of Caithness and parts of Sutherland, his visits parsed out to two or three times a year for remote places like Thurso. Last year, however, the once papist chapel in which they now sat had been rebuilt under the leadership of local landed gentry and reconsecrated by the Episcopal Church of Scotland. With the arrival of a vicar, the recently ordained Reverend James Oswald, Thurso finally had its own

Episcopal clergyman.

In the absence of an organ, the vicar employed a fiddler for the processional, a Mr. Archibald Donaldson, whose interpretation of church music on his instrument created what Declan thought an unholy racket. Add to that the square tones of wee Jemma's caterwauling, and it was a wonder everyone didn't bleed from the ears.

At last, the vicar crossed the transept, and the music mercifully ended. The congregation exhaled a collective sigh of relief, which Mr. Donaldson, no doubt, construed as appreciation. The vicar began the service in a clear and pleasing voice, a Lowlander from his accent, Declan thought. Admittedly, this was only his first time in attendance. He preferred to spend his Sunday mornings working on his house rather than nodding off in kirk. Besides, it wasn't as if God could hear him any better in kirk.

Halfway through the gospel, Jemma's attitude toward the Word of God turned decisively negative. No amount of jostling or knee dandling would redirect her determination to free herself from her father's lap. Most everyone in the church had focused their interest on Alex and Lucy's obstinate offspring, the child's discourse having more compelling content than the vicar's. Alex passed her to Uncle Fergus who, in turn, passed her to Aunt Agnes. Once engulfed in Agnes's ample bosom, Jemma settled.

The congregation rose, murmured the appropriate responses, then launched into song. "Alas! And Did My Savior Bleed." At first, the singing produced a jumble of notes as people searched for a beginning chord. Then the vicar's baritone rang out, and everyone fell in.

One voice, a clear, silvery soprano, floated above all the others. Heads swiveled to and fro, searching for its origin, seeking the creator of the singularly beautiful refrain:

At the cross, at the cross where I first saw the light,
And the burden of my heart rolled away,
It was there by faith I received my sight,
And now I am happy all the day!

What earthly being made such a heavenly sound? Who was this angel among them? This songbird?

Declan knew.

Eventually, everyone else found the source, as well. Even wee Jemma smiled and reached a hand out to touch the divine creature, Caya.

• • •

After taking communion, Caya returned to her seat, slid down the pew, and settled next to Flora. Lucy slid in after her, and kneeling together, caught between the two female pillars of Balforss, Caya began to pray.

She had always enjoyed being alone with God among a crowd of people. For as long as she remembered, the church had been the center of her world. It was there, in God's house, where she found contentment, renewed hope, and the answers to life's difficult questions.

But today everything was off. This wasn't her church. These weren't her people. And the vicar—she didn't even know his name. The comforting accompaniment to communion, Mrs. Dewey's organ music, was missing, replaced by rustling skirts, shuffling feet, and the vicar's repeated phrase, "The body of Christ." She closed her eyes and clasped her hands, experiencing a moment of panic. Would God hear her if she wasn't in her proper place at home in Penzance? Would he be deaf to her prayers here in Scotland?

She thanked the Lord for watching over her, for shielding her from harm, for delivering her into the kind hands of Laird John and the people of Balforss, and she promised she would find a way to be of service to them.

She prayed, too, for forgiveness for not having the strength and wisdom to save Jack. And, as always, she said a prayer for her mother and her father. She was about to finish when, on impulse, she thanked God for Declan Sinclair. She didn't know why, but she felt the need to single him out. And with that connection, with Declan as her touchstone, she knew she had found God in this place.

An odd noise distracted her from prayer. What was making that curious wet sound behind her? Like smacking lips. Not the sort of sound one normally heard in church. She said a quick, "Amen," and turned to see what or who was disturbing her prayer.

Jemma, in a muslin gown trimmed with lavender ribbons, stood in Declan's lap, his big hands wrapped around her middle, stabilizing her wiggling body. She had tight hold of his nose with one fist. The other outstretched toward Magnus, who entertained her with googly eyes and fish faces. Her head of bright red curls wobbled on her shoulders as she focused first on Declan, then Magnus, then Declan. Huffs of excitement turned to shrieks and giggles, the child's joy echoing through the church.

Jemma grunted as she pulled and twisted at Declan's nose while he patiently endured her treatment. Caya had to smile. Magnus and Declan looked like two bears playing with a baby.

Lucy made a noise of disapproval. "Jemma. Let go of Cousin Declan's nose," she whispered.

Hearing her mother's voice, Jemma twisted in Declan's hands and reached for her mummy.

"No mind." Declan pretended to mold his nose back into shape.

"She's a sweet wee thing," Magnus added.

Declan darted a glance at Caya. She got that same

heated sensation of intimacy every time she met his dark eyes, leaving her breathless and guilty. She shouldn't feel this way in church, for goodness' sake. His gaze fixed on her, but there was nothing disquieting in it. Was he thinking, as she was thinking, that, if they married, they might have their own children one day?

As she turned away from him, albeit reluctantly, she caught Lucy looking sideways at her, cheeks sucked in, trying not to giggle. She narrowed her eyes at Lucy, who immediately assumed a look of total innocence.

Though she'd known her less than a day, she suspected that Lucy FitzHarris Sinclair was a calculating woman. Not in a devious or duplicitous way. Lucy was far too honorable to practice upon innocents. But there was definitely some kind of mischief bubbling behind Lucy's beautiful blue eyes.

"What's so funny?" she whispered.

Lucy shook her head.

"Tell me."

"Later," Lucy said. "I promise."

After the service concluded, Flora and Caya stepped out of the church into the gray daylight. She still hadn't thought of what she could contribute to Balforss and the people who lived there. It had to be something of value, some assistance only she could provide.

Her thoughts were interrupted when the vicar, a handsome-looking man of about thirty, greeted them. "Lady Sinclair. I'm happy to see you."

"A lovely service, Vicar James. You'll be pleased to meet our dear friend, Miss Pendarvis. She's come all the way from Cornwall to stay with us."

"How do you do?" She made a curtsy.

"Welcome, Miss Pendarvis." He stared down on her with an expression she would call...dazed. "Beautiful," he said absently. The vicar's eyes flew open. "I mean, your beautiful voice." He seemed to recover his wit and laughed lightly. "I heard you sing. God has gifted you with the voice of an angel."

"Thank you." She curtsied again. The vicar had a warm, genuine demeanor Caya found appealing.

"Cornwall. It's a long way from here to Cornwall, is it not? What brings you so far north, Miss Pendarvis?"

Her mind went blank. By the change in the vicar's face, she must look as addled as she felt. What should she say? That her brother gambled her away to strangers and only by the grace of God did she end up with Flora and John Sinclair of Balforss?

"Will you join us for supper this evening, Vicar?" Flora asked, rescuing her from having to answer the difficult question.

"What?" Flora's invitation seemed to wake the vicar from a trance. "Oh yes. Tonight." He smiled again. "I accept with joy."

She and Flora said their goodbyes, then proceeded across the churchyard toward the wagon. The vicar's question bothered her. No doubt others would ask the same thing, and Flora wouldn't always be there to deflect the question. How should she answer? Laird John said she need not tell everyone the whole of her story. But what account would do as a substitute? And would that be the same as telling a lie?

"Caya."

She recognized his voice. No one said her name the way Declan did. He turned the simple word in his mouth like it was something exotic. She spun toward the sound.

His eyes shone bright with…what? Hope? But before he said another word, Laird John loomed behind him and wrapped an arm around his shoulders. "A word with you, nephew."

Declan cast a forlorn look at her over his shoulder as

Laird John led him toward the horses. That was the second time Laird John had intercepted Declan today. Yesterday, he had insisted he wait before courting her. His reason for imposing the delay seemed to be on her behalf at the time. Perhaps his concern was more for Declan than for her. But why?

The answer to her question came to her suddenly, a painful jolt of realization. Laird John would think it unwise for him to consider marriage to a plain and penniless woman with no title and no family. The laird would be obliged to dissuade his nephew from marrying out of a sense of duty. No doubt a man like Declan could find a far more suitable match among his peers. To ensure his future, the laird had offered to be Caya's guardian. A small price to pay, she supposed. The motivation for Laird John's kindness came to her on a wave of disappointment.

Lucy, Flora, Aunt Agnes, Mrs. Swenson, Haddie, and Caya squeezed into the Balforss carriage, a large wooden box on wheels, really. Lucy held Jemma in her arms, the baby's head resting on her shoulder. Light blue veins showed beneath the delicate translucent skin, and blond lashes fringed the edges of Jemma's sealed lids. Blissfully asleep. Even the violent jouncing of the wagon didn't wake her. The other women in the wagon, filled with the Holy Spirit, closed their eyes and enjoyed the contemplative ride.

Until Alex rode up to the window and shouted, "Mind taking a detour? I'd like to see what progress Declan's made on Taldale."

"That's a wonderful idea, Alex," Flora called back.

Caya felt a sudden frisson of excitement. Taldale was Declan's house. She was curious to see the home he had built for—*I built the house for you*—for the woman who would become his wife. Yet, she had to admit, the idea of walking around inside his house felt intimate, almost as if he had invited her to take a stroll inside his mind. *I built the house for you. You and me. No one else.*

The wagon pulled to a stop, and she gaped out the window. "Oh, it's lovely," she breathed, her words lost among the other compliments spoken by the wagon passengers. The two-story house was modest in size, but beautifully made from cut stone the color of wheat and topped with a slate roof. Again, she felt a rush of excitement. What would it be like to be the mistress of this house?

Declan ushered his guests through a heavy wooden front door into a central entry hall with wood-paneled walls and a winding staircase leading to the second floor. She removed her bonnet. The brim impeded her view of the world. She saw much better without it.

Declan explained he had built the two-story home with double chimneys. "To the right is the study, to the left, the drawing room, and behind that, the dining room." All the rooms had roughhewn wood floors and smooth plaster walls, just as she had always imagined her own house would have. All the rooms were empty of any furnishings, though she didn't find that fact disappointing. The house's mistress should have first choice how the rooms would be appointed.

As Declan led his guests through the house, he commented on things he planned to finish. The men remarked on the good workmanship while the women suggested what items of furniture he would need to purchase. She breathed in the smell of fresh wood shavings, plaster, and varnish. This was a good house.

Magnus invited everyone to follow him above stairs. "You'll want to see Caya's new bathing tub."

Her eyes flew open wide, and she darted a look toward Declan. He had turned crimson, whereas she felt the blood drain from her cheeks.

Alex punched Magnus in the arm, and Magnus looked at

him as if he'd lost his mind. "What did you do that for?"

Laird John said, "Let's not get ahead of ourselves, aye," and he escorted Flora and the other women to the second floor.

Caya froze. She didn't dare go above stairs. Lord only knew what she'd find.

"I'm sorry." Declan stood behind her very close.

Her voice had taken flight. She nodded.

"I was wondering …" he began hesitantly. "I was wondering if you'd lend me your opinion."

Taken aback by his request, she whirled around to face him. "You want my opinion about something?"

"Aye." He motioned for her to follow and walked toward the back of the house. "I've yet to finish the kitchen. I dinnae ken where to build the larder or where to put the sideboard. Would you come and have a keek?"

She didn't move.

"Please?" he asked and smiled sweetly. One of his irresistible smiles. The kind that made her smile back whether she wanted to or not.

• • •

Declan walked through the dining room toward the kitchen, hoping Caya would follow. She was so skittish. Like a foal that would follow only if one's back was turned, she trailed behind, leaving plenty of distance between them. He waited in the center of the kitchen until her footsteps echoed within.

They were alone. Together. For the first time. Forever after, this room would hold that significance for him. For an insane moment, he wanted to bar the kitchen doors, sweep her into his arms, and kiss her. Kiss her until—

"Declan?"

He jerked to attention.

"Is something wrong?" she asked. Her delicate blond brows drew together. Oh God, those freckles. Like someone had sprinkled cinnamon on her bitty nose.

"Ah, no. I'm fine. How are you?" Christ, he sounded like a dafty.

She curtsied. *Again.* "I'm fine, thank you." She tilted her head and waited. She must have read his blank expression, for she kindly prompted him. "You wanted to ask me something about the kitchen?"

"Oh, aye." His mouth had gone dry, and he didn't know what to do with his hands. He propped them on his hips. Not liking them there, he crossed them in front of his chest. Still uncomfortable, he let them drop to his side. "The larder and the sideboard, what do you think?" he asked, glancing around the room.

She circled the kitchen, pausing to inspect the brick oven and the cooking hearth. She opened the shutters on the window overlooking the spot where he planned to plant the kailyard.

"Is there a root cellar?"

"Aye. The hatch is outside the back door." Footsteps clacked above them. Magnus was showing everyone Caya's bathing tub. Declan's ears flamed again.

"I would build the larder against the north wall. It will be cooler," Caya said. "And I would place the cupboard on the opposite wall, where the dishes will be closer to the dining room."

"Good. I'll do that." He liked that she expressed a definite opinion so freely with him.

"Our first decision as husband and wife," he said and smiled broadly.

"But, we're not married, yet."

"Och, dinnae fash. We're as good as married," he reassured her. "The wedding is only a formality," he said, shrugging one shoulder. "I should build a bunker in the center, aye?"

"Bunker?"

"A workbench. But I dinnae ken how high to make it."

Caya held her hands out, palms down, as if testing the approximate height she would want for working. "About this high, I suppose."

He stepped closer to her. Close enough that he could gauge on his body the height of her palms. They came to the top of his hip. She had removed her bonnet, the silly wee thing. He closed his eyes and inhaled. Her hair smelled of rose water. Without thinking, he reached to touch her hair and startled her.

"No," she said, pulling back. "You mustn't. Laird John says we must wait to court."

"There's nae need to court. I already know you're mine." He advanced a step forward. If he couldn't touch her, he needed to be close to her.

"Laird John expects us to court."

"There's no use wasting time courting. We're meant to be married." Only inches away from her now, well within her orbit. He could bend down and steal a kiss if he had the nerve.

At the sound of footsteps, he jerked his head up.

Laird John entered the kitchen, one awful eyebrow lifted. "Time to go."

Declan took two guilty steps back from Caya.

"The others are waiting for you in the wagon, lass," his uncle said.

She curtsied. Damn. She was always curtsying. He wondered at what point she would stop. Then she dashed out of the room as if she'd caught fire.

Once she'd gone, his uncle turned a dark look his way, and he felt like he was fourteen again. "Sorry, Uncle. I was just… I was just…"

"I ken what you were *just* doing. Dinnae do it again."

His shoulders drooped, and his head lolled sideways. "I cannae help it," he said. It was true. Caya had become something like an addiction to him. He couldn't stay away from her.

His uncle issued an angry warning. "Caya is under my protection. She is my ward, and I demand you respect her like any other member of our family. Do not compromise her by being alone with her, or I'll give you a thrashing you'll not soon forget."

His uncle was right, and though twenty years his senior, he could indeed give Declan a damn good thrashing. But, having experienced the singular pleasure of her sweet company, he would be alone with her again at the next opportunity, no matter the consequences.

• • •

Caya swept the sides of her hair up and anchored them with a set of tortoiseshell combs, leaving the back down. She hadn't worn her hair this way since she was a girl, but after her visit to Declan's house, after talking to him in the kitchen, she felt young again.

He had declared he would defy his uncle's wishes. His words, *You're mine,* fluttered inside her chest like a trapped bird. But what did he mean when he said there was no need to court her? She must have misunderstood him. Of course he should court her. Shouldn't he?

She checked the small mirror above her washstand again. Her complexion was still clear, her features regular, and she had all her teeth. The face reflected in her glass wasn't all that changed from when she was eighteen, an age when most women chose their intended. At five and twenty, she was teetering on the brink of spinsterhood. Would she seem ridiculous with her hair down?

Someone knocked on her chamber door. "Come in."

Lucy entered, taffeta gown rustling, her pretty—and very young—face aglow. "Are you ready to go down for supper?"

Caya plucked at her skirts. "Is this all right?"

"Lovely."

"You don't think I look foolish with my hair down?"

"Nonsense. It shines like spun gold." Lucy flounced down on the bed. "If I had hair like yours I'd show it off all the time."

"My gown isn't special."

"My dear, you could wear a flour sack and Declan wouldn't care." Lucy's words chuckled out of her. "He's absolutely besotted. I've never seen a man so afflicted. Can't you tell?"

The idea that Declan's pledge to marry her was borne of feeling rather than honor made Caya deliriously happy. She turned her head, not wanting Lucy to see how pleased she was with her assessment of Declan's condition, which only seemed to make Lucy laugh harder.

She remembered something Lucy had said earlier. "This morning at church you said you'd tell me what amused you. Was it something about Declan?"

Lucy chewed her thumb as if deciding how much she should tell. "All right." She patted the bed, inviting Caya to sit. "I overheard Alex and Magnus teasing Declan about…" She covered her giggle with a hand.

"Tell me," Caya said, nudging Lucy with an elbow.

"They tease him about women."

She sat back. "What do you mean?"

"He's shy. Or at least he always has been until now. He seems rather bold with you."

Caya turned away, feigning interest in the bed curtains. "I hadn't noticed."

Lucy laughed again, that elegant laugh one expects from highborn ladies.

"Has Declan arrived yet?" she asked, trying and failing to sound indifferent.

"No, just the vicar."

"The vicar and his wife?"

Lucy shook her head. "He's not married. As a matter of fact, mothers have been peddling their unmarried daughters before him ever since he arrived in Thurso, but he's expressed no interest. He asked after you, now I think of it." Lucy gave her a curious look Caya could not interpret.

"What?"

Lucy's face cleared, and she popped to her feet. "Nothing. Come on. Let's make our grand entrance together."

Family and guests had gathered in the entry hall for a glass of Mrs. Swenson's milk punch. She suspected the beverage contained spirits and demurred when offered a glass. She searched the crowded hall for Declan among the mob of tall Sinclair men, but it seemed he hadn't yet arrived.

Vicar James approached. "Good evening, ladies." After they made their polite gestures, the vicar asked Lucy, "Did the new foal arrive?"

"Yes, just yesterday. A colt and he's beautiful," she said. "Would you like to see?"

"Most definitely."

"I need a word with Alex, but Caya can show you to the stables."

Caya stared at a smirking Lucy, who batted innocent eyes, waved, and swished away, leaving her alone to entertain the vicar. Lucy was full of the devil. Whatever could she be up to?

Remembering herself, she said, "I would be delighted. Just this way, Vicar."

She led Vicar James through the back of the house,

passing the kitchen, alive with activity—banging pots, female laughter, and Mrs. Swenson calling out orders. The heady smell of roasted lamb wafted out of the open kitchen door, and she hoped the vicar wouldn't hear her stomach growling.

Outside, the yard was empty of the usual clamor of farm work, everyone having gone home for supper. She and the vicar rounded the candle shed and the hatchery and continued on toward the stable. He walked at her side, clearing his throat every so often. She was quite at ease with him, even though they'd only met this morning. He was a tall man, but his presence was comforting rather than imposing. Perhaps that was why he'd been called to serve the church.

The vicar said, "I never found out how it is you've come to Scotland all the way from Cornwall."

She slowed to a stop. She had considered telling people that her parents had died and left her in the care of their longtime friend, Laird John. It wasn't too far from the truth. She opened her mouth, but the lie died on her tongue. Vicar James was a man of the cloth, a man so close to all that was holy it would be like lying to God.

"I'm glad to have this chance to speak to you alone," she began.

Vicar James faced her, his eyes blinking furiously. "Dear, dear, Miss Pendarvis. I don't know what to say…"

"I seek your spiritual advice on a personal matter."

"Oh… Yes, of course. That's—that's my purpose. Please continue."

"I'll tell you why I'm here, but I beg you not to judge me too harshly."

As they walked, a little slower now, she told him an abbreviated version of recent events, including Declan's gallant gestures. The vicar remained silent throughout except for a grunt of disapproval when she spoke of her brother's wager.

They had reached the stable and were peering over the door to the loose box by the time she finished her story. Vicar James folded his arms and rested them on the top ledge of the chest-high stall door. A gleaming blue-black mare stood, ears forward, alert. Behind the mare, a big-eyed, spindly legged colt found its feet and staggered forward. The vicar smiled at the pair.

"You are blameless in all this, Miss Pendarvis." His words were kind and his voice soothing.

"Was I wrong to leave my brother?"

"Your brother betrayed your trust. I understand your reasons for leaving him."

"Still, I'm embarrassed. What should I say when people ask me how I came to be here? It's a sin to lie, but if I tell my wretched story, it can only reflect poorly on the house of Balforss. These people are good to me. I wouldn't harm them in any way."

"I think telling an untruth to protect the ones you love is not a sin."

A weight lifted from her chest. Both Laird John and Declan had said she was guiltless. Even Flora and Lucy had found no fault when she told them her story. She only half believed them. But now that she had the priest's absolution, she was finally freed of Jack's oppressive grip.

"One thing concerns me, though," Vicar James said.

"What?"

"I would caution you not to be too hasty about affairs of the heart. Especially when it comes to Declan Sinclair. You barely know the man."

"He's been nothing but kind and considerate. I'm so thankful—"

"That's just it. What you are feeling is gratitude. Gratitude and obligation," he said, his voice firm but warm. "Indebtedness is a poor way to establish a union. You must give yourself time to adjust. I support Laird John's wish for you to wait and advise you not to become entangled with Declan at this time."

"But he said it was his honor to marry me."

"I hesitate calling Declan's character into question, but gambling for your hand was not an honorable thing to do. In addition, he is a soldier by trade, a man of blood. A good woman like you, a woman of faith and integrity, would not be well-matched with such a man. No. I cannot in good conscience recommend you entertain his attentions." The vicar took a deep breath. "At least, not at this time."

His assessment of Declan's character rang true, and perhaps her attraction to Declan, her desire to be near him, had stemmed from gratitude. Moreover, the vicar confirmed her suspicion that Declan's desire to marry her was fueled by his promise to her brother, now a matter of honor. As lighthearted as she had been when the vicar absolved her a minute ago, she was doubly downhearted to hear his reproof. She almost regretted having consulted him.

"Thank you for your wise counsel. I will consider your advice carefully."

Declan sat next to her at supper. It saved her from having to meet his eyes—those eyes that seemed to look inside her, read her, know her—but not from the physical reaction his proximity had on her body. Occasionally, his arm would brush against hers. Wherever they touched, that spot on her body would burn white hot. She hoped the effect wasn't apparent on her face. The vicar sat directly across the table, his eyes darting up and down from his plate to Declan to her and down again. Her stomach twisted into a knot. The lamb on her plate smelled delicious, but she couldn't eat a bite.

Declan leaned toward her, his breath warm on her cheek. "Are you all right, lass? You havenae touched your supper."

Vicar James paused mid-bite, his crystal blue gaze flicking from Declan to Caya.

She gave her head a slight shake. "I'm fine." She collected her fork and shifted the potatoes around on her plate.

The vicar smiled across the table and began to chew again.

Two people whose opinions she respected—Laird John and Vicar James—opposed Declan's advances. She should follow the advice of these two wise men. Yet, she couldn't shake her attachment to the way Declan smiled at her, the way he looked at her, the way he said her name.

"I propose a toast to the newest member of our family," Laird John said, lifting his glass. "Welcome, Caya. We are, every one of us, pleased you've come to stay. We hope you will find happiness here at Balforss."

The others at the table raised their wineglasses and toasted with a strange word that sounded like *slan-jeh*. Gaelic, she thought, so like the Kernewek, and she was reminded of her home near the shores of Penzance, a world away from this place.

"Thank you, Laird John. Thank you, everyone. I hope what skills I have might be worthy of your kindness and generosity." She looked to Flora. "I want to contribute, to be of value to you and Balforss."

Flora reached out and covered her hand with hers. "Dinnae fash, dear."

"I have an idea."

Everyone turned to Vicar James, who had until this moment remained rather quiet since blessing the food. "I have an excellent idea. That is, if Miss Pendarvis is agreeable and you provide your consent, Laird John."

"Please continue," Laird John said and tipped his head in

her direction as confirmation.

"Miss Pendarvis, I wonder if you might lend your beautiful voice to the church. I think ours would benefit from practiced voices. Many churches are forming choirs these days. You are just the person to help organize one."

All eyes shifted from James to her.

Lucy added an enthusiastic endorsement. "You have a glorious voice. You'd be perfect."

Almost simultaneously, Laird John and Flora said, "What a wonderful idea."

A choir? She loved to sing, but to direct a choir? "I'm not sure…"

"Do say yes," Lucy insisted. "I'm no songbird, as Alex loves to point out, but I'll join the choir. And Haddie has a pretty voice. I'm sure she'd like to take part."

A choice. She was being given another choice. Yes or no.

Declan turned to her and said in his quiet, silky burr, "I ken you can do it, lass, and they'll love you for it."

Caya's chest filled with all the air in the room. "Yes," she said and exhaled a laugh. "Yes, I'd like that very much." Her cheeks burned when her acceptance met with applause and cheers. She smiled her thanks to Vicar James. Such a kind man to consider her in this way.

Before the applause died down, Flora patted her hand and said, "There now, you see? You've found your place. You do Balforss great honor taking on such an endeavor."

Her appetite returned with a vengeance. She devoured everything on her plate. When dessert was served—a raisin pudding soaked in treacle and drenched with custard cream—she all but licked her bowl clean.

The wine went to her head, and she forgot she wasn't supposed to encourage Declan. When he shoveled his last spoonful of pudding into his mouth and made a satisfied *mmm* sound, she giggled like a girl.

Vicar James cleared his throat convulsively and winked. She sobered and nodded an acknowledgment. He asked, "Shall I come tomorrow afternoon, and we can discuss plans for the choir?"

She looked to Flora.

"Four o'clock," Flora said.

Shortly after the meal ended, the diners gathered in the entry hall to say goodbye to the vicar. He thanked Flora and John, then turned to her. "I shall see you tomorrow, Miss Pendarvis. Good night." He spoke low, as if he was telling her something personal, something private, flattering her with his full attention. Then he placed his hat on his head and left.

Once the door closed, Declan draped a cloak on her shoulders. "Alex and Lucy have invited us to walk with them in the garden. Will you come?"

All gaiety drained from her body. What she was obliged to do next might not please Declan Sinclair, but she couldn't dodge him forever. Some decisions would be easy, like the one she'd made about the choir. Others, like whether to receive Declan's attentions, would be much, much harder. Yet, that was what it was like to make one's own life choices, was it not?

• • •

"I ken you'll be warm enough. It's a fine night." Declan adjusted the cloak around Caya's narrow shoulders. Without thinking, he slipped a hand under her long tail of yellow hair and freed it from the neck of the cloak. Her hair was soft and sleek like the pelt of a seal.

Caya whirled around. "You mustn't do that."

"Sorry."

She was sensitive again. Every turn of her head, every flick of her eyes, every twitch of her lips cried, "Stay back."

But he couldn't, because every inch of his skin demanded he be near to her. She'd been changeable all day. Cool at kirk. Warm in the new house. Quiet at dinner. Giddy during dessert. Now, she was troubled again. What made her mood so unpredictable?

Ah, well. At least she wasn't curtsying. That was an improvement.

They all four stepped out into the night air, damp and threatening rain. Rain would be good, but not until after their walk. Declan hoped the troublemaker in heaven would hold his *wheesht* one more hour.

One of the grooms, an orphan named Peter whom Alex had rescued some years ago, finished lighting the torches surrounding the garden. Alex mussed the lad's hair and sent him off to bed. Peter had endeared himself to everyone at Balforss, including Declan. No doubt Caya would come to like him as well.

Moths flitted dangerously close to the flames, and pleasant nighttime sounds floated on the air. Their walk took on a figure-eight pattern around the rectangular kitchen garden bisected into two squares by one center path. Auntie Flora had planted herbs as both a decorative border and a deterrent. Bugs, worms, and flies didn't care for basil, borate, and calendula. His mother had taught him that. His mother. Fiona Sinclair. He wished she'd lived long enough to meet Caya. She would have liked the lass. Everyone did.

Several yards ahead, Alex and Lucy walked side by side at a lazy pace, their arms wrapped around the other's waist, linked, synced, and swaying. He yearned for that kind of familiar contact with Caya. To know the slight weight of her relaxed against his side. His hand on her slim back. Her head resting on his shoulder. His face buried in her hair. His lips on her—bloody hell. He had to stop imagining her in that way before he embarrassed himself.

They completed two silent circuits around the garden. Still, Caya remained distant. He clasped his hands behind his back and sighed. "Why do you shy from me? Have I done something wrong?"

"No. It's not that."

He stopped walking and tugged on Caya's cloak to get her to face him. She turned, but she wouldn't meet his eyes.

"You dinnae want me, then?"

"I can't."

Her words practically shattered him. "You…you want someone else? Someone better?"

She stepped closer and turned her face up to his, the torchlight shining in her eyes. "No, it's not that. Truly."

"What, then?"

Even though she was breaking his heart, he wanted to kiss her. He wanted to gather her into his arms and run away with her, keep her until she understood that they were meant to be together. He was just about to reach for her when she spoke again.

"Aren't you concerned that my feelings for you might only be ones of gratitude?"

"Gratitude?" He shook his head, puzzled by the word. What did gratitude have to do with marrying the lass?

"I'm grateful to you for bringing me to Balforss. I need to be certain that what I feel is real affection and not obligation."

"I dinnae want your gratitude. I want your hand."

"But the vicar says—"

"What? You told the vicar about us? About Jack and what happened?" He felt exposed, as though she'd shared his secret. It was one thing for his family to know the details of his life. But James Oswald was not family. Declan didn't even know if he liked the man.

"I spoke to the vicar because I needed counsel."

His heart banged a wild tattoo inside his chest. She

seemed perfectly calm, whereas he thought he might fly apart into a million pieces. "And what did he say?" He could guess what the God-botherer said, but he wanted to hear it from her.

"Keep your voice down. Alex and Lucy will hear."

He answered with something akin to a growl.

"He advised me to wait." She lowered her eyelids and turned her chin away.

"Did he now?" So angry he could no longer stand still, he paced back and forth on the narrow path.

"Yes. And I think it's sound advice."

"Oh, aye? And did he say how long you must wait?" There was a nasty edge in his voice. He couldn't help it. He was frustrated. Thwarted by a bloody priest. If the bampot weren't a clergyman, he'd go thump him right now.

A flicker of lightning illuminated Caya in blue light for a second, making her look like a life-size porcelain doll. Thunder made an ominous roar. The storm was near.

"Everything all right, man?" Alex asked.

"Oh, aye," he said.

Alex and Lucy squeezed past them and continued walking.

Caya huffed. "Your uncle asked us to wait as well. Why are you so angry?"

"I'd like the vicar to keep his nose out of my business."

"It's my business, too, is it not?"

"He doesnae know you like I do," he insisted. Why was she talking this nonsense? "You're mine."

"Declan, you can't bully me into marrying you, and you can't just disregard formalities like courting."

"Courting? Why must I court you? You already know we're to be married."

"That's what I mean. How can you be so certain we should—I mean, aren't you concerned that your reason for marrying me is entirely owing to your sense of honor?"

"You'd reject me for being honorable?" What the bloody hell was she talking about?

"I'm not rejecting you," she said. "I'm asking you to be patient."

Her voice sounded bruised. He had done the one thing he promised himself he'd never do—hurt her. He was instantly remorseful. "I'm sorry." Another flash of lightning. Declan saw the pain in her expression. Oh Jesus. "Forgive me. Please."

Her head wobbled, a half nod, half shake. Did she mean yes, no, maybe?

Then…she curtsied.

Damn.

He bobbed his head like a numpty. When she took a step toward the house, he blurted, "Will you not forgive me, Caya?"

She paused for a moment as if about to say something, but the heavens opened up and released a punishing rain. Lucy broke away from Alex and linked arms with Caya, and the two ran toward the house, skirts aflutter.

Alex approached him from behind and shouted over another clap of thunder. "I take it things didnae go so well."

Declan spun around, fists clenched, his belly on fire. He shouted back through the pelting rain. "Did you ken that ferret-faced dog-collar told Caya not to see me?"

"James the Vicar? Why?"

"I dinnae ken for certain," he said, blinking away the drops collecting in his eyelashes. "But I have a good idea why."

Chapter Six

The next afternoon, a vague sense of dread gripped Caya as the hour for the vicar's arrival approached. Though it was unfair, she laid the blame for her altercation with Declan on Vicar James. Per his advice, she had discouraged Declan's attentions, or at least postponed them. A risky move. If Declan became impatient, he could lose interest in her altogether, and her one chance of having her own house would vanish. And then where would she be?

The answer: she would be without a house, without children, and...without Declan. That last bit worried her overly much. She and Declan had parted on shaky terms last night. His angry reaction had startled her. It did not please her that he had a hot temper. Still, when he asked for forgiveness, she should have given it. It had been mean of her not to forgive him, and it had left a sour taste in her mouth.

Vicar James arrived at precisely four o'clock.

"Good afternoon." She bobbed a curtsy and welcomed him into the house.

He swept his hat off and bowed. "It is indeed a most

excellent afternoon."

The vicar's broad smile seemed to make the whole entry hall glow with his presence. Again, she saw the vicar for what he was, a kind and gentle man who cared for the welfare of every member of his congregation. How could she begrudge his counsel? Even though the vicar's advice had felt harsh, he had meant to protect her and Declan, not punish them. She would do well to remember that.

"Lady Sinclair thought we might take refreshments in her parlor," she said, indicating the grand center staircase. "Just this way."

Vicar James cleared his throat. "Em, I hope I didn't upset you with our talk last evening," he said.

"I appreciated the time you took to listen."

Though not as tall as the Sinclair men, he still towered over her in his clean, well-tailored coat and neatly tied stock—no doubt a reflection of his clean and blameless lifestyle. She smiled to herself. Declan's stock was always untidy.

"Did you think about what I said regarding Mr. Sinclair?"

"Yes. I took your advice and asked him to…to wait."

The vicar smiled down on her with eyes as kind as God's own. "Good." He was quick to add, "I mean, I think that's for the best."

"Of course." She smiled back at the vicar. She had been wrong to blame him for her quarrel with Declan. How could she have doubted a clergyman? Vicar James's intentions had been true and his judgment sound.

Between savory scones, plates of ham and cheese, and Mrs. Swenson's heavenly treats, Vicar James and the ladies of Balforss exchanged comments on the weather, plans for repairs to the church's crumbling north transept, and speculation as to whether Mrs. Ross would give birth to a third set of twins this fall.

Caya remained quiet, as she could contribute little to the

discussion. Vicar James favored her with frequent glances. Conversation eventually came around to the purpose of their meeting, the choir. All at once, everyone had suggestions based on their favorite hymns. Her head spun with the possibilities.

"Does the church have an organ?" she asked.

"Alas, no. Do you play, Miss Pendarvis?"

"A little. My mother taught me. We had a pianoforte." She didn't mention that she had sold the instrument months ago in order for her and Jack to eat.

The vicar produced a hymnal, the church's only hymnal, and moved his chair next to her so they could page through the book together. She didn't mind being close to his person, big and solid and serene. And he smelled like...well, like church.

Flora and Lucy seemed to enjoy the vicar's company as well. He didn't talk about himself like many men did. He laughed easily at Lucy's stories about Jemma, dispensed heartfelt compliments on Flora's home and family, and offered generous words of encouragement to Caya when she expressed doubt about her abilities.

"You mustn't worry at all," he said. "People will be delighted to take part, and I will be there with you." He punctuated his promise with, "Always."

"Thank you," she said.

"Which reminds me, we haven't discussed the best time for practice."

"Have another scone." Flora held out the tray of sweets.

"Yes, thank you." He selected one with red currants and icing and washed it down with a gulp of tea. He coughed. "Will Saturdays work for you, Miss Pendarvis?"

"Of course." She smiled politely. Sunday after church was her preference. But, no doubt the vicar knew what was best.

He removed his handkerchief and dabbed at his brow,

which was odd because the room was rather cool.

"It's decided," he said. "Saturday afternoon from one to three. I'll post a notice on the church board and make an announcement this Sunday. We'll begin the Saturday after next. I'm pleased we are in agreement." He stood. "Lady Sinclair, Mrs. Sinclair, Miss Pendarvis." He bowed to each. "Thank you for your hospitality. Always a pleasure."

The three women bobbed their heads.

"You are most welcome," Flora said.

"I would like to drive you to choir practice in my phaeton, Miss Pendarvis."

"You are kind to offer, but there is no need," Flora said, rising.

He waved off her objection. "No trouble at all."

"Really," Flora insisted. "Alex will escort the ladies to choir on Saturdays." Flora offered to see James out, and they exited the parlor, leaving Caya alone with Lucy and little Hercules.

Lucy made a *humph* sound.

"What?" Caya asked.

She lifted her chin. "Just *humph*."

"You must mean something by that *humph*."

Lucy looked right, then left, as if she was about to say something terribly wicked.

"I find the vicar's offer to drive you highly suspicious."

"Why?"

"Returning you so late in the day, he would expect an invitation to supper." She leaned back in her chair with lowered lids, looking prim.

"The vicar is a bachelor. You can hardly blame him for catching a meal here and there from parishioners."

"Oh, Caya," Lucy said, shaking her head. "You are so naive."

"Whatever do you mean?"

"Why do you think Vicar James asked you not to receive Declan?"

"I told you last night. He believes I should wait until I'm certain I have real affection for him."

"And while you wait, the Reverend James Oswald makes a quiet play for your hand."

"*Whaaat?*" She couldn't find words strong enough to object to Lucy's outlandish statement.

Lucy pursed her lips and raised her eyebrows. "You heard what I said."

"No." Incredulity lowered her voice to a hoarse whisper. "The vicar would never do something so—so deceitful."

Just then Flora returned to the parlor and said matter-of-factly, "Looks like you have another suitor, Caya. The vicar is obviously taken with you."

She closed her eyes and put her head in her hands. "Oh dear."

"There's nothing to be fashed about, lass." Flora patted her back on the way to her chair. "It's a lucky woman to have two suitors. And what fine choices. Both fit. Both successful. Both kind. I'd be hard-pressed to choose one over the other. Neither Lucy nor I had a choice. Our fathers betrothed us to men we hardly knew. Fortunately, the Sinclair men make excellent husbands. Do they not, Lucy?"

Lucy and Flora had a private chuckle while Caya had a private panic. She lifted her head, feeling more confused than ever. "Vicar James lied?"

"Not exactly," Flora said. "He gave you good advice, but for selfish reasons. You shouldnae let Declan court you out of obligation. Wouldnae be fair to you or to him. Do you feel indebted to Declan?"

"Well, yes. I can never thank him enough for bringing me to Balforss. But…"

"But what, dear?" Flora asked.

"There's more." There was the house, of course, but then there was that other thing. That fluttery sensation she got whenever Declan looked at her. "I feel something more. Something more than gratitude."

"Well then, what's the problem?" Lucy asked.

"Declan believes he is honor-bound to marry me. I don't want to marry someone who feels obliged."

Flora leaned back, chuckling to herself. "In my experience, men often substitute the word 'honor' for what they really feel." She sighed. "They think it's more manly than expressing their affection."

Declan didn't seem to be the kind of person who would say one thing and mean another. But men often lied to get what they wanted.

"I'll tell you what I think," Lucy said, collecting Hercules off the carpet and folding him into her lap. "Two suitors are better than one."

Flora raised her eyebrows and said to no one in particular, "I wouldnae want to be around when Declan learns about the vicar's intentions."

"Nonsense. A little competition never hurt anyone." Lucy lifted Hercules to her face. "Isn't that right, my darling?"

Caya stared at Lucy, transfixed. She was the most designing woman Caya had ever met, and she adored her for it.

That night, the full moon streamed through slats in her bedchamber shutters. Caya lay abed, studying the patterns of light on the wall. Four bars of blue light. One for each day in Scotland: the day she first saw Declan in the tavern, the day he brought her to Balforss, the day she told him he mustn't court her, and today, the day she spent without him.

Lucy's laughter floated up from the garden. She and Alex were taking their evening walk. Only twenty-four hours ago Caya and Declan had walked among the sleeping blossoms. She missed him. Odd. She didn't miss her brother at all, but she missed Declan, a man she had first laid eyes on only four days ago. That was a good sign, another good sign that her feelings for him were more than gratitude.

The bars of light flashed on the wall, and a roll of thunder rumbled in the distance. It would rain again tonight.

She hadn't forgiven Declan last night when he'd asked, because she'd been angry. No, that wasn't the truth. He had hurt her feelings. Maybe not on purpose, but when he hadn't denied her accusation that he only wanted to marry her out of a sense of duty, she'd been injured. She should forgive him, explain that she had received poor counsel from the vicar.

Oh dear. The vicar.

Both Lucy and Flora insisted Vicar James was keen for her. Caya was doubtful. The priest didn't look at her with the same intensity as Declan. From the moment she had first seen Declan in the tavern, he'd intrigued her, stirred her, made her body experience sensations she was unaccustomed to—passion. Should she take that as a sign they were meant to be together or as a warning?

Declan had been quick to anger last night, something she found troubling. And she had glimpsed his barely contained rage when he had held Jack by the throat. But he could have snapped Jack's neck like a twig. He hadn't. Nevertheless, Declan was, as the vicar said, a man of blood.

Vicar James was a man of God, a peaceful man, kind, a good shepherd to his flock. Most likely his beliefs would be in line with hers. His version of morality and sin would be in keeping with her convictions. Life as the wife of an Episcopal priest would be comfortable.

Her priest from home—the Reverend William Pearce—

he and his wife had always seemed happy with their rabble of seven children. A clergyman would never be rich, but his family would be well-fed, suitably clothed, and decently sheltered in a vicarage provided by the church—a home she could call her own even if she didn't hold the deed. The Reverend James Oswald would give her security. What more could a plain girl like herself wish for?

Could she dare wish for more? Passion? Love? Declan could provide that, and a house—a home that was well and truly her own. Forever.

The wind blew the shutters open with a *shoosh* of rain. She rose and pulled the window closed, then latched the shutters. The front door opened, and the voices of Lucy and Alex gasping from their dash indoors echoed up the stairs. Another flash and a loud crack of thunder. Jemma began to cry. Poor thing. Caya moved to put on her robe and go to the child.

She heard heavy footsteps on the stairs, and then Alex's soothing voice making nonsense sounds to comfort his child.

"There now. There now, *a leannan*. Daddy's here. It's all right. *Wheesht, a nighean*. Cuddle doon the night. All is well. All is right."

Alex hummed a melody, one Caya had never heard, a haunting, bittersweet tune. She climbed back in bed, closed her eyes, and rolled to her side. Alex had a fine baritone. She should remember to ask him to join the choir.

She shifted to her other side, feeling restless. Lucy believed she should receive the attention of both admirers. Caya had never been courted by a man, and suddenly she had two. She had loved once, but that had been when her heart was young. She was a woman now, full grown with the same needs and desires as any other woman. She wanted a home, a family, and a husband who loved her, wanted her, and looked at her with beautiful…dark eyes…

In the morning, Caya went to the kitchen after breakfast. Mrs. Swenson, the cook, a robust, rosy-cheeked woman, balked when she proposed making Cornish pasties. The kitchen was the cook's domain, and Mrs. Swenson ruled supreme.

"There's someone who deserves my pardon," she explained. "I thought it best to make my expression of forgiveness with a gift of food. Surely you understand."

Not one to surrender territory easily, Mrs. Swenson allowed Caya a corner of the workbench, all the while keeping one chary eye on her. The culinary tyrant scrutinized every ingredient, made sounds of disapproval when she didn't sieve the flour, and was openly aghast at her liberal use of butter. She endured all with patience, and by the time she finished her dough, most of Mrs. Swenson's rancor had dissipated.

She and the cook exchanged bits of conversation in the form of kitchen wisdom while she prepared the filling. Gradually they established a comfortable working rapport. By the time the pasties were ready to assemble, she felt accepted by the woman, who was, as it turned out, very agreeable. Mrs. Swenson stopped stirring to watch her crimp the edges of the pasties.

"That's clever," Mrs. Swenson said. "And pretty, forbye, the way it looks like a rope."

"It has a purpose, too," Caya said, deftly turning the dough and pressing. "Men in the tin mines take these to work with them for their dinner. The edge serves as a handle to protect them from the arsenic dust on their hands."

"Arsenic?" Mrs. Swenson said, sounding horrified and fascinated at the same time. "Poison, ye mean?"

"Yes. The crust has another purpose, too."

"What purpose would that be?"

"The miners, being very superstitious, believe there are spirits down below called knockers. When they finish their elevenses—their midday meal—the miners toss the pasty crusts down the shafts to feed the knockers, so they won't shake the earth and cause the mine to collapse."

"Knockers?" Mrs. Swenson whispered the word as if saying it out loud might conjure them.

Using the tip of a knife, Caya poked vent holes in the sealed crust in the shape of a *D*.

Mrs. Swenson gasped. "Is that the mark of the devil, then?"

"Not at all," she reassured the cook, who was, unconsciously or not, making the sign of the horns with the fingers of one hand to ward off evil spirits. "It's a Cornish tradition. The *D* is for Declan so he knows these pasties are his."

"Ah, so that's the young man who's wanting your pardon." Mrs. Swenson nudged her with an elbow. "A fine choice, if I do say so. A braw and canny young man, Declan." The woman's ample bosom jiggled with knowing laughter.

Caya, thoroughly pleased with Mrs. Swenson's endorsement, marked a half-dozen pasties with a *D* and the other six with a *B* for Balforss, as the balance would be served with dinner. She brushed the tops with a beaten egg and positioned the pan at the cooler end of the oven.

"There. In the time I take to clear away and wash, they should be done."

One of the young grooms popped his head through the door. "Got an extra bannock, Mrs. Swenson?"

"You ate four for breakfast," the cook scolded. "Dinnae tell me you're hungry again."

"I cannae help it. I'm always hungry." Spotting Caya, the boy executed a courtly bow quite at odds with his filthy clothes and hair. "Your servant, miss. My name is Peter."

She dipped a low curtsy worthy of the boy's bow, and said, "I'm pleased to make your acquaintance. My name is

Miss Pendarvis."

Mrs. Swenson pointed to a basket on the sideboard. "Och, take another bannock and be off with you."

"Wait," Caya said. "Peter, do you know the way to Mr. Declan's distillery?"

"Oh, aye."

"Would you take me there?"

"You cannae go there yourself, lass," Mrs. Swenson cautioned her. "It wouldnae be proper. The malting shed is hotter than the hinges of hell and the men work half naked." Her blue eyes sparkled. "It's a braw sight to see, forbye, but no' for a maid like yourself."

"I wanted to bring the pasties to Mr. Declan for his dinner."

"Dinnae fash. Peter will be your cupid. Won't you, laddie?" Mrs. Swenson patted the boy on the head, glanced at her hand, and wiped it on her apron.

· · ·

Stripped to the waist, Declan and Hamish kept the grain moving to release the moisture with rakes fashioned for the task. Malting generated a lot of heat, and he felt like he was roasting along with the barley.

He had found Caya at the beginning of the malting process, the first stage of whisky making, a time-consuming business. The barley had germinated over the weekend and for the following two days he and his brother-in-law had kept the barley turning. They worked together all day and all night, occasionally spelling each other for a few hours sleep.

The thought of not seeing Caya for days bothered him. A lot. He suspected James Oswald would try to woo her away from him in his absence. Thinking about that made him jealous and angry.

He dropped his rake and cursed.

Thinking about Oswald and Caya made him clumsy, too. He consoled himself knowing that his dreams never lied. She would be his wife, vicar or no vicar. Nevertheless, he tried to keep his mind occupied with things other than Caya. Counting helped. Twenty-seven boards on the north wall of the shed. A hundred and fourteen knots in the wood. If Hamish stood still, he could count the freckles on his back. Caya had freckles on her nose. Such a sweet wee nose. Pretty lips, too. If he could touch those lips with his own lips, what would she taste like?

Bloody hell. No good. His thoughts continually circled back to Caya.

After she had rejected him Sunday night, he'd ridden Gullfaxi home in the dark at a reckless pace, then walked through the empty rooms of his house for hours, too restless to find his bed. The kitchen had held him for a while. She had been there that afternoon, had stood where he stood, had spoken to him and smiled. But all that had remained of her was a ghost of a memory.

Sometime during the wee hours, he'd finished off the whisky in his flask and fallen asleep fully clothed in Caya's zinc-lined tub. He'd dreamed of her. Like in previous dreams, she sat in a field of gowans with her back to him. Only this time he'd known her name and called to her, but she didn't turn to face him. He'd called again and tried to go to her, fighting hard, reaching out, kicking frantically. The harder he'd kicked, the farther she'd drifted from him. His dream of her had become a nightmare.

"Declan."

He flinched as if he'd just come awake.

Hamish leaned on a rake handle, examining him thoughtfully. "Looks like your end of the shed needs another turn, man."

"Thanks." He swiped at the sweat dripping from his chin. Hamish handed him a wooden ladle full of tepid water. He took two swallows, dumped the rest on his head, and handed the ladle back to the likable fellow. Hamish was short, stocky, and losing his light red hair, but his sister loved him fiercely, and he was good to her. He was a good worker, too, and Declan enjoyed laboring alongside the man, as his company was agreeable.

"Another twelve hours, would you say?" he asked.

Hamish squatted on the malting floor, rubbed a few sprouting grains between his fingers, and nodded. "Aye. Tomorrow morning, to be sure."

Tomorrow morning. Wednesday. It would take most of tomorrow to finish the malt—to shake off the chaff and rootlets. By day's end Thursday, he'd have the lot ready to grind for the mash. Friday. He'd find a good reason to visit Balforss on Friday. Even if Caya didn't want to receive him, she could hardly refuse to say hello. Seeing her face, hearing her voice, if only for a few minutes, would ease his mind enough to get by for another few days without her.

A light rapping outside the shed door caught his attention. "Mr. Declan, sir. It's Peter. Can I come in?"

"Aye," he called back.

The young groom slipped in through the narrow door, carrying a cloth-covered basket. On the cusp of becoming a man, the spots on the boy's forehead showed the signs of the cataclysmic battle taking place inside his body.

"Shut the door behind you, man."

"Miss Caya sent me," Peter said, and he bumped the door closed with his backside.

Declan perked up. "Miss Caya?"

Peter held out the basket. "Aye. She bid me bring you these meat pies. Only she calls 'em 'pah-stees.'"

Declan inhaled. Something wonderful was under that

cloth. Something baked and buttery. He lifted the corner and peered inside. "Oh God."

"My belly's been talking to me all the way here. I never smell't anything so good." Peter slurped and wiped drool from the corner of his mouth. Declan's mouth watered as well. And Hamish, who had been drawn in by the seductive aroma, licked his lips and edged closer. All three of them stared down at the six shiny golden pockets of pastry, sealed at the edge with a turn of the dough, and made to look like a braided rope. *And* they were still warm.

"Miss Caya made these?" he asked.

Peter nodded without looking away from the basket.

"And she asked you to bring them to me?"

"Aye," the boy said, still fixed on the treats.

Declan reached into the basket and plucked one from the bunch. He pointed to the holes in the top of the pastry pocket. "What's this?"

"Miss Caya says the *D* is for Declan so's you know these are for you."

He took a bite and let his eyes roll to the back of his head. Juicy minced beef, neeps, onions, and parsley baked inside a tender, flaky, buttery crust. He spoke with his mouth full. "Oh God. This is the best thing I've ever eaten."

Peter and Hamish looked at him like vultures waiting their turn at a carcass. He motioned for them to take one, as his mouth was already full with a second bite. Ten minutes later, three torpid Scots sat on the malting floor, leaning against the wall, their bellies full, and the basket empty. He was transported with happiness. Caya had made him dinner, had labored in the kitchen on his behalf, had touched the very food he had in his stomach, an oddly arousing thought.

Peter let out a loud belch and mumbled, "S'cuse me," more to himself than to anyone else in the room. Strange for a groom to have such good manners, he thought absently.

The belch roused the men from their temporary stupor. Hamish went back to turning the grain with the rake, and Peter collected the basket from the floor. His distended stomach looked comical on his skinny body.

"Give my thanks to Miss Caya for the delicious pasties," he said.

"Och, I almost forgot. Miss Caya said to say…"

He waited motionless while Peter stared into space with his mouth open. "Well? Out with it. What did she say?"

"Oh, I remember now. She said she's sorry and that all's forgiven. Do ye ken what she means by that?"

Declan drew up to his full height. He felt a smile break out all over his face. "I do." He called to Hamish over his shoulder, "Back in a trice." Then he gestured to Peter. "Follow me."

He and Peter left the shed and walked a ways up the hill to a fallow field undulating with wildflowers. Was she simply sorry they'd had a row, or had she flung open the door to marriage? Either way it didn't matter to him. She had sent him a gift. That had to mean something good. He'd give her flowers in return. Gowans, of course. Gowans—daisies—had to be the most potent flower in God's garden. They'd worked when Hamish courted Margaret. They'd worked when Alex courted Lucy. Surely, they would work for him.

He picked a fistful and placed them in the basket Peter was carrying. "Give these to Miss Caya from me. Then come see me this time tomorrow, aye."

"Am I your cupid?" Peter asked, eyes narrowed with suspicion.

"What?"

"Mrs. Swenson told Miss Caya I could be her cupid. Do you know what's a cupid?" The boy's adolescent voice broke on the word "cupid."

He chuckled. "A messenger of love."

"Yeck." The gangly groom made a face and pointed a warning finger. "Dinnae ask me to do any of that kissing stuff."

"Dinnae fash, laddie," he said. "Leave me to do the kissing stuff."

• • •

Caya sat on a boulder at the edge of the River Forss and waited. And waited. And waited. Growing bored, she found a stick and used it to poke at pebbles and scratch swirls in the muddy bank while she sang "Sweet Nightingale" to herself.

Pray sit yourself down
With me on the ground,
On the banks where sweet primroses grow.
We will hear the fond tale
Of the sweet nightingale,
As she sings in those valleys below.

Having exhausted all the lyrics she knew, she rose and paced the river bank. She had followed the young groom as far as this shallow crossing, then watched him stumble down a long dirt path and disappear over the ridge. Peter said this was the secret path to Declan's whisky distillery. Not much of a secret if Peter knew the way. He promised he'd be no longer than an hour. The way he salivated over the basket, she worried the pasties might not make it to Declan before being devoured by the boy along the way.

She would have liked to have made the delivery in person so she could watch Declan enjoy the pasties, but Mrs. Swenson had cautioned her. *The men will work half naked, a braw sight, but not for a maid.* Caya didn't know the exact meaning of the word "braw" but gathered it meant something good. What would Declan look like without his shirt? Something fluttered inside her chest, reminding her not to think wicked thoughts.

Female laughter floated in the air. Seeking the source, she leaned out over the river's edge. About forty yards down river, a group of women was washing laundry on the opposite bank. She could go introduce herself. Chatting with the other women would make the waiting go faster, but she might miss Peter on his way back.

Wherever was the boy? He'd been gone way more than an hour. Had she missed him somehow? She shaded her eyes and fixed her gaze on something moving in the distance. Peter running along the path, his dirty hair sticking every which way, legs churning, and the basket snugged under one stick-thin arm. She waved to him. He waved back, tripped over a stump, and tumbled ass over teakettle. Peter landed spread-eagle on his back in the middle of the trail and didn't move.

"Oh dear."

Caya lifted her skirts and waded across the river, soaking her boots through to her stockings. By the time she reached Peter, he had picked himself up and was examining his skinned elbow.

"Are you all right?"

"Oh yes, miss. I fall all the time."

"Let me see." He had a scrape, bleeding only a little, but covered in dirt. "Let's go clean that wound in the river."

"Wait." In his fall, the basket had upended. Its contents, daisies, were strewn about on the path. Peter collected them and handed her the mangled bunch. "These are for you from Mr. Declan."

"Thank you." She accepted the flowers and bobbed a curtsy, and Peter bowed to her with a flourish. Who on earth had taken the time to teach a groom the manners of a gentleman?

At the river's edge, she dipped a corner of her apron in the water and dabbed at Peter's elbow.

"So, did Mr. Declan like the pasties?"

"Oh, aye. We ate them all." He patted his belly with his free hand, then jerked his gaze back to his elbow and hissed.

"I'm sorry it hurts, but I have to clean the cut or it may fester."

The chatter from the women doing laundry caught her attention again. The tone had changed from relaxed to frantic. Screams of distress. Calls to God. She scrambled to her feet.

"What's that?"

"Dinnae ken," Peter said.

She started toward the commotion, walking slow at first and then faster.

Following on her heels, Peter said, "I think we shouldnae bother them, miss."

"Something's wrong. They might need help."

Ahead, five women shin-deep at the river's edge were bent at the waist, peering into the water, searching, calling. An agonized cry halted the commotion, and a woman pulled a small body from the water.

Caya ran. Oh God. Oh dear God, no.

From behind her, Peter shouted, "Miss Caya, where are you going?"

The woman slogged out of the river, her child's limp and dripping body clasped to her chest. One long, low, mournful cry rolled out of her. The sound trailed off, but her face remained frozen in a rictus of pain.

None of the women spared Caya a sideways glance when she entered their circle. They were focused on their anguished friend, holding a little boy no older than two. Why wasn't the mother trying to save him? Why wasn't anyone doing anything? Someone should try reviving the boy. It might not be too late.

"Do something," she said, her words disturbing the air of grief surrounding the mother. "Someone, do something."

She felt a tug on her arm. "Please, miss. Come awa' with me," Peter said in a hushed tone.

A collection of startled faces turned toward her, noticing her for the first time.

"At least try." Her voice sounded shrill and desperate. She looked from one confused face to another. Meanwhile, the mother moaned and rocked the child, oblivious to anyone else.

A woman with white wispy hair said, "What's wrong with you? Can you no' see he's gone?"

"He may still live." Caya darted looks from woman to woman. "Doesn't anyone know how to revive a drowned man?" They answered with wary stares. "I've seen it done. I know it's possible."

She had seen someone attempt a revival. A man had been pulled from the water by his fellows, and they'd made him breathe again.

"Let's go, miss," Peter said more urgently.

Caya spoke without thinking. "Lay the child on the ground."

The mother paid her no mind, her moaning having turned to hysterical sobs.

The white-haired woman gave her a hard look. "Why? What good will that do?" She seemed resentful of her intrusion.

"At least let me try to revive him." She reached for the child. "It might not be too late."

The mother turned frightened eyes on her. She stopped her sobbing long enough to ask, "Can you bring him back?"

"He may yet be alive. If so, it's possible. I might fail, but at least let me try." She gently took the child from the mother's arms. He was heavier than she imagined he would be. And cold. She had to work quickly. The revivals she'd witnessed were vigorous, almost brutal on the victims. This was a small child. She risked injuring the boy if she was too forceful.

She laid the boy facedown on the grassy bank, turned his head to the side, and pressed on his back. Water trickled out of his nose, but she didn't hear the life-affirming intake of air. She tried again. Nothing. She instructed the mother to cover him with her shawl. "Rub his arms and legs. Make him warm." The mother went to work immediately.

She felt Peter at her elbow. He whispered into her ear. "This isnae a good idea."

She ignored him and said to the others, "Say the Lord's Prayer out loud. When you finish, the boy will either be with the living or with God."

The women began, "Our Father which art in heaven …"

She rolled the child on his back, pinched his nose, and blew into his mouth.

"…Thy will be done…"

Someone shouted, "What are you doing?"

"Keep praying," Caya said, and blew into the child's mouth again.

"…Forgive us our debts as we forgive…"

Caya paused, listened, nothing. She said her own silent prayer asking God to grant her the strength to save this boy.

"…Lead us not into temptation…"

She breathed into his mouth once more.

"Amen."

Silence. The boy's body remained still, pale, lifeless.

Please, please, please. Dear Lord, spare this one. Please.

The mother began her wailing again. She had failed. God had been deaf to her prayer.

Peter tugged at her sleeve. "Come away with me now, miss."

She attempted to comfort the mother. "I'm sorry. I was too late."

Ignoring her, the woman continued to keen over the boy's body with a high-pitched howl that cut through Caya's soul.

Suddenly, the child's body convulsed. The women made a collective gasp. She turned the boy on his side. He coughed, spit up, coughed again, and started to cry, the most welcome cry she'd ever heard. She fell back to leave room for the mother to gather the boy in her arms. The mother repeated nonsense into the boy's ear while he clung to her neck and howled.

At last, Caya got to her feet, shaken and drained from the last few minutes. The other women, the white-haired one in particular, stared at her with an assortment of looks—most of them of horror. A prickle crept up the back of her neck. Her efforts to save the child were obviously suspect.

The white-haired one hissed, "What kind of trickery was that, bringing the dead back to life?"

"The boy wasn't dead. I only helped him to breathe again."

The white-haired woman spat on the ground and said something in Gaelic.

"Come. Now." Peter grabbed her hand and pulled. He sounded frightened. She saw the wisdom in his words. She had best leave now before sentiment turned violent. Peter led her away with a breathless, "Dinnae look back. Just keep walking, miss." She wanted to run but made herself walk.

When they reached the narrow river crossing well away from the laundry party, Peter let go of her hand, and they paused to catch their breaths.

"Who were those women?" she asked.

"They're from a fishing village called Scrabster. Presbyterians. They dinnae take to outsiders. You shouldnae have interfered."

"But what else could I do? I had to try. If I hadn't that boy would be dead."

"Most likely they saw what you done as witchcraft. You best stay far away from those women. I dinnae trust them at all."

Peter was right. What she had done was risky. The child could have died and those women might have blamed her. The experience served as a strong reminder that she was a stranger here, an outsider.

Peter retrieved her basket of flowers and helped her across the slippery river stones and up the riverbank to the path that led to Balforss. Her stockings were soaked to the knees, and they both made rude squelching sounds as they walked. Wanting very much to put the unpleasantness behind her, she fussed with the daisies to keep her mind off the ugly business with the women.

"What did Mr. Declan say when you gave him my message?"

Peter's face lit up. "He said they were the best thing he ever et. I ken he was happy and then we went to the field to pick the gowans."

"Gowans? You mean flowers?"

"Gowans are a *kind* of flower, ken? Like these with the yellow centers and white bits."

"They call these flowers daisies where I'm from."

"Where are you from?" Peter asked. He picked up a stick and, using it like a sword, jabbed and swiped at some invisible foe.

"Have you ever seen a map of the British Isles?"

"Miss Lucy showed me in a book once. Balforss is at the very top of Scotland."

"I'm from a place called Cornwall at the very bottom tip of England."

"Is that a long way?" Peter held the branches of a bush

for Caya to pass.

"A long way by boat. An even longer way by foot."

"What's it like?"

"In many ways, Cornwall is a lot like the Highlands. The land looks similar. The people look the same. There's lots of fishing villages and sheep farms. We even have an old Cornish tongue just like you have the Gaelic."

"Do you have pirates?" Peter asked, round-eyed.

"Yes, actually. Penzance, the village where I'm from, has a long history of pirates and smugglers. Not so much anymore."

"Did you ever see one?" Peter's interest had turned feverish.

She hated disappointing him, but she couldn't lie. "No. I've never had the pleasure. Have you?"

"No, but Mr. Alex saw land pirates once. He said they were a lowpin' lot."

"What does that mean?"

"Ugly and smelly."

"Yes, of course," she said. "I've often heard pirates described as such."

They were quiet for the rest of the way back. No doubt Peter was daydreaming about pirate adventures. When they arrived at the kitchen door, she thanked the boy for running her errand.

"Nae problem at all, miss. I told Mr. Declan I dinnae mind being the cupid as long as I dinnae have to do any kissing stuff. Will you be sending pasties every day, miss?" The hope in his question was unmistakable.

"I don't think Mrs. Swenson will like sharing her kitchen every day. Oh, and..." She caught him by the arm before he slipped inside the kitchen door. "Perhaps you shouldn't mention the Scrabster boy to anyone until I've told Laird John."

"Aye, miss."

Lucy swooped toward them, swathed in lavender satin with Hercules bounding joyously at her side. "There you are. You've been gone for hours." She bent a low curtsy to Peter, and he made his courtly bow to her. "Well done, Peter. You'd better go inside or you'll miss your dinner."

Peter bowed to Caya. "It's been my infinite pleasure, miss," he said, and scampered into the kitchen.

"Did you teach him that?"

Lucy beamed. "He's quite the little gentleman, isn't he? When he bathes and dresses in his best, you'd never know he was a stable boy."

"What was your purpose?"

Lucy shrugged. "It started out as a game when he had a case of the mumps—a way to cut the boredom. Then I thought, why not teach him to behave like a gentleman? He may not want to be a stable boy for the rest of his life." Lucy cocked her head. "Caya, are you all right? Did something happen?"

"No, no. I'm fine."

Lucy glanced at the contents of Caya's basket. "Daisies?"

"Yes. Declan sent them."

Lucy craned her head forward and asked her incredulously, "He sent you daisies?"

"Yes."

"Caya, dear, do you know what that means?"

"He liked my Cornish pasties?"

Lucy made an impatient face as though she were dealing with a simpleton. "In the language of flowers, daisies mean true love."

"Really?" She had never heard of flower language.

"Don't you see? Declan is trying to tell you he loves you."

"Oh." Something inside her—something she had no name for—opened and spilled a warm sensation across her shoulders and down her body. Declan had sent her a message of love.

• • •

Less than an hour after Peter had left, Declan's sister Margaret arrived at the malting shed with dinner. He put his shirt on, a useless measure to shield himself from his sister's wrath.

"Sorry. I would have told you had I known."

"And what am I to do with this?" Margaret punctuated her question by setting a cast iron kettle on a stool with more force than necessary. Her kertch was on askew, and wild coils of black hair sprang out from under. Tall and rawboned and red in the face, Margaret fired a look at Declan he knew well. She had been pushed past the limit of her patience, and there would be no reasoning with her.

Declan and Hamish exchanged glances. His brother-in-law looked as frightened as he felt. They were both sorry cowards—bawfaced fearties, the two of them. Hamish, the braver of them, took a wary step toward his wife. "It smells good, love. Is it the lamb stew you've made?"

Margaret jammed her fists on her hips and turned her black glare on Hamish. "I suppose you've stuffed yourself as well?"

Hamish was an inch shorter than his wife. He shrank another inch and took two steps back.

"Did you no' beg me this morning to bring you some scran for the midday lest you perish?" she said, her curls vibrating with anger. "And me, fool enough to take pity on you, spending all morning slaving over the fire, wrapping the heavy kettle so's it stays warm, and walking all the way from the cottage bearing victuals for my men, only to find you've filled your gluttonous bellies with someone else's food."

"It would have been rude not to accept the gift. Miss Pendarvis is a guest of Laird John's," Declan said, appealing to his sister's Highland sense of hospitality. Unfortunately, the comment only fanned Margaret's fiery temper.

"And who am I, your maid?" Her voice reached an ear-piercing crescendo. "Do you think I have nothing better to do than wait on you two gomerils?"

His brother-in-law approached the kettle cautiously. "Ye know, love, the smell of that stew has got my appetite up." Hamish's voice took on a seductive quality. "The pasties werenae all that filling. And I can never resist your lamb stew." Hamish smiled a smile that said, *I know you cannae stay angry wi' me for long.*

Declan was impressed with his brother-in-law's skill. Hamish reminded him of a snake charmer he'd once seen in Edinburgh. Still, he was grateful his sister wasn't carrying a kitchen knife. She looked angry enough to run him through.

Margaret folded her arms and turned away from her husband. Pouting was one of the many weapons in her arsenal of female manipulation. With the indifference of a cat, she allowed Hamish to put an arm around her and kiss her forehead. He said something in her ear, and she smiled in spite of herself. She gave him a playful slap, and all seemed well between them. Margaret served Hamish a generous helping of rich stew. He accepted the bowl and spoon, took a deep breath, and dug in with valiant determination.

Wanting his sister's dispensation, Declan admitted a taste for her stew as well. She wordlessly ladled a bowlful and accepted his kiss on her cheek. It would take longer for him to get back into Margaret's good graces, he knew, but at least she didn't look as though she might injure him. He chewed a tender chunk of gravy-coated lamb, swallowed, and prayed to God it would stay down, all the while wondering if anyone had ever died from eating too much good food.

By noon the next day, he and Hamish were deep into the process of cleaning the malt. They had both ends of the shed open for a cross breeze that carried the tiny bits of husk out with the wind. Still, the chaff filled the air, stuck to their skin, and settled in their hair like snow. They wore kerchiefs over their mouths to keep from choking on the stuff, but nothing stopped the flakes from getting in their eyes.

"Mr. Declan, sir." Peter stood at the opening, waving away floating chaff. "I come like you said."

"Over here, lad." He motioned Peter to follow, and collected two dozen daisies from a bucket of water. He'd plucked them earlier that morning but hadn't provided for a means of delivery. Peter had no basket with him, so Declan pulled the leather thong from his hair and used it to tie the gowans into a neat bundle.

"Give these to Miss Caya. Tell her…" What should he tell her? What dare he tell her? He trusted the flowers to carry the message that he was thinking of her. But what words should he trust with Peter, and would the loon say them in the right order? "Tell her I hope she likes gowans." A simple message, he thought. One Peter could remember.

"Aye, sir," Peter said and dashed off.

"Wait." Declan called for him to return. He tested Peter's memory. "What will you tell Miss Caya?"

Peter opened his mouth, slid his gaze sideways, and went perfectly still.

Declan rubbed his face vigorously with both hands. The boy must have a brain the size of a peach pit. Finding his patience, he asked, "Did you forget already, man?"

"I recall exactly," Peter said, indignant. "You said, 'Give these to Miss Caya. Tell her I hope she likes gowans.' But you wouldnae want me to say it like that, aye? You'd want me to say it more like…" Peter paused to ponder again. After a moment, he held the flowers out with one hand, placed the other over his heart, and spoke with adolescent earnest. "These are from Mr. Declan. He says you're prettier than all the flowers in the field."

Declan stepped back, somewhat in awe of the boy.

"I ken something else, too," Peter said.

"What's that?" he asked, interested but wary.

"Miss Caya and Miss Lucy were outside the kitchen door, and I was inside having my dinner. I heard them talking—not a'purpose," he added quickly. "Just accidental like."

He shifted his weight and cocked a skeptical eyebrow at the boy. "And…"

Peter glanced over his shoulder like one about to say something treasonous. Then he leaned toward him and whispered. "I heard Miss Lucy tell Miss Caya that daisies mean you love her." The boy made a face as though repeating the words had left a bad taste in his mouth.

Declan reared back. It hadn't occurred to him that flowers had meaning beyond their beauty. However unintentional, his gift conveyed a more powerful message than a simple thank-you.

He looked the boy up and down. "Seems you've taken awfy fast to your job as cupid."

Peter grinned stupidly at the compliment, destroying whatever newfound respect he had for the lad.

"Go on," he said, making a shooing motion. "And dinnae forget to come back tomorrow."

Chapter Seven

Caya had meant to tell Laird John about the incident with the Scrabster women. But he was a busy man and rarely available for a private talk. And anyway, would he want to be bothered with something so trivial? Peter had said those women were nothing but a suspicious lot. No doubt religious zealots, all of them. Her father had always told her not to take notice of such individuals. Perhaps her best decision was to forget the whole thing had happened and move on. That was the kindest thing to do. Forgive and forget like a good Christian. At least, that's how she justified her silence.

Friday came. Caya woke with the sun, performed her morning ablutions, then joined Mrs. Swenson in the kitchen before breakfast. Declan had sent her daisies via his cupid, Peter, on Tuesday, Wednesday, and Thursday. Today she would answer Declan's gifts with one of her own—revel buns—yeasty sweet rolls flavored with saffron, cinnamon, currants, and sultanas. Her brother, Jack, had allowed her to bring only what she could wear on her back or fit in her travel bag. One of the precious few things she had packed was her tiny supply of saffron, expensive and difficult to come by. Lucky, too, because Mrs. Swenson had no saffron nor did she know of any use for the delicate spice.

She sprinkled a pinch of the burnt orange–colored threads into a few teaspoons of warm water to soak and watched the bowl turn the color of a summer sunset.

"What a bonnie color the wee things make. Like tansy flowers," Mrs. Swenson said, peering over her shoulder. "Wherever do they come from?"

"I'm told they come from the centers of crocus flowers that grow in the East. In Cornwall, we only make the revel buns on special occasions like Easter or Christmas because the spice is so dear."

"And what's the special occasion today?" Mrs. Swenson poked her in the side.

She pursed her lips. Today was market day in Thurso. She and Lucy were going into town to purchase a few necessaries. Afterward they would visit the home of family friends, Dr. and Mrs. Farquhar. She planned to deliver the saffron treats to Declan on the way. Mrs. Swenson knew very well her purpose for baking. Nevertheless, she wasn't about to admit her affection for the tall, dark Scot.

"Today we celebrate the Visitation of Mary, do we not?" she said in exaggerated reverence.

"Ooooh. I see," Mrs. Swenson teased. "The buns are for the Virgin Mary. Silly me. And I thought they were for the young man who's been sending you flowers."

Caya disintegrated into laughter, something she'd done more often in the last week than she had in the last few years. The stress of losing the farm, the creditors threatening the workhouse, and the fear of leaving her home had taken a toll on Caya's capacity for happiness. It felt good to laugh again. Laughter made her feel…new. New country, new home, new friends. She even had a new gown to wear.

She and Magnus's mother, Aunt Agnes, had spent most of the last two days cutting down one of Lucy's old gowns—a light blue frock made of airy lawn cloth with a delicate chain of daisies embroidered down the length of the sleeves. The bodice had become too tight in the bust for Lucy's comfort— or so she said. Caya suspected Lucy made up the excuse to make a gift of the gown. Still, she was thankful for Lucy's generosity and excited to add a new gown to her meager clothing cupboard.

While the revel buns baked in Mrs. Swenson's oven, she returned to the house to get ready for her trip to Thurso. The finished blue gown lay on her bed. She traced a finger around the embroidered daisies. Would Declan notice them on the sleeves of her gown? Would they be satisfactory acknowledgment of his gifts? More importantly, would they serve to return his sentiments of love?

She heard a light rap on the door. "It's Lucy. May I come in?"

"Please."

Lucy swept into the room with a gust of the citrusy bergamot Flora used to make soap. She moved with the confidence all beautiful women seemed to share. Caya wondered if confidence rose from being beautiful or if being beautiful came from having confidence.

"Almost ready?"

"I'm glad you're here," she said. "I need help fastening my gown." All of her clothes fastened in the front, a design common among women who lacked a lady's maid. The altered gown, like all of Lucy's, closed in the back, making dressing impossible without assistance.

After finishing the last button, Lucy stepped back and looked her up and down. "My, you and Aunt Agnes have done a fine job. This gown never looked so lovely on me."

It was a generous thing for her to say. "Thank you, Lucy.

When I'm wearing it, I don't feel quite so plain."

Lucy laughed as though she had told her a joke. "Who on earth said you were plain?"

"Well." She thought for a moment. "My brother, I suppose."

Lucy dropped her smile. "Darling, your brother is a blasted idiot."

Her batch of revel buns had produced two dozen. She packed six for Declan and six for Mrs. Farquhar. Anticipating Peter's insatiable appetite, she wrapped two lavishly buttered buns for his immediate consumption and included another two for him to eat at his leisure. The balance she left for Mrs. Swenson to serve with the afternoon meal.

The same wagon used to transport the women of Balforss to church clacked and rattled into the dooryard. Lucy fondly referred to the rig as "The Crate" because it looked like a large wooden box on wheels. And that, in fact, was what it was.

The spindly groom, Peter, looked insubstantial driving something as big and cumbersome as the Balforss wagon. The draft horse alone was at least a hand taller. Yet, the boy managed the wagon with surprising skill as he maneuvered The Crate up the drive to the front of the house. After pulling the brake and securing the reins, he hopped down, opened the wagon door, and offered Lucy and Caya a gentlemanly hand.

"We're stopping at Mr. Declan's house on the way, Peter," she said, and she held out the bundle of bakery.

Peter's social airs vanished in a heartbeat. He extracted one warm buttered bun, stuffed the whole thing in his mouth, and uttered a muffled, "Fank you, miff."

They reached Taldale Farm just after one in the afternoon. She remembered her last visit, the time she'd spent alone in the kitchen with Declan, and how he had so passionately declared she was his. She must remember not to be alone with him again. Laird John hadn't objected to their exchange of tokens—the daisies and her baked goods—but he hadn't yet lifted his ban on courting.

When The Crate creaked to a stop, she stared at the large front door in the center of the stone house—the house that would be hers one day if...she swallowed. What if her visit was not welcome? What if he was not alone? What if Declan saw her unannounced arrival as an intrusion? So many "ifs." Suddenly, she felt foolish—her visit, the revel buns, her gown—everything must look foolish. Oh dear. This was the wrong thing to do.

Lucy leaned forward and caught her attention. "Caya, is something wrong?"

"I don't think this is a good idea. We should go."

One of Lucy's elegant dark eyebrows lifted. "Nonsense. You made those revel buns especially for Declan. Now, go deliver them. No need to stay long. I'll wait here for you."

Peter hopped down and opened the wagon door.

"What if he's not home?"

"Then go inside and leave the bundle in the kitchen. He'll know who it's from." Lucy patted her arm for reassurance.

Caya wobbled on shaky legs to the front door. She knocked. Waited. Knocked again. Waited. Knocked a little harder. Still, no one answered. She looked back at the wagon. Lucy made a *go inside* gesture.

She lifted the iron latch and swung open the heavy oak door. Right away she heard sounds coming from the back of the house. She called to Declan before walking through the dining room. She called his name again when she reached the door to the kitchen.

A tall, dark-haired woman in an apron about Caya's own age greeted her with a hardened face. "Who are you?"

She stumbled backward. "I...I...I'm looking for..."

The woman folded her arms under her bust, lifted her chin, and said, "You're the wee bizzum what's bringing my brother that Cornishy scran. Did ye think you'd buy his affection with a few meat pies?"

Caya gasped. Of all the rude—

"I most certainly did not." Caya was so shocked, so taken aback by this woman's accusations, she couldn't think of a response strong enough to express her outrage.

"Oh, no?" The woman pointed at her bundle of bakery. "What's that you got there, then? Put a love spell on those, did ye?"

"Never."

"My little brother is a gullible sot when it comes to women, but you willnae put one over on me with your fancy cooking and pretty blue kirtle."

"You are the most, the most...inhospitable person I have ever met." She thrust her bundle at the woman. "Please give these to Declan." She sprinted out of the house as if her hair had caught fire, not forgetting to give the big front door a good slam behind her.

Lucy opened the wagon door, looking startled. Flinging herself inside the wagon, she shouted, "Drive, Peter. Get us out of here."

"Aye, miss." Peter made a sharp whistle. The wagon lurched forward and then trundled down the lane at a clip.

"What on earth happened in there?" Lucy demanded.

Caya was so spitting angry she couldn't speak at first. At last, she growled, "That *woman*."

"What woman?"

"Declan's sister. She's, she's... I dislike her."

The alarmed look disappeared from Lucy's face. "Oh, Margaret." She flapped a hand. "Don't mind her. She's been in a bad mood for years."

Caya leaned forward. "She accused me of trying to buy

Declan's affection with food."

Lucy tilted her head and let her gaze slip sideways. "Well, she's not completely wrong."

"What?" She couldn't believe her ears. Lucy was supposed to be her friend. Friends didn't accuse each other of such underhanded—oh my Lord, Lucy was right. Her jaw dropped open, and she fell back in her seat.

Lucy laid a hand on her knee. "Forget Margaret. Once she realizes Declan is in love with you, all will be forgotten and everyone will be happy."

Feeling dazed and numb around the edges, she nodded, not believing Lucy, but not wanting to further the conversation by arguing.

"You're upset. If you like, Peter can take you home. I'll go to the Farquhars on my own, and the boy can return for me later."

"No." She straightened her spine and her resolve. "I'm fine. Really." She wasn't fine, but she wouldn't ruin market day for Lucy. It was Lucy's favorite day of the month.

The market was crowded and loud. She welcomed the noise. The fugue of voices made conversation impossible. The last thing she wanted to do was chat about figs and fish. Buffeted between bosoms and backsides, she squeezed past people haggling over price and quality.

How could she have been so ridiculous? Why hadn't she known that enticing someone with food was no honest way to establish tenderness? A woman's attempt to snag a husband with her cooking was sad and desperate. And yet that's exactly what she'd gone and done with Declan. Humiliating.

Lucy paused in front of each booth to examine every apple, every cabbage, every blank-eyed salmon. Occasionally, she would hold something out for Caya's inspection. She would give whatever she held a dull nod. She knew Lucy had looked forward to sharing the day with her. She didn't want to spoil things for her friend, but good Lord, would this day never end? How many hours before she could climb into bed and pull the covers over her head?

Lucy slipped her hand into hers and pulled her inside a shop. The door shut behind them with a jingle. Sudden quiet made the clack of Lucy's heels on wood floorboards echo inside Caya's head. Clean linen and wool smells tickled pleasant memories of Cornwall. They were in a dry goods store very much like the one she had frequented in Penzance. She remembered Lucy's primary shopping mission: buy new trim to replace the frayed cuffs of her peach-colored gown.

"Which one do you like better?" Lucy asked, holding out two cards of fine Belgian lace.

She stared at them. They looked identical. She pointed to one.

Lucy sighed and handed the clerk one of the cards. "A yard of this one please, Mrs. Gordon."

"I'm sorry," she said. "I've ruined your market day."

"Never mind that. I'm sending you home with Peter. Listening to Mrs. Farquhar prattle about her grandson will be torture for you."

"But what about the saffron buns?"

"I'll give them to Mrs. Farquhar, if Peter hasn't eaten them all."

When they stepped outside the dry goods store, she and Lucy came to an abrupt halt. Three women blocked their way. Caya caught her breath and froze when she recognized the one with the white hair.

"Witch," the old woman hissed. Her companions repeated, "Witch," and made the sign of the horns to ward off evil spirits.

"Whatever do you mean?" Lucy demanded, standing regal under the darkening afternoon sky.

Taking no note of Lucy, the old woman pointed at Caya

and shouted to anyone within earshot, "She's a witch. I saw her charm a dead boy back to life with my own eyes."

Black talons of fear swooped down and clutched her shoulders. Her arms and her legs shook. She wanted to run, to break free, and flee this moment, return to the safety of Balforss, but her legs wouldn't move. Curious folk gathered behind the wretched-looking Scrabster women. The crowd, like the weather, was growing ugly.

"Stand back, all of you, and let us pass." Lucy's tone was firm, but the three women held fast. Lucy raised her voice. "Madame, I mean what I say."

The white-haired woman screeched, "I'm telling you, she's a witch."

Caya felt her knees buckle. She'd heard of women accused of witchcraft being drowned or burned, a practice that had been abolished in England nearly a hundred years ago. Did they still do such things in Scotland?

"Here now, what's all this?" Vicar James pushed through the crowd of people. "Stop your nonsense and let these women by." He thrust his way between Caya and her accusers.

The vicar seemed to have materialized from the ether, but she didn't care. She practically crumpled with relief. Lucy wrapped an arm around her waist, and they clung to each other.

"She's a witch," the old woman repeated, with murmured assents from her fellows.

Vicar James bellowed, "Take your wicked tongues and leave. Go home and pray to God he forgives you for your evil talk."

The women stood fast for a moment.

The vicar pointed an awful finger. "Go. Now," he commanded, looking and sounding like an avenging angel. At last, the three Scrabster women turned away and shuffled off, casting furtive glances behind them.

"The rest of you, go about your business and forget all this unpleasantness." The vicar waved a hand and waited until most everyone else had moved off. He turned and asked Caya, "Are you all right?"

She found she could breathe again. "Yes, thank you."

"Will you see us to the wagon?" Lucy asked.

"Of course." Vicar James placed a firm hand on Caya's back and guided them toward where Peter waited with The Crate. Supported between the two, she found she could relax somewhat. In fact, the vicar's large presence was a comfort.

"It was lucky you came along when you did," Lucy said. Caya detected a ripple of fear in Lucy's regal veneer, an armor she had thought was impenetrable.

"What were those women talking about?" he asked.

"Absolute nonsense, that's what." Lucy tightened her arm around Caya's waist.

It was wrong not to have told Laird John about the incident straight away. Caya could see that now. She would have to tell everyone about the boy at the river, and her silence on the matter would make her behavior seem worse. "It was my fault."

"Did something happen, Miss Pendarvis?"

"A child fell into the river while his mother was doing laundry. When she pulled him out, she and her friends assumed he was dead. I begged the mother to let me try what I'd seen fishermen do when their mates were thought drowned. I breathed into the boy's mouth. He woke and… well, the other women were angry."

The vicar stopped walking. "You breathed life into him?"

"I swear he wasn't dead. I did nothing wrong." Oh God, would Vicar James condemn her as well?

"No. No. I'm not angry. I've heard of this way of saving people. I thought it was fiction." He started walking again. "Don't trouble yourself. These women are simple folk, uneducated and prone to superstition."

"*Merde*." Lucy covered her mouth, looking shocked that the word had escaped.

The corner of Vicar James's mouth twitched. "I'll see you at services, then, on Sunday." He was teasing, and Caya appreciated his attempt to lighten the mood after what had been a frightening encounter.

Crystal blue eyes marked with infinite patience looked down on her. The expression on the vicar's face was so different from any she had seen from him before. She stole a glance at Lucy, whose raised eyebrows and pursed lips communicated an unmistakable, *I told you so*. For goodness' sake. Flora and Lucy were right. The vicar was fond of her.

• • •

Declan looked up from his work on the new bunker. "You what?" He stood in the center of his kitchen, unable to sort out the meaning of his sister's words.

"She has no right coming 'round with her fancy pies or pasties or whatever you call 'em." Margaret jutted a pugnacious chin at him.

The skin on his back sizzled like bacon in a hot pan. "What did you say to her?" He was taut, ready to snap, and he held his fists at his sides for fear of reaching out and shaking his sister.

Margaret's head wobbled on her neck with uncertainty. She looked to her husband. Hamish offered her nothing but an accusing look. With barely an ounce of shame, she said, "I might have called her a wee bizzum."

Declan exploded. "You what!"

Margaret flinched. He'd never frightened his older sister before. But then he'd never been this angry with her, either. She twisted her hands in her apron. "She left you these."

Margaret reached for the bundle of rolls. "I wouldnae eat them. They're probably charmed."

"What the bloody hell do you mean by that?" Declan bellowed.

"Everyone's calling her a witch."

"Who's calling Caya a witch?"

Margaret folded her arms across her chest, returning to her inherent state of belligerence. "Everyone in town. It's common knowledge. At least a dozen women witnessed her conjure wee Bobby Campbell from the dead."

Declan frowned at Margaret. His sister was making no sense at all.

"Explain yourself, woman," Hamish said with an implied *or else.*

"The Scrabster wives were doing laundry by the river, and Mrs. Campbell let out a skelloch. When she pulled her wee Bobby frae the water it was plain to everyone the boy was drowned." Margaret's lips curled back. "Then, out of nowhere, yon woman appeared and snatched the babe from the grieving mother's arms. She blew a charm into the bairnie's mouth." Margaret's eyes opened wide. "And he come alive again. She's a witch."

Declan leaned down and roared in Margaret's face. "Dinnae say that about my wife."

Hamish set down his rasp and calmly inserted himself between the two. "Best leave off before things come to blows."

Declan staggered toward the dining room door, panting from the effort of restraining himself. "You're the witch, Margaret," he shouted. "You and those gossiping bitches from town. Never repeat that evil lie again." He left the kitchen and stormed up the stairs to his bedchamber.

By the time he had washed and changed into his good clothes, his rage had reduced to a seething boil. He was struggling with tying his stock when he heard a light knock on his door. "Come."

Margaret entered his bedchamber cautiously. "Your dinner is ready."

"I'm no' wanting dinner." He continued to fumble with his stock, refusing to look at his sister.

"I'm sorry," Margaret said. She sounded as sorry as a prideful woman could be.

He ceased his battle with the stock and turned. "It's not me you should apologize to, is it?"

Declan and Gullfaxi kept a good distance ahead of Margaret. She was riding an old mule named George. Gullfaxi didn't like George. No one did. George was an ornery beast who, if given the chance, would bite you as soon as look at you. The only person George ever let sit on his back was Margaret. He supposed the crabbit animal saw a kindred spirit in his sister.

His older sister hadn't always been disagreeable. When she was young, she had been everyone's favorite, with her bonnie curls and her sweet disposition. Her one heart's desire—aside from Hamish—had been to be a mother. She would have been a good one, too. But she had slipped two bairns in the ten years she'd been married to Hamish, and those ten years of disappointment had made Margaret a bitter woman.

She called to him. It was the first time she'd spoken since they'd left his house. "What did you mean when you said, 'Dinnae say that about my wife?' Are you married to her?"

"No," he said. "But I will be."

"Ye've asked her?"

"Nae."

"Then how do you ken she'll marry you?"

"I dreamed she was my wife."

Margaret snorted. She didn't believe him. Most people didn't. Laird John certainly didn't. *Don't tell Caya about your dream. She'll think you're daft*, his uncle had said. His uncle was most likely right.

When they rode into the dooryard of Balforss, he saw the back of a red coat and tensed. British soldiers could only mean trouble. He relaxed when he recognized the man wearing the uniform of the Highland Regiment, Alex's younger brother, Ian.

Declan dismounted and strode across the yard, overjoyed to see Ian again. "Good to see you, man."

"And you," Ian said, clasping forearms with him and giving him a couple hearty slaps on the back.

"When did you return?"

"A few hours ago. The wars with France and America are over. I'm furloughed indefinitely." He spotted Margaret and went to help her down from the mule. "Hello, cousin."

George the mule curled his lips back and sank his teeth into Ian's arm before anyone could call a warning.

Ian jumped. "Jesus, that nasty bugger bit me."

Margaret slid off George's back. "Sorry, Ian. Did he break the skin?"

"Nae." He rubbed his arm. "But if that ass tries me again, I'll remove his ears with my dirk."

She kissed Ian on the cheek. "I'm glad you're back safe from France."

"Never made it to France. Only got as far as Flanders." He took Margaret's hand in his. "I saw my sister, Maggie, in Edinburgh last month. She sends her love to you."

Margaret smiled. She and cousin Maggie, the two Margarets born in the same year, had always been the best of friends. Declan remembered how they had done everything together. Even their weddings had only been months apart.

But Maggie had moved to Edinburgh with her husband soon after her marriage. Margaret rarely saw her best friend anymore, something Declan knew added to his sister's sadness.

"I miss her," Margaret said.

"She's with child again." Ian made a gesture in front of his stomach to indicate her size. "Her third."

Margaret whispered, "Three."

Declan opened his mouth to stop what he knew would come next, but he was too late. Ian had already spoken the words.

"You must have bairns of your own now. How many?"

She turned to stone for a moment. In words that could have easily been tears, she said, "No, Ian. We havenae been so fortunate."

Ian looked stricken. "I'm sorry, cousin."

She patted his chest. "Pay it no mind."

Ian turned to Declan, looking at a loss. "Em…I'm afraid you've missed dinner."

"We're here to visit Miss Pendarvis. Have ye met Caya yet?" he asked.

"Oh, aye. She's an awfy quiet wee thing. Does she ever speak?"

"Perhaps she's shy of your uniform," he said, feeling the need to make an excuse for her. "Is she in the house?"

"Last I saw, she took the path to the duck pond."

"Thanks, man. We'll talk later, aye? You and Alex and me, we'll have a dram."

This was a rare day in the Highlands. The sun had come out and burned off the storm clouds that had threatened earlier. Caya wasn't at the duck pond. He and Margaret continued down the path toward the field where Flora kept her hives. The afternoon sun flickered through the western line of trees. A light wind picked up, bringing with it the hum of bees. The biting midges would hatch soon, and the river would be good for fishing.

He spotted her in the distance. The sun cast a glow around her yellow hair like a halo. She had her back to him, walking through the field of waist-high wildflowers. She held her arms out and let her fingers trail over the tops of the flowers as she walked—almost but not exactly like the image in his dream. Odd, that. He couldn't put his finger on it, but the image was different. Why didn't she look like she did in his dream?

Rather than call to her, Declan increased his pace to catch her up. He was a few yards away when she turned and inhaled sharply. He'd startled her.

"What are you doing here?"

The grass stirred behind him and Margaret stepped forward. Caya's lips tightened, and she looked down.

"You've met my sister Margaret. She's married to Hamish Clouston, who works for me at the distillery. I told you about them. Do you not 'member?"

Caya said nothing.

"Margaret, meet Miss Caya Pendarvis."

Caya hesitated for a moment and then bobbed a curtsy.

Margaret attempted an awkward curtsy in return.

"My sister wants to say something to you." He elbowed Margaret in the side.

Back rigid and voice clipped, Margaret said, "I came to apologize for my rude behavior this morning."

He felt a twinge of sympathy for Margaret. It had to be difficult for her to bury her pride and apologize.

"I have no excuses," his sister said. "But I wanted you to know, the sweet rolls you brought were delicious." Margaret sounded as if she was ordering meat from the butcher. Short and to the point. She pulled a scrap of paper from her apron pocket and fumbled for her next words. "This is my receipt for raisin cake. I ken you're a crack cook, so..." Margaret thrust the paper in Caya's direction.

Declan's jaw dropped. Margaret never shared her receipts.

Caya had gone still. She looked at the proffered receipt for a long while before she reached for Margaret's peace offering. After reading the receipt, her face lit up as bright as her sunlit hair. There was joy in her smile. Declan felt a tightening in his chest. If Caya's unhappiness caused him pain, her happiness would likely kill him.

She released a short burst of laughter. "Thank you, Margaret. Thank you so much." His heart burst with feeling for them both—the prideful sister who would humble herself and the injured Caya who would offer forgiveness at once.

Margaret's shoulders relaxed. To his amazement, the two women turned their attention toward the silly receipt and chattered nonsense about sultanas and currants and nutmeg and whatnot. They walked past him as though he were invisible and headed back toward the pond, fastened at the shoulders.

"Caya?" he called.

She paused to look at him. "Yes, Declan."

"Thank you for the yellow rolls."

Her smile was sweet, but not as bright as the one she'd given Margaret in answer to the receipt. "They're called revel buns, and you're welcome." And then she curtsied again.

Bloody hell.

He trailed behind, feeling out of sorts listening to Caya and Margaret havering about food. A part of him was pleased they got on well. Another part of him resented his sister drawing Caya's attention away from him. He had hoped to have a word or two or three alone with her. Perhaps he could convince Margaret to toddle along home to Hamish.

"Caya."

She turned to him, her face unreadable. Damn, what he

wouldn't give to know her thoughts right now. "May I have a word with you? Please?"

Margaret slipped off toward the house, but Caya, thank the Lord, remained. He approached cautiously. How close, he wondered, would she let him get before she took a step backward?

"Margaret tells me you saved a boy's life. That was a brave thing you did, lass."

She twisted her hands and shifted her weight. "Yes, well, my help wasn't appreciated by the Scrabster women. They think I'm a witch."

"Will you look at me, please?" After a moment's hesitation, her eyes flicked up and met his. "Pay those nasty women no mind. You've nae need to fear. I will never let anything bad happen to you. I'll protect you with my life, and that's a promise."

"Thank you." She let her gaze slide away.

His skin cooled as if the sun had disappeared behind a cloud. All he wanted at this moment was to scoop her into his arms, squeeze the fear from her body, and stroke away her uncertainty. She was like a magnet, and he trembled from the effort of holding himself back.

"Is there something else that bothers you? You've but to ask and I'll—"

She stepped back, her jaw set, determined. "I wasn't trying to buy your affection with food."

"What?"

"I was simply thanking you for the—I wasn't—I didn't think I could make you—the buns were a gift, not a—"

The leash on his impulse broke, and he lunged. Before she could react, she was in his embrace, her small self engulfed by his awkward limbs, his cheek pressed against hers, his heart banging in his chest. Instead of resisting or attempting to free herself, Caya did the most remarkable thing. She let her body ease against his, melting, softening, forming her curves to match his angles, a warm, sultry, dizzying sensation.

She whispered in his ear, "Thank you for sending me daisies."

His cock sprang to life with no prelude, no warning. Was this how it would always be when he held her, instant arousal? He breathed her in, her silky cheek against his, her voice sounding sleepy, her words so intimate, familiar, wife-like. Jesus, he needed to take her home with him. Now. All this waiting was unnecessary.

Margaret shouted his name, and Caya pushed away as if she'd touched a hot stove. Damn his sister. Still, the way his body was on fire, he could hardly blame Caya for reacting as she did.

Margaret shouted again, and they turned their attention toward the house. Wild braying sounds echoed from the dooryard. It had to be George. Only the racket wasn't the typical complaint of an irascible mule. The calls sounded more like an alarm.

"What do you suppose has got him riled?" he asked.

Caya ran toward the front of the house, with him following close behind. They found Margaret attempting to calm the mule, but George continued to honk and screech at something farther down the lane. A riderless horse trotted toward the house, a wild-eyed Belgian, mane and feathers dancing, its loose harness trailing in the dust.

George stopped his braying, and for a moment, the four of them stood in silent confusion, watching the black giant approach.

"That's the horse that pulled The Crate," Caya said, almost to herself. Then more urgently, "Declan, Peter took the wagon to collect Lucy from the Farquhars."

He ran for Gullfaxi, heart drumming in his chest. He was already swinging his leg over the saddle when he shouted,

"Tell Alex and Ian." One swift kick and he and Gullfaxi were flying down the lane. They skidded into the turn at the road to Thurso, and he kicked harder.

"Come on, laddie. Come on!"

There was only one route to Thurso from Balforss. Peter had to be on this road. He slapped a hand to his hip. Bloody hell. He didn't have his dirk. He'd been in such a temper when he left his house he'd forgotten to arm himself. No time to take a detour home. He needed to find Peter and Lucy.

What could have happened? His mind hopped from one thing to another, a broken axel, a crash, a robbery gone wrong? Highway robbery was becoming more and more commonplace in the south of Caithness. Not so much here in the north. Until, perhaps, now.

Up ahead, he saw a single horse pulling a familiar looking gig.

"Whoa, laddie. That'll do, now."

As the gig neared, he recognized the driver, Dr. Farquhar. He had a woman passenger with him. The woman lifted a hand and waved.

Lucy.

Declan let go the breath he was holding. Thank the Lord. Lucy looked fine. But, when the gig was only a few yards away, he saw a slender body slumped over in Lucy's lap, and the relief he felt only a moment ago vanished.

Aye, me. Not wee Peter. He would be saddened by the loss of the boy, everyone would. But, having saved the boy's life and acted as his adopted father, Peter's death would devastate Alex.

Rather than stop them, he turned Gullfaxi and fell in step with Dr. Farquhar's gig.

Lucy shouted over the clopping of the horses, "When Peter was late, the doctor offered to drive me. We found him lying in the road next to the wagon."

Lucy had a good deal of blood on her gown. Peter's blood. It looked as though he'd received a blow to the head.

"Is he alive?" Declan asked.

"Yes. The doctor needs to stitch him up," she called.

Ian and Alex came barreling down the road, spewing clots of mud in their wake. They, too, pulled up short when they spotted Dr. Farquhar's gig.

"I'm all right, Alex," Lucy called out. "But we need to get Peter home straightaway."

Alex carried Peter upstairs. Lucy and Dr. Farquhar followed them, leaving Declan and the others standing in the entry hall, looking anxiously at their backs.

Laird John broke the charged silence. "Peter is in good hands. There's nothing more to do for the time being but wait and pray for his swift recovery."

"I'll be upstairs in my parlor should anyone need me," Flora said.

Laird John and Ian slipped into the library. No doubt for a tot of whisky. Declan could use one, too, but he remained in the entry, wanting to be near Caya.

"Is Peter hurt badly?" she asked him, her face covered in worry. She was a kindhearted lass. No doubt she had developed an attachment to the likable lad, he having acted as their cupid. He wanted to reassure her, smooth the trouble from her brow, tell her all would be well, but he couldn't. He didn't know for certain.

"I dinnae ken, *a leannan*." *A leannan*. He'd called her sweetheart without thinking. Would she know the meaning of the Gaelic word? If she did, would she like him calling her sweetheart?

Caya turned to Margaret. "There was so much blood."

His sister waved off her concern. "He's got a dunt on the head is all," Margaret said as though Peter had skinned his knee. "Head wounds bleed something awfy. He'll be fine."

The shadow lifted from Caya's face. Again, Declan resented Margaret's ability to do for her what he could not.

"I should go," Margaret said. "Hamish will worry if I'm not back before dark."

"You shouldnae go alone," he said.

Margaret released a sharp bark of laughter. "Do you honestly think that ornery mule would let anyone near us?"

He smirked. His sister had a good point, and for the first time he saw the wisdom in her choice of mount. "Still, take the seaward trail while it's still light and stay off the main road, aye."

He kissed her cheek, and she slipped out the door.

For a heartbeat, Declan thought he had Caya alone again. Then Alex thundered down the steps. He'd strapped on his sword belt and armed himself with dirk and pistol. There was a ferocity in Alex's eyes Declan knew well. Bloodlust.

"How fares the lad?" he asked.

Alex shook his head. Either he couldn't talk or didn't want to talk in front of Caya. He jerked his head toward the library door, a signal for Declan to join him.

"Wait here," he said to Caya. He added, "Please?"

She curtsied.

Damn.

Inside the library, Ian and Laird John waited with identical expressions of concern. Anyone would make the two for father and son they looked so alike, whereas Alex was the male reflection of his mother.

"Did the boy say what happened?" Laird John asked.

"The only word he said was 'pirate.' He was attacked. I'm sure of it. Lucy said the wagon wasnae damaged." Alex shook his head. "This was no accident. Some bampot bent on mischief must have tried to steal the draft horse."

"Aye," Laird John said, sounding weary. "Cottars, no doubt. Run off their land and so desperate they turn to thievery."

Ian, Alex, and Declan waited silently for Laird John to give them orders.

"I have sympathy for those left homeless, but I cannae let an attack on one of my people go unanswered." After a moment's thought, Laird John said, "Right then. You three search for Peter's pirate while there's still light."

"And if we find him?" Ian asked.

A disturbing grin formed on Alex's mouth. "We'll feed him to the fish."

• • •

Caya followed the men outside to watch them leave. They acted nonchalant and said Scottish things like, "Back in a trice" and "Dinnae fash yourself," which she had come to know as phrases of reassurance. But there was an intensity in their movements that made gooseflesh rise on her arms. Ian and Alex took off at a gallop with the draft horse in tow.

Declan walked toward her, holding the reins of Gullfaxi, a muscular dark gray gelding with a white mane and tail. She reached out, and the horse met her palm with his muzzle.

"Promise me you'll stay close to the house until we sort this out, aye?" His voice was as soft and velvety as Gullfaxi's nose.

"I promise." She found it difficult to meet his eyes when she added, "You'll be careful, too."

A puff of laughter escaped him as if she had said something silly. "I'll be fine."

He stood close. Very, very close. The setting sun cast shadows on his face, sharpening the lines of brow and cheek.

Had he grown more handsome since they met? Since he'd given her daisies? Since he'd held her in his arms and pressed his hot arousal to her stomach? What a wicked, wicked feeling. And worse, she had encouraged him. But oh Lord, she'd do it again, if given a chance.

He leaned closer and her heart beat faster. He was going to kiss her. Right here. Right now. Should she let him?

He touched her arm. "Oh, look," he said, as if he had discovered something small and pleasing. "You've got bitty gowans running all down the sleeve of your gown." Their eyes met, and he chuckled lightly. "You do like the daisies, then?"

She nodded.

"Good." He spun, stepped into the stirrup, and swung a long, graceful leg over Gullfaxi's back. Then he took off down the lane, standing in the stirrups, his coattails flapping in the wind.

He hadn't kissed her. She placed her disappointment in her box of guilty sins, along with the depraved sensations he provoked with his hot, hard, lanky body, and promised to account for them on Sunday.

She went up to Flora's parlor to inform her of the men's plan to retrieve the wagon. "They said not to worry, but I got a queer feeling. Will they be in danger, do you think?"

Flora took a deep breath and sighed. "Aye. Most likely." She lifted an eyebrow. "If there's danger, my Alex will find it. I shouldnae have named him Alexander. The name means *defender of men*."

"What does the name Declan mean?"

Flora gave Caya a knowing smile. "Declan means *full of goodness*."

She returned a look of perfect understanding. "Yes. He is."

Flora set aside her knitting and crossed the carpet to a

cabinet where she removed a bottle and poured two small glasses of a dark amber liquid. "Like John said, there's naught to do but wait. This will help." Flora handed her a glass of the stuff.

She smelled the contents and jerked her head back. "Whew."

"Brandy. Drink. It will settle you."

She rarely took spirits. She didn't trust them. Look what they'd done to Jack.

A yelp came from down the hall. She and Flora turned toward the open door to the parlor and heard a pitiful cry of pain. Poor Peter. Dr. Farquhar must be stitching his wound.

She and Flora tossed back their brandy and swallowed. A warm sensation blossomed inside her belly like a flower unfolding. Not at all an unpleasant feeling.

"Sit yourself doon, *a nighean*."

Flora's voice was calming, as was the endearment *a nighean*. The way Flora used it, it meant, "my girl or dear girl." Caya dropped into a cushioned chair by the fire and held her glass steady while Flora poured her another finger of brandy.

"Mrs. Swenson is sending up a cold supper," Flora said.

Another howl echoed down the hall, more tortured than the first.

"I don't have much of an appetite."

"Och, dinnae concern yourself with Peter's cries. He's awake. That means he'll be fine. I'd worry more if he made no sound at all."

The brandy must have emboldened Caya, for she asked, "Were you always so brave?"

If Flora was surprised or offended by the personal question, she made no sign.

"When you marry a Highlander, you learn to be brave." She gave more thought to her answer and added, "A Hieland man is, and always will be, a warrior at heart. It doesnae matter if he wears a uniform or an apron, fighting is in his bones, ye see." She took another sip of her brandy and leaned back in her chair. Addressing the fire this time, she said, "A Hieland man can be gentle as a lamb. Sweet as bees' honey." She smiled. "And charming. Very charming." Flora's eyes darkened. "But cross him, threaten his kin, or the ones he holds dear, and there will be blood." She looked up as if remembering she wasn't alone. "You cannae change that about a Hieland man. Dinnae even try. But know this, *a nighean*: he will love you with body and soul until the day he dies."

Flora turned back to the fire, apparently seeing something in the glowing peat that pleased her. Caya didn't move. She didn't want to break the bubble of safety Flora had built around them. She sat for a long while, listening to the *pop* and *hiss* of the fire and thinking about what Flora had said.

Scotland was a strange place, full of contradictions. Life in the Highlands seemed unpredictable and often extreme. In these past seven days, she had experienced fear, anger, sadness, joy. She had lost and found a family. Lost and found her self-worth. She'd been swept up in the happy chaos of Balforss, all the while more fully engaged with the world around her than she had been in all her life.

And the one constant throughout this whirlwind week was Declan. Even if he wasn't with her in the flesh, he was in her thoughts, pictured in her mind, his smile, his gleaming black brows, and the way he looked at her. The feelings he aroused in her melded into one. She could no longer separate the sexual attraction she had for him from mere fondness or admiration. Regardless of the reason—honor or desire—he was determined to marry her and she was determined to be his wife.

He will love you with body and soul until the day he dies.

Heavy footsteps popped their tranquil bubble. Dr. Farquhar appeared in the parlor doorway, looking tired and stooped. He ran a hand through his gray-streaked hair and sighed.

"Come in and have a dram," Flora said.

The doctor nodded his thanks and went to the cabinet, seeming well acquainted with where Flora kept her spirits and thus, Caya assumed, had a long association with Balforss. He poured himself a good amount from a different decanter. Whisky, perhaps?

"*Slainte*," he said and took a substantial swallow of the golden liquid.

Almost at once, the doctor's body remolded itself before Caya's eyes, gaining two inches of height and losing a score of years from his age. Whisky must have amazing restorative qualities as well as destructive ones. Perhaps, like medicine, the dosage is what made the difference.

"The lad will be fine," the doctor said.

Caya and Flora exhaled their worries in unison.

"Oh, good," Flora said. "Thank you, doctor. Will you stay for supper?"

"My thanks, but no. Tess will have my supper waiting. But, might I have a word with you, Miss Pendarvis?"

She startled at his request. "Me?"

Flora rose, but the doctor gestured for her to remain. He pulled a chair from the games table close to where Caya was seated by the fire. "I've heard talk. Gossip, no doubt, but I thought I'd speak directly to you."

A cold lump formed in Caya's belly, dousing the fire lit by the brandy. Dr. Farquhar must have sensed her unease.

"Dinnae fash, lass. It's only I hear you saved a wean who appeared to have drowned in the river. Is that so?"

"He wasn't dead," she insisted, her voice trembling with a mixture of fear and anger.

Dr. Farquhar leaned back and smiled as if her confirmation brought him pleasure. "Ah. So, it's true. I ask, you see, because, not long ago, I read a paper written by Dr. Trossach from Glasgow regarding the practice of resuscitation. The doctor recommended the application of tobacco smoke by fumigator and bellows into the patient's— em." Dr. Farquhar darted a look at Flora and made a delicate cough. "Em...to the patient's backside. But he also stated that, when those implements are not to hand, sharing one's breath with the drowned person can sometimes achieve the desired effect." Dr. Farquhar leaned forward. "Is that how it was, lass?"

She looked to Flora and received an encouraging signal. "I don't know about the tobacco part, but back home, I have seen bodies revived by breathing in their mouths. I'd never tried before, but the mother was so—and there was a chance the boy..." Heart racing, she bolted to her feet, her fists clenched. "I'm sorry. I didn't mean to cause trouble."

"*Wheesht, a nighean*," Flora said. "Dr. Farquhar's no' angry, lass. He's only curious. Sit."

"That's right," he said. "I had my doubts about Dr. Trossach's method, but now, well..." He stood with effort. "I see I've upset you, Miss Pendarvis. That was not my intention. I hope you will let me discuss this further with you at another time. As a doctor, I would want to know how you saved the boy." The doctor swallowed what was left in his glass and set it down. He made a polite bow to both Caya and Flora. "Good night, Lady Balforss. I'll see myself out."

After the doctor left, Flora said, "Caya, why did you no' tell me about this?"

"I was afraid. The women at the river were so angry. Like I had done something evil. And now they're telling people I'm a witch." Her chin wobbled. "I'm not a witch."

Flora took her hand and squeezed. "Of course you're not.

No one here would ever think such a thing. Scrabster women, were they?" Caya nodded and sniffed. "Covenanters," Flora said and made a *pssht* sound. "They see the devil in everything they dinnae understand. Pay it no mind, dear."

Mrs. Swenson entered with a tray of food. She took one look at Caya wiping away tears and gasped. "Peter? Has he?"

"Nae, nae, the laddie's fine. Caya's just a wee bit fashed over nothin'."

Mrs. Swenson made a trill of relief ending in, "Thank the Lord." She set the tray on the games table. "There's cheese, cold ham, bread, the last of the gooseberry jam, and some good ale."

Lucy swept into the room. She had changed her blood-soaked clothing but looked exhausted. "Peter's asking for you, Caya. He wants to tell you about the pirate." Lucy sniffed the air, and her face changed like quicksilver. "Supper." She fell upon the food. "Thank goodness. I'm positively famished."

As always, Lucy's presence in the room lifted everyone's spirits. All of Caya's earlier fears and regrets seemed to evaporate. She even managed a smile when Lucy took a large bite of jam-coated bread and reverently closed her eyes.

"I'll go say good night to Peter."

"Take this broth with you." Mrs. Swenson handed her a warm mug.

She slipped inside the open door to the room adjoining Lucy and Alex's bedchamber. Peter, his head bandaged, was sitting up in bed, reading a book by the light of an oil lamp. He looked up from his reading and his face contorted. A pitiful moan escaped on his sigh.

"How bad?" she asked.

"Just a scratch," Peter said, sounding valiant.

"I brought you some warm broth."

"Thank you, miss." He took the mug with both hands and gulped the contents down without a breath. He'd been washed thoroughly and dressed in a man's nightshirt. Lucy's doing, most likely. Even though Lucy insisted she had only fond feelings for the groom, it was apparent from her reaction to Peter's injury that she and Alex loved the boy.

Finished with the broth, he set the mug on the bedside table, wiped his mouth with his sleeve, and pointed at his head. "Dr. Farquhar gave me three stitches," he said with a measure of pride.

She sat on the edge of his bed. "Did it hurt very much?"

"Aye. Like the devil. But, I didnae mind it." He shrugged, a mannerism she had noticed was common among Scottish men, especially when talking about their injuries. "Doctor said I'll have a terrible scar." The boy looked enormously pleased, as though the scar was a badge of honor commemorating his battle with the pirate.

"What's that you're reading?"

He held the tattered volume up for her to read the cover. *A General History of the Pyrates.* "I'm looking for the pirate what attacked me," he said, flipping the pages to the next crude engraving. The title beneath the sword-wielding rogue read *Calico Jack Rackham.*

Caya didn't have the heart to tell him the volume had probably been published fifty years earlier, and the pirates enumerated within would be long dead, not roaming the Scottish countryside.

"What did the pirate look like?" she asked, humoring the boy.

"Not like this one," Peter said, pointing to the tricorne hat in the engraving. "My pirate wore a tall black hat what looked like a chimney pipe."

"A tall black hat?" she repeated.

"Aye. I ken he was maybe a Cornwally pirate on account he talked like you, miss."

Blood pounded in Caya's head.

"Miss? Are you all right, miss?"

She stared into space, imagining Jack attempting to rob a stranger. She had left her brother to fend for himself with no money, no skills, no connections, with no means to survive on his own. She'd hoped he would've found work, let go of some of his arrogance, and done something constructive to earn his way rather than cheat his way through life. She was a fool. She should have known. Jack had no sense at all. She might as well have left a child on the streets. And now he had broken the law and caused someone injury.

"Miss?" Peter touched her shoulder. "Please, miss. Shall I call someone?"

"No." She gathered herself into a semblance of calm again. "No, I'm fine. Get some rest now. I need to speak with Laird John."

She slipped downstairs and peered into Laird John's study. He was standing before the hearth, gazing into the dying fire. She hesitated at the door, wondering how the man would react when she told him of her suspicions. Would he be angry? Ask her to leave Balforss? Would he end all hope of her marrying Declan?

Laird John sensed her presence and turned. "You're up late. Were you worried, lass?"

"I was wondering what will happen when you find the man?"

"We'll bring him to the magistrate and he'll be tried for theft and assault."

Her stomach churned at the thought of Jack being arrested like a common criminal. She may be angry with her brother, she might never want to see him again, but she didn't want him to suffer. "Will they hang him?"

"Nae." Laird John made a doubtful face. "They might only fine him. If not, there's a chance he'll be indentured and deported to Canada."

The time to tell Laird John was now. She should say, "I think Peter's pirate might be my brother, Jack." She should say the words now. Now before it was too late.

"Caya? Is there something else?"

She wanted to speak the words, but they would not come. "N-no."

"Dinnae fash, *a nighean*. You're safe here at Balforss. Go to bed and sleep well."

She left the library with the weight of sin on her shoulders. Though she hadn't spoken a falsehood, she had, by omission, lied to Laird John just as she had when she didn't tell him about the Scrabster boy. Her father had always said omitting the truth was the same as lying. What was worse, she didn't know if she had lied to save Jack or to save herself. Either way, she had to get Jack out of Scotland. And to do that, she needed help.

. . .

Declan met his cousins at the abandoned wagon. While Ian hitched up the draft horse, he and Alex rode up and down the road to Thurso, searching for signs of Peter's attacker. They found nothing beyond the traces in the dirt marking the boy's scuffle. When the sun gave up its last bit of light, they quit the search.

The excitement generated by the hunt ebbed once they headed back to Balforss. Declan didn't need to return to the house. Alex and Ian could report to Laird John without him, but he hoped he might see Caya. Perhaps she waited up for his return. If so, he might continue what they'd started in the bee field. Maybe coax her to a secluded spot near the back staircase where he could have a word alone with her and… and what?

Yes. That was the question. What would happen next? If

they were married, he and Caya would retire for the evening. They would find their bed and do what married people do before they sleep. But what happened when one wasn't married? Jesus, he hated this waiting, this time in between finding his wife and marrying her. Why did his uncle insist they wait? Laird John must see by now, Caya was his. To dither about made no sense at all. Worse, his uncle had Caya believing courtship was necessary. Nonsense. Courtship was for people who didn't know each other, people who didn't already know for certain they were a perfect match. Damn, if only Caya would see that they were meant to be together.

He was still brooding about his stalled marriage when they entered the laird's study. He accepted a whisky from Ian and drank while Alex made his brief report. When he inquired after the ladies, Laird John indicated they'd all retired for the evening. Declan hid his disappointment, finished his whisky, and said his goodbyes. On the way out of the house, his stomach growled. Fine then. He'd go home to Taldale Farm and eat the remaining revel buns Caya had made him, the next best thing to seeing her.

Gullfaxi waited where he had left him near the garden, but there was something odd about the horse's demeanor. He seemed bothered by something in the shadows. Declan tensed.

"Who's there? Show yerself."

Caya stepped out from behind Gullfaxi, her eyes as round as two silver shillings. The warmth of the whisky in his belly rushed up his chest, over his shoulders, down his back, and settled in his loins. Alone. He had her completely alone, and she had come willingly.

"Caya."

"Please, I need to talk to you." She sounded frightened, and the hot rush of blood he'd felt a moment ago turned chill.

He glanced around. Certain no one was watching, he

led her a short way down the path toward the mill. "What troubles you, lass?" As they walked, he pressed a hand to her back to reassure her. More than that, he needed to make physical contact with her.

Once hidden by the trees, she stopped. "I need your help."

"Anything. You have but to ask and—"

"Wait until you hear what I have to say before you say yes." They were cloaked in darkness, and he couldn't see her features, but he could tell by the quality of her voice she was upset. One didn't grow up with three women in the house without learning to recognize the sound of one who had been weeping.

He fumbled in the dark until he found her hand and held it between his two. "Tell me, and I will do whatever needs to be done to take away your tears."

"I—I think Peter's pirate," Caya sobbed, "is my brother Jack."

Through her gasping and hiccupping, he gathered that Peter's pirate spoke like Caya, and wore a hat that sounded a lot like Jack's foolish topper. He didn't want to believe it at first, but the more he thought about it, the more it made sense.

"I don't want to see him arrested and jailed," she said, squeezing his hand. "Will you help me find him and get him out of Scotland?"

Hell. What she was asking of him was wrong. If the fugitive was Jack, he'd become a criminal. He'd assaulted and tried to rob a member of his clan. As his uncle had said, these actions could not go unanswered. How could he go against his laird's wishes and help a criminal escape justice?

"I know Jack didn't mean to hurt anyone. He was just frightened. Please help him. He's lost."

She was his wife. How could he refuse her? "Dinnae fash,

a leannan. I'll find him. Somehow. And I'll find a way to get him out of the country."

Caya pressed her cheek, wet with tears, to his hand. He wanted to hold her, kiss her, carry her home with him. But she was too upset to receive him. Instead, he guided her to the house and through the back entrance. He pointed her in the direction of the servants' staircase, and said, "It's all right. Go on to bed and I'll see what can be done."

On the way back to Taldale, he ruminated over his promise. He should have gone directly to his laird and told him the truth. Instead, he'd chosen to risk his laird's wrath in favor of his wife's affection. Had another man done what he'd done, Declan would have broken his sword arm. He turned his face up to heaven and shouted, "Lord, why do you make it so damn hard to get a wife?"

In answer, God took one last swipe at him. The skies opened up and began to piss down on his head.

He felt an uneasiness as he approached Taldale. No surprise to find the house dark. Still, he sensed something almost sinister about the place. He slid off Gullfaxi and led him to the as-yet-unfinished stable. Neither he nor the horse needed light to find his way. His eyes were good in the dark, a quality that had made him the best reconnaissance man in his regiment.

He removed harness and saddle and filled the feed trough with oats. Just as he finished rubbing the horse dry, the hair on the back of his neck bristled. He glanced over his shoulder, feeling as though he were being watched. Seeing nothing, he shrugged and went back to his work.

By the time he'd finished putting Gullfaxi away, the rain had let up, and the moon peeked out between fast-moving clouds. On his way to the house, Declan noticed something had disturbed the fence around the henhouse. Damn. A fox must have gotten inside. Lord only knew how many chickens he'd lost. No doubt the eggs were gone as well. He'd go without breakfast tomorrow morning.

Bloody hell.

Soaked and shivering, he returned to the stable for a mallet and some twine to mend the fencing. He hoped the makeshift repairs would prevent further damage during the night. He'd finish the job properly tomorrow.

Damn. The kitchen door was ajar. Hamish would have been the last to leave and it wasn't like him to be so careless. He fumbled for the flint and struck it repeatedly, cursing his cold stiff fingers. At last, lamp aglow, he turned the flame higher to let the golden light warm the room.

Bloody, bloody hell.

Something—a fox or a polecat maybe—had gotten into the kitchen and raided his meager pantry. He spun around and searched the top of the new work table Hamish had finished for him. All the way home in the rain, he'd been looking forward to eating the last two revel buns. They were gone. Declan nearly wept.

He held the oil lamp over the bunker. Both the rolls *and* the towel they were wrapped in were gone. In fact, the telltale mess common to animal pillage was absent altogether. He examined the pantry more carefully. Various items were missing, but no broken jars or wreckage of any kind. Not something, but *someone* had robbed his pantry.

A jolt of panic sang through his body. Lamp in hand, Declan raced through his empty dining room and drawing room, then bounded up the stairs to his bedchamber, the only room where he kept anything of value. He stood in the doorway and let the light of the oil lamp cast shadows on the empty hooks where he stored his weapons—his sword, pistol, and dirk. Gone.

The top of his clothing chest yawned open. He rummaged through the contents. At least the jakey bastard had had the good sense to leave his old uniform alone. Alas, any clean clothing of value had been taken. Even the good socks his oldest sister, Lizzie, had made for him this past Christmas were missing. He reached toward the bedside table, in need of whisky. The bottle was gone.

Bloody fucking hell. Jack Pendarvis had robbed him blind.

Chapter Eight

He reached out and called her name. He couldn't hear her answer over the clamor. The gowans were everywhere. They almost enveloped her. He called to her again, but something choked him into silence. He kicked harder. Harder. Reaching out. He almost had her.

"Declan."

The sound of his name jerked him awake. He lay naked, his legs tangled in the bedclothes, hair and pillow damp with sweat.

"Declan." His sister Margaret pounded up the stairs.

He sat upright and covered himself before Margaret burst into the room. Her wild-eyed expression relaxed into relief.

"Do you ever knock, woman?"

"Someone's robbed the—" She stopped to catch her breath.

"I ken it," he said. "Is Hamish with you?"

"Aye, outside seeing what damage is done to the chickens."

"Go home to your cottage, Margaret. Lock the doors and

load the musket. Dinnae leave until Hamish returns."

Still half in a dream state, Declan went to the basin, poured water from the ewer, and splashed his face until he returned to his skin. His dream of Caya had left him shaken. Why couldn't he reach her? What did it mean? His shirt and britches lay on the floor where he'd dropped them last night. They hadn't dried completely, but he pulled them on, cold and uncomfortable. He was hungry.

A short time later, Declan and Hamish followed the wake of rubbish the thief had left. An empty jar of jam, a grimy stock, the tea towel that had held Caya's revel buns, a discarded crust of Margaret's meat pie, a pair of tattered breeks, and one filthy stocking with a hole in the toe. The bampot had taken the path that led to his stillhouse. Shite.

He and Hamish left their horses to graze on a patch of sweet grass, then crept through the stand of trees surrounding the malting shed and stillhouse. Most people who lived nearby knew approximately where the distillery was hidden. Those folks also knew to stay the hell away.

"Do you see him?" Hamish whispered.

"Nae. But the lock on the door is broken."

"Could be someone's inside."

"Could be. Go canny, man. He's got my pistol."

The two Scots slipped silently through the grass. When they reached the structure, stertorous vibrations from within rattled the timber walls. Declan rolled his eyes at Hamish. This was the most incompetent thief in all of Christendom.

Inside, shafts of morning sunlight angled through the line of windows on the east side of the stillhouse. One hit the belly of the copper still, making it glow like it was on fire. Another bathed the sleeping form of a man. He lay snoring on the dirt floor, sprawled on his back, an empty bottle of whisky in one hand and a pistol in the other. When Declan bent and retrieved his dirk and firearm from the man, he wrinkled his nose. Vomit crusted the man's spotty beard and hair. From the stain on his britches—Declan's britches—he'd pissed himself, as well.

"Jesus," Hamish muttered and went back outside.

Declan kicked a booted foot. "Get up."

No movement.

He kicked harder and shouted, "Get up, ye mingin' clot-heid."

The dung heap stirred slightly, making incoherent sounds. Hamish returned with a full bucket of water and dumped it on the man's head. He rose, sputtering for breath. Declan grabbed him by the back of his jacket and dragged him out into the daylight, whereupon he curled into a ball like an exposed grub.

"Stop your grietin' and pull yourself together, ye silly wee man," Declan said. "I'm no' going to kill you."

He uncovered his head. Eyes like two pee holes in the snow blinked up at Declan.

"You," the thief hissed.

"You ken who he is?" Hamish asked.

Declan had hoped he was wrong. No such luck. "Aye. Caya's brother, Jack Pendarvis."

Hamish whistled the *I'm glad I'm not you* tune. *Traitor.*

The Cornishy bastard reeked. "Here," said Declan. He handed Hamish his pistol. "Take him down to the river and make him bathe. I cannae take the stink of him."

"Wait!" Jack shouted. "Where's my sister? I want to speak with my sister."

Hamish shoved Jack in the direction of the river. When Jack resisted, Hamish grabbed his wrist, twisted, and marched him to the water's edge, the Cornishy devil squealing and cursing all the way.

While they were gone, Declan paced. What the hell was he going to do with the bastard? If it had been anyone else, he would have taken the thief into Thurso and handed him to the magistrate. But no. As usual, things were far more difficult for him. His stomach growled, a loud angry gurgle. Bloody hell, he was hungry.

He had no doubt Pendarvis was the man who had assaulted Peter and tried to steal the draft horse. Failing that, the bampot had robbed Taldale. Jack should be tried for robbery and acts of violence. Unfortunately, this same thief was also Caya's kin. Jack had already hurt the lass deeply by his disregard for her welfare. The last thing Declan wanted to do was further upset his sensitive bride with her brother's arrest. Plus, he'd promised her he would help get Jack out of the country.

On the other hand, he had an obligation to protect Balforss and all the people within. The right thing to do was to bring Jack to Laird John and allow his uncle to deal with the matter. But what about Caya? Shouldn't his sweet wife come first? Shouldn't he see to her well-being before all else? True, they weren't yet married. But they would be. His dreams told him so, and his dreams never lied.

He had a sudden murderous thought. He could drown Jack in the river. Jack was a hazard to the public. How many other people had Pendarvis robbed along the way to Balforss? The world would be better off without the man. Hamish wouldn't tell anyone, and Caya would be none the wiser.

But God would know, and he would make Declan pay double. He sighed.

Hamish returned from the river with Jack at gunpoint. Jack looked marginally improved. His hair lay slick against his small, misshapen head. Finding his tall beaver hat in the dirt, he brushed it off and set it atop his head, making him look all the more like a numpty.

"I want to see my sister."

Declan refrained from laughing at the ridiculous-looking

fellow and addressed his brother-in-law instead. "I've a dilemma of sorts."

"Oh, aye?"

"I demand to see my sister now," Jack said.

Declan turned a deaf ear to Jack and continued his conversation with Hamish. "The bastard is Caya's brother, my future brother-in-law."

"He's also a thief," Hamish said.

"Are you listening to me?" Jack shouted.

"True, but put yourself in my place," Declan said. "I'm your brother-in-law. Would you turn me over to the law?"

Hamish rubbed his chin as if considering the notion.

Declan chuckled. "Right, but even if you could catch me, how do you think Margaret would react?"

"She'd skin me alive." Hamish nodded. "I see your point. Would you have me turn him in for ye?"

Jack screamed at the top of his lungs. "I said, I want to see my sister now!"

"Quiet!" Declan barked. He turned back to Hamish. "Nae, but thanks. In any case, I cannae let this"—he jerked a thumb at Jack—"complication make us lose a day of whisky making. With the rain last night, the malt is liable to mildew."

"True. We need to grind the malt today or risk losing the entire harvest."

Declan pressed his lips together, considering his next move. "Fine then. Only one thing to do." He spun around and stormed toward Pendarvis.

Jack backed away. "No. No, wait," he said, cowering like a child. He stumbled over a clump of grass and fell on his ass. His foolish hat toppled off his head, and Declan crushed it under his boot.

He reached down and pulled Jack to his feet, shook him once, and released him. "You have a choice, Mr. Pendarvis," he said, careful to keep all traces of rage from showing on his face. "You can work for me or go to the magistrate's office. Which will it be?"

Jack straightened his jacket with a tug. "Neither. I am a gentleman and demand to be treated—"

"Which one?"

"Gentlemen are not born to labor like common—"

"Hamish, tie him up and take him to the magistrate."

"Wait, wait, wait." Teeth on edge, Jack capitulated. "Fine. I'll work."

Hamish instructed Jack to lug sacks of grain from the malting shed to the mill. The Scots suffered through nonstop complaints, groans, and curses until the man's whining became background noise to the loud process of grinding the malt for the mash.

At midday, Declan sent Hamish home for food and to let Margaret know all was well. His gnawing hunger only compounded his irritability. The fact that Jack, having consumed the contents of his pantry, was the cause of his hunger, made him hate the man more.

"Where's the whisky?" Jack asked.

"You drank it all." The memory galled Declan.

"No. Where do you store your whisky?" Jack addressed him as if he were a halfwit.

"This is our first making. It willnae be suitable to drink for three years." Jack must truly think he was a numpty if he expected him to say where he kept his cache of aging whisky.

Desperation in his voice, the man persisted. "I'm parched. I need something to drink."

"Hamish will return with ale, no doubt."

Jack made a derogatory snort and tripped over the bag of oats he'd just set down. What the hell was he going to do with the man? He was about as welcome as a turd floating in the beer. And how did he and Caya come from the same sire? They were so different.

"Did you wed my sister as you promised?" Jack asked him.

"I will."

"Where is Caya? What have you done with her?"

"Stop pretending you care a whit about her." The man had no right to speak her name, much less inquire after her.

"I want to see her."

"She doesnae want to see you. And if you go near her, I swear I'll tear out your throat with my teeth."

Jack turned back to his work, mumbling something about Scottish savages.

Declan would be damned if he would upset Caya by bringing her brother to Balforss. Worse, she might forgive Jack and want to keep him. The thought of having to look at the man, speak to him, work beside him every day, made him want to retch.

Hamish returned with food, and they found a shaded spot near the river to eat. Jack drank off his ale in one go, then stuffed his face with Margaret's cottage pie. It was the first time he'd been quiet all day. Declan's mood improved once he'd eaten. He even laughed at one of Hamish's bad jokes.

Hamish jerked his thumb in the direction of the Cornishy whelp having a piss in the bushes. "Have you decided what you'll do with Gentleman Jack over there?"

Declan sighed and closed his eyes. "I need to find a place to stash him until I can locate a boat that'll take him as far away from here as possible."

Hamish lifted both hands and shook his head.

"Nae, I wouldnae do that to you and Margaret," he assured his brother-in-law. "Besides, your place is too close to the big house. No. I have to get him off the property."

They were quiet for a while as they watched Jack Pendarvis pour himself another tankard of beer and then slop it on the ground when a bee startled him.

"I've an idea," Hamish said.

"Oh, aye?"

They both continued to stare at the Bee versus Man dumb show taking place before them.

"Do ye ken Mr. Kinney what runs the public house in Scrabster?" Hamish asked.

"Neil Kinney?"

"That's him."

Jack dropped his tankard on the ground and flailed both arms at the bee.

"For the price of a cask of your best, he'd keep yon loon pickled and out of sight until the next free trader comes through." Hamish applauded when a sharp cry signaled the bee had won the battle.

Declan liked the idea. For the first time that day, he believed things might work out to his advantage. By month's end, if all went according to plan, Jack Pendarvis would be out of his hair, and Caya would be his wife.

Declan got to his feet. "Thanks, man. That's what I'll do."

$$\cdot \cdot \cdot$$

Caya followed Flora and Lucy up the gravel path toward the church. They passed a knot of women who fell silent and turned their backs, the same women who had been so welcoming last Sunday. Had she imagined the snub? And where was Declan? She needed to speak with him about her brother.

Another woman crossed herself and pressed her child behind her—a gesture that looked suspiciously like she was shielding the boy from her. Or was Caya being overly sensitive since Friday's encounter with the Scrabster women at the market? She could be mistaken.

Once inside, she scanned the dozen or so heads already

seated. Where was Declan? He hadn't met her outside the church as he had last week. She swept past a fat man who made a disapproving sound. The grunt was meant for her. There was no mistaking it. Then someone whispered, "Witch," and her heart took off at a gallop. Where was Declan? He should be here with her, by her side, to protect her from these people as he had promised. Why wasn't he here? Had something happened?

Or was he still searching for Jack? Upon waking this morning, Caya realized she had asked too much of Declan. She was wrong to beg him to save her brother, especially after Jack had attacked poor Peter. Asking him to intercede on Jack's behalf—on her behalf—was selfish and put Declan in danger, compounding her guilt and adding to her mounting pile of wrong-doings. Now that she was thinking clearly, she wanted to retract her request, but where was he? She needed him here.

Flora and Lucy slid into the pew and made room for her to join them. She paused at the end. Once seated, she would be trapped. No way to flee from the suspicious stares of the congregation. Did everyone think her a witch?

Lucy patted the space next to her. "Ignore them."

"Where's Declan?"

"Making whisky, most likely. Sit down."

Whisky? How dare he make whisky when she needed him here with her. Her fear molded into anger. Odd how the two emotions felt almost the same. Caya took the proffered seat next to Lucy and reminded herself she was in church. No place for anger. No place for fear. She took a deep breath and tried to pray. When the processional began, the screech of Mr. Donaldson's fiddle drove a spike of pain through her forehead.

It was Whitsunday. Pentecost. She gathered the frayed ends of her nerves and listened to the sound of the vicar's voice rather than his words. Soothing. Calming.

Alex sat next to her, looking the proud father with Jemma in his arms. She'd never known a man to be as engaged in the care of his child as Alex. She'd even seen him change the baby's napkin. Twice. Were all Scots as demonstrative, or was it only the Sinclair men who exhibited the trait? In any case, she was glad for the distraction sweet Jemma provided.

She rose with the congregation and sang "Away with Our Fears, Our Trouble, and Tears." It was one of her favorite hymns. She knew all the verses. The congregation sang the first verse with confidence, then stumbled through the second before stopping altogether. Not everyone in church had a prayer book. No one had hymnals.

It came to her with a rush of clarity. That's what she would do. She would write down the lyrics she remembered from her favorite hymns and make copies for the members of the choir. Laird John would provide her with ink and paper. If not, surely Vicar James would find the necessary supplies. Four copies would be enough to start with. People could share. And...

The quality of Vicar James's voice changed from soothing to deep and booming, the kind of voice that demanded her ear.

"It has come to my attention that many members of our congregation believe in witchcraft. *Witchcraft!*" He smiled and people laughed. A few glanced in her direction. She wanted to hide.

"Absurd, is it not? My parishioners speaking of witchcraft? You might ask yourself, 'Why would the vicar mention witchcraft in church?'" He pulled the corners of his mouth down and made a face. More nervous giggles. "I will tell you." He paused, waiting for quiet. "Because I hear nothing but talk of witches among you. No talk of our Lord. No talk of our Savior. No talk of good deeds. Only talk of witches."

He paused again for a few uncertain titters this time. Then Vicar James slammed his Bible shut with a crack and shouted, "Blasphemy!"

Caya flinched, as did most everyone in church. He cast a critical eye over the crowd like a disapproving schoolmaster. Mouths hung open, not knowing what to make of the vicar's outburst.

"I would expect this from the simple folk of Scrabster. Poor. Uneducated. Taught to fear anything they don't understand. But from people of privilege, people who know better, people like you?" His face turned an angry red, and his eyes glowed like twin torches of fury. "Outrageous. Your talk is for no one's benefit but your own idle entertainment. Worse, you chatter at the expense of the innocent. I am ashamed by your behavior, and you should be ashamed as well."

The vicar paused, breathing hard. Perspiration beaded on his forehead. His jaw muscle flexed and jumped. "A young woman new to us performs what seems like a miracle, using knowledge gifted to her by God. Knowledge we lack." He was shouting now. "And the way we thank her is to spread unfounded rumors about her, blacken her good reputation, and assign wicked motives to her actions."

Caya glanced around. No one was looking her way now. Many dipped their heads and closed their eyes. Others still had faces frozen with astonishment. These people had probably never seen their vicar angry before.

James banged his fist on the pulpit. "Why spread these lies? To make ourselves seem superior? Holier? To tarnish her spotless soul so as to make ours seem cleaner? Why would we do such a thing?" In a tone that might as well have come from the heavens, James raised the Good Book. "What does the Lord have to say about such behavior?"

He flipped the Bible open to a marked page. "'They are filled with unrighteousness, wickedness, covetousness, maliciousness; full of envy, murder, debate, deceit, malignity; *whispers.*'" He paused to breathe, then leaned out over the pulpit, and in a voice low and deadly, said, "Search your souls. Confess your sins. Ask for forgiveness and remember Him always. Above all, recognize His gifts and give Him thanks."

James said a short prayer, crossed himself, and stepped away from the pulpit.

Perfect silence. Not a rustle of skirts. Not a scuff of a boot. Not a cough or a sneeze. Everyone seemed to have stopped breathing. Then, with the perverse timing characteristic of all toddlers, Jemma shattered the silence with a shriek. Standing on her father's lap and facing him, she clapped her hands on his cheeks, repeating, "Da, da, da, da, da."

A smattering of nervous laughter broke the tense atmosphere in the room.

"Thank you for reminding me, dear Jemima," Vicar James said, smiling, his good nature somehow restored. "We have not one, but two baptisms on this auspicious day. Will the parents and godparents please come forward?" The congregation made a collective sigh. Everyone loved a baptism.

She hadn't needed Declan by her side after all. Vicar James had come to her defense in a way Declan could not. Declan might have intimidated the nasty wagging tongues. But the vicar had swept aside the rumors and shamed the gossipers into silence. James had been her champion today.

Following communion, Vicar James made an announcement about the formation of a church choir. "Anyone interested in taking part, our first meeting will be held here this coming Saturday at one in the afternoon." He gestured toward the Sinclair pews. "Miss Pendarvis has accepted my request to lead the choir." He sweetened the offer with, "And Mrs. Swenson will provide refreshments at the first meeting." His charm having returned, Vicar James added, "You won't want to pass up Mrs. Swenson's molasses cakes."

After church, Caya found the vicar outside, talking to an older couple. She lingered until he was finished and then approached him. He looked down on her with an apologetic smile.

"I expect those words were for my benefit," she said.

Vicar James pulled his chin in and furrowed his brow. "Absolutely not. Every member of my congregation needs an occasional talking to about the sin of gossip."

The blood rose in her cheeks at his teasing. She looked down, hoping her bonnet would conceal her reaction. "Even so, thank you."

"It was my pleasure to be of service to you, Miss Pendarvis." The playful tone had left the vicar's voice. She looked up. He was watching her intently. He spoke again, but Lucy interrupted them.

"Caya, darling, Mother Flora is looking for you." Caya curtsied low to Vicar James. As she left them to look for Flora, she heard Lucy say, "That was the most entertaining homily I've ever heard."

Caya met Flora with the other women of Balforss by the church gate. "Lucy said you wanted to see me."

"Aye. I'm sending Alex to fetch Declan for supper. I thought I'd check with you first in case you'd rather I ask someone else?" Flora flicked her gaze toward Vicar James.

Flustered, she tripped over her words. "No. The vicar—Declan. I mean—"

"Take a breath, dear."

She did and found her composure. "I'd be happy to see Declan at supper. Thank you, Flora." Worry over her brother still plagued her. She needed to speak to Declan.

"Very well," Flora said. "Wait for me in the wagon."

Lucy was the last to wedge herself into The Crate. With the six women squeezed into place, Flora signaled Ian to drive on. A sharp whistle, a snap of the reins, and they were bumping and jostling along the road home.

"The vicar's lesson today would rival that of any Presbyterian preacher," Flora said. "You do know that was for your benefit, Caya. Nae doot quelling the gossip about you rescuing the Scrabster boy."

The other women made sounds of agreement.

She dipped her head. "I thanked him after services."

"I spoke to Vicar James, as well," Lucy said. "He suggested we visit the Presbyterian minister, Reverend Linklater, and little Bobby Campbell's mother tomorrow afternoon."

"In Scrabster?" Caya gasped. Visiting Scrabster, walking among those hateful women, even talking to their clergyman, made her shiver. "Why should we do that?"

"To show them you don't have horns and a tail, of course."

The other women uttered sounds of shock and dismay.

"Oh, stop it. I'm joking," Lucy said, piqued. "Why is everyone so solemn? I always feel lighthearted after service." She brushed away their sounds of disapproval with a wave of her hand. "Anyway, the vicar thinks it's a good idea, and so do I, but it's up to you, Caya."

She looked down at her gloved hands. She would like this business to be over—to go away for good. "If you and the vicar think it will help, then, yes. I'll do it."

"Good. Vicar James will collect us at the noon hour tomorrow."

"I'd feel better if Declan went with us," she said.

Lucy turned her blue eyes on Caya like a cat who'd spotted a juicy mouse, and her insides squirmed. "Do you expect him to protect you from the Scrabster women or from the vicar?"

Everyone in the wagon laughed. Everyone except Caya, whose face burst into flames.

• • •

Declan finished making the mash by early afternoon and was just locking up the distillery when Alex rode up.

"I came to see your progress," Alex called, and he hopped down from his favorite horse, a warmblood named Goliath.

Always glad to see his cousin, Declan clasped his forearm in greeting. "We'll be ready to fire the pots on Tuesday."

"Need help?"

"I'd be glad of it." It would be a relief to have another set of hands to work the stills.

"We missed you in kirk." Alex gave him a sidelong look, and he wondered what the hell he meant by it.

"Oh, aye?" he said, fastening the new lock on the stillhouse door.

"Caya was asking after you."

Ah, that was it. Alex meant to nettle him about his affection for Caya. "Did she now?" He'd be damned if he'd give Alex any satisfaction.

"Ma invites you to supper, if you've the time."

"Thanks. I will."

The two cousins walked the path toward Taldale Farm, their horses trailing behind them. After a few minutes of silence, Alex cleared his throat.

"It's too bad the whisky season falls right in the middle of courting season," Alex said.

"I didnae ken there was a particular season set aside for courting."

"I speak metaphorically, ye ken. I only mean now might be your best opportunity."

"Why now and not a week from now?" He refused to fall

prey to his cousin's goading. He'd already won Caya by saving her brother. No worries about courting from now on.

"Because, well..." Alex pulled at his collar as though he'd tied his stock too tight. "Someone else may beat ye to it."

Alarm seized Declan in his tracks. He growled out one coherent word. "Who?"

Alex paused and tugged at his collar again but didn't answer.

He grabbed the front of his cousin's coat and jerked on it once. "Who!"

Alex's face remained impassive. He blinked and said cordially, "Declan, let go a' me."

The air went out of his passion all at once. He relaxed his grip, smoothed his cousin's coat, and stepped back, embarrassed by his outburst. "Sorry."

Alex cast a resentful look at him before untying his stock and loosening his collar with irritable tugs. At last, he said, "You were right aboot the vicar. He's most definitely pursuing Caya."

"That bloody Bible-beating God-botherer—" He stopped himself, a horrifying thought having occurred to him. "Does she return his interest?"

"I dinnae ken, cousin. But ye best be about your business soon, or she might." By "business" his cousin meant courting, a thing about which Declan was not well versed.

"There's nae need to court Caya. She's mine."

"Oh really? Does Caya know that?" Alex was a little too smug sounding for his liking. "Because I dinnae think the vicar knows she's taken."

Gullfaxi stomped and nickered.

"Has he asked permission to court her? Has your da agreed?"

Alex shrugged. "Dinnae ken, but why would he say no?"

Bloody hell. Was the vicar good at courting? Would the

vicar's skill at wooing Caya outshine his own clumsy efforts?

"He's got no business sniffing around my woman, and I'll tell him that first chance I get."

"Seems to me you ought to make yourself plain to Caya."

Gullfaxi nudged Declan in the back, and he pushed him away.

"I have. Repeatedly. But your da and that blasted vicar keep getting in my way." And anyway, wasn't saving her brother from arrest enough to secure her commitment? "Why do I have to suffer the indignity of courting when it's a simple matter of marrying the lass and taking her home?" Gullfaxi nudged him in the back more forcefully. "Christ, you're an impatient beast."

"Aye, you are," Alex said. "And if you don't slow down and listen to what Caya wants, she'll find it somewhere else."

The truth of Alex's words burned their way through his conscience. He was an impatient beast. He knew very well that women expected romance. Aside from three bunches of flowers and a scant few words about gowans and revel buns, he hadn't bothered with any of that. Though humiliating, it was time to admit he knew nothing about courtship and ask Alex for help.

Alex started to walk, and he fell in beside him. "Did you court Lucy?"

"Och, me? Well, ye ken we were betrothed by our fathers. Marriage was assumed, of course, but I still needed to win her favor if we were to be happy, so I tried to court her." He chuckled and leaned his head back. "Oh God, I made such a mess of it, it's a wonder she didnae turn around and head straight home for London."

"You mean the trick you played on her?" When Lucy had first arrived in Scotland, Alex had pretended to be a common soldier. She'd discovered his chicanery and had been so livid Declan thought she'd never forgive Alex, but she had.

"That and other stupidity. I was thoughtless, jealous, arrogant."

Declan cringed a little. Alex had just described his own behavior.

"I even forgot to ask her to marry me." Alex shook his head. "I was too proud to tell her."

"Tell her what?"

"To tell her that I loved her. I almost lost Lucy because I couldnae stop long enough to court her properly, to woo her like a man. And you'll lose Caya if you neglect her."

"I dinnae ken how to court." He ran a hand through his tangled hair.

"Och, it's easy, man."

"Easy? What did you do? I mean, how did you do it?"

Alex leaned toward him and spoke low as if he were about to disclose the secret to making gold. "You've got to get close enough to kiss her first. If you kiss her, and she kisses you back, then you know you can bind her to you."

"Oh?" He'd kissed women before and was confident he'd done it right, but couldn't recall any of them kissing him back. However, the thought of kissing Caya and Caya kissing him *back* pleased him very much.

"You've got to ask her to marry you. Dinnae forget to do that. And you need to tell her things, true things, things you feel in your heart."

"Like what?"

"Tell her she's pretty. That's a good start. She'll also want to know why you want to marry her."

They walked in silence for a much longer time. Declan debated the wisdom of telling Caya why he wanted to marry her. He wanted to marry her because his dreams told him it was the way it should be and he trusted his dreams. He also wanted to marry Caya because if he didn't, he thought he might die.

Perhaps if he kissed her, and she kissed him back…yes, if she kissed him back, he would tell her about his dream. If she kissed him back, then she would believe him when he told her why they should be married. And if she kissed him back that would mean she liked his kissing. Wouldn't it?

"Alex, do women like the kissing?"

"Oh, aye. They like kissing a lot."

"And do they like the bedding, as well?" Declan couldn't imagine any woman enjoying his ugly bits.

Alex snorted. "Do you mind the time we hid up in the stable loft? The time we were in trouble wi' my da?"

"Which time? We hid there every time we were in trouble with your da."

"That time we saw Geordie with Tottie in the loose box."

He flushed with the memory of the two half-naked bodies grunting and struggling in the hay. He and Alex had been barely thirteen. At first, they'd thought Geordie was hurting Tottie. But it soon became clear that both parties were enjoying the frenzied tussle. The alarm he had felt had quickly turned to arousal when Geordie had abandoned his breeks and waved his considerable cockstand lewdly at Tottie. Tottie in turn had pulled her skirts up to her waist and, for the first time, Declan had caught a glimpse of a woman's private parts.

He and Alex had lain frozen on their bellies in the loft above, staring wide-eyed at the activities below. After spending some time fondling Tottie while she panted and moaned for "more, more, more," Geordie had climbed aboard and begun his business in earnest. The final indignity was when Geordie had yelled, "Put yer finger up my arse. Put yer finger up my arse." Tottie obliged him, after which Geordie had assaulted her with a string of curses until he'd finally collapsed on top of her.

The event had raised conflicting emotions of arousal and

disgust in Declan. He and Alex hadn't talked about it for some time. Weeks later, though, when they'd been playing a game of attack-the-keep with Ian and Magnus, Alex had spontaneously used it as a battle cry. He'd charged Magnus and Ian with Declan at his side, yelling, "Put yer finger up my arse! Put yer finger up my arse!"

The boys had laughed so hard, Ian had wet his breeks. It had been a private joke between the four of them. Even when they had become grown men, whenever they heard someone boasting about his female conquests, one would lean to the other and mutter, "Aye. But did she put her finger up his arse?"

He smiled at the memory. "Oh, aye. I mind it."

"It's like that," Alex said. "I mean, no' all of it, of course, but, aye, your wife will like your bed fine."

"Oh. Good."

"Go slow the first time, mind you. Let her get used to you. Take all night if you must, but, Declan…"

"Aye?"

"I wouldnae ask her to put her finger up your arse."

They laughed. Hard. It was a joke that never stopped being funny.

Declan knocked on the front door to Balforss, nervous as hell. And no wonder. He'd rather fight a wild boar armed only with a knife than what he was about to do. He'd been trained to fight with a knife. What training did he have for courting? A few jumbled words of advice from Alex?

Alex?

Why the bloody hell was he listening to Alex? And where the hell was Magnus? Magnus was much better with women than his clot-heid cousin, Alex.

He was about to turn and run when Auntie Flora greeted him at the door, saying he'd arrived just in time. "The men havenae returned from visiting the tenants. Will ye go and fetch the ladies for me? I ken they took Jemma to feed the ducks."

"Sure, Auntie. Will you—" His voice warbled like a chicken. "Will you tie this stock for me? I can never manage it."

Flora chuckled. "Of course." She smelled of beeswax and bergamot, and the ruffle of her starched white kertch tickled his chin. The combination of those smells and her nearness triggered a memory of her blowing on his skinned knee and kissing away his tears. In all this time, nearly twenty years, she'd barely changed a whit.

"There," she said stepping back. "Not too tight, is it?"

"No."

"You look real smart."

Her words had the same effect as her kisses had on his tears when he'd been a boy. He smiled. "Thanks, Auntie."

On the way to the duck pond, he repeated Alex's advice to himself. "Tell her things. Get close. Kiss her. No. Wrong order. Get close and kiss her first, then tell her things. Propose. Tell her…tell her…" Damn.

Alex had given him too many things to think about. Bloody hell, courting was complicated. When Hamish had come to court Margaret, things had seemed straightforward enough. Hamish arrived with gowans, asked her to marry him, and she said yes. Why was there so much more involved with courting Caya?

The light laughter of women fanned across the tall grass. Waist-high daylilies laden with their orange blossoms bent over the path and left their ruddy pollen on the sleeve of his coat as he brushed by. He rounded the tall juniper and saw her surrounded by gowans, her yellow hair loose and swaying on her shoulders, facing away. Just like in his dreams.

But *not* like in his dreams. Like when he'd seen her in the bee field two days before, everything about her was the same—her hair, the flowers, her gown—and yet everything was *not* the same as his dream. How could that be?

. . .

Caya heard her name and turned, knowing whom she would see. He smiled that impossibly charming smile that demanded hers in return. For a moment, she admired his lanky lope, so lithe, graceful. Then she considered her own appearance. Oh dear, her hair had come down.

Lucy scooped Jemma into her arms. "Come on, sweetheart." Jemma screeched an ear-piercing protest that made everyone wince. "Hello, Declan. You'll excuse us. Jemma's cutting a tooth, and she's been in a foul temper today." Lucy hurried back toward the house with Jemma squirming and flailing in her arms, leaving Declan and Caya alone.

She searched her apron pockets for something to bind her hair. Finding nothing, she wrapped her kerchief around her head.

"Don't," Declan said.

She lifted her head and met his warm brown eyes. His look was so shockingly direct it made her heart stutter.

"Leave it," he said, his voice velvety. "Your hair is too pretty to hide."

Caught in his gaze, she was powerless to do anything but obey. She slipped the kerchief off and stuffed it back into her pocket. "You weren't—" Her voice sounded like a squeaky hinge. "You weren't at church this morning."

"I'm sorry." He stepped closer to her. "I'm here now, though."

"My brother—"

"He's fine. He's safe." Declan took another step closer. And then another.

"I'm sorry. I shouldn't have asked you—"

"*Wheesht* now. Dinnae fash aboot that."

He was close. Close enough she could feel the heat of his body. "We should go back to the house or we'll be late." Her statement was so lacking in commitment even she didn't believe herself. She should back away for modesty's sake, but she couldn't.

No. That was a lie. She didn't want to.

"Caya."

Her eyes closed at the sound of his voice speaking her name low and rumbly. His sweet breath brushed her cheek with cinnamon and clove. He pressed his soft lips to hers and she reeled. She clutched at his coat to keep from swaying. No need. Declan had her in his arms, his big warm hands on her back. His lips released hers for a moment and then fell back into place, fitting perfectly. His kiss grew urgent, and she answered him, pulling him closer, slipping her hands over his shoulders, her fingers finding and stroking the downy hair on the back of his neck. Oh dear, how could anything so wrong, so sinful, feel so wonderful?

This was bad, lovely but bad. She shouldn't. They must stop. Now.

She broke the kiss and pushed against Declan's chest. Goodness. He was out of breath, and so was she. Who knew kissing would be so strenuous?

He looked down on her, surprised. "I kissed you," he said, and blinked.

"Yes, but we need to stop. You must release me."

"But you kissed me back." Somehow, that aspect of the kiss was causing him confusion.

"Yes, I did. I'm sorry. It was very wicked of me."

"God, no," he said, looking at her as if he was seeing her for the first time. "You kiss like an angel."

"Thank you very much, but I'm afraid all this kissing has to stop."

"Why?" He closed his eyes and touched his forehead to hers.

Caya felt her resolve weaken and her lids begin to droop. "Because we're not supposed to...not supposed to touch... this is too..."

He whispered in her ear. "But you kissed me back."

She was definitely in trouble, sinning with her mind *and* her body. How could she ever face Vicar James in the confessional? She grasped at the only lifeline left to her, the residual anger and fear from the ugly business in church, and freed herself from Declan's embrace.

"You weren't at church this morning," she scolded. "I had to face all those people on my own while you stayed at home making your stupid whisky."

"What people?" he asked, baffled.

"The people at church. They were calling me witch behind my back and—"

Declan jerked to attention and clapped his hands around her shoulders. His face contorted with anger. "Who called you a witch? Who?"

She twisted away. "Never mind. It's over now."

"Och, lass. I'm sorry," he said, truly remorseful. "Had I been there, I would have run anyone through who'd said a cross word to you."

"Yes, well, that's just the problem, isn't it?"

"Problem?" he asked, back to his former state of bafflement.

"You and your swords and your whisky. I don't understand those things, I don't trust them, I don't approve of spirits and violence. I require a life of temperance and quietude. I can't abide whisky drinking in my house or swords or, or, or all these passionate kisses in broad daylight. You and I are very different, Declan."

"But you kissed me back. You liked the kissing part," he said. "Husbands and wives are passionate with each other. Did you not know that?" He raked a hand through his hair, pulling wild strands free of his queue. "Whisky making, that's who I am. I cannae change that. And it's true I was a soldier once, a bloody business, I know, but I cannae change that, either, and I'm not ashamed, I'm not sorry. A man must protect his family, and I can do that. I will always protect you."

"There are ways to protect someone other than with violence. Vicar James protected me—"

"What?"

Declan dipped his head, and his brow cast a dark shadow across his face. She had waded into dangerous territory by naming Vicar James.

"He put a stop to the gossip this morning. The vicar didn't have to use a sword. He used a more powerful weapon, the Word of God."

Declan staggered back as though she'd struck him. "You think the vicar is a better match for you because he's a man of God and I'm a man of blood?"

"I don't know what I think," she said, feeling her anger slip away. "All I know is that this, what happens with us, it's too strong so it must be wrong."

"Nae, nae, lass." Declan's voice was gentle, beseeching. He clasped her hands in his. "It's no' a sin to burn for the one you're meant to marry. And you and I are meant to marry. I believe it. I ken you believe it, too." He smiled down on her. "You kissed me back."

She looked down, unable to bear the intensity of his gaze. He was so sure. But how could she be certain? "You really think so?"

"Aye. There's no need to doubt." He pulled her a little closer. "When we're married, you'll see." He slapped his forehead. "Oh. Wait. I'm supposed to ask you first." Declan cleared his throat, straightened, and braced himself. "Caya Pendarvis, will you marry me?"

The question left her speechless. She shouldn't be surprised. He'd declared his intentions all along. Still, it was the way he proposed that gave her pause. "What did you mean by, 'I'm supposed to ask you?' Did someone say you must propose?"

He looked unmistakably guilty. "Nae...well...aye. Alex said I should."

Alex? Alex made him propose? Caya withdrew her hands and backed away. Hurt feelings seared their way up the back of her neck.

"Alex told you to ask me to marry you?"

"Aye." Declan cocked his head. "Did I do it wrong?"

"Alex made you propose?" She felt hot tears gather.

"Well, no' exactly." His Adam's apple bobbed again. "He explained the proper way—"

"Proper?" Caya asked. Her voice quavered, and she fought to steady herself. "You mean, honorable? He asked you to do the honorable thing, then?"

Declan seemed unsure. "It goes without question, does it not? It *is* my honor to marry you."

"So, you admit it? You'll marry me to satisfy your honor?" Hurt turned to humiliation.

Declan's face flushed an angry red. "I am an honorable man, Caya. I value my honor. Would you no' want to marry such a man?"

The vicar was right. Declan didn't want to marry her because he loved her. He just needed to prove he was a man of his word. "I release you," she shouted before she thought her words through.

"What?"

"I refuse your offer of marriage."

The color drained from Declan's face. "But, you kissed me back."

"You asked. I refused. You've satisfied your obligation, and now your honor is restored." She stormed off, then remembered her shawl and returned for it, ruining her dramatic exit and making her even more infuriated. Caya dashed away angry tears and sniffed. "In any case, you are the last person in the world I would marry."

She gathered herself on the way back to the house. Declan could just take his blasted house and his kisses and his big brown eyes and...damn and double dammit to hell. She was shaking, and her face was probably blotchy. It would not do to arrive at supper looking discomposed. If anyone asked her what the matter was, she'd burst into tears. She quickly tied her kerchief around her hair. When she entered the back door, she removed her apron and took a deep breath before stepping into the dining room.

Supper had already been laid out. Ian, Alex, Laird John, and Flora were all waiting. She and Declan had obviously held things up. She moved to take a seat next to Flora. Ian held out her chair for her.

"Sorry I'm late," she said. Her movements were jerky and mechanical, as was her speech. She stole a quick look at a puzzled-looking Alex. Most likely, he expected her to return beaming with happiness. Well, he and Declan could just go... She wouldn't finish the nasty thought.

The men took their seats. Everyone passed platters and served themselves with none of the usual friendly chatter. Only the clank and scrape of serving utensils and forks echoed in the dining room. Though her back was to him, she sensed Declan's arrival when all heads lifted toward the door.

"Sorry I'm late," he said.

She sank a few inches in her chair. Against Laird John's strict instructions, they had spent time alone. His identical apology most assuredly gave them away. Laird John shot him a hard look, confirming her assumption. Declan dipped his head, then sat directly across from her, blast him. His face looked the color of a frog's belly. She experienced a perverse sense of triumph seeing the effect her refusal had on the Scot, then felt a stab of pity for him. He looked so miserable. Like a lost puppy.

Last to arrive, Lucy swept into the room on a dramatic sigh. "At last. Jemma's down for the night. No, no, no. Sit," she commanded the men. "I thought she'd never settle. Thank goodness for Haddie. She's always so good with Jemma." Her words died off as she glanced around the room, no doubt sensing the tension and trying to suss out the origin. She settled in and heaped vegetables and meats onto her plate. Lightening her voice, she said, "I've never seen such unruly behavior from a child so young. She obviously gets it from you, Alex."

"Nae," Alex said, matter-of-factly, and swallowed what was in his mouth. "She gets her red hair from me. Her temper is from you."

Lucy made an English, "*Hmmph*."

Alex made a Scottish snort.

Declan said nothing and ate nothing.

Ever the hostess and mother to all, Flora placed a thick slice of ham on Declan's empty plate, tapped his fork, and said, "Eat."

Through surreptitious glances, Caya saw that he did eat, though she didn't think he enjoyed the ham one bit.

Toward the end of the meal, Laird John asked to have a word with Declan in the study, and the two excused themselves. Alex and Ian made a hasty exit as well, leaving

Flora, Lucy, and Caya alone in the dining room.

Muffled shouts from behind the closed library door reverberated across the entry hall and into the dining room. Was Laird John angry they'd been alone? Or that Declan had proposed? Or that she had refused? She shouldn't care. It had taken courage for her to refuse Declan. Another less scrupulous woman would have accepted his offer regardless of the fact that it had been made under duress. Now that he had satisfied his honor, he must be relieved to be free of his promise at last. A lump the size of a walnut formed in her throat. She tried to swallow, but it would not go down.

Lucy stood and peeked out the dining room door to see if anyone was listening and then rounded on her. "What on earth has happened? I left you alone with Declan for five minutes and you return to the house looking like you've both swallowed poison."

"Did he do something to upset you, dear?" Flora asked. "Did he…rush things? Men often do."

"No, nothing like that." She twisted her serviette into a knot and wished she could hide.

"What, then?" Lucy crossed the room to stand behind Flora's chair. "Tell us." They waited.

"He asked me to marry him."

Flora and Lucy cocked their heads to the side in unison, the question *So?* etched on their faces.

"Declan and I are not meant to be together." She struggled to keep her chin from wobbling. "He only asked me because he felt obligated."

"Why do you think that?" Flora asked.

"He said as much."

"And what did you say?" Lucy asked.

Her vision blurred. "I said he was the last person in the world I would marry."

"*Merde.* I'm going to have a word with Alex. Maybe he

can tell me what the *D-E-V-I-L* is going on."

"It's still a curse even if you spell it, lass," Flora said and rose from the table. "Let's go up to my parlor."

Caya and Lucy followed Flora toward the staircase. As they passed the library door, she overheard Declan shout, "Doesnae matter! She willnae have me."

The library door swung open, and Declan, his cheeks dark with anger, stormed out. He stopped for a moment in front of her, his face a mask of torture, then he turned and flung open the front door.

Standing on the stoop, a fist poised to knock, was Vicar James. Caya's hand flew to her mouth. From behind her, she heard a collective female gasp. Of all the ill-timed entrances, the vicar's had to be the worst.

In the next instant, Declan and the vicar were rolling and thrashing on the ground in a flurry of coattails.

She ran toward the fray, having no idea how to stop them but knowing she must try before one of them, most likely the vicar, was hurt.

Flora called to Laird John for help.

"Stop," Caya shouted. "Please, stop this instant."

Laird John pushed past her, grabbed Declan by an arm, and yanked him off the vicar. Declan struggled until he freed himself from John's grip. He was breathing hard and covered in dirt.

Vicar James scrambled to his feet, looking much less affected by the unexpected skirmish. He brushed the dirt from his trousers and coat and then retrieved his hat from where it had landed in a bush.

Declan wiped blood from his nose. She couldn't bear to see his face, his hurt, his anger. She was the center of this discord. When she stepped forward to apologize, Declan turned and strode away, back rigid and shoulders hunched.

"I see I've come at a bad time," the vicar said.

"Declan received some unfortunate news today," Laird John said. "But that's not an excuse for his behavior. I'm sure he'll offer you his apologies when he's recovered."

"No harm done." The vicar tested his jaw.

"Will you come in?" Flora asked.

Caya closed her eyes and willed the vicar to refuse her offer. The last thing she wanted to do at this moment was conduct idle conversation with the man Declan had just attacked.

Vicar James declined the invitation, and she exhaled her relief.

"I shan't stay. I thought Miss Pendarvis might like to borrow my hymnal." The vicar brushed the dirt from the cover and handed her the book. "I forgot to give it to you this morning."

She bobbed a polite curtsy. "Thank you."

"Well, em." Vicar James backed away a few steps. "I'll collect you tomorrow at the noon hour for our trip to Scrabster. Til then." He tipped his hat, mounted his horse, and trotted away.

Caya dropped her eyes and said to Flora, "If you don't mind, I'll retire to my room."

And never come out again.

• • •

Declan rode Gullfaxi home hard. Angry tears pricked at the corners of his eyes. He told himself it was the wind, sand in his eyes, anything but what it was, gnawing defeat. She didn't want any part of him, his whisky, his honor, his protection. To Caya, he was a godless, violent, unprincipled man—the last person in the world she would marry.

He found his bed and lay there, blank and flat as the ceiling. Where had he gone wrong? For the hundredth time, he thought back on every detail, every moment, every word said. Over and over, he replayed those fifteen minutes of nervous anticipation, arousal, joy, and then bitter disappointment. Bloody hell. He had done all the things Alex had said to do. And he had done them in the right order.

Exhausted and saddened beyond anything he'd experienced since the death of his mother, Declan started the process over again. He closed his eyes and laced his fingers together over his chest. This time, though, he went back further in his memory. He'd arrived at Balforss and handed Gullfaxi over to Peter. Peter had shown him his stitches, and Declan had congratulated him on his bravery. Flora'd tied his stock for him. Afterward, he'd gone to the duck pond to call Lucy and Caya inside for supper. On the way, he'd reviewed everything he and Alex had discussed on the off chance he found himself alone with Caya. And then...he'd seen her. Standing among the gowans. Just like in his dream, but...*not* like his dream.

Declan opened his eyes. Just like in his dream, but *not* like his dream. Why didn't she look like the wife in his dream? Her hair, the flowers, even the color of her frock— all the same, but not the same. Damn. Why? What was different? He squeezed his eyes shut and tried to picture his dream. Nothing *looked* different. Things only *felt* different.

You are the last person in the world I would marry.

The pressure of his hands folded across his chest was too much. He was having difficulty breathing. Self-doubt catapulted him out of bed. The edge of the basin table was within reach, and he grabbed hold. Had he misremembered? Misinterpreted? Had he...no, no, no. Oh Jesus God, no.

He'd chosen the wrong woman. Caya wasn't the woman in his dream. He'd taken her from her brother, snatched her from the man who would have been her husband, changed her life forever because of his selfishness, his bloody impatience.

A cramp twisted his bowels into a knot, and he doubled over. He cried out to no one because no one could hear him, alone in this empty husk of a house. When the pain subsided, he straightened and brushed the hair from his eyes. His knuckles were scraped from having attacked and beaten the vicar in front of everyone. Caya must hate him.

He hadn't been able to stop himself. Already furious from his altercation with Uncle John, he'd seen the blasted God-botherer at the door, and the next thing... It hadn't been much of a fight. He'd gotten no satisfaction from it, and maybe that was a good thing. Jesus. The vicar. He'd assaulted the bloody vicar.

Declan sat down on the edge of the bed. Now that the horror of misinterpreting his dream had subsided, he could see things more clearly. The vicar wasn't a bad man. In fact, he was surely a better man than himself. He supposed Caya would do well with a man like James Oswald. He would have to apologize. To everyone. And then he would have to explain things to Caya. While he consoled himself with the belief that marrying the vicar would make up for all she had lost because of his mistake, Caya's devastating words repeated in his head.

You are the last man in the world I would marry.

Chapter Nine

At noon the next day, Lucy and Caya gathered in the entry hall, ready to leave the house. "Do you think it's wise to bring Jemma with us to Scrabster?" she asked. "Those women frighten me."

Lucy handed Jemma to her. "Hold her while I tie her bonnet." Lucy did battle with the ribbon while Jemma made "eh-eh-eh" sounds. "Those women may be an angry, superstitious lot, but they'd never jeopardize the safety of a child. Besides, I can't think of a better way to show them we're not afraid."

She took Lucy's confidence as reassurance and relaxed enough to ask the question she had been meaning to ask all morning. "Did you talk to Alex about what happened yesterday? With me and Declan, I mean."

Lucy pressed her lips into a thin line of disgust and shrugged. "Alex told me not to meddle." She yanked on her gloves with angry tugs. "Men." She uttered the word like it was the explanation for all that was wrong with the world. And maybe she was right.

They stepped outside when the vicar's carriage jangled up the drive right on time. He drove a smart-looking phaeton with a calash top that offered its passengers a modicum of protection from the elements. He climbed down and brushed the damp off his jacket. The day's weather was what Laird John called "soft," meaning the rain came down in a light mist rather than drops. The women were well-prepared with cloaks and bonnets.

Vicar James called to Jemma with a voice pitched higher, the way adults talk to dogs and children. Jemma flapped her arms and made excited squeals, anticipating Vicar James's attention. Caya transferred the bundle of churning arms and legs into the vicar's arms, admiring his gentle way. He did seem to have an easy hand with children.

Not for the first time, she considered Vicar James as a man rather than a priest, appraising his worth as a potential husband, judging his good qualities and balancing them against his shortcomings. He had only one shortcoming that she could ascertain. Vicar James didn't make her heart flop about inside her chest the way Declan did.

True. The Reverend James Oswald had several advantages over Declan Sinclair. He had a more even temper, and he didn't deal in spirits—something she disapproved of strenuously. But her skin didn't burn the way it did when Declan stared at her with his dark brown eyes.

Vicar James interrupted her thoughts with, "Good morning, Miss Pendarvis."

"I should apologize for yesterday, the fight—"

Vicar James waved a hand and smiled. "Forgotten."

"Thank you."

With Lucy and Jemma already snug aboard the phaeton, he held a hand out. "Ready?" he asked. He had that look on his face again, a look of affection. She wanted to return his interest if only because he was so kind to her, but to do so felt unnatural. He helped her into the phaeton. Even that simple gesture was lacking. When Declan helped her in and out of the wagon, he cradled her as if she were something breakable, his hands lingering a moment too long, almost reluctant to let her go. Vicar James handled her like baggage.

The vicar climbed in after her and eased himself into what space was left. The phaeton was made for two passengers to travel comfortably. It would be a cramped ride with the three adults wedged together as they were. The vicar arranged a blanket over their laps and gave the reins a snap. His body felt stiff and awkward pressed to her side. If Declan were here…

Merde.

It was Lucy's French word. Caya didn't know what it meant. It sounded like a curse word, so it served her well for the moment. She had to stop comparing Vicar James and Declan. There was no point. Declan offered to marry her only out of his misguided sense of honor. A sadness formed in her mind like a dark and bottomless pit. One more step and she would fall in and never find her way out.

The tiny fishing village of Scrabster, located halfway between Balforss and Thurso, was situated on a cliff-lined promontory jutting into the North Sea. Dwellings dotted one side of the narrow dirt road, and boats bobbed in the water on the other. The ramshackle houses seemed to cling to the sides of the cliff that towered over the small harbor. Sheltered from the west wind, the village reeked of rotting fish and dead seaweed. By all visible indications, the people living here were barely eking out an existence culled from the sea.

Caya saw a line of four women blocking the road ahead. She felt a jolt of recognition—the women from the river.

Vicar James stopped the phaeton, pulled the break, and

secured the reins. "Good afternoon, ladies." He climbed down and offered the women a courteous bow.

They remained unmoved, arms crossed, feet apart, standing shoulder to shoulder.

"We've come to pay Mrs. Campbell and little Bobby a visit," he said. "Can you tell me, please, which is her house?"

The white-haired woman lifted her chin. "The unholy are not welcome in Scrabster. Turn your cart around and go."

Ignoring the warning, Vicar James approached her with a genial smile. "You're Mrs. McConnechy, are you not?"

The white-haired woman startled at his recognition.

Clever of the vicar. Troublemakers prefer anonymity. By calling the woman by name, he had made her responsible for her actions.

"How do you know me?" Mrs. McConnechy demanded, obviously agitated to be singled out.

"Reverend Linklater says you make the best fishcakes in all of Caithness." Vicar James oozed charm.

Bewildered, Mrs. McConnechy's comrades turned to her for guidance. She brushed a wisp of white hair from her forehead. The vicar's flattery had worked. "Ye speak with the silver tongue of the devil."

James laughed. "I've never been accused of having a *silver* tongue before. Still, I'd be obliged if you'd let me purchase two of your fishcakes for my supper."

Jemma had remained motionless during the exchange, seeming to sense the tension among the adults. But Lucy's shoulders jiggled with stifled laughter.

The old woman lifted her chin again and considered the vicar's request. "Ye've coin?"

"Yes."

"It'll take a while to make them."

"My companions and I will wait at Mrs. Campbell's house."

Mrs. McConnechy's ethical debate between commerce and creed played across her forehead. Commerce won. She pointed up the cliff to a cluster of wooden shacks. "Second from the right."

Vicar James bowed to the women and returned to the phaeton with a sheepish look on his face.

Lucy cocked an eyebrow at him. "Silver-tongued devil?"

The corner of Vicar James's mouth twitched.

They left the phaeton behind and took the footpath up the cliffside. The steep climb along the muddy slope left them all winded. The shack looked as though it had room for two people at most. How would they all fit inside? The vicar rapped his knuckles on the weathered door and an older gentleman answered. He stepped out of the shack, wearing a rumpled coat and black-brimmed hat, his face pinched and severe looking.

James greeted the man with reserve. "Reverend Linklater," he said and dipped his head.

The old man responded with an icy, "Father Oswald." Though not incorrect, she thought addressing Vicar James as "Father" was the Presbyterian minister's way of pointing out a significant difference between their faiths. After all, Anglican clergymen had retained the papish moniker of priest.

The minister stepped outside the shack and motioned for the women to enter. She cast one last look at Vicar James, silently wishing him luck with the dour Reverend Linklater.

The two clergymen remained outside the tiny shack while she and Lucy visited with Mrs. Campbell. Having absolutely nothing in common, their chat was brief. Lucy gave Mrs. Campbell a loaf of honey cake. Mrs. Campbell murmured a shy thank you to Caya for saving her boy's life. And Jemma poked a curious finger at little Bobby, who remained stoic throughout her prodding.

Reverend Linklater accompanied them back down the cliffside to the phaeton, where Mrs. McConnechy waited with a cast-iron pan of hot fishcakes. James gave the woman two bits, and Lucy produced a lace-edged handkerchief to wrap the delicacies.

Jemma fell asleep in Caya's arms as soon as the phaeton got rolling.

"I have to admit, the cakes smell delicious," Lucy said, clutching the bundle on her lap as they flew down the road to Balforss. "But I'd think twice about eating them."

Vicar James gave her a sideways look. "I don't plan to." He looked up to heaven and crossed himself.

Caya asked the vicar, "What did you and Reverend Linklater talk about while we visited with Mrs. Campbell?"

"I asked him to explain to his congregation that your actions were the work of God and not the devil."

"Do you think he will?"

Vicar James turned his head and gave her an apologetic smile. "No. He would never do that."

"Then why did we make this trip?"

"Evil is a coward. It hides in the shadows. Goodness is courageous. It lives in light. We showed our goodness and bravery by visiting in daylight."

The weight of Jemma's slumbering little body in Caya's arms prompted a memory from when she was a girl resting comfortably against her father's shoulder, feeling loved and contented, oblivious to all the ills of the world. Nothing and no one could ever harm her while she lay safe in her father's embrace. She wondered if she'd ever feel that safe again. Declan had once said to her, "We will marry, and you need nae be frightened ever again." She'd chosen him that day, but when he'd tried to make good on his promise, she unchose him. Had she been a fool?

When they arrived home, Vicar James asked her to walk

with him a while. She agreed, and without any attention to where they were going, they ended up at the paddock fence, where the colt, now a week old, was trotting wild circles around his mother.

"The last time we were here, you confessed to me," he said. "I would like to confess something to you and hope you won't judge me too harshly."

"Of course."

"I warned you off Declan Sinclair unfairly. It was wrong to do. I was jealous, I suppose."

"Jealous?"

"Miss Pendarvis, Caya, you must know by now that I hold you in high regard." He removed his hat and held it to his chest. "This may sound sudden, but trust me when I say I have been thinking about it since the first day I met you. Though we've only been acquainted a short time, I believe we could make a happy life together. Do you think you could feel the same way?"

"W-what do you mean?" Was he really asking her to… Her world tilted sideways, and she grasped the fence post to steady herself.

"I would speak to Laird John first, naturally, but…" Vicar James reached for her hand and said, "What I'm asking you is, would you be my wife?"

She stammered for a moment, not able to find any words that made sense.

"I see I've shocked you. Take as much time as you like to consider my offer. But know it is my most fervent desire to wed you." James's open, trusting face shone down on her.

She found her voice at last and asked the first question that came to her. "Why?"

"I beg your pardon?"

She slipped her hand out of his. "Why do you want to marry me?"

He looked blank for a moment, laughed nervously, and then stammered, "For the usual reasons, of course."

"And those are…"

"Well." He held the brim of his hat by the fingers of both hands and turned it in circles. "Like me, you strive to live by the Word of God. And like me, the church is central to your life. You value faith and prayer, as I do. We are well-matched, I think."

"Yes, but are there other ways in which we are matched? Ways that are more personal, more intimate?" She held her breath. Would he speak of love? And if he did, would that be enough to spark love in her heart for him?

He searched again for what to say. "You would take good care of the vicarage, be a good mother to our children, visit the sick, organize church functions—" He stopped mid-thought and smiled. "You're teasing me. You know what's expected of a clergyman's wife."

Should she be surprised by his answer—a list of all the things she would do for him? Nothing about what he would do for her in return. Nothing about love or passion. Nothing about a burning desire for each other. Did she really expect declarations of the heart from a clergyman? Of course not. The vicar was a man of the cloth, a man of peace, a man of reason. Exactly the kind of man she should marry. Had she met Vicar James a month ago, she would have been grateful for his attentions.

"One more question: Will I have my own home?"

Relief flushed his face. "Yes, of course. Once I marry, the church will provide for us."

She nodded, feeling slightly dizzy, weightless. "Thank you. I promise to give your offer careful consideration."

"I'll see you Saturday for choir practice—five days hence. Can I hope for an answer by then?"

"Yes." Caya walked back to the house as fast as she could

without actually breaking into a run.

• • •

On Tuesday afternoon, Declan, Alex, and Hamish paused on the bench outside the distillery to enjoy the cold beef and cheese Margaret had sent along in the morning. Alex removed the cloth covering the jug of ale, filled a tankard, and handed it to Declan, then poured one for Hamish and another for himself.

In a conversational tone, Alex said, "I gather things are not going well with Caya."

Declan drank and wiped his mouth with the back of his hand. He directed his gaze off in the distance, focusing on nothing. "I was wrong." He felt empty and defeated, but the sooner he admitted his mistake, the sooner he could make things right for Caya.

"What do you mean?" Alex asked.

"I was mistaken. Caya isn't the woman in my dream."

Alex snapped his head around. "What?"

Hamish coughed and excused himself to take a piss. Why did his friends always desert him when he needed them most?

"Forget the bloody dream, man," Alex said. "I thought you had feelings for the lass. Have you changed your mind?"

He had spent most of yesterday mulling over his dream and coming to the conclusion that he was indeed wrong about Caya. He'd made a mistake, a terrible mistake he could not undo. As much as it hurt his heart to say it out loud, he had to try and make things right. "Aye. I've changed my mind. She's no' the woman I am to marry."

Alex gasped repeatedly like an astonished trout. "Where does that leave Caya?"

"She doesnae want me. I'm stepping aside. I leave her to the vicar. That's the best I can do to make up for my mistake."

Angry splotches formed on Alex's cheeks. "You're a bloody fool, cousin."

Declan shouted back, "She doesnae want me. She said so."

"You think because a woman you love turns you down once that's the end? Do you ken how many times Lucy pushed me away before I finally got it right? Ye cannae give up, man."

"It's no use. She's not the woman in my dream."

"You were certain before. What's changed?"

"It shouldnae be this difficult."

Alex smacked himself in the forehead. "It's always difficult with women, ye numpty."

Shaking his head slowly, Declan repeated, "It shouldnae be this difficult."

"Oswald has asked Caya to marry him."

Declan shot to his feet. "What?" How had things progressed so quickly with Caya and the vicar?

"I said—"

"I ken what ye said. What did Caya say?" His heart pounded a rapid *thud-a-thud-a-thud-a-thud-a-thud*.

"She hasnae given him an answer."

He gulped in air, willing his heartbeat to slow. At least Caya had not yet chosen.

"What will you do if she says yes?" Alex asked.

"I dinnae ken."

"Do you love her?"

He hesitated. "I dinnae ken."

"Come on, man. Two days ago, you wanted to marry the lass. Is your heart so changeable?"

"I said, I don't know if I love her." He wanted to yank his own hair out by the roots. "Everything is mixed up, and nothing makes sense anymore. I cannae tell which is the right thing to do."

"It's time to stop dreaming and act like a man." Alex tossed back the rest of his ale and strode toward the stillhouse, calling over his shoulder, "You've got till Saturday morning to sort yourself out. That's when Caya will give the vicar her answer."

• • •

At her request, Laird John supplied Caya with ink, quills, a sheaf of paper, and full use of his study. Using small, careful lettering and the vicar's hymnal, she wrote out all the verses for two of her favorite hymns, then copied them four times.

Not a thing from Declan since Sunday. No flowers, no note, no word sent by cupid. Nothing. What did she expect? She had said those awful words to him. *You are the last person in the world I would marry.* On top of that, she had another decision she had to make. Sometime before Saturday, she had to decide whether to accept or decline the vicar's proposal.

The peaceful atmosphere of the laird's study made what could have been a chore a meditation. The light *scritch* of the quill on vellum comforted her until she would come across the word "love" and her hand would hesitate over the surface, quill trembling, nib dripping inky black tears.

Midafternoon, she paused to massage her cramped hand. The days had grown warm enough that no fires were necessary until after sunset, and the tall windows let in plenty of light. She stretched and inhaled the room's particular perfume: musty books, chair leather, and a sweet smoky smell she'd come to recognize as whisky.

Whisky. Flora said Alex was at the distillery helping Declan and Hamish store this season's whisky. Apparently, they transported the casks to a secret place known only to a few. Perhaps she hadn't heard from Declan because he was busy with his whisky. More likely, he hadn't come around because he was done with her. Free to pursue some other woman for a wife.

And what would it be like to see him with another woman on his arm, to know he would be kissing her like he had kissed Caya? To have to sit in church with them every Sunday, go to his wedding, congratulate his wife when she bore Declan's children—the children Caya could have given him. Bring gifts to their house—the house that could have been hers. Would she be able to bear the pain of it all?

She closed her eyes and, as she had at least a hundred times since Sunday, she remembered how Declan's soft lips had fit so perfectly with hers. How he'd held her, pressed against her, the low groan he'd made when she slipped her hands around his neck. He'd said, *Husbands and wives are passionate with each other. Did you not know that?* And then she'd said those awful words. *You are the last person in the world I would marry.* She opened her eyes and fell back in her chair.

Laird John entered his study to tell her dinner was ready. She showed him the copies, and he complimented her skill with a pen.

"You have a fine hand, lass. May I call on you to pen a letter for me on occasion?"

"That would make me very happy."

Indeed, after his kindness, she would gladly perform clerical tasks for the laird. But she doubted if she would ever be truly happy again. At least, not like she'd been in that one perfect moment when Declan had kissed her.

Lucy and Flora were aware of her misery. How could they not be when she arrived at the breakfast table each morning with puffy eyes and a stuffed-up nose? They avoided the subjects of Declan, marriage, courting, Vicar James, Scrabster, the choir, or anything else that could lead to bad thoughts. Even Mrs. Swenson and the upstairs maid, Haddie, were careful about what they said around her.

Unfortunately, their pointed attempts to avoid sensitive subjects had the opposite effect. Conversation at mealtime was stilted and forced. Caya decided that if one more person cleared her throat, she would scream.

"I'm going to accept the vicar's offer of marriage." The words were out of her mouth before she thought to say them.

Lucy and Flora slowly lowered their teacups to their saucers.

"You've decided to marry Vicar James?" Flora asked.

She had wanted Declan to *want* to marry her. That wasn't meant to be. But Vicar James wanted her, so he must be the correct choice. Right?

"Yes." Her answer held no conviction. She repeated with more confidence. "Yes."

"Do you want to marry James?" Lucy asked.

"It's a very kind offer." A mercy, really. An offer for which she would always be grateful. Grateful? Hadn't Vicar James said she shouldn't accept an offer of marriage out of gratitude?

"But, do you want to marry Vicar James?" Lucy asked again.

She ignored the little voice in the back of her head screaming, *I want to marry Declan.* "He'll make an excellent husband. You said yourself that every unmarried woman in Thurso wants to be the vicar's wife."

Lucy leaned forward. "Caya, do you *want* to marry James?"

Her continued badgering annoyed her. "Don't be silly. Why would I accept his offer if I didn't want to marry him? Excuse me. I need to get back to my writing." She left the parlor. The conversation was over. She'd made her choice.

• • •

Jack Pendarvis pounded on the locked door again. Where was that blasted woman? The tavern owner's wife should have returned hours ago with his meal. He was out of whisky and his head hurt. Hungry, too, but that was secondary to his need for drink.

How many days had he been holed up in this room? He'd lost track of time. When Sinclair had left him here, he'd sworn he was not a prisoner, that the lock on the door was for his welfare only. He'd received assurances from the tavern owner, Mr. Kinney, that as soon as a passenger ship took anchor in Scrabster Harbour, Sinclair would purchase a packet and see him safely aboard. That had to be days ago. Mrs. Kinney had kept him well-supplied with whisky and food for the duration. But he was beginning to sober, and as he did so, he was growing bored. He scratched at his scalp, but there was no way to satisfy the itch. It was coming from the inside.

The narrow slat that served as a window offered no more light. With the darkness came garrulous sounds from the tap room. He'd gladly lower his standard of company to the likes of the tavern owner's custom if the man would let him out of this cage to mingle for a few hours among other humans. For the first time in days, he considered his appearance. He hadn't bathed, and his clothes smelled like his mattress. He'd blend right in with the other peasantry. No one would take him for a gentleman. Odd. He'd never before seen advantage in appearing anything but a gentleman.

"Mrs. Kinney." He thumped the side of his fist on the door several times. "Mrs. Kinney!"

At last, the tavern owner's wife called from down the hallway, "Hold your *wheesht*, man. I'm coming." A grunt as she bent to set the tray on the floor outside his door. A jangle of keys from her chatelaine. The clunk of the lock. He stepped back, and the door swung open.

Jack gave the older woman a brilliant smile meant to charm. "Please. Allow me," he said, and he collected the tray off the floor himself rather than waiting for her usual service. He set the tray on his mattress. "I haven't adequately thanked you for your hospitality, madame." Jack made a polite bow.

The woman let her mouth hang open, replacing her normally half-intelligent countenance with a witless one.

"You will forgive me, of course?"

She regained her senses and replied, "If you like, sir." Mrs. Kinney turned to leave.

Before she shut the door, he said, "Would you mind terribly if we left it open? As you know, I have no intention of going anywhere. It's just that these four walls have become rather confining."

She hesitated for a long while, considering his request, the key in her hand, aimed at the lock.

Jack increased his smile and winked as if to say, *This will be our little secret.*

At last, the tavern owner's good wife nodded and marched away, leaving the door open. He tore a few bites off the joint of meat she'd left for his supper while he waited for her footsteps to fade. His appetite sated for the moment, he grabbed the decanter of whisky and headed down the hall in the direction of the tavern room noise.

As he anticipated, no one took note of him. He found a corner and sat alone, enjoying his whisky. He was beginning to acquire a taste for the spirit and understood why the golden liquid was so precious to the Scots. About halfway through his bottle, he was feeling pleasantly drunk and in need of a piss. He squeezed through bodies that smelled more of fish than man. Someone shoved him aside and spat out a Gaelic curse, igniting his temper. Yet, he refrained from answering the cur for fear of calling attention to himself.

It had been so long since Sinclair had delivered him

to this establishment, he'd forgotten that the building was situated on the side of a steep incline. He stepped through the door into the night, and the ground failed him. He missed the stairs and landed in a crumpled mess.

No damage done, but he'd lost hold of his bottle when he reached to break his fall. He groped in the dark on his hands and knees. Finding the bottle unbroken and still stoppered, he breathed a sigh of relief and got to his feet. He rose a little too quickly, as it turned out. The blood rushed from his head and he staggered. The blasted earth slipped away yet again, and he went tumbling backward, picking up speed as he rolled, cracking his head, crashing through bushes, knocking over barrels, banging his knee, and bowling over someone. Dogs barked, chickens squawked, and a woman cried out. When his body finally came to a stop sprawled on its back, the stars above continued to swirl clockwise, making beautiful patterns in the sky.

The head of a dog haloed in white fur slavered over him, blocking out his view. "Are ye deid?" the white dog asked.

Odd for a dog to talk. But this was Scotland. Absurd things happened here all the time, as he well knew.

"Are ye deid, man?" the dog asked again.

"I live," he said.

The dog straightened, and by the shadowy moonlight, he could see she was in fact a woman, an old woman with white hair.

"Didnae ken should I fetch the preacher or the healer," the old woman said and cackled. "You look a right mess, laddie."

Jack attempted to sit up. Lifting his head took great effort. Someone had weighted it down with sand.

"Give it here," she said, extending a helping hand.

He lifted his arm, grateful for the assistance. Instead, she took the whisky from his hand, still stoppered and miraculously undamaged. The old woman pried his fingers from the neck, twisted the cork out with a pop, and took a deep swallow.

Rolling first to his hands and knees, Jack managed to get his feet under him and stand, slowly this time. When he stumbled forward, the woman caught his arm.

"Steady, lad."

A pulsating pain at the back of his head made itself known. He reached back to assess the damage. Wet. Sticky. Blood? He checked his hand. Not blood.

The old woman cackled again. "Looks like ye landed in the shite this time, laddie."

"Blast this whole sodding country." Jack snatched the decanter of whisky back and took several swallows. "Damn you and every whoreson in this fucking town."

He turned and banged a shoulder on the side of a building, ricocheted off into a post, tripped, and landed in a horse trough. Someone yanked him out by the back of his jacket. He coughed and sputtered.

"Let me help. You need a baptizing, ye heathen." The old woman shoved his head in the trough again and rubbed the cack out of his hair.

He came up, gasping for air. "Enough. Enough. Release me."

She hissed in his ear. "You're the sassenach bastard what's wanted for robbery."

Fear cut through his anger. "No, you have it wrong." He tried to free himself to run. She was alarmingly powerful for an old woman. Before he had recovered from his near drowning, she'd dragged him through a dark doorway and shoved him into a chair. He sat shivering, dripping, still smelling like shit.

"Nae need to be afeart, laddie. You and me, we're on the same side." She set the whisky on the table in front of him, and he took a greedy gulp. "I'll no' give you away. You're safe as a lamb with Mrs. McConnechy."

He doubted he was safe. He judged Mrs. McConnechy to be either a murderer or a lunatic. Maybe both. "What do you want?"

"Best keep your voice down so's not to wake my man." She jerked her head in the direction of another room. Then she sat across from him and leaned into the candlelight. Her half-toothless grin reinforced his opinion that she was doddering. "I ken you want to get away. The Sinclair would see you off with nothing but a boot in the arse. Better to go with a wee bit a silver in your pocket, aye?" Mrs. McConnechy picked up a knife, and Jack tensed. Would he have to fight this old woman? Did he even have the strength?

She sliced off a chunk of bread, slathered it with jam, and handed it to him. "The publican, Kinney, doesnae ken how to treat a gentleman such as yerself."

She was damn-well right about that. He had been dealt with shabbily, and the Sinclairs were chiefly responsible for dishing out his egregious treatment.

"You'll fare better here with me, sir." Her eyes glittered with cunning.

At last, someone who appreciated his circumstance and had the decency to acknowledge his position in society. Jack relaxed back into his chair and let out a noble sigh. "They say clothes make a man, but rags cannot conceal the character of a true gentleman, I suppose."

She smiled again, this time with what he recognized as the adulation underlings had for their superiors.

"You, um, mentioned something about silver," he said and canted his head to the side.

"Och, aye." She leaned forward and crooked a finger for him to do the same. "I have it in mind how we can ruin the Sinclairs whilst making a small fortune for ourselves—you, being of high birth, taking the larger cut, of course."

"Go on," he said.

"I ken it best to keep this a'tween us. Nae need to tell my man, aye?"

"Of course, madame. It will be our little secret."

"You're going to find the Sinclair whisky stash, and I'm going to show you where to look."

Jack gave her his most charming smile. She had earned it.

Chapter Ten

At the breakfast table on Wednesday morning, Caya was finishing her toast when a horse-drawn carriage jangled into the yard. Alex and Ian exchanged a look and scrambled to the window.

"Magnus has returned from Inverness," Alex said. He and Ian darted into the entry hall, with Ian calling over his shoulder, "Meet us outside."

Laird John, his face alight, hustled Caya and the baffled Sinclair women out of the dining room toward the front door. He paused with his hand hovering over the latch. "Are you ready for a surprise?"

"I love surprises," Lucy breathed, bouncing on her heels with her hands clasped under her chin.

Laird John swung open the door and swept his arm in a graceful arc. "Dear ladies, your carriage awaits."

A gleaming black lacquered carriage—a real carriage— stood in the yard, complete with red wheels, glass windows, running lamps, and a pair of perfectly matched black horses with a gold trimmed harness.

"Is it ours?" Lucy asked. Laird John nodded, and she squealed with delight. One of the carriage horses snorted and swiveled a wary eye her way.

"Oh, John. It's beautiful." Flora kissed her husband on the mouth in front of everyone. Caya didn't know which shocked her more—the carriage or the kiss.

When Magnus leaped from the driver's seat, his family engulfed him with fond embraces and congratulatory backslaps. She hadn't seen Magnus in almost two weeks. The explanation given for his absence was that he and his stepfather, Fergus Munro, had gone to Inverness on business. Magnus, therefore, was oblivious to the recent unfortunate turn of events that had made her miserable.

So no one could upbraid him when he smiled down on her and said, "Are you and Declan married yet? I hope I didnae miss the wedding."

She heard several gasps. Magnus shot a confused look over the top of her head. When she turned, she caught Lucy shaking her head and Alex drawing a finger across his throat, signaling Magnus to shut up.

The look on Magnus's face darkened. "What has that eejit done now? Has he upset you, lass? Because if he has, I'll break his bloody neck."

"We're not getting married," she said.

Magnus shook his head. "A'course you are. Declan dreamed it so."

"Dreamed?"

"Did he no' tell you aboot his dream?" Magnus looked to John and Alex, who scratched their heads and averted their eyes.

"What dream?" she asked.

Lucy crossed her arms and stepped forward. "Yes. What dream are you talking about, Magnus?"

Caya's heart tripped and stumbled.

Magnus frowned at Lucy. "He dreamed Caya was his wife. That's how he recognized her at the tavern." Magnus looked down at Caya again. "So, you see, you two are meant to be married. Declan's dreams never lie."

Three hours later, Caya followed the path she had seen Peter take the day he'd delivered pasties to Declan. After making sure the Scrabster women weren't lurking about doing their laundry downstream, she tucked up the hem of her skirt and waded across the river, balancing on the slippery rocks with boots and stockings in one hand and a basket of freshly baked Cornish pasties in the other. Now that she was certain Declan's desire to marry her had nothing to do with honor, she was determined to make things right.

She paused on the far side of the river and used a handful of grass to clean and dry her feet before pulling on her stockings and lacing her boots. She arranged her skirts and bent to collect her basket of pasties, smelling hot-out-of-the-oven good.

When she straightened, she turned to stone.

"You're looking well, sister."

Bile rose in her throat, and she swallowed. "Hello, Jack."

He was filthy, disheveled, and much thinner than she remembered. "What are you doing here? I thought you were—"

"Hiding? Yes, your man stashed me in the back of some stinking hovel unfit for animals. I had to leave. Is that food?" His arm shot out like a striking viper and snatched the basket from her embrace.

She covered her yelp with both hands.

He tore open the towel, grabbed one of the hot treats, and stuffed it into his mouth, wolfing it down in gulps, devouring it almost whole. He took a bite out of another pasty and spoke, crumbs and juices tumbling from his lips. "I've been looking for you."

"I know you tried to steal a horse the other night," she said. "Have you become a thief now?"

"It's your fault. You left me in Wick with nothing. O'Malley found me and threatened me. I barely escaped with my life." He stuffed another bite into his mouth.

"What you did was wrong. You could have killed that boy."

"You care more about a dirty little groom than your own brother, your blood?"

"Leave here. Now. Laird Sinclair is looking for you. If he catches you, he'll turn you over to the magistrate. Declan will find you safe passage—"

"I intend to leave, but not without what you owe me."

Caya stepped back. "I don't owe you anything."

"O'Malley would have given me another twenty quid when I delivered you. Instead you took off with that imbecile Scot and left me with nothing."

"I don't have any money, Jack."

He grabbed her arm and yanked her close. "Then get me Mother's jade ring. You owe me that much, at least. You'll find me at the home of Mrs. McConnechy in Scrabster. Bring it to me there."

Mrs. McConnechy was the terrible woman who had called Caya a witch. The old woman must have known Jack was her brother. "I can't go there. And you mustn't trust that woman. She means you harm."

He shook her. "Never mind about that. You have to get me that ring. There's a passenger ship in the harbor that leaves the day after tomorrow."

She dug her heels in. "No. Let me go."

As soon as she freed herself, he struck her in the face

with the back of his hand. The blow took her by surprise, and, failing to break her fall, she hit the ground hard.

He stood over her. "Look what you made me do." He twisted his fist in her hair and pulled her to her feet.

Her ribs expanded, her lungs filled, and her rage released like a thousand arrows, a scream that shook the leaves on the trees. She fought back, kicking and scratching and clawing.

He protested but kept hold of her. "Stop it, damn you. Be still." Something crunched beneath her fist and Jack cried out, "Shit. Fuck. You broke my fucking nose, you bitch."

Freed from his grip, she ran, fear and fury blinding her, branches and bushes slapping at her face. Someone called her name, but she kept running, running. She fell once and got to her feet. She fell again with a sob, then picked herself up, swiping at the tears and wild strands of hair blurring her vision. Someone grabbed at her. She struck out. Fought hard. Fought to save her life. She screamed again, her lungs burning for air.

"Caya, stop. It's me, love. It's me."

She stilled, panting like an animal. Her sight returned, and she saw Declan's handsome face. Declan held her in his warm hands, his gleaming black brows drawn together with concern. Her knees gave way, and she collapsed against him.

He gathered her into his arms as if she were an injured bird. All her strength had dissolved. Every muscle had expired. She had been reduced to a trembling mess of bones and flesh. But he held her safe in his arms. Safe from Jack. Safe from all the ills of the world.

She closed her eyes and nestled her face in the crook of his neck, breathing in his scent, listening to his strong heartbeat, his soothing voice murmuring Gaelic words of comfort. It seemed like he carried her for miles and miles.

She roused when he shouted, "Hamish."

From a distance, a voice answered, "Aye?"

"Go tell my sister I need her. Caya's hurt."

Declan reached a building and set her down on a bench. "Are you all right?"

She nodded, not yet able to talk.

"Dinnae move. I'll get you something."

A moment later, Declan knelt before her, pressing a cool tankard to her lips. She winced. Something was wrong with her mouth.

"Sorry. Try to drink this, love."

Declan's worried face came into focus. She took two swallows of the bitter ale, then signaled she'd had enough.

"I'm sorry." When he shook his head in confusion, she tried again. "I was angry. I didn't mean what I said."

He held her face in his hands like a chalice and smiled into her eyes. "My fault. I made a mess of things."

She started to smile back but winced again and touched her mouth. "I think I cut my lip."

"It's bleeding. Let me see." Using the tip of his thumb, he delicately pulled her lower lip out and leaned his face close. "It's no' so bad." He placed a light kiss near her mouth, then touched his forehead to hers. "Who did this to you, love? Tell me." The tone of his voice had dropped to a low menacing rumble.

"I fell." The lie made her lip hurt all the more. Why would she lie for her brother after everything? Was it to protect him? Or to protect herself? How many times could she bring chaos to Balforss before they would politely ask her to leave? She closed her eyes.

"Caya, tell me who did this?" he asked again.

"Jack."

She heard Declan rise on an angry growl and she reached for him. "Wait! Don't go. Please. Stay with me. I don't care about Jack anymore. Can't we just leave him to his fate?"

He tilted his head, considering her request. After a

moment, his shoulders lowered, and he dropped to his knees before her. "Your brother deserves a good thumping."

She stroked his cheek. "I know."

"He hurt you, and he should pay for—"

"I know." Caya took hold of his hand and pressed her lips to his knuckles.

Declan's wrath cooled, and he exhaled a ragged breath. Then she remembered the pasties.

"*Merde.*"

He made an amused snort. "You've been spending too much time with Lucy."

"I lost the pasties I was bringing you."

"What? You made me those delicious meat pies again?" He popped to his feet. "I'll go and have a look for them."

"No, don't. Don't leave me. I'll make you more tomorrow," she said and smiled as much as her cut lip would allow.

His eyes sparkled in the afternoon light. "If you didnae have a fat lip, I'd kiss you."

Margaret came tearing into the yard, red-faced and gasping between every other word. "Is she all right?"

"I'm fine."

Margaret bent and grabbed her side, her face contorted. "I've got a stitch." When she finally caught her breath and straightened, she rounded on her brother. "You said she was hurt." Margaret kicked her brother's backside.

"Och!"

"That's for making me run all the way here," Margaret snipped. Then said to Caya in a gentler voice, "I'm glad to find you well, *a nighean*."

• • •

Declan sent his bad-tempered older sister on her way. He wanted to be alone with Caya. Perfectly alone.

"Can you walk, *a leannan*? I'll take you to our house, and you can rest a bit. Gullfaxi and I will give you a ride back to Balforss…when you're recovered." He wanted to say "when I've finished kissing and holding you" but didn't think it wise. Plus, if she allowed him to kiss and hold her, he would never want to stop, and what would that lead to?

He shortened his normal stride so as not to tax her, but she kept even with him without difficulty. She stayed close, too, bumping his arm now and then. He liked that. She faltered once. He caught her and liked his arm around her narrow shoulders so much, he didn't let go. Caya made no protest. In fact, she wrapped her arm around his waist for support. He liked that a lot.

After a long silence, she asked, "Why did you name your horse Gullfaxi?"

"Gullfaxi is the horse the Norse god, Thor, gave to his son. I ken the name means something like *one with the golden mane*." Her golden mane had come undone and hung in loose ringlets down her back. Unable to stop himself, he touched her hair. Rather than object, as she had in the past, she smiled up at him.

"Do you believe in that sort of thing, the Norse gods?"

"My grannie did," he said. "Up here in the north, all of us have some Viking blood running through us." He stopped walking and turned Caya to face him. "I need you to know, I'm no' a heathen. I mind the first commandment, but until two years ago, we didnae have a kirk. The old clergyman visited but three times a year. I'm not accustomed to attending every Sunday. But I will if that's what you want."

She nodded. "Thank you."

He didn't think he'd done a good enough job of convincing her of his faith, so he added, "I believe in God. I do. It's just that he and I, well…"

"You don't always agree. I know."

When he looked at her again to measure her response, he saw her suppress a shy smile. She might be laughing at him, but he didn't care. He'd be her fool if it made her happy.

"I'm fair angry with him at the moment, to be honest."

She chuckled out loud. "Why?"

"Three times I've asked him to help me win you, and three times he's rained on my head."

They both laughed and continued walking down the path, her arm linked with his, a connection he never wanted to break.

She was quiet for a good while longer before she asked, "What were you doing when you found me in the field?"

He thought for a moment. He couldn't remember what had fueled his decision to leave the stillhouse and take the drover's path to Balforss. "I suppose I was meaning to find you and beg you not to marry James Oswald."

Her only reply was, "Oh."

He was on shaky ground again. He would have preferred if she had said, *"Don't worry. You're the only man in the world I would ever marry."*

They emerged from the woods into the backyard of his house—their house. The view from the rear did not impress. The stable was, as yet, unfinished, the fencing around the henhouse needed repair, and stacks of uncut lumber waited for him under a lean-to shelter. Project after project, all of which required time, time he needed to spend making whisky, time he needed to spend courting Caya.

He held the back door open and followed her inside. They were alone again in the kitchen, and God save him from his uncle's wrath, but he was glad of it. She opened the shutters, turned to face him, and leaned back on the window ledge, silhouetted in the early afternoon sunlight. He stepped toward her, but she lifted a palm to stop him.

"What was the dream Magnus told me about, the dream

you had about me?"

So, she knows about the dream.

He sighed. His dream was not something he wanted to discuss. His uncle had warned him not to tell Caya lest she think him daft. Worse, he had misinterpreted his dream. "It's a doaty dream, and you wouldnae believe me even if I told you."

"Have you ever lied to me?" she asked.

"No. A'course not."

"Then I have no reason to doubt your dream."

He wanted to be close to her when he told her about such personal things, sit beside her as he had in the wagon on the way to Balforss, but he had no chairs in the house. What was he thinking? He hadn't a bloody place for her to sit. The only stick of furniture in the house was… No, he couldn't invite her to the bedchamber.

"Sit with me on the bunker." Before she could object, he gathered her by the waist and lifted her onto the worktop, then hopped up next to her, both their legs dangling. "It's like this: I sometimes have dreams, special dreams, dreams different from regular ones because they feel real. And while I'm dreaming I say to myself, 'This is real. This will happen.' Then, whatever I dream of always happens the way I dreamed it."

"I see," she said. "And you dreamed about me?"

"Sort of. I dreamed of a yellow-haired lass sitting in a field of gowans—daisies you call them. Even though I couldnae see her face, I knew the lass was my wife." He swallowed hard. "And when I saw you in the tavern, I was certain you were the lass in my dream."

"So, even before you gambled with my brother—before you promised him—you dreamed about being married to me?"

"Aye. My dreams never lie." He looked away. "Or at least they hadn't until…well, now I'm none so sure."

"Why?"

"I cannae say why. I'm just not sure I have it right."

"Is it because you're not sure I'm the woman in your dream?"

"I want you. More than anything I've ever wanted in my life. But, if I'm wrong and you aren't the lass in my dream, then I've taken you away from your life. I've ruined the plans you had—"

She stopped his havering with a hand to his chest. "Declan, you're not wrong. In fact, I know your dream is right. I know I'm the woman in your dream." She winced and put her fingers to her hurt lip. It had started to bleed again.

"Och, lass, does it hurt?"

She brushed away his concern. "Do you know the meaning of my name?" she asked, and a fat tear trickled over her pretty freckles. "Caya is the Cornish word for daisy."

Declan closed his eyes and let her words glide down his back like warm honey. He felt himself bend and sway toward her. Their foreheads touched, and her breath tickled his chin.

"Caya, I love you."

• • •

A warm rush of emotion flooded Caya's entire body. "You love me?"

Declan sat up straight and blinked. "Did I say that out loud?"

She adored the stunned look on his face. "Too late to take it back."

He broke out into one of his winning smiles. She wanted to fling her arms around his neck and kiss him. Never had she felt this kind of joy.

"You dinnae mind me saying it, then?"

"Not at all."

He hopped down off the work bench and stood in front

of her, eye level. "Look, I cannae change the past, but if my sword and dirk frighten you, I can put them away."

She remembered what Flora had told her. *A Hieland man is, and always will be, a warrior at heart...You cannae change that...Dinnae even try.* She touched his cheek. "Your weapons don't frighten me."

"Are you sure? Because I can sell the whisky business—"

"No. Never. I don't want you to change for me. Truly."

He favored her with another brilliant smile. "Feel my heart," he said and held her palm to his chest.

The organ pumped under her hand with such force and at such an alarming rate, she worried for him.

"Do ye feel it, *a leannan*?"

"Yes." She thought she might fall right into those fathomless dark eyes of his.

He slipped an arm around her waist and lifted her from the bench, held her against him high off the ground so she looked down at his handsome face. All at once the boundaries of their bodies seemed to meld. She cupped his cheek and felt the rasp of his bristly beard. Slowly he let her body slip down the length of his until her toes touched ground. The room began to spin.

Declan's lips brushed against the cup of her ear. "I'd do anything for you, Caya. The only thing I willnae change is the passion I feel for you. You cannae let it frighten you, love." His body shuddered, sending vibrations through her as if they were already one.

"Kiss me," she said.

"I dinnae want to hurt you."

"Kiss me."

His lips pressed a light touch on hers. Hers parted, and his tongue, wet, tentative, and alive, slipped inside her mouth, delicately searching for an answer. As if directed by his desire, her hips surged forward against his. Declan gasped.

Shocked by her own wanton behavior, Caya pulled away. They stared at each other wide-eyed and breathless. How did he do it? How did he stir her desire into a frenzy with just one kiss?

He swallowed. "Dinnae be afraid, lass."

"Has passion ever overcome you in that way before?"

He shook his head. "No. Never. But …"

"But what?"

"I liked it." A slow grin appeared on his face, an irrepressible, rakish grin with a promise of mischief behind it. "I'd marry you now, if I could. Take you to my bed and make you mine forever. I want you so."

She put a hand to her heart, certain hers might be beating dangerously fast, too. "You would?"

He straightened to his full height and stepped back, looking as if a new idea had just occurred to him. "Aye. We can marry now—today if you'll have me. I know a way."

"How?"

"We can ask my uncle permission to handfast."

"Handfast?"

"Aye. It's the same as marriage. Then, later, we can marry in the church."

She slapped a hand over her mouth and turned away. The church. The vicar. *James.* She'd completely forgotten about Vicar James.

"It's a legally binding marriage ceremony in Scotland," Declan said, a note of supplication in his voice.

"I need to tell the vicar."

He let his head tip back and groaned. When he lifted his head, he pleaded, "Why do you talk of that God-botherer at a time like this? I'm asking you to marry me."

She understood his agitation, yet he had to know how important it was that she spare Vicar James any unnecessary embarrassment. "I need to tell the vicar I can't marry him.

It's only fair."

He stared at her for a long time, motionless. Then the air seemed to go out of him. His shoulders dropped, his head tilted to one side, and the buckle in his brow disappeared. "You've a kind heart, *a leannan*." He gave her a crooked smile. "Yet another reason I love you. But I ken the Reverend James Oswald is a grown man. He can take it."

She went to him, slipped her arms around his waist and hugged. "Please."

"All right." He crushed her to him, then released. "I best wash before I take you back. It won't help with Uncle John's temper, but Auntie Flora might take pity on me."

"What do you mean?"

"My uncle is going to give me a thrashing for being alone with you." His face had that green tinge she'd seen before when he was upset.

"Don't worry," she said. "I'll protect you."

Instead of laughing at her silly joke, he said quite seriously, "You would, wouldnae you?"

"With my life," she said, and knew it was true.

He left her to drift idly through the empty house while he went above stairs to wash. Standing in the dining room, she imagined a long table filled with friends and family come to supper. She and Declan would sit at one end. Flora and John at the other. Alex, Lucy, Jemma, and Ian, on one side. Agnes, Fergus, Magnus, Margaret, and Hamish on the other. My, she had a large family.

She hadn't seen the second floor of his—of their house. The bathing tub was up there. What else? Declan, of course. A bed, perhaps? The combination of the two could only mean danger. Was she thinking wicked thoughts again?

Her footsteps, slow and purposeful, echoed through the drawing room and into the cavernous entry hall. Halfway up the staircase, she paused to consider the weight of sin. What drew her upward? Curiosity? Desire? Love?

At the top of the landing to the right, she could hear movement behind a closed door. Declan was in there. The door to the back room had been left open, and she went inside. The fireplace caught her attention immediately. Declan had tiled the surround in Delft ceramic, the pastoral depictions painted in indigo on white. In the corner of the room angled toward the center, a dark green bathing tub patterned with a raised garland of flowers around the rim. A tub fit for a princess.

Muttered curses came from the next room, and she caught sight of Declan through an open connecting door. As if sensing she was near, he turned. He flapped the loose ends of his stock at her. "Will you help me with this bloody thing?"

She knew how to tie a stock as neatly as anyone. She looped the ends of Declan's stock and tugged them into a gentlemanly knot. He smiled down on her, and she felt domestic, adored, and grown-up.

An issue that had plagued her early on jabbed her in the side.

"I'm twenty-five," she blurted.

He cocked his head. "You mean you're twenty-five years old?"

"Yes." She waited for his disappointed reaction.

He stared at her for a moment. Was the gap too great? Did he consider her too old? After all this, would he cast her aside? Declan swallowed hard, pain etched on his face. Whatever he was about to say would likely cut her in two.

"I dinnae care about that, but if we're telling secrets… I've never been with a woman. I mean"—he shot a quick look at the bed—"that way."

She shook her head. "I think that's lovely."

"You dinnae mind?"

"No."

Relief and joy transformed his face. Dear Lord, he was

beautiful. "Good," he said. "We'll figure it out together, then?"

She nodded.

"Did you see your bathing tub?"

"It's perfect. Thank you."

"That wee room is yours for bathing and dressing and, well, whatever it is women do in private. And this..." He swept his arm to indicate the entire room. "This is our bedchamber." His gaze paused on the bed, and his ears turned pink. "Erm, that's our bed," he added low and quick. He shrugged a shoulder backward and craned his neck as if she had tied his stock too tight.

She imagined the two of them lying naked, locked in a passionate embrace, kissing. Only this time, Caya didn't shut the box on her fantasies. She threw the lid wide open and let her wicked thoughts run wild. She sat down on the edge of Declan's bed, their bed.

His eyebrows nearly met his hairline.

"I'm not afraid of your passion. I've never been afraid of *your* passion. It's my own I don't trust when I'm with you. You make something inside me spin out of control." Lightheaded, out of breath, her body began to float off the mattress. "Every time you...you..."

He pounced, hooked his hands under her arms, dragged her across the mattress, and settled the length of his body against hers. He groaned something in Gaelic and then covered her mouth with an almost brutal kiss. The weight of him, the trembling restraint in his hands, and the power behind his kiss threatened to undo her. Dear God, would she come apart in pieces if she just let go?

When he finally broke the kiss, he rested his forehead against hers, breathing hard, pressing himself onto her, swollen and hard, which made the need to feel friction between her legs even more urgent.

She heard herself whimper, "Please."

Declan rucked up her skirts in jerky, desperate moves, then rolled between her legs and pressed hard, rocking against the…yes…there… right there.

"Oh God. I love you," he rasped in her ear. Suddenly he scrambled to his knees. Why? She was about to protest when she saw him unbuttoning his fall as fast as he could. He flicked the last button, and it tumbled out. Caya lifted herself to her elbows and stared, fascinated at its size, the way it stood by itself, belligerent and blunt-ended, jutting from a thick growth of black hair. Then Declan lifted her skirts and took the same long look at her parts.

"Jesus. You're beautiful."

He leaned forward, weight on his forearms, and kissed her, a long and lingering kiss. Just as his tongue slipped inside her mouth, he lowered his hips until flesh met flesh. She sighed. At last, what she had desired, what she had long anticipated, fantasized about, was happening. Declan was loving her. He began a slow, rhythmic, rocking motion, letting his solid member slide against that slippery spot, that point of no return spot, that place between her legs that needed his touch, ached for his touch. Then he, he…he stopped. What was wrong?

Declan lifted his head. "What was that?"

"What was what?"

"That."

She heard a clopping, rattling, jangling sound in the distance. "I don't know."

He pushed himself off the bed, lurched toward the window with his britches around his knees, and caught himself just in time. She tugged down her skirts and joined him. Outside, twin horses pulling a gleaming black carriage careened toward the house.

"They've come to show you the new Balforss carriage."

"Jesus." He yanked up his britches. "If my uncle catches us alone upstairs, he'll have my balls for breakfast."

Chapter Eleven

Declan hustled Caya out of the bedchamber and down the stairs. They hit the bottom step just as Alex swung the front door open. *Doesn't anyone knock anymore?*

"There you are, Caya," Alex said. "Lucy got worried, and we came looking for you."

"Is Uncle John with you?" Declan asked.

"Nae."

He exhaled. At least his life wasn't in immediate danger.

"I'm sorry to trouble you," Caya said.

"Dinnae fash yourself. You gave Lucy a good excuse to go for a ride in the carriage. She's calling it 'The Chariot.' Want to come along?"

Caya pranced out the front door, presumably to join Lucy in The Chariot. He would have followed her, but Alex blocked his way.

"Who else is here?" Alex asked, sounding critical and way too much like Laird John.

"No one. Why?" he challenged.

"You were alone with the lass?"

In Declan's opinion, Alex had no right to gather a head of steam over something that was none of his business. "Hold your *wheesht*, man. Dinnae try to pretend you disapprove. I ken you spent time alone with Lucy before you married."

"Aye, but we were betrothed."

"As are we." He folded his arms, and cocked his head, defying Alex to contradict him.

Alex grinned like a rogue. "You sly devil. Congratulations, man."

He endured a back pummeling and his cousin's enthusiastic felicitations.

"By the way, what the hell happened to the lassie's lip? Ye didnae bite her, did ye?" Alex asked, one eyebrow cocked just as Laird John would do when riled.

"She was on her way to see me at the stillhouse and ran into her bloody fucking brother."

"He did that to her?" Alex asked aghast.

"Aye. And when I find him, I may kill him."

"Not if I find him first."

"Come on," Declan said. "I'll saddle Gullfaxi and follow you back. I need to talk to Uncle John."

When they reached Balforss, Declan helped the women from the carriage. To see Caya with her face aglow, havering and laughing with Lucy, the both of them bubbling with excitement, and to know that she was his, filled his heart to bursting. He should remember to thank the gods, old and new, for his wife, the most beautiful gowan in the field.

"Will you come wi' me to talk to your da?" he asked Alex.

"For all the good it will do. He's going to murder you for being alone with Caya."

"I know it." His legs shook. Odd. He could stand before Napoleon's army without breaking a sweat, but provoking his uncle's wrath had him about to fill his boots.

Laird John was at his desk when they entered the library.

Without lifting his head from his writing, he asked, "You found Caya?"

"Yes, sir," Alex and Declan spoke in unison. They stood at attention. Force of habit.

Laird John dipped his quill and continued to write. The room was so still Declan could hear the nib scratch the paper. "Where did you find her?"

"I met her by chance on the drover path."

His uncle stopped writing and slowly lifted his head from his work.

Declan launched into the rest of his tale, rushing to get it out, as quick and painless as he hoped his uncle's retribution would be. "She was injured and upset so I carried her to the stillhouse. When she felt better, we walked to Taldale. I was about to give her a ride home when Alex and Lucy arrived."

"You were alone with Caya again? After I've told you repeatedly I forbid it?"

Alex scratched the side of his neck, a casual gesture. "Ah, I ken Margaret was about somewhere. Was she not, cousin?"

He gave Alex a look of sincere thanks. "Oh, aye. Margaret saw to her injury, to be sure." Neither of them had lied. They simply hadn't told the whole truth.

Laird John made a skeptical-sounding grunt.

"We're engaged," Declan said. "To be married," he added just to clarify.

Laird John rose from his desk and walked toward him, one awful eyebrow cocked. He stopped four inches from his face, and Declan resisted the urge to back away.

"I didnae say you could court." Laird John inhaled. "But, I suppose enough time has passed." His uncle dropped heavy hands on his shoulders, a rough benediction. "Congratulations. I trust the lass is informing your auntie Flora as we speak."

"Aye. Thank you, sir."

Laird John headed toward the cabinet where he kept his whisky. While his back was turned, Declan summoned the courage to ask, "So, it's all right if we handfast?"

John's back stiffened, and he turned a face of unmasked anger toward him. "What did you do?" he ground out between clenched teeth.

"Nothing, Uncle. I wouldnae. It's just, I dinnae want to wait. I want to marry her now. Tomorrow, maybe. Or Saturday. Soon."

Laird John stared with narrowed eyes for what felt like an eternity until, seemingly satisfied Declan was telling the truth, he flopped into one of the wingback chairs and rubbed his forehead. His uncle had no idea how close he and Caya had just come to consummating their marriage.

"I sympathize with you, lad. I do. If Caya were a Scot, I would agree. But handfasting is not the way of her people. She needs a church wedding."

His head felt too heavy for his neck to support and let it drop. "Aye. You're right, sir." A month. At least. The banns had to be read out loud in kirk three Sundays before he could wed her. Having tasted her passion, how could he wait that long?

He became conscious of his uncle, who was still speaking, the quality of his voice having altered from authoritative to exigent.

"Sorry, sir. What did you say?"

"The chief magistrate, Lord Assery, visited today. He delivered bad news. Jack Pendarvis is wanted for murdering a sailor in Wick."

"Bloody hell," he and Alex said at the same time.

"He wanted to ask Caya if she's seen anything of her brother. I told him none of us has seen the man."

Declan felt sick to his stomach.

"I'm sorry to dampen the good spirits of what should be a

happy day, nephew. Would you want to tell Caya, or shall I?"

"Oh God, no," he said, nearly buckling from the pain in his gut.

"I ken the news will upset the lass, but it's best she hears it from you rather than from someone else," Alex said.

"No. I mean aye, but...oh God." He unburdened himself to Alex and his uncle. He told the whole shameful story about Caya suspecting Jack had attacked Peter and begging him to find and help her brother.

"I found him the next day dead drunk inside the stillhouse." He appealed to his uncle. "I'm sorry but I had to do it, Uncle. Caya asked me to help her. How could I say no?"

"Where is he?"

"I dinnae ken. I had stashed him away in Scrabster, but he must have gotten away because Caya came across him on the path to the stillhouse this afternoon. The bastard assaulted her. I would have gone after him, but she was injured and so upset."

"Pour me a dram," John said. "Pour all of us a dram and sit."

Alex filled three pewter cups and handed them around. After downing his, Declan sank into a chair and put his face in his hands.

"I understand what you did and why you did it. I dinnae blame you," his uncle said. "But why did you no' come to me?"

"You ken well enough why," he said miserably. "You are Laird. It would be your duty to find Jack and deliver him to the magistrate."

John finished his whisky and rose from his comfortable chair. The man had made a decision. "You are right, nephew. And now you know what I must do."

Declan went above stairs to break the news to Caya while the others readied the horses. He dreaded this duty.

It was like delivering news of a death. From behind Flora's parlor door he heard female laughter, Caya's blended with Lucy's like a sweet chorus. He cherished the sound, would do anything not to take this happy moment away from her. But he could see no way around it.

He knocked. Flora's voice beckoned him inside. Three smiling faces greeted him. One in particular took his breath away.

"I'm sorry to disturb you."

"Nonsense. Come in and sit down, dear," Flora said.

He crossed the room and knelt before Caya.

Her smile faded. "Is something wrong?"

There was no other way to say it but to just say it. "I'm sorry, love. Terrible news has reached Balforss. Your brother is wanted for murder."

Flora and Lucy gasped, but he cared only for Caya's response. At first, there was no change in her face or her breathing. He thought she might swoon or cry or shout a denial. Instead, her eyes became unfocused. Her lips formed the word "murder."

Then she whispered, "When?"

"I dinnae ken. It happened in Wick."

"Who?"

"A sailor. That's all I know." He took her hands in his. "Look at me, love. Please."

She appeared stunned, the same look she had the morning he took her from the tavern.

"I need to go with the men now and find him before someone else does. It'll go easier for him if we take him to the magistrate. Do you understand?"

"This is my fault," she said.

"No." He shook his head adamantly. "This is not your fault. You are not to blame for anything your brother does. Believe me."

She turned to Flora, eyes brimming with tears. "I brought this trouble to your doorstep. I'm so sorry. Please forgive me."

He rose and let Flora take his place.

"Hush now, *a nighean*. Come. You'll rest a bit." She helped Caya to her feet, then put an arm around her for support and walked her out of the parlor.

Lucy patted his arm. "We'll take good care of her."

Outside, Gullfaxi stomped and nickered with impatience. Declan had taken longer than the beast had liked. "Sorry," he said and swung into the saddle. Alex, Ian, and his uncle ambled up the path on horseback and paused.

"What are we waiting for?"

Alex hooked a thumb over his shoulder. "Him."

A shaggy pony trotted up the path with Peter's stick-thin body bouncing in the saddle, his blond hair flying in the wind, making him look more like a dandelion gone to seed than a boy.

"He wanted to come along," Alex said with resignation. "When I told him no, he said it was his pirate, and he was coming whether I liked it or no'."

"You cannae argue with that," Ian said.

"Are you armed?" Declan asked Peter.

"Aye, and I brought the rope." The boy held up a coiled length of hemp.

"We're no' going to hang him," Uncle John said.

Peter set his jaw. "When we catch him, I'm going to tie him up tight so he cannae get away again."

Declan stood in the back hallway of Kinney's tavern, staring into the room where he'd left Jack Pendarvis. "How can you lose an entire person?"

Mr. Kinney flung his arms up and down like he was about

to take flight. "Feed and water him like a cow," he shouted at his wife. "That's all I asked ye to do."

Mrs. Kinney wept into her apron.

"Ye've gone and cocked it up, woman." Kinney shook his head in disgust. "I'm sorry, Sinclair."

Jesus. Laird John and the others were waiting just outside Scrabster to take Jack to the magistrate in Thurso. What the hell had happened to the bampot? He elbowed Mr. Kinney aside and pried the weeping woman's apron away from her face. "Here now, Mrs. Kinney. There's no use crying. Did you take him somewhere else?"

She shook her head.

"Did someone come for him?"

She shook her head again.

"Did he escape?"

Mrs. Kinney said in a small voice, "He said he jess needed some air an' could I leave the door open. He wasnae goin' anywhere."

Bloody hell. "He left on his own then?"

"Oh, aye."

"Can you tell me where he's gone?"

She sniffed and hiccupped, then chanced a look at her husband.

"Go on, woman. Tell him what you know," he commanded.

Mrs. Kinney waddled down the hall and into the tavern. Declan followed her to the window, where she pointed to the lights aboard a ship anchored in the middle of the harbor.

"Old Mrs. McConnechy telt me her mister rowed him out yesterday."

Declan stormed out the tavern door.

Kinney called after him, "What aboot that cask of whisky?"

"Not a chance in hell."

Declan related the news of Pendarvis's escape to the

Balforss men waiting by the highway. "I'm sorry, Uncle." He expected Laird John to be angry, but the man made no response.

Eager for action as always, Alex suggested they take a skiff out to the ship, find Pendarvis, and drag him back to shore.

Laird John shook his head. "Nae. We're done here."

"But, Da, he's a murderer."

"I said we're done." He turned to Declan, well out of Peter's earshot. "If I can spare Caya pain, I will."

Declan bowed his head, grateful for his uncle's kindness.

"It's late," Laird John added. "Go to the magistrate tomorrow morning and tell him what you know. If he wants Pendarvis bad enough, he and his men will take him from the ship."

Declan breathed a sigh of relief. "Please dinnae tell Caya anything until after I speak to the magistrate tomorrow."

Laird John gave a sharp nod, then called to the others, "Alex, Ian, Peter, let's go home."

Declan watched them ride back toward Balforss. If luck was with him, the ship would sail tomorrow morning, too late for the magistrate to capture Jack. Then he could tell Caya her brother was safe away. She would not have to watch him hang. They would be free of her brother forever, and everything would be good again. He looked up to the heavens. The sky was darkening.

Bloody hell.

• • •

Images of Jack dangling by his neck at the end of a hangman's rope had made Caya's insides swirl until she thought she might be sick. Flora and Lucy visited her room several times, offering her comfort, but their kindness only made things worse. How could they be so forgiving after all the grief she'd brought to Balforss?

She paced circles around her tiny bedchamber, waiting for the men to return. Declan promised her Jack would be safer if found by the men of Balforss. But what would happen after they left him with the magistrate? Would they hurt him? Hang him without a trial? She'd never seen a hanging, but she had heard that, for some, the end was not quick. At last, exhausted with heartache and worry, she collapsed on her bed and sobbed herself to sleep.

The next morning, she dressed in a trance. Haddie entered her room to change the bed linens and offer her pity, something she wanted no part of. She struggled to maintain her patience with the maid.

"That's a pretty gown, miss, but are you sure you want to be wearing the white muslin? It's a sunny day, to be sure, but there's a chill." She was sweet, solicitous, and overly mindful, but Caya wasn't fragile, she was just upset.

"It doesn't matter." Nothing mattered anymore. "Did the men return last night?"

Haddie's pretty smile dimmed. "Aye, but they didnae find your brother."

Her legs wobbled, and she grabbed hold of the bedpost to keep herself from crumpling to the floor. The maid dropped the linens and helped her to sit on the side of the bed.

"It's all right. I'll be fine."

"Can I get you anything?"

"No. Thank you. I'll be fine. Just give me a minute."

Haddie excused herself, leaving Caya alone to think. They hadn't found Jack. What did that mean? More in need of news than nourishment, she went downstairs to the breakfast table and found Flora and Lucy already sipping tea.

Flora greeted her with, "Good morning, dear. The men came back late last night. John is in his study, and Alex and

Ian are still abed." She touched Caya's arm. "Dinnae fash yourself. Declan will find him."

Jack had said he'd be at Mrs. McConnechy's house. She should tell Declan. Again, she worried about the rough treatment Jack would receive if captured by strangers. New visions of Jack being beaten and dragged by an angry mob flashed through her mind. She flinched when Lucy interrupted her nightmare.

"Have a bite of toasted bread with jam. You ate nothing for supper last night."

"I'm sorry, but I've no appetite this morning." She excused herself from the breakfast table. "If you don't need me for anything, I'll go for a walk."

"Stay close, *a nighean*. They still haven't—" Flora stopped herself before she said, *They still haven't found the murderer.* Or at least that's what she thought Flora would have said.

She fled the house at a trot and kept up the pace until she was well away from the people working the farm. She needed to be alone with such terrible thoughts. Jack had betrayed her trust, lied, tried to steal a horse, harmed Peter, and murdered a man. Yesterday he had been violent with her. Struck her in the face. Still, she couldn't forget the once gentle, sweet young boy who had buried his face in her skirts when it thundered, called her name when he'd had a bad dream, or given her gifts of frogs and beetles. The Jack she knew couldn't have killed deliberately. It had to have been an accident or self-defense. But who would believe him now after everything else he'd done?

She hadn't made it all the way to the duck pond when a barking Hercules bounded down the path after her, ears flapping in the wind. When he reached her, he danced on hind legs, pawing at her skirt. The sight of his little wiggling body lifted her spirits.

"Caya," Lucy called, waving her hand. "Vicar James

would like a word with you."

Oh no. Not the vicar. Not today. Not now. Caya glanced from side to side like a cornered animal ready to flee. Should she run and hide? Lie and say she was too ill to see him? Tell Lucy to turn him away?

Her shoulders sagged with the uncharitable thoughts. James was a good man. He'd shown her kindness. He deserved better from her.

"On my way." She waved back. She willed herself into a better disposition. Sometimes it was necessary to pretend to be untroubled for the benefit of others.

Lucy directed her to Laird John's study. Two faces etched with emotion greeted her—Vicar James's with dread, Laird John's with anger. No doubt, the vicar had arrived with bad news. Had he come to tell her Jack was dead? She braced herself, feeling empty, hollow, her senses dulled. Even the tips of her fingers were numb.

Laird John rose from his desk and shot the vicar a hard look. "Ten minutes and I'll be waiting right across the hall." He exited the room, leaving her alone with James in an altogether too quiet room.

"Is something wrong?" she asked.

He gestured to the wingback chairs in front of the hearth. "Please sit. I need to talk with you about something."

The vicar had on his coat and held his hat in his hands. Either he hadn't been invited to remove them or he'd refused. Either way, it was a bad sign. He sat with a sigh and leaned forward.

"Yesterday I learned that your brother is wanted for…" He halted and looked away.

"Murder," she finished for him. Surprising how she was able to say the word more easily than Vicar James.

"Yes, and I'm very sorry for you and for him. There's another matter. Something I neglected to tell you about for fear of causing you grief."

"Go on. Nothing could cause me more grief than hearing my brother is a murderer."

"A man came to the church door last week seeking refuge. He said his name was John Chisholm, but his looks and his speech led me to believe he was your estranged brother. I took him in, fed him, and made a place for him to sleep in the rectory." Vicar James smiled ruefully. "I suppose I imagined I might reform him and reunite you."

"That was kind of you."

He turned the brim of his hat in his hands. "Yes. Well, the next day, I found the strongbox pried open and church funds gone, as well as John Chisholm. There were only thirty pence within, but…" He took a deep breath. "He'd drunk all the sacramental wine."

She was wrong. She was not yet at the bottom of her misery. The shame of Jack robbing a church brought her even lower. "I'm sorry. I'll do what I can to replace—"

"No need. It's just that the incident, combined with the charge of murder…" Vicar James gave her a look of sheer torture. "I must withdraw my offer of marriage, you see. The church elders will insist."

She touched his arm, and he stopped twisting his hat. "I understand, and I accept your decision."

The vicar's shoulders relaxed. "Thank you." He glanced at the door uneasily. "I should go."

They both stood and stared at each other for a moment. What did one do in this circumstance? Not knowing the protocol, she bobbed a polite curtsy. He bowed and put on his hat.

He paused at the door as if he'd forgotten something. "Perhaps, it's best to postpone plans for the choir until this business is behind us."

"I agree," she said.

She was relieved to see the vicar go. Relieved she didn't have to tell James she had chosen Declan over him. At the same time, the vicar's apology brought to light the sad realization that marrying Declan was out of the question. How could she expect him to wed the sister of an accused murderer? The shame of it would haunt them always. Whenever people would see them in church, they would think, *"There goes poor Declan Sinclair, who had the misfortune of marrying into a family of murderers and thieves."* That was the way of things. A person's actions colored public opinion of his whole family tree. But Caya might spare Balforss additional embarrassment if she took action right away.

Flora and Lucy were engrossed in the day's project—taking inventory of home goods and assessing the need for additional comestibles—a perfect time for Caya to slip out of the house and make her way to the stable. She smiled in spite of her dark mood when Peter greeted her with a courtly bow. She couldn't help noting that the boy practiced his good manners only on the women of Balforss.

She curtsied in return. "Good afternoon, Peter. Please saddle an agreeable horse for me. I should like to ride today."

The groom's blond eyebrows crinkled together. "Alone, miss?"

"Yes. I find a long ride in the countryside helps clear my mind."

"Oh no, miss. The laird wouldnae like you to go alone. There's a pirate prowling about. It isnae safe." Peter seemed unaware of the pirate's true identity.

"I don't plan to go far. Just to Scrabster and back." Not a lie, she told herself. If she could find Jack and give him their mother's ring, he could buy passage to Canada or America. She could spare the Sinclairs the shame of Jack's criminal behavior if she could smuggle him out of the country before he was captured.

Peter fidgeted with the curry brush he was holding. He glanced toward the house, then to the line of stalls, looking as though he was considering her request.

"Please, Peter. It's very important."

The boy straightened like a soldier at attention. "As you wish, Miss Caya, but I shall accompany you."

"That's kind of you but unnecessary."

Peter tilted his head forward and cocked his eyebrow, looking so like Laird John she almost laughed.

Caya considered him for a moment. Peter would foil her plan if she left him behind. He would tell Flora where she'd gone. If he accompanied her, he might be of service. At the very least, he would make certain she found Scrabster without a problem.

"Fine," Caya said and waited while Peter saddled the shaggy pony he had been grooming. Afterward, he pulled a magnificent white gelding from the last stall.

"This is Apollo," he said, introducing her to the horse as he saddled him. "He's used to a lady rider. He belongs to Miss Lucy, and I ken she willnae mind. You'll make a pretty picture upon his back with your white frock."

"What's your pony's name?"

"Heather." He patted her neck. "She's a sweet wee thing."

Peter positioned a mounting block for Caya, adjusted the stirrups, and handed her the reins. He disappeared into a back room for a moment and returned armed with a knife of fourteen inches or more. Declan had referred to the long knives as dirks. She shuddered to think what a weapon like that would do to a man.

"Do you really need that?" she asked, pointing to Peter's blade.

"I hope not," he said, his voice cracking. Using his lowest register, he added, "But I'll use it if I have to."

. . .

Declan woke refreshed, having had a deep and dreamless night of sleep, the first in a long time. He bounded out of bed, washed, dressed, and ate the supper Margaret had left him the night before, humming to himself between bites. Then he ambled outside, smiling at the animals, talking nonsense as he fed them.

"Did ye ken I'm getting married," he said to the chickens. "Soon Miss Caya will be collecting your eggs."

After Gullfaxi had his fill of oats, Declan got him ready to ride into town. "Laird John ordered us to visit the magistrate this morning. Nae need to rush, man. We've plenty of time." He yanked the girth tight and buckled it. "There's one thing I've got to do before, though. It willnae be pleasant, but I ken I should set aside my pride just this once. For Caya, mind you. No one else." He hooked a foot into the stirrup and slung a long leg over Gullfaxi's back. "Then we'll fetch a ring for my wife, aye?" He clicked his tongue and Gullfaxi headed off toward Thurso.

Declan knocked on the rectory door, his insides twisting. The last thing he wanted to do was apologize to James Oswald. There was, of course, the possibility the vicar might refuse his apology, but he doubted it. Oswald might be a bastard for trying to steal his Caya, but he was a man of the cloth. He was obligated to forgive minor infractions like brawling.

He knocked again. Louder this time. He waited a few more minutes for an answer and when none came, his guts relaxed. "Ah, well," he said, climbing on board Gullfaxi again. "I'll try this evening after we finish what we've set out to do."

Chapter Twelve

Caya's more-than-conspicuous arrival in Scrabster caused a stir. Was it her fine white horse or the way she rode Apollo like a man? She arranged her skirts to hide as much of her legs as possible. Riding astride was immodest for a woman but far safer than riding sidesaddle. Modesty was not the issue, however. No white horse or white frock would disguise what the people of Scrabster considered her dark soul. The Presbyterian residents had branded her a witch, and perhaps they were right. Hadn't she brought pain and discord to Declan and the people of Balforss?

"Miss," Peter called out and rode up next to her. "I dinnae like this place. We should go."

She pulled Apollo to a stop. "I have private business with Mrs. McConnechy." Caya surveyed the faces in the crowd, their furtive glances, their secret murmurs. Peter was right. This was not a good place.

A boy with a shaved head about Peter's age showed some daring and inched his way closer for a better look at her.

"You, boy," she said. His eyes flew open wide. "Where is

the home of Mrs. McConnechy?"

The boy pointed and stammered. "B-b-blue door."

"Wait for me here, Peter. I'll only be a minute."

"I cannae leave you to go alone."

"Believe me. I will be safer alone." She clicked her tongue, and Apollo stepped forward, the horse showing the bold demeanor she didn't possess.

Mrs. McConnechy's home was a weather-beaten shack at the far end of the harbor road, the chipped and faded paint on the door barely discernible as blue. People watched, but no one offered to help her dismount. The good-tempered Apollo seemed to sense her intention and held still while she leaped from his back. She wound his reins around a garden post and patted the beast on the neck, careful not to speak to him lest the watchers assume the horse to be her familiar.

The door opened before she could knock. Mrs. McConnechy barked a sharp, "She's here. Remember what I said," over her shoulder, then shoved passed Caya in such a hurry she almost knocked her down.

Jack spoke from the darkness within. "You came. I was beginning to think you'd abandoned me again."

She fumbled in her pocket, eager to deliver her mother's ring and be away from this place.

"Come inside, fool. Don't let people see you with it."

He was right. People were looking. A woman alone with a fine horse, dressed in fine clothes, in possession of fine jewelry… Best not to tempt fate. She stepped inside, and the door closed behind her. She waited a moment to let her eyes adjust to the dim. Jack sat in a chair by the fire, a drink in hand. It was midafternoon. If he'd fallen into old habits, he would be well into his cups by now.

"I've brought Mother's ring like you asked. It should buy you passage somewhere safe with money to spare."

"Come sit with me a while. I want to apologize for my

rough treatment the last time we met." He sounded different. Not his usual angry, arrogant self. He sounded uncertain. Frightened, even.

"I need to go or I'll be missed. I'll just leave the ring here on the table. Take care of yourself, Jack."

"Wait. You can't go yet," he barked. "I mean." His voice softened. "Will you at least let me kiss you goodbye, sister?" He stood and took two measured steps toward her, his arms held wide.

She was tempted. This was goodbye forever. The golden afternoon light blazed through the one window and shone on his blond hair. His voice, light and sweet, was so like when he was a boy. If only he were that boy again. If only they could start over. If only... But then, she would never have met Declan Sinclair.

The door swung open with a crack. She gasped and spun around to face the silhouettes of two figures squeezing through the low opening.

"Who are you?"

One wrapped a meaty fist around her upper arm, hurting her. She cried out, "Jack, tell them to let me go."

The man yanked her outside. She'd been in the dark house long enough that the afternoon sun hurt her eyes.

"I'm sorry," Jack called out, as the other man dragged him roughly through the doorway. "The old woman tricked me, and O'Malley said he would kill us both. I had to. I'm sorry."

• • •

Peter didn't like Scrabster or the fisher people who lived there. He definitely didn't like the suspicious way they stared at his pony as if estimating her value. Every bone in his body urged him to grab Apollo's reins and lead Miss Caya away from this village.

Against his better judgement, he'd agreed to wait for her at the edge of town while she visited with Mrs. McConnechy. He'd watched her maneuver Apollo around carts, through crowds of people, and past stray dogs. Why would she want to come here, of all places? And why visit that nasty woman who had called her a witch?

Private business, she had said.

He didn't know what private business was, but he recognized the queer feeling rising in his belly. Miss Caya was headed for trouble, and she needed his protection. He just knew it. Before he lost sight of her, he slid off Heather's back and followed Caya at a reasonable distance, his pony trailing behind him. When she dismounted and entered a shack, he paused at the end of a dock twenty yards away and watched.

Mrs. McConnechy left the shack right away, but Miss Caya went inside anyway, which was a curious thing. Miss Caya had said she had business with Mrs. McConnechy. Should he go inside the shack and see if she was safe?

A bluebottle buzzed by his ear, distracting him for a moment. Out in the harbor, a graceful double-masted sloop had dropped anchor. He could identify any ship, as he had studied the pirate book Laird John had lent him. It was his dream to one day board a ship like that and sail around the world, looking for adventure like the pirates do, only he wouldn't rob other ships. No. He'd explore places no one else had visited and make maps for the King and…

Just then, laughter drew his attention. Mrs. McConnechy was returning to the shack with three men. One, dressed like a gentleman with a good coat, a clean stock, and tall black boots, had a ghastly looking smile that revealed a mouthful of rotting gray teeth. The other two wore filthy shirts, their hair clubbed in tight knots. Sailors. He could tell by their slops, those loose-fitting breeches like sailors wore. *Like pirates wore.* Bloody hell. They were headed straight for Miss Caya.

Peter's heart bumped and wobbled inside his chest so hard he had to rub the pain away. Should he sound the alarm? He doubted anyone in Scrabster would come to his aid. Ride back to Balforss and get help? Aye, and what good would that do if the pirates took Miss Caya to parts unknown? His grapple with indecision left him paralyzed.

Two men went inside the shack, leaving the well-dressed gentleman and Mrs. McConnechy waiting outside. Peter tensed. They wouldn't dare harm Miss Caya, would they? He had his dirk. He could run into the house and stick the two men before they had a chance to fight back. But then what? Lord, why had he let Miss Caya talk him into this? Laird John would gut and stuff him if he lost her.

Calls of distress spilled out of the shack, along with the two pirates dragging Miss Caya and another man. A man he recognized. *The Cornwally pirate.* The blackguard who had nearly dashed his skull in. The one wanted for murder. What was Miss Caya doing with a murdering pirate? He tied Heather to a bollard and crept closer. Close enough to hear them speak.

Miss Caya sounded scared. Her voice warbled when she asked, "Jack, who are these men?"

She knew the Cornwally pirate? Had it been part of her plan to meet him?

"I'm just trying to set things right again," the Cornwally fellow whined. "You left me no choice. Captain Sean O'Malley, meet my sister, Caya."

Jesus. The murdering Cornwally pirate was Miss Caya's brother. Did Laird John know about this?

The rotten-toothed captain-man bowed. "Ah, darlin' Caya, at last we meet. I feared you might be lost forever, but your brother has delivered you to me after all."

Miss Caya lifted her chin. "My brother is mistaken. I am engaged to another. I apologize for the misunderstanding. Please allow me to leave."

She tried to free herself from the pirate holding her by the arm.

The captain stepped closer to her, and Miss Caya turned her face away. "No, ye see, I can't let ye go, darlin', because you're already paid for."

"Jack, give him Mother's ring and tell him to let me go. Please, I want to leave."

Peter thought Miss Caya's murdering pirate-brother might do as she asked. Instead, O'Malley shook his head. "Sorry, darlin'. Your brother and I had a deal. You're coming with me."

Miss Caya broke free long enough to slap O'Malley in the face before the pirate got hold of her again. "You had best let us go before the men of Balforss arrive," she said. "They are looking for my brother and they will kill you if you lay a hand on me."

The pirate holding her placed the point of his knife to her cheek. Peter gasped out loud, almost giving himself away.

"Keep your mouth shut now, darlin'. I don't want my man's blade to slip and cut that pretty face of yours. Just relax and come with us. Your brother is leading us to a stash of whisky."

"Jack, no," Caya gasped.

"Don't worry, Caya. We'll show them the stash and then they'll let us go. Just do as O'Malley says and we'll be all right."

Miss Caya begged her brother. "Please, Jack. Don't do this. The Sinclairs will kill you. They'll kill all of you if you steal from them."

She was right. Mr. Declan stored his whisky somewhere on Balforss land. Its location was unknown to Peter, but he knew well of its value. Miss Caya's murdering brother must have discovered the location and intended to lead these men to Mr. Declan's stash. If the Sinclairs caught them stealing, they would kill the thieves.

The back of Peter's legs trembled all the way up to his backside. He was scared. Scared for Caya. Scared for himself. Scared for the whisky. But he had a sworn duty. He had to protect Miss Caya. He lingered nearby, not wanting to get too close lest the Cornwally pirate—he couldn't stand to think of him as Miss Caya's brother—recognize him from the night of the attack.

The captain said something to Caya that Peter couldn't hear, but her face turned sad, so he knew it couldn't be a good thing. His stomach growled, angry with him for having missed his midday meal. He willed it to be silent.

No time to think aboot food, ye numpty. Miss Caya is in danger.

Heather was hungry, too. And thirsty. He'd just made up his mind to lead Heather past the public house to the village well when a driver and his dray came rattling down the road with three more pirate men seated in the back.

"Here comes my man," Mrs. McConnechy said. "He'll drive you to the stash and help you bring the load to your ship." The captain handed her a big gold coin. That evil woman was in on the plan to rob Mr. Declan as well. Peter would be sure to report that fact to Laird John.

Jack and the captain's men piled into the back of the dray. "Lead the way, Pendarvis," the captain shouted, and the dray rolled forward. The captain helped Miss Caya mount Apollo. When he climbed into the saddle behind her, Miss Caya batted away his roving hands and elbowed him good in the stomach, making it plain she didn't like the arrangement.

"Relax, sweetings," O'Malley said. "No reason to blush. We're practically married."

The man's voice made Peter's insides turn liquid. Poor Miss Caya. One way or another, he had to save her. He couldn't let that disgusting Irishman take her away.

. . .

O'Malley leaned close to Caya's ear and said, "If you give me any problem, darling, I'll have that towheaded lad that's following you killed. Understand my meaning?"

He meant Peter.

She cast a furtive glance to her right and caught sight of Peter crouching behind a tangle of netting and ropes. Why had she agreed to let him come along? She'd placed them both in danger. So foolish. So utterly foolish.

"Yes," she said, finding it difficult to catch her breath. "I understand you. Just leave him be. I'll do what you want."

"That's a good girl," O'Malley said. "Now, up ye go into the saddle, and keep your pretty little mouth shut."

Heart racing, legs and arms shaking, she let the Irishman boost her on top of Apollo. Then he climbed up behind her, and they began the slow, inexorable ride out of Scrabster.

The man wedged behind her in the saddle made her skin crawl; his fetid breath, his lewd suggestions, the familiar way he rested his hand on her thigh. And she was certain he was enjoying the ride in an indecent way.

O'Malley's hand roamed up her leg and settled near her belly. She jabbed another elbow into his side as hard as she could.

He only laughed. "Tut-tut, sweetings. Remember the boy. You wouldn't want to see me slice him open, would you?"

What had she done? She'd ruined everything. That's what she'd done. She'd forsaken Declan, the man she loved, to help her worthless brother. A brother who'd demonstrated time and time again that he cared nothing for her well-being. How could she have been so stupid, so foolish? And now Peter's life was in jeopardy, as well. Even if she found a way out of this mess, even if she and Peter were able to get away from O'Malley, she could never undo the damage. Laird John would never forgive her for bringing scandal and chaos to Balforss. Even if Declan still wanted to marry her, Laird John would never allow it now that she'd stolen away to help her fugitive brother, and been party to what would likely be Declan's financial ruin. With one thoughtless, selfish act, she'd tarnished the Sinclair name. She deserved every ill-turn that came her way.

· · ·

Peter followed at a safe distance on Heather. Even when the dray turned off the main road onto a drover's path, he had no trouble keeping track of them with all the noise they made. They reached a thick grove of pines, and the sound of the rattling dray stopped.

Peter led Heather out of sight and hobbled her. "Stay here, horse," he whispered. "Dinnae make a sound or we're both dead."

The days were longer now but it was near dusk. The sun, low on the horizon, cast long shadows on the ground. Peter crept through the thick stand of trees until he reached the clearing. They were near the shore of Loch Calder. About thirty yards away, the men gathered around what looked like a cairn. The hair on the back of Peter's neck felt funny. No one went near a cairn if they knew what was good for them. Bad fairy people lived in such places, and to disturb them was to ask for trouble.

Cornwally Jack and two of the pirate men, looking like shades themselves, descended into the ancient burial ground. A hush fell on the party. Caya remained atop Apollo, but

O'Malley dismounted and held the reins. Peter waited for some frightful creature to rise out of the loch and devour everyone.

Shouts came from the cairn, and Peter crouched lower. If the fairy people were attacking the pirates, he might be able to run across the field and grab Apollo's reins from O'Malley in the commotion. That plan dissolved instantly when one of the pirates stepped out of the cairn carrying a cask. Whisky. Mr. Declan was a canny man. He'd hidden his precious goods where no reasonable Scot would ever look.

The men brought up cask after cask and loaded them onto the dray while Caya, the captain, and the driver looked on. Peter was having trouble hearing their exchanges, so he slithered on his belly through the tall grass for a closer listen.

When Jack walked past her, Miss Caya called, "Why did you do it, brother?"

"It wasn't my plan, I swear. The McConnechy woman convinced me to follow Sinclair and find out where he hid his whisky. We were only going to take a couple barrels and sell them. I needed money, Caya." Jack rubbed his forehead. "The old lady must have met O'Malley and figured she could make more money by double-crossing me."

"Hey, you!" O'Malley shouted. "Quit yer gabbing or I'll cut yer tongue out. Back to work. Jiggity-jig."

Jack Pendarvis ran back to the cairn.

After an hour of labor, one of the pirates said, "That be all of them, Captain."

They draped a tarpaulin over the stacked casks and secured the dray's load with rope. Peter counted thirty-three casks, give or take one or two. Only the three-year-old barrels would be good for drinking, but the spoils represented a fortune in whisky. Plus, O'Malley wouldn't have to pay the exciseman a single tot since they were smuggling the spirits out of the country.

"Higgins," O'Malley called. "Get your arse back to *The Tigress* and tell Richardson we'll meet the ship at the usual place."

"Aye, Captain," the man said and took off at a trot.

O'Malley called to his back, "And dontcha be stoppin' for a nip or I'll have you keelhauled."

Peter went perfectly still as the pirate ran past his hiding spot. He let out his breath once he was well beyond the tree line. *Usual place.* O'Malley said they'd meet at the *usual place.* Where would that be? Bloody hell. If the Irishman had been plain about it, Peter could race back to Balforss right now and tell the laird where to find the scalawags.

"Well, our business is complete," Jack said. "I'll take Caya and we'll be on our way."

"Not so fast, laddie." The captain smiled in that too, too friendly way. "To be fair, son, I'm not letting your sister go. She's mine."

"But I-I-I led you to the whisky, more than adequate compensation for the bridal payment."

"The whisky is payment for the life of my best gunner, Mr. Boyle. You still owe me a bride."

The Jack fellow made a nervous laugh. "Yes, of course. And then we're square."

"I'll be taking that wee bauble, as well. Give it here. Jiggity-jig." O'Malley crooked an impatient finger, and Jack put something small into the Irishman's hand.

"And you won't be going anywhere, Mr. Pendarvis. I need your company to assure your sweet sister's cooperation, ye see." Captain O'Malley chucked Miss Caya's chin as though they were already well acquainted. If Mr. Declan saw that, he'd cut off the man's offending arm.

While Pendarvis and O'Malley argued over the terms of their arrangement, the driver slipped down from the dray and attempted to steal off toward the wood. Peter supposed the

Scrabster man would rather lose his horse and dray than end up dead at the hands of these banditti.

"Stop him," O'Malley shouted. The remaining pirates tackled the driver and dragged him back to the dray. "Tie his hands and feet and leave him in the cairn. By the time he gets his bindings loose, we'll be long gone."

"I'll not tell a soul, sir," the driver said. "Please. You have my word."

"Put a gag in his mouth, as well." O'Malley mounted Apollo again and wiggled his backside into place behind Caya. "You haven't said a word, sweeting. Cat got your tongue?"

"I have no words strong enough to tell you how much you disgust me," Miss Caya said.

"You wound me, darlin'. Not even one kind word for your future husband?" O'Malley laughed and didn't wait for her response. He turned Apollo around and headed back the way they came.

Jack and the other pirates scrambled on board the dray. When the one driving snapped the reins, the draft horse leaned hard, but the dray wouldn't move. The men had to get off and push. Once rolling, the horse huffed and snorted with effort. One of the pirates nearly stepped on Peter as they passed. Thank God it had grown almost dark.

When he was certain they'd gone, he walked toward the pile of stone rubble that was the cairn. He was more scared now than he had been all night. Would he become a victim of the fairy peoples' wrath if he trespassed on their sacred place? Heart thumping in his chest, he peered down into the cairn's dark maw.

"Are you still alive?" he called. He heard the driver struggling.

"Right then. I'm coming down." He crossed himself, took a deep breath, and crossed himself once more for good measure.

He stumbled down the rough stone that served as stairs. It was pitch black below. The cairn smelled of earth, charred wood, and the sour sweat of the pirates. He stooped and groped for the squealing and thrashing man.

"It's all right. I'm no' a fairy person. Hold still."

Peter talked while he worked the knot loose on the man's gag. "I can help you get your horse and wagon back, but first I need a favor from you."

The driver made a muffled sound of agreement. Once Peter had removed the gag, the man cried, "My feet, boy, untie my feet."

"Then be still. I cannae find the knot."

Peter drew his dirk and cut the man free. The two of them were quick to leave the cairn. Above ground, Peter and the driver sighed.

"Thanks, lad. I thought I would surely die in that tomb."

"Do you ken the way to Balforss, sir?" he asked, untying the rope around the man's hands.

"Aye."

"Go as quick as you can. Tell Laird John pirates have stolen Caya and the whisky. Tell them to gather what men and arms they have, go to the northern highway, and wait for Peter. That's me."

"I'll do that straight away, you can be sure. What will you do?"

"I'm going to follow them and find out which beach they'll use to smuggle the whisky to the ship."

"Take care and God go with you."

"Wait. What's your name, sir?" Peter asked.

"Gavin McConnechy."

"Mrs. McConnechy's husband?"

"Aye. This is all her doing, foolish woman. Almost got me killed for a few quid." McConnechy hobbled off into the darkness. He was an old man, older than Laird John even. The way Mr. McConnechy was wheezing, he might expire at any moment. Peter hoped he had enough life in him to make it to Balforss.

He picked his way through the woods, dry pine needles crackling under his feet. He'd left Heather to graze on the west end of the clearing behind a rough patch of gorse. Though the evening air was cool, trickles of sweat inched down his temples. When he reached the spot where he thought he'd left Heather his blood turned icy cold. Heather was gone. She'd broken her hobble.

Oh God, oh God, oh God.

He turned in circles, searching the ever-growing darkness.

"Heather, where are you?" He cupped his hands around his mouth and called again and again. Each minute spent searching felt like an hour. He grew more and more desperate and more and more fearful for Miss Caya. Tears of frustration threatened to break loose. He closed his eyes. "Please, God. I cannae fail. I dinnae mind if I die, but please help me find Miss Caya."

He opened his eyes, and Heather stood before him. She made a disgruntled snuffle and shook her mane.

Peter hopped up and struggled his way into the saddle. "Thank you, God." He gave Heather a nudge. "Come on, girl. We've got to hurry."

Chapter Thirteen

A cold wind roared in from the sea, threatening to topple her from Apollo's saddle. Tangled strands of hair whipped around her face, but Caya made no attempt to brush the mess aside. She no longer cared to see what lay before her, a long unhappy life without Declan. Jack had betrayed her yet again. Why be shocked? And why blame him? She knew exactly who and what he'd become. It had been wrong to help Jack; she knew it, and yet she'd done it anyway. She had only herself to blame.

Things had come full circle. Back to the way they were meant to be. She was in the hands of Sean O'Malley, as was the original plan. How could she be angry? If she'd never met Declan Sinclair, if she'd never known the kindness of the Sinclairs of Balforss, she wouldn't feel anger, sadness, or betrayal at this moment. Besides, even if O'Malley hadn't captured her, she couldn't marry Declan. Not with the stain of her brother's sins on her name. This unexpected turn of events had actually spared her the pain of having to tell Declan she would leave Balforss.

Her only real regret was the whisky. Because of Jack, Declan would be ruined. She had hoped that, years from now, Declan would think of her and smile. That he might always hold her in his heart with some measure of fondness. Now, he would have only bitter memories of her. For, if not for Caya, he would be whole and happy as he should be. As he deserved to be.

Peter. Was he still following them? She didn't dare turn to look. O'Malley seemed to have forgotten the boy. Drawing attention to him might mean his death. She didn't dare provoke O'Malley until she was certain Peter had stopped following. A part of her wished he had gone for help. Perhaps Declan or Laird John would look for her. At least they might be able to save the whisky. But then, O'Malley and his men were a ruthless bunch. If there was a clash, one of the Sinclair men might be injured or killed. No amount of whisky was worth a life.

She fretted about the driver, too. Had they killed the poor unsuspecting man? No. They wouldn't have bothered to bind him if they'd planned to murder him. But he was an older man. Would he be able to free himself before he died from thirst or starvation?

O'Malley reined in and called for the wagon to halt. They paused where the road west came close to the coastal cliff's edge. The moon cast a corridor of light across the rough surface of the North Sea. O'Malley pointed to a ship silhouetted in the moonlight.

"There she is. *The Tigress*. A pretty ship, but she's got claws."

"That's the boat you use to ship herring?" Caya asked.

O'Malley made a nasty chuckle deep in his throat. "That I do, sweeting. I've got a cargo of little fish aboard my ship, to be sure." He laughed out loud as if he'd just told a hilarious joke. Phlegm rattled in his chest, and he coughed convulsively. "Fish." He coughed and wheezed. "Fish in my hold." He laughed, coughed up the phlegm, and spat on the road.

Caya's stomach rolled over inside her belly.

O'Malley called to the men. "Unload here, lads. One cask at a time. Jiggity-jig. It's a long way down. Anyone drops a cask, and it breaks, he'll pay dearly." O'Malley slid off the horse and beckoned for Caya to dismount.

When her feet touched the ground, she felt the effect of having been in the saddle for hours. Her legs wobbled, and she staggered to the side.

"The horse needs water," she said. "And I need to make water."

"You'll need to *hold* yer water till we reach the beach, sweeting." O'Malley grabbed her hand and pulled her toward the cliff's edge. For a moment, she thought he might toss her off. With what little light the moon provided, she was just able to make out a steep but navigable path along the side of the cliff that led down to the beach. And, like O'Malley said, it was a long way down.

The loose shale pathway was carved out of a wall of crumbling rock on one side. On the other, a sheer drop to the slate-strewn beach. She had never been fond of heights. They terrified Jack. She hadn't descended but twenty feet when she heard Jack shouting from above, balking at having to carry a five-gallon cask down the incline. Caya felt a stab of pity for him and cursed herself for being weak.

She made it down the jagged picket path by clinging to the wall despite the dark and her fear. The soft soles of her boots failed to protect her feet from the shards of shale that cracked apart like sheets of ice when stepped on.

O'Malley, rather sure on his feet for a man of forty-odd years, stood on the beach and coaxed her down the last thirty feet or so.

"Good girl," he said, when she arrived at the bottom. He pointed to a huge black hole in the side of the cliff. A cave. "Find yourself a private spot in here to do your business while I get the fire started." O'Malley disappeared into the dark hole and re-emerged with an armload of firewood. This *was* their usual place. They'd been here often enough to see it supplied.

The moon was high but shrouded in thin clouds. Still, it offered enough light for her to see four shadowy figures, each carrying a cask on one shoulder and creeping down the cliffside like ants.

"Best to have your wee before my men arrive, sweeting." O'Malley turned his back and went about starting a fire.

She ducked inside the cave far enough into the darkness to not be seen, yet not too far. The absolute blackness was terrifying, and Lord only knew what kind of strange creatures lived inside a place like this. Caya finished as quickly as possible and hustled back out. Unscalable walls of rock and churning sea sheltered the beach cove on all sides. Nowhere to run, even if she had the strength or the will.

O'Malley had the fire going. "There now. My crew will see the signal and send a launch from *The Tigress*. In a couple hours, we'll be safe aboard my ship. My men will take care of the rest."

"What do you mean the rest?"

"*The Tigress* has only the one launch. Lost the other in a storm. The boat can handle two men on oars and eight casks of whisky each trip. It'll take four more trips to transfer all the whisky. We'll set sail at dawn."

"What will happen to my brother?"

O'Malley straightened as if she'd called his honor into question. "I'm a fair man. Jack Pendarvis will get what he is owed."

The way he said "what he is owed" made Caya back as far

away from the man as possible. She wandered to the shore, close enough that the water licked at the toes of her boots. O'Malley wasn't a herring merchant as Jack had told her. The Irishman and his crew were, at best, smugglers. More likely they were pirates. Had they duped Jack, or had he always known he was selling her to criminals?

In England, when she had first agreed to marry Mr. O'Malley, she'd imagined life would be pleasant enough as the wife of a sea merchant. After all, the man would be out to sea most of the year. When O'Malley had resurfaced this afternoon, when she'd seen him in the flesh, watched his behavior, she'd understood what kind of hellish life awaited anyone married to the odious man. Right at this moment, though, Caya doubted all her imaginings. She even doubted if O'Malley's intention was marriage.

Good Lord, she'd traded a life with Declan for her worthless brother's safety. She'd made a hash of everything. Her anger at Jack for gambling with her life had set in motion a terrible string of incidents. If she hadn't left Jack behind in Wick to fend for himself, he wouldn't have killed that man, he wouldn't have robbed the vicarage, he wouldn't have attacked Peter. If she hadn't asked Declan to shield her brother, Jack would be answering to the law for his crimes, as he should. He wouldn't have had the opportunity to betray the location of Declan's whisky. If only she hadn't made mistake after mistake, Declan would still have his whisky and the Sinclairs wouldn't be entangled in this mess, the mess she had created.

If only she could do everything over, start again, she would go to Declan right now, declare her love, and give herself to him completely. She wouldn't care about marriage or handfasting or houses or furniture. She would just be his, the woman in his dream, and she would spend the rest of her life loving him. And maybe, just maybe, one day, she would be worthy of his love in return.

A sharp cry made her whirl around and look up to the cliff-lined path. Jack stumbled, lost his balance, and let go of his cask. The cask bounced once on the narrow path and crashed into the man in front of him, causing that man to lose hold of his cask as well. As a result, both casks rolled off the side of the cliff and hit the slate beach with a terrible crack and a tall splash of whisky. For what seemed like one awful minute, the man Jack's cask had hit teetered on one leg with arms pinwheeling in a desperate attempt to grasp on to something, anything to keep his balance. The fall happened so fast. Two hundred feet took all but a second. A short, "*Eeee*," and then abrupt silence.

The silence lasted only a moment before her brother tried to scramble back up the path toward the cliff-top, but the last man in the line blocked his way.

"No," Caya shouted. "Stop."

Jack had no chance of passing the big man. He could only hope to shove the giant off the cliff as well. He tried. He barreled into the fellow as hard and as fast as the treacherous path would allow. But the man was unmovable. He batted Jack off the cliffside with nothing but a swipe of his arm.

She screamed. Jack did not. She ran to him. He lay half in shadow, half in moonlight with his eyes open. Dear unmerciful God, he was not dead. Caya knelt beside him, the sharp slate digging into her knees through her skirts.

"Jack. It's me," she said, smoothing his cheek. "I'm here with you, dear brother."

His eyes searched hers, frightened and pleading. His lips moved but she couldn't make out what he was trying to say.

"I forgive you, dear one. Close your eyes now." She fumbled for his hand, grasped it, and recited the Lord's Prayer. Jack slipped away before she finished.

From behind her, O'Malley said, "You see? He got what he was owed. Though I dearly regret losing the whisky."

• • •

Gullfaxi carried a weary Declan into the churchyard well after dark. It had been a long day, but he still had one more thing he needed to do before finding his bed. The dim light of an oil lamp glowed in the rectory window. The vicar was in.

Declan dismounted and patted Gullfaxi on the neck. "This will only take a minute, horse. Then we can go home and eat."

The vicar greeted him at the door, tight-lipped and frowning. After a moment's hesitation, Oswald invited him inside, but he refused.

"Nae. I've just come to say—"

Oswald held up a hand. "Before you go on, you should know I've withdrawn my proposal of marriage to Caya."

Declan stepped back from the vicar and cut him a look. "Oh, aye?"

"I had no choice. When the church elders found out about her brother…" He sighed. "I regret having to do it, but my life is ruled by the church."

For one fierce moment, he wanted to punch Oswald in the neck. The man had no bloody right to withdraw his offer of marriage to a blameless lass like Caya. The next instant, he wanted to blurt, "*You never stood a chance, ye numpty. She was mine from the start and always will be.*" But a charitable feeling toward James Oswald overcame him quite unexpectedly. How could he condemn the man for loving Caya?

He nodded to Oswald, a gesture of understanding, and said, "I'm sorry, man, and I'm sorry for thumping you the other day, too. I was out of line."

"It's forgotten." Oswald stepped out over the threshold and sat down on the steps with a sigh. He produced a flask from his coat, took a long pull, and held it out.

Accepting, Declan sniffed, tipped the flask to his lips, and let a welcome swallow of good whisky slide down his throat. He took a seat next to Oswald and returned the flask. "Thanks. I needed that."

"What's going to happen? With Caya's brother, I mean."

Declan took a deep breath. "It seems he's escaped. Managed to board a ship in Scrabster Harbour. I doubt the magistrate will expend the effort of chasing him." He tipped his head to the side until he heard the satisfying pop and crackle of his spine.

"Long day?"

Declan nodded. "I rode all the way to Keiss and back. I needed to see my oldest sister, Lizzie. She was keeping this safe for me." He retreived his mother's wedding ring from his coat pocket, polished it on his shirt front, and held it up to catch a bit of lamplight.

"Will you be marrying Caya, then?"

He smiled. "Oh, aye. I expect I will." He returned the ring to his pocket.

"I would be honored to bless your union."

Before he could accept his offer, the sound of racing hoofbeats disturbed the evening calm. They rose to meet the dark rider as the horse trotted to a stop before them.

Magnus.

"Someone's kidnapped Caya and stolen the whisky." Magnus and his horse panted in unison.

What he heard clearly were *Caya* and *kidnapped*, words that felt like a blow to the head. He reached for Gullfaxi's reins and untied them from the post.

"Who?" he demanded.

"The Irishman Jack Pendarvis had talked aboot," Magnus said. "The herring merchant Caya was supposed to marry. He and his men took her."

Still he could make no sense of his cousin's words. All he

could comprehend was the urgency in Magnus's voice. "They took her from Balforss?"

"Nae. She went to Scrabster to find her brother. That's where they got her. Pendarvis led them to your whisky stash. Peter followed them all the way to the landing cove north of Dunreay. Their ship is anchored off shore."

Magnus's sobering words finally sank into Declan's thick skull. He hauled himself into the saddle, grateful he'd brought his dirk and pistol.

"I'm coming, too," Oswald said.

"We cannae wait," Declan shouted.

"I'll catch you up!"

Declan called on Gullfaxi to fly for him. Gullfaxi would run until his heart burst if he asked it. Without a care for the dark or the danger to the horses, he and Magnus raced up the road toward Dunreay full tilt.

Prayers for Caya's safety were useless. He'd leave the praying to the vicar. What Caya needed now was action. Tonight, he would make the North Sea red with the blood of those who had stolen his woman. Taking O'Malley's life was the only thing that would slake his bloodlust.

They weren't too late, he assured himself. They would find Caya, and she would be unharmed, untouched. She was a brave, sensible woman.

She had to be fine.

The whisky was a lucky thing. Lucky because it would take time to get the barrels on board the ship. Had they not stolen the whisky, O'Malley would have already raised anchor and set sail.

No. They would not be too late.

A quarter-mile from Dunreay, a dark figure stepped into the road, waving his arms. He and Magnus slowed. It was Alex. The sight of his cousin, the fiercest warrior he had ever known, made his heart slow to a dull thud. His uncles were there, too, John and Fergus. Ian and his brother-in-law, Hamish, as well. And Peter, bless the lad. Had he not been so clever, they'd have lost Caya for certain.

"Where's Caya?" Declan asked, hopping off a lathered and blowing Gullfaxi.

Alex made signs for all of them to quiet. "We've been spying on them from the cliff above the beach about two hundred yards north."

Ian leaned close to Declan's ear. "We think they've taken her aboard," he said, as if Caya had already died. He wanted to shout a denial, but held back.

Just then, another horse rode up and skidded to a halt. Vicar James. The men spared him a curious glance before turning back to Laird John.

"They've taken the last load of whisky and left four men ashore," Laird John said. "My guess is the launch will return in another hour for the men. That leaves us little time to plan."

Fear began to consume Declan by chunks. It had crept up the back of his legs and was now making its way along his spine. Every muscle in his body strained to keep himself from charging down the cliffside and slashing every man he met into pieces. But he knew any rash action now would mean certain death for Caya.

"Kill the men on shore, and attack the ship," Alex said, as if the solution to the problem was obvious.

"Aye, but it takes time and effort to board a ship like that," Fergus said. "The crew will spot us and call the alarm. We'll all be dead before one of us gets on deck."

"Not if you're dressed like pirates." Everyone turned to stare at Oswald. He stammered for a moment. "I mean, can't we arrest the men on shore and disguise ourselves in their clothing? In the dark, the crew won't discover the ruse until we've boarded her."

"We?" Alex asked. "You're a priest."

"They've got Caya. I need to help get her back."

Declan looked the vicar over. If Oswald loved Caya even half as much as he, the man was dying inside. "The vicar is with us."

"Are you sure?" Alex asked.

Oswald nodded. "I'm positive."

"Fine," Laird John said. "The vicar poses a reasonable plan. But there's no use trying to take the pirates alive. They know they'll be hanged so they'll fight to the death. Best we try and take them unawares."

Alex twirled his dirk in his hand. "There's only four of them on shore. Six if you include the oarsmen who will arrive in the launch. We can take them easily enough."

Magnus added, "That means they'll be expecting only six returning in the launch. Six of us against how many more on board?"

"I ken how many." All eyes shifted to Peter. "That's a double-masted sloop. The crew numbers twelve to fourteen."

"How do you know, laddie?" John asked.

"I ken everything about pirates and their ships. O'Malley called the ship *The Tigress*. I saw her in Scrabster Harbour this afternoon. She's a howker or maybe a collier, about eighty-seven feet long. Say she has fourteen crew plus the captain. Two lie dead at the bottom of the cliff. We'll take six on shore. That leaves seven men, at the most, aboard ship. And they won't be expecting us."

"You've learned your numbers well, man," Alex said, as proud of the boy as if he were his own son.

"That still leaves the problem of how to sneak up on the men on the beach without being seen. There's only one way down. The crew will spot us and send up the alarm," Fergus said. Everyone grunted their agreement, but no one offered a solution.

Declan appreciated Peter for his knowledge and enthusiasm, but he was straining at the bit to take action. He felt as though every second they stood on shore debating was another second shaved off Caya's life. He paced while he tried to think of a way to get down to the beach and across the water to the ship. Something about this place was familiar to him. But how? Why did he know this place?

And then it came to him, and his body went slack.

"I ken another way." Everyone turned to listen. "There's an opening to the cave farther north. Do you mind it, Magnus?"

"Aye. We used to play here when we were lads."

"It'll be a treacherous climb down in the dark, mind you," Declan said. "But it's the only way."

. . .

O'Malley wouldn't allow her to bury Jack. No time, he had said. And no shovels. Caya's worst suspicions about O'Malley were proving true. Perhaps the best she could hope for at this point was an early death. Such were her dismal thoughts as the oarsman rowed away from shore. Away from Scotland. And Balforss. And Declan.

When they reached *The Tigress*, she was obliged to climb into a kind of swing, whereupon the crew hoisted her aboard like cargo. O'Malley climbed a rope netting that hung down the side of the ship. Once standing on the deck, she felt that queasy sensation she'd had on the voyage to Scotland. Sailing did not agree with her.

She counted at least eight shadowy figures standing motionless on deck. They seemed to be staring at her, though she couldn't see their eyes in the darkness. O'Malley shouted at them to load the whisky. He delivered a few more orders, to which Caya took no heed. Suddenly, she raced to the railing and retched. She vomited up bile and the strong spirits O'Malley had made her drink after witnessing Jack's death.

"Poor child," O'Malley said. "Come with me, sweetings."

"I would like to lie down, please."

"Of course." O'Malley opened a hatch and motioned for her to climb down a ladder into a dark space. He lowered a lantern to her and followed down the ladder.

She held the lantern out, casting a short glow of light on various items: sacks of grain, barrels, cannonballs. It looked nothing like the cabin space aboard the ship to Scotland.

From behind her, O'Malley said, "Keep going, sweetings. Just ahead there. I want you to see my shipment of herring."

The lantern threw light on what looked like an animal pen made of horizontal wooden boards spaced three to four inches apart. Something rustled inside the pen, living things shifting and moving about. O'Malley produced a key and unlocked the hasp. When he pulled the door open, she shined the lantern inside the pen.

Four big-eyed, disheveled-looking women huddled together in a corner.

"Behold, my cargo of little fishes," O'Malley said and laughed.

"What?"

O'Malley lifted a boot to her behind and shoved her inside the pen. As he slammed the door and locked the hasp, he said, "There you are, sweetings. Get acquainted with your new sisters."

She grabbed at the door and rattled it. "Wait. Come back. Why are you doing this?"

O'Malley offered no answer. She listened to his receding footsteps and the thump of feet on the deck above.

"How do you do?" She turned to look for the source of the refined English voice.

The four women bobbed polite curtsies her way.

Speechless, and operating as if in a dream, she returned a curtsy.

The tallest of the women squinted at her as if she had trouble seeing in the dim. "My name is Miss Virginia Whitebridge."

"I'll take that for you," another woman said, and she relieved Caya of the lantern. She hung it on a hook overhead and introduced herself. "I'm Lady Charlotte Goulding of Black Port Lodge."

"I'm Caya Pendarvis of, of…Balforss." Her heart hurt when she said the name. But for her, Balforss would forever after be her home.

The other two introduced themselves. Her head was still reeling from this unexpected turn. She could barely retain their surnames, much less their places of origin. One thing she noted, though. All were from good homes. Miss Whitebridge and Lady Charlotte were from England, Miss Tucker from Edinburgh.

The fourth woman, the youngest, Morag Sinkler, had been taken from her home in Wick. Wick? Oh dear Lord. When O'Malley hadn't found Caya in Wick, had he taken Morag in her stead?

"Please have a seat, Miss Pendarvis." Miss Whitebridge indicated an overturned crate. The others found similar spots on which to sit. "I'm afraid I can't offer you tea," she added. Lady Charlotte laughed lightly at the absurdity of Miss Whitebridge's jest. English to the core.

"Why are we here?" Caya asked. "And what's going to happen to us?"

The women exchanged furtive looks.

"Please. I want to know."

At last Lady Charlotte said, "It's not good news, I'm afraid. The captain plans to sell us in the West Indies to—" She pressed her lips together.

"To who knows who," Miss Whitebridge finished for her. "The good news is that, so far, none of us has been molested by captain or crew, they feed us—"

"My uncle's pigs eat better slop," Miss Tucker interjected flatly.

"But they do feed us."

The last brick of fear fell into place. With the layers of lies peeled back, she could at last see the reality of what lay ahead. O'Malley was not a gentleman, he wasn't a herring merchant, he wasn't even a mere smuggler. He would not be her husband, and she would not be his wife. Caya was his merchandise. She would be sold to a house of prostitution, where she would live a short, unhappy life.

Miss Whitebridge tilted her head in sympathy. "We've all been through what you must be experiencing now. You'll weep for a while. Be seasick for a while. But in a day or so, you'll be yourself again." Miss Whitebridge turned to the others. "We must all remember to remain true to ourselves." It was odd. The other women seemed to defer to Miss Whitebridge, even though Lady Charlotte held the rank of nobility.

Caya pretended to agree. They all pretended to agree. That seemed to be their way of dealing with this nightmare. But she knew the truth. She would never be herself again.

. . .

Searching for the cave opening in the dark, Declan and Magnus were reduced to crawling on hands and knees. Had the opening been sealed? Had he somehow misremembered? Was this even the cave he and Magnus had explored when they were nine and ten? His heart had been beating double time since Magnus had delivered the news of Caya's abduction. Now he was growing short of breath. He fought back the urge to panic.

"Found it," Magnus rasped.

He scrambled to Magnus's side and helped tear away the rough grass covering the opening.

Alex leaned over his shoulder. "Jesus."

"It's much smaller than I remember," Magnus said.

The opening was the ideal size for a boy of ten, a slit in the rocks approximately two and a half feet long by ten inches wide. From what he recalled, another four feet farther down, the opening expanded. Being lean, he thought he could slither inside. But Magnus could not fit his great chest through the cleft. Nor could Alex.

"I'm going down," Declan said, and he slipped his feet into the hole.

"Wait," John said. "We need four men of stealth and deadly skill. I think I can make it. Who else?"

"Me," Ian said.

"I can," Peter said.

"Nae, lad. We need your knowledge of the ship. We cannae afford to lose you."

"I'll do it." Fergus stepped forward.

Hamish wrapped a hand around Fergus's arm to stop him. "Nae. I'm the best man with the knife. I'll go."

Though not blooded in battle like the other five former soldiers, Hamish was undeniably good with a knife. Declan had seen his ruthless precision cutting leather for saddle and harness.

Alex demonstrated for Hamish. "Approach from behind, one hand over his mouth, pull him to your chest, and slide the blade across his throat quick and deep as ye can, aye?"

Hamish nodded once.

"Right then," Laird John said. "Declan, Ian, Hamish, and I will go down through the cave opening. Once we've dispatched the men on shore, the rest of you take the cliff path, but be careful. More than one man has already fallen to his death."

Confident, Declan and his team of assassins removed their shirts and shoes and slithered one at a time through the rough rock. Declan went first, holding on to a rope, glad of the dark. Had he been able to see his suffocating surroundings, he might have balked. When he had cleared the narrow stone channel and could stand upright in the opening, he tugged on the rope.

Ian went next, followed by Hamish, then Uncle John. As each man emerged from the slotted entrance, he was helped by the others and held steady on his feet until he adjusted to the inky black. The air in the cave was not still. Wafts of salty sea breeze swept over Declan's face, and he inched toward the source.

The four men remained connected, one hand on the wall, the other hand on the shoulder of the man in front of them. Declan moved forward, guiding them down, down, down—partly by memory, partly by instinct, mostly by his need to reach Caya.

None of them spoke. The only sound was their collective breathing, which echoed eerily inside the cave. At last, he saw the literal light at the end of the tunnel. The half-moon cast a pale blue glow on the beach. To their good fortune, the four pirates huddled downwind of their fire, their backs to the cave opening. The swoosh of the wind and waves, the crackle of the fire, and the talk among the pirates covered the sound of blades being drawn and bare feet padding over stone.

Working as one, the gruesome job was over in an instant. Declan signaled the others waiting above, then pulled the dead men into the shadow of the cave and removed the blood-soaked clothing while Alex and the others descended the cliffside path and hid inside the cave.

Upon reaching the beach, Alex joined Uncle John and Ian inside the cave. They made their transformations into pirate clothes and resumed positions around the fire. Declan breathed in. Taking action, taking a life, helped assuage his fear. He calmed himself and readied his mind and body for battle. There would be more blood spilled tonight. Payment for Caya's abduction. Hopefully, none of it would be Sinclair blood.

He took a moment to inspect the two dead bodies lying at the base of the cliff. One of them was Jack Pendarvis. A small part of him felt sorry for the foolish man, sorry for the grief Caya must feel for losing her brother. But the greater part of him was relieved he wouldn't have to kill the man himself. Caya might never have forgiven him.

Taking the oarsmen was child's play. Ian and Declan made the killings. Magnus and Uncle Fergus donned the bloody garments of the oarsmen. They doused the fire and readied the launch.

Laird John stopped Hamish. "I need you to remain on shore. After we take the ship, we'll signal, and you can relight the fire." John turned to Vicar James. "You'll lie facedown in the bottom of the craft, covered with the tarpaulin until the six of us are over the rail and the battle has begun. You'll stay with the boat. We'll get Caya off the ship first, and you'll row her back to safety."

"Understood," the vicar said.

Peter, Oswald, and the six disguised men climbed into the launch. As they rowed toward *The Tigress*, Peter asked, "What about me?"

"Ah, yes. You'll be the diversion," John said. Declan heard a smile in his uncle's voice.

After a desperate struggle and vehemently whispered protests, Alex and Laird John had dressed Peter in tartan plaid and head kerchief to look like a lass. If Declan weren't worried to the point of madness, he would have laughed.

"There now, laddie," John said. "The crew will be so busy

looking at the whore we've brought them, they willnae pay any mind to the rest of us."

"But I want to fight."

"Peter, listen," Declan said, turning the boy to face him. "You ken the layout of the ship. As soon as we're on board, point me to the captain's quarters. That's most likely where Caya will be, aye?"

"Aye," Peter said grudgingly.

"Then throw off your women's clobber and check the hold. There's a chance he would lock Caya in a cabin below. I want her freed and off the ship as quick as ye can. Do you understand, man?"

"We're halfway there," John said. "Time to start the performance, men."

Chapter Fourteen

A resounding *thump* came from the deck, sending a shower of dust down upon the women's heads. O'Malley shouted curses and warnings of bodily harm should any of the crew damage his cargo.

"Whatever is going on up there?" Lady Charlotte gazed upward as if she might see through the ceiling boards.

"They're loading a cache of stolen whisky." Caya noted the unnatural calm in her voice.

"I see," Lady Charlotte said. "If you don't mind my asking, are you really from around here? You don't sound like a Scot."

"You sound Cornish, actually," Miss Whitebridge put in.

"I am Cornish. I'm from Penzance to be exact, Miss Whitebridge."

"I knew it." She clapped her hands, pleased for having guessed Caya's origins. "But you must call me Virginia. We use our Christian names just as sisters would, do we not, Mary?"

"Yes, but what on earth is a Cornish lass doing in the

Highlands?" Mary plunked herself on a crate, elbows on her knees.

"Long story."

"Believe me," Charlotte said, "we have the time."

Virginia brightened. "I know. We'll each share our own stories to make you feel more comfortable. I'll begin."

In the following hours, while the light from the lantern held, each woman retold her story for Caya's benefit. Interestingly, telling the story of their pathways to bondage seemed to calm them, as if speaking the names and places of their homes kept their pasts alive, kept their hope for salvation alive, kept *them* alive.

Virginia Whitebridge, daughter of a wealthy spice merchant, had been snatched from the streets of London while shopping.

"I blame myself to a certain degree," she said. "I should never have gone to the bookshop alone. On my way, a boy called to me for help. I followed him down an alley. Harmless, I thought. The next thing I knew, someone knocked my spectacles off my nose, covered my mouth, and dragged me to a carriage. I must have fainted because I don't remember being carried to the ship. I wouldn't mind so very much if I had my spectacles. I'm positively lost without them."

Charlotte Goulding had an even more sinister tale to tell. She had inherited the bulk of her father's sizable estate. Though Lord Goulding had left a substantial jointure to his second wife, Charlotte's stepmother made it plain she was unhappy with the settlement. "I have no evidence, but I would bet my life that witch sold me to O'Malley."

Morag Sinkler wept openly when she told her story. The girl couldn't have been more than fourteen years old. She had made the mistake of stopping at the candy store for a lolly on the way home from church.

"If I hadnae been sae greedy for the sweets, I wouldnae

be here."

Virginia placed an arm around Morag and comforted her.

"I wasn't so much sold as passed off," Mary Tucker said. Her brother was secretary to a member of Scotland Parliament. They had lived in a flat in Edinburgh off High Street. The flat was suited for two, but when her brother announced his engagement, he also announced that he had arranged for Mary to wed a well-to-do herring merchant named Sean O'Malley.

"That sounds familiar," Caya said.

And so she began her story. She was surprised by her own candor. There seemed no reason to hide any detail. Rather than stupefaction and shock, she received nods of sympathy, sounds of understanding, reassurances of their similar bond. They embraced her and welcomed her into their sisterhood of exile.

Though their stories were unique, they had two things in common: all five women were from good families and all were unmarried. O'Malley had told them virgins would fetch a better price.

Mary leaned forward. "If the captain thinks for a minute yer no' a maid, he'll pass you among the crew—"

"Mary, please," Virginia said.

"She's right, though," Charlotte added. "From the things the captain has said, I don't think he'll sell us to a brothel. Most likely some lonely man who desires a…a…" Charlotte's voice quavered, showing for the first time a crack in what seemed to be her impenetrable English armor.

"Have you tried to escape?" Caya asked.

"And go where?" Mary said. "We're surrounded by the sea."

"The captain doesn't lock us in to keep us from escaping. He locks us in to keep his crew out," Virginia said. "That's one thing to be grateful for."

"That doesn't stop them from—"

"Mary, don't say it," Virginia cautioned. "You'll upset her."

"Don't say what?" Caya asked. The women looked at the floor. "Tell me. Please."

Mary lifted her chin. "Some of the crew come down here and…expose themselves."

"We never look," Charlotte said.

"But you can hear them do unspeakable things," Mary added, her face twisted with disgust.

"If ever I get the chance," Morag said, her small hands clenched in fists, "I'm going to stab Captain O'Malley in the heart."

Caya imagined for a moment how satisfying stabbing the man would be. Never once in her life had she thought to kill someone before. Today, though, she understood the hatred and loathing that drove men *and* women to murder.

The regular thump of footsteps above changed to shouts and raucous laughter.

"What's happening?" Lady Charlotte raised her question to the ceiling again.

"Dinnae ken." Mary stretched and yawned.

"They've finished loading the whisky. They'll be raising anchor and setting sail," Caya said in a flat voice. "It'll be morning soon."

Suddenly, shouts shot across the deck above them. Screeching, howling cries. Roars so loud, so long, and so murderous all the hairs on Caya's arms stood on end. The five women rose, their faces upturned.

"What is that?" Virginia asked.

Mary laughed. "That, my dear ladies, is a Highland war cry. We've been boarded by Scots!"

"Someone's come to save us." Morag flung her arms

around Mary.

Caya hesitated. She wanted to believe it. Dare she hope?

"Miss Caya, are you down there?"

"Peter, is that you?"

"Aye, miss. Anyone else down there with you?"

"Just women. There are five of us ladies. We're locked inside a cage."

"Coming."

She heard Peter stomp down the ladder, run, stumble, hit the floorboards, curse, and pick himself up. "I'm all right."

"We're over here."

"I can see ye now."

Peter pulled at the hasp, kicked it, then used his dirk to prize open the lock. When that didn't work, he used the handle of his knife as a hammer. The sounds from above grew more and more disturbing. Peter continued to pound on the lock while Caya's fear they might not escape in time mounted.

"Peter, whatever you're doing isn't working," she said.

"Aye." He panted from the effort. "I've got an idea."

Tinny sounds, like someone hammering a nail, resonated through the slatted door. All the while, shouts of agony, the *clang* and *zing* of steel blades, and the occasional crack of gunfire emanated from above.

"Hurry, Peter. Hurry," she said, desperate for freedom.

"I'm taking the hinge pins out, miss. Almost done." He grunted once. "There."

Caya pushed hard, and the door crashed to the floor, revealing a grinning Peter holding a dirk. She'd never been so happy to see his dirty face. Her sisters stood wide-eyed, clinging to one another. Except for Mary. She'd smashed the wooden crate and held a jagged piece of it in her hand like a club.

Peter swept them a courtly bow. In his most manly voice,

he said, "Follow me, please, ladies, and keep your heads doon."

He scampered up the ladder. "All's clear. Come up one at a time." Caya held the base of the ladder for Virginia to climb into the air above. They waited at the bottom, gazing up through the hole. It seemed like forever. Then Peter called for the next.

"You go," Charlotte said to Caya.

"No. Morag, it's your turn. Go quickly." Morag hiked her skirts and ran up the ladder.

Again, the women waited.

"Next," Peter shouted. "And hurry."

Mary and Caya took Charlotte by both arms and shoved her up the ladder. While they waited, she and Mary looked at each other, smiling, knowing full well they would argue over who would go next.

"Even or odd?" Mary asked.

Caya knew the game. "Odd," she said, and put a hand behind her back.

"One, two, three."

Their hands shot out, and the dawning light shone down through the cargo opening on Caya's two fingers, and Mary's one.

"I stay," Caya said. "You're next. Up you go."

When Mary disappeared, Caya felt a ball of panic swell in her chest. What if she didn't make it off the boat?

"Next," Peter called, and Caya hiked up her skirts.

Above and out in the open, she squinted in the dawn light. The deck was a hellish chaos filled with curses, gun smoke, and blood. One man she didn't recognize lay on the boards screaming. His belly had been slashed open, and he held his insides in with both hands.

"Come on, Miss Caya." Peter pulled her toward the railing.

She coughed and waved away the gun smoke. Then she saw him, Declan, in a ferocious battle with a large sailor. It looked as though the sailor had the upper hand. His attacker advanced a step, and Declan retreated two. He blocked each blow of the blade with his own.

"Come," Peter pleaded.

But she couldn't leave until she knew Declan was safe. He stumbled and Caya caught her breath. The sailor's blade came down. She shut her eyes, unable to watch. How could she watch her beloved killed? And yet, she had to know. Caya forced her eyes open in time to see Declan's blade thrust up and through the sailor. He rolled, and the big sailor dropped to the deck, flailing.

With effort, Declan withdrew his blade from the man's body.

"Declan," she called out.

His head snapped up, eyes tracking the deck until they fastened on her. A sudden burst of shame flooded her body. The danger they were in, this battle, all this blood and carnage was her fault. What if one of the Sinclair men was injured or killed? Would Declan ever forgive her? For that split second, her fate teetered in the balance. Had Declan come for the whisky? Or had he come for her?

And then he smiled with such relief in his eyes she thought her knees would buckle under her. He had come for her. He'd risked everything for her, and she knew by the look on his face that nothing could have stopped him. True to his promise, he was there to protect her, and for a moment she felt safe again, sheltered, as though she were in his arms. Safe from all the ills in the world. Forgiven.

He took a step forward, and another figure loomed up behind him.

"No!" she screamed.

Declan's head jerked and his body slumped sideways

against the ship's railing. A man had clubbed her beloved in the head with the blunt end of his pistol. She ran to Declan, but before she could reach him, the pirate pushed his slack body overboard.

"Declan!" Caya reached for the railing. Declan couldn't swim. He would drown. She had to save him. A hand slapped around her wrist, halting her forward motion, holding her fast.

"You're staying with me," the blood-spattered face growled.

Caya kicked, punched, scratched, and twisted. Anything to free herself and get to Declan. "Let go of me, you bastard. I'll kill you. I'll kill you!"

When the man released her, she stopped her flailing, surprised he had obeyed her wishes. The look on his face went from vicious to blank. Then, he crumpled to the deck, a slow graceful fall. Peter stood behind him, holding his bloody dirk and looking surprised.

"Thank you, Peter," Caya called, and she vaulted over the railing.

· · ·

Flashes of white light sparked behind his eyes. The world had gone dark, and he was flying. No. Floating. No. Falling. He seemed to be falling forever. Was this what dying was all about? If so, why did the back of his head hurt like the devil?

Something smacked him square in the face. He gasped from the shock of it and choked violently. Shite. He couldn't breathe. He was choking to death in the freezing blackness. Then he stopped his struggling. Let his arms and legs go limp. He shouldn't fight back. Let death take him. A fair trade for Caya's life. And she was alive. He'd seen her.

Wait. Did Caya make it off the boat? Did the Sinclairs

prevail? Shite. Was the battle yet won? He had to finish. He kicked and waved his arms about until he broke the surface of his death. He coughed and spit up sea water. Bloody hell. He'd been tossed in the drink.

"Declan."

Caya's voice.

"Declan."

She sounded close. He spun around in the water, searching. And then he spotted her. Just there. Her back to him. Her yellow hair waving on the surface of the water. Her white shift spread out around her like she was sitting in the middle of one huge gowan.

Exactly like his dream.

"Declan!"

"I'm here, Caya."

She turned her head, and the terror in her eyes changed to blessed relief. She swam toward him, cutting easily through the black water.

"Are you all right, love?" he asked.

She smiled. "Yes. Why are you looking at me funny?"

"It's my dream. This is my dream."

"Hey," a male voice called out.

They looked up at Alex leaning over the ship's railing, lowering a basket contraption.

"Grab hold of this and I'll pull you up," Alex called.

Caya swam toward the basket, then paused to look back. "Declan?"

"Swim, ye numpty," Alex called.

Bloody hell. He didn't know how.

"Kick your legs and paddle your arms like this." Caya demonstrated.

He swallowed a mouthful of water and coughed. His head slipped below the water, and he kicked hard. When he broke the surface again, Caya was bobbing in the water before him.

"Come to me, Declan," she said, her voice sultry like a siren. She drifted backward toward the ship and the dangling basket. "Keep your eyes on me, my love. Kick your legs and paddle your arms and come to me."

He kicked and kicked and kicked, never taking his eyes off his beloved, his Caya, the most beautiful gowan in the field.

They both tumbled out of the basket contraption and onto the deck, clinging to each other and shivering in the morning chill. Alex and Laird John helped them to their feet. Out of the corner of his eye, Declan saw Ian and Magnus stacking dead bodies on the opposite end of the deck.

"Anyone injured?" Declan asked.

"Magnus was cut on the chin, but he'll do," his uncle said, removing his coat. "There were more of them than we anticipated, but they're all dead." Laird John wrapped his coat around Caya's shoulders. "Take her inside the captain's quarters. You'll find blankets in there and maybe another shirt for you."

He was grateful his uncle had covered Caya with a coat. Her thin wet cotton gown clung to her round bottom, leaving little to the imagination. Although he appreciated the sight of her backside, he didn't want anyone else looking at her.

Before she would let him lead her away, Caya called out to Peter.

"Yes, miss?"

"There are clothes in the hold where they kept us. Will you bring me something dry to wear?"

"Aye, miss." Peter ran toward the hatch opening.

"And, Peter," she said, teeth chattering, "you were very brave today. You saved us."

The boy grinned and swept a deep bow. "Your servant, miss."

Declan ushered Caya through a door under the quarterdeck and into what he assumed was the captain's cabin. The ceiling was too low for him to stand upright. A wide window spanning the aft end of the room allowed the morning light to warm the jumbled contents of the chamber, including a table with a map anchored at one end by a plate of half-eaten food and a flagon of ale at the other. Declan righted a chair lying in their way and sat Caya down on a berth with rumpled bedclothes.

"It smells terrible in here," she said.

He imagined the room carried the stench of O'Malley, a man she wouldn't like to remember. He threw open the window, letting the sea air inside, then turned to her.

"Better?"

She nodded and whispered, "I'm sorry."

With the battle over, uncertainty settled in. "Why?" he asked. "I ken why you went to warn your brother, but why did you go away with O'Malley?"

"He was going to hurt Peter if I didn't go with him. And…"

"Did you change your mind? Do you not want to marry me anymore?"

"How can you marry me knowing Jack was a thief and a murderer? With everyone knowing he was a criminal?"

"His crimes are not yours, love. I dinnae care at all aboot him. I ken you're sad he's dead, but truth be told, it's for the best."

Caya's face crumpled. "You're not angry?"

"Never."

"You still want to marry me?"

"Oh, aye." He felt the ground under him growing solid.

"Why? Because I'm the woman in your dream?"

"Nae. I dinnae care about the daft dream. It's you. You're the reason. I want to marry you because..." This was it. This was the moment Alex had told him to expect. He would have to tell Caya things, true things, things he felt. Declan took a deep breath. Smiling, half embarrassed, but determined to reveal his soul, he began.

"I want to protect you, provide for you, give you a fine house and a good life. I want to see you every day. Not just now and then. You are the first person I want to see when I open my eyes in the morning. You are the person I want sitting across the supper table from me. I want to hear you laugh and sing and shout my name. I wouldnae mind if you scolded me now and then, as long as I can be with you, hold you in my arms every night. I could bear anything as long as we can live together as husband and wife."

A beam of sunlight slanted across her face. Those eyes, those lips, those precious freckles, he'd almost lost them forever. He crossed to her in two steps, gathered her in his arms, and kissed her, knowing he was too rough. But he was desperate. "And this," he said, breathing hard. "I need this— what's between us—this passion. I need it." She kissed him back with equal hunger. He never wanted the kiss to end. He never wanted to let her go.

"Yeck."

He broke their kiss and whirled around. Peter stood in the cabin doorway with a gown wadded in his hands and a look of disgust on his face. Declan's initial impulse was anger for the interruption, but the sound of Caya's laughter made his irritation melt away.

"Thank you, Peter," she said. "Where are the other ladies?"

"The vicar and Mr. Fergus rowed them to shore. They'll be back with the boat in about a quarter of an hour, I ken."

"Leave the gown on the chair. I'll meet you on deck in a

minute or two," Declan said.

"Are you going to kiss some more?" Peter asked, his nose wrinkled.

Declan lost what little patience he had left. "Get out!"

Peter darted away, slamming the cabin door shut behind him.

"You mustn't be mean to Peter," she said, sounding like she was teasing him.

"No one," he said, dead serious, "will ever keep me from you again." He had just placed his lips on Caya's when he heard Laird John shout his name from outside the cabin door. He pulled away and closed his eyes. "Except my uncle." He sighed. "Change your wet clothes and rest. The boat will be here soon."

Before he slipped out the door, Caya said, "I love you."

He caught his breath, and for a moment his world went perfectly silent, perfectly still. "I love you, too," he said and answered her smile with one of his own.

Still reeling from the thrill of her words, it took him a while to orient himself. Outside in the open, the specifics of their situation came into focus—eight dead bodies, a blood-soaked deck, his precious whisky on board, and no one knew how to sail the damned ship.

Magnus leaned against the railing, holding a cloth to his face. Ian, Alex, and Laird John stood facing Declan, arms folded, still wearing their ridiculous pirate clothes, faces and shirt fronts soaked in blood. He glanced down and remembered he looked just as absurd in loose-fitting slops still wet from his swim in the sea.

"How fares the lass?" his uncle asked.

"She's uninjured."

His uncle tipped his head, and he understood his meaning.

"Nae. I dinnae think anyone…violated her."

"Sir," Peter called from the other end of the ship. Laird John held up a finger for the boy to wait.

"Good," his uncle said, still looking grim. "That's good."

"What's next, Da?" Ian asked.

Laird John inhaled deeply. "We get Caya and Magnus to shore. Hamish will see them home. Then, we unload the whisky."

"Laird John, sir," Peter called out again. Still, the laird paid the boy no mind.

"We've got hours of work ahead of us, men," Laird John sighed.

"Sir," Peter shouted. At last, the boy got the laird's full attention.

"What is it, lad?"

Peter stood before the eight dead bodies, frowning. "The captain's not here."

No one said a word.

The boy looked up, his eyes wide. He pointed a shaky finger at the bodies. "The captain's not among the dead."

Declan lunged toward the captain's cabin, threw open the door, and froze.

• • •

Caya had no warning before a greasy hand clapped over her mouth and cold steel pressed at her throat.

"Don't make a sound, darlin', or I'll slice your pretty little neck," O'Malley's saccharine voice rasped in her ear. "That's the flat of my blade yer feelin'. Try to get away and I'll turn the sharp edge on yer skin."

O'Malley pressed her head against his shoulder. His grip was brutal. She moaned.

"We'll wait here a while. Your billy boy will be back soon." O'Malley's breath smelled rotten and his body odor sour. "Let go my arms, pet."

Caya loosened the grip she had on his forearms and crossed her hands over her chest. O'Malley had watched her change into the dry gown. Bastard. She burned with anger from the inside. When Declan found out, he'd—oh Lord, no. Declan. He'd return to the cabin as soon as he ran out of patience waiting for her. What foolish thing would he do?

The cabin door banged open, and O'Malley tensed.

"Let her go!" Declan bellowed, teeth bared and eyes black with rage.

The look on Declan's face frightened her. She hoped it scared the devil out of O'Malley, too.

Laird John and Ian's faces peered over Declan's shoulders from behind him.

"Top o' the mornin' to ya, gentlemen," O'Malley said, sounding like he was welcoming them to breakfast.

"You'll never get off this ship alive," Laird John said.

"Then I'll take the little lady with me. She'll be fine company in hell."

Declan made a move and froze when O'Malley jerked his knife around, the sharp edge against her tender flesh. She felt the sting of it, followed by a warm trickle of blood.

"Back away from the door. Jiggity-jig. I'm comin' through. Try anything and I open the lady's throat."

"Take me instead," Declan said. "I'll change places with her. I'd be of more use to you rowing the launch. Just let her go."

"Back away."

Caya heard the first note of panic in O'Malley's voice.

Declan, Ian, and Laird John backed out of the doorway, never taking their eyes off her.

"Come on, darlin'. Right foot, then left foot, real slow." Caya and O'Malley inched toward the door. At the threshold, O'Malley said, "I'm not a fool, Sinclair. There's someone above ready to cave in my skull as soon as I come out. I heard the boards creaking. Tell 'em to come down."

Laird John signaled, and Magnus leaped down from the quarterdeck, holding a wooden mallet.

"Back. Farther. Farther." She and O'Malley stepped into the sunshine. The bright light made her squint. Declan was looking at her, his gaze unwavering. He seemed to be telling her something. Whatever it was, her fear receded. Perhaps that was his message. Don't be afraid. A tear trickled down her cheek.

O'Malley ordered the men to lay their swords and dirks on the deck where he could see them. The Sinclairs obeyed.

"Tell the launch to pull up alongside," O'Malley said. "Then hoist the basket to the deck. Caya and I are taking our leave."

"Vicar," Laird John shouted. "The captain and Caya are coming down. You're to row them ashore without trouble."

Caya heard Vicar James call back, "Right."

"Magnus, Ian, hoist the basket to the main deck," Laird John ordered.

The two men took hold of the rope and pulled hand over hand.

O'Malley kept his eye on Declan and Laird John as he backed up to the railing with her gripped close to his body. "I mean it, gentlemen, one false move and I'll slaughter this lamb."

Everyone but the ship went silent. The timbers groaned, the water slapped the sides, and the pulley squeaked as Ian and Magnus continued to hoist the basket.

Peter stood next to Declan, almost glued to his side. Declan did a strange thing with his eyes. He flicked them downward to the deck. Repeatedly. Was that a signal?

Suddenly, a roar came from behind her. "Put your finger up my arse! Put your finger up my arse!"

She felt the blade leave her neck and O'Malley's grip on her mouth loosen. She understood Declan's signal. The deck. Drop to the deck. Everything seemed to happen at the same time. She slipped to her knees, Declan drew a dirk from the back of Peter's belt and sailed through the air above her with the blade held high over his head. She curled into a ball and shut her eyes. A sickening sound similar to a cleaver smacking the flesh and bone of a pig, followed by a gurgling cry of agony. A heavy body landed on her back, forcing the air from her lungs.

She drew in a breath and called out to Declan.

In an instant, the weight rolled off her back, and Declan was at her side, pulling her into his lap, rocking her, murmuring Gaelic words, holding her tight. Too tight.

"I can't breathe," she said.

When he released her, he fumbled to look at her bleeding neck. "He hurt you. Bloody hell, he cut you. I wish I could kill him a hundred times."

She glanced back at O'Malley's body, the handle of Peter's dirk protruding from the juncture of his neck and shoulder, blood seeping out onto the wooden deck. His blank stare upset her, and she turned her face away.

"Get him out of here," Declan said.

Alex hopped out of the basket and helped Ian pull O'Malley's body away. It took her a moment to piece together that Ian and Magnus had hoisted the basket up with Alex inside. It was Alex who had distracted O'Malley by yelling… What had he said? *Put your finger up my…*

"You three loons, pull yourselves together," Laird John growled.

Alex, Ian, and Magnus stood at the opposite end of the deck, doubled over laughing so hard no sound came out of them. They had turned red in the face and were holding their stomachs. Had they lost their minds?

"What's wrong with them?" Caya asked. She looked to Declan, who, like the others, was shaking with laughter. "I fail to see what's so funny?"

"Ignore them, Caya," Laird John said, and he offered a hand to pull her to her feet.

"Hey," came a call from the waters below.

Caya stepped around the pool of O'Malley's blood and went to the railing.

Below, Vicar James stood in the rowboat, shading his eyes. "What's going on up there?"

. . .

Declan retrieved Caya's ring from O'Malley's coat pocket at her request and slid it on her finger. When he was confident she'd stopped shaking, he took her hand in his and approached his uncle, determined to get the intractable patriarch to allow her to remain aboard ship with him until he went ashore.

"She's mine. I need her with me. I have to protect her."

"Until you're wed, Caya is my responsibility."

"Then let us handfast now. Today."

Taking him aside, his uncle said, "Look at the lass, son. She's been through hell. What she needs is the comfort and care of other women."

His uncle was right. He always was. In the end, he was allowed to hold her for another five minutes before Magnus rowed Caya and Laird John back to shore.

"We'll be together soon. I promise you," he called down. He stood at the railing, watching until he was certain Caya reached the shore safely.

She loves me and that's all that matters.

The vicar had come aboard *The Tigress* to take charge of the dead. He demonstrated the kind of strength and endurance Declan never thought possible in a man of the cloth. While he and his cousins brought the whisky barrels up from the cargo hold, James Oswald tied each body into a canvas hammock and weighted the makeshift shrouds with cannon shot. When Oswald had finished, they gathered on deck for a final prayer before dropping the bodies into the sea. The vicar treated each man with dignity. Declan doubted the pirates would have seen such care had they been hanged publicly.

They let wee Peter sleep cradled in a coil of rope, while the four remaining men, Declan, James, Ian, and Alex, took turns ferrying the casks of whisky from the ship to the beach. Around midafternoon, Peter awoke ravenous. They stopped to eat the bread and cheese Ian had found in the cook's larder.

Alex emerged from the captain's cabin with a bottle. "Wine," he announced. "There's two crates of it. Good, too." He passed the bottle around. "They'd stocked the ship for a long voyage. The charts on the captain's desk suggest they were headed for the Indies."

"There's a fortune in spices, wool, and silk in the hold," Ian said. "And dozens of muskets and ammunition. Nae doubt there's more. I havenae looked in all the crates. All stolen goods, I'd venture."

"What will happen to the ship and the cargo?" Declan asked.

"Law of salvage," Alex said. "It's ours."

They all stopped chewing.

"What do you mean?" Ian asked, his mouth full.

"The ship is ours," Alex said, as if it were obvious to any fool. "Equal partners. All of us that fought for her. You, me, Da, Fergus, Magnus, Hamish, Declan, the vicar, and Peter."

Peter popped to his feet. "Me?"

"Not I," Vicar James said. "I'll take a crate of wine for the church, but I can't be part of this venture."

"What will we do with a ship? None of us kens how to

sail," Declan said.

"Well," Alex said. "We can sell the ship and the cargo and split the profits, and that would be the end of it."

"Or we can sail it." Peter shot both fists in the air in a gesture of victory.

He laughed at the boy's enthusiasm for a moment before he realized the lad was serious.

"We'll hire a crew and an honest captain. We'll sail the ship to Canada or America and sell the cargo." Peter's eyes glittered with excitement. "Then we'll gather another load of furs or tobacco or cotton and sail back to Edinburgh. We'll be rich."

Alex looked around the circle of men. "What do you say, Declan? You'll need someone to ship your whisky. You'd fetch a better price in America."

He nodded, still considering.

"And you, Ian? You're furloughed indefinitely. The rest of us have duties here. You've always wanted to see America. You could be our chief mate, watch over our investment, see we get a good price. Take Peter with you, if you like."

"I'll be your cabin boy," Peter said, breathless. "I'd be a good cabin boy."

Ian laughed. "Nae, Peter. You ken more aboot ships than any of us. You'll be our quartermaster."

Chapter Fifteen

Balforss had been turned upside down with the arrival of four new guests. The staff ran themselves ragged bathing, clothing, and feeding the rescued women. Haddie, the two girls from the kitchen, and the woman from the laundry ran up and down the stairs, carrying buckets of water, armloads of clothing, and trays of food. Everywhere Caya turned, she was bumping into someone shouting down the hallway or bustling in and out of bedrooms. And everyone was talking at once.

"Haddie, I need more hot water."

"Has anyone seen my other stocking?"

"I'll have more tea and perhaps a little jam with my toast."

Caya gave Morag Sinkler her green gown, as she was closest to her size. Then she washed, changed her clothes, and went below stairs to escape the chaos.

She passed the door to the laird's study, where Dr. Farquhar and Flora were tending to Magnus's injury. Magnus bellowed Gaelic words that sounded suspiciously like curses. It was necessary for Dr. Farquhar to shave off Magnus's beard to stitch him up properly, and the angry Scot was having none of it.

"If ye come near me wi' that straight razor," Magnus growled, "I'll ram it up your—"

Unable to hear herself think, she left the entry and wandered toward the back hallway. Her body was at odds with her mind. Too exhausted to sleep. Too weary to keep still. Too relieved not to worry. What was wrong with her?

She groped blindly through a haze of emotions. Guilt over having been the cause of the recent violence was the pervasive feeling, and yet battering away at her guilt was relief that the other women had been saved from what surely would have been a hellish existence. She felt anger, too, and resentment for her brother's selfish behavior, and at the same time a perverse sadness for the loss of Jack. But mostly, she felt loved. Declan still loved her. In spite of everything, he loved her, and she loved him. He'd forgiven her. Could she forgive herself? After all that had happened, would she be right to marry Declan?

She woke from her thoughts standing in the kitchen, wondering how she'd gotten there. Mrs. Swenson had five pots on the boil and was cutting up three ducks for roasting. As harried as the cook was, she found a corner for her to sit.

"There now, lassie. Help yerself to scones and tea." Mrs. Swenson resumed her work on the ducks.

"Thank you, Mrs. Swenson, but I don't think I can eat anything just yet."

"Poor lass. Did they hurt you?" Mrs. Swenson gasped and inspected her neck. "Did someone try to…?"

"Yes, but Declan stopped him."

Mrs. Swenson trilled her relief, grabbed a jar of salve, and applied a gooey dollop liberally to Caya's wound. "Such a fright ye must have had, being taken by pirates, of all things." She stilled for a moment, then cupped Caya's chin in her hand. "That's an awfy sad face for a lass what's getting married soon."

Caya's lower lip trembled. "After Jack and the ship and the whisky…" She swallowed hard. "After everything that's happened, do you think it's right for me to marry Declan?"

"Whyever would you think that?" Mrs. Swenson pulled a stool close and sat. "Have you changed your mind?"

"No. I love him. I suppose I've wanted to be Declan's since the first night I saw him. But Laird John, he doesn't seem to want us to marry. After the battle, Declan asked him again if we could handfast and he wouldn't allow it."

"He told Declan you weren't allowed to wed?"

"Well, no. He said I'd been through too much and I needed to be with the other women."

"Och, lass, that doesnae mean he won't allow the union. The laird's just looking after you. Sometimes men think they know us women. They think we need their protection all the time and that we need to be handled with care. They forget how strong we are. They forget who brought them into the world in the first place." Mrs. Swenson brought the edge of her apron to Caya's face and dabbed away her tears. "If you know in your heart that you're ready to be Declan's wife, then it's time to pack your things and go to him."

Caya searched all over the house and the grounds for Laird John. She checked everywhere. No one had seen him. Finally, she stopped Flora on her way out of Laird John's study.

"If he's not in the house or in the cow byre, he's down by the old mill," Flora said. "There's a spot he goes when he's hiding from me. He thinks I don't know aboot it. Silly man."

Caya carried her travel bag and a basket of food down to the old mill and found Laird John sitting at the river's edge, sipping from a silver flask.

"Did Flora tell you where to find me?"

"Yes."

"She thinks I don't know that she knows about this place, the wee bizzum." He took another pull from the flask and pointed to her bag. "I see you're going somewhere," he said. "Did it get too loud in the house for you, too?"

She set her basket and bag down and sat next to Laird John.

"You had us scared to death with worry," Laird John said, his voice gentle like he was talking to a child. "We thought we'd lost you."

"How can you be so kind after all the trouble I've caused you?"

"Your brother's sins are not yours, lass. You needn't atone for them. He has paid the ultimate price for his folly."

"I'm sorry. I put everyone in danger, and Declan almost lost all his whisky."

"Och. That was only a quarter of his stock. The rest is stashed in other places."

"Oh." She thought for a while and said, "That's a lot of whisky."

Laird John smiled. "You've only been here a little while, *a nighean*, but we've come to love you like a daughter."

"I love you all, too. And I can never thank you enough for caring for me and for saving my life."

"Then why are you leaving?"

"I'm going to live with my husband now. Declan needs me." She squeezed Laird John's arm. "But I didn't want to go without your blessing."

"I knew from the beginning you were perfect for Declan."

"Then why—"

Laird John stopped her with a gesture. "You needed time, both of you," he said. "Declan needed time to realize that one doesn't win a wife in a game of cards and expect everything to unfold like in a dream. He needed to work hard for your hand. And you needed time to know Declan, to understand the man, to believe him worthy of your love."

"I do love him."

"Do ye understand what it means to handfast, lass?"

"Declan said it's like a temporary marriage until a clergyman can perform a ceremony."

"And do you want to marry Declan?"

"I love him, and he loves me."

He leaned down and gave her a whisky-breath kiss on the forehead. "Then you have my blessing."

· · ·

The sun hung low in the west by the time they finished. Ian and Peter remained aboard *The Tigress*, guarding the newest Balforss business venture and arguing about which new name would be best for their merchant ship—*Challenger* or *Sea Wolf.*

Declan, Alex, and the vicar made the last trip to shore with the launch. His shoulders ached as he pulled on the oars.

"Vicar," Declan said, "last night, when I told you I would wed Caya, you offered to sanctify our union."

"Yes."

"Caya would like that…as would I."

Oswald's face rippled with sadness for a moment then brightened. "With joy."

"You're a good man."

Vicar James smiled. "As are you."

"Thanks for helping."

"You can thank me by coming to church regularly."

Declan and Alex laughed.

"What day is it?" Declan asked.

"Saturday," Vicar James said.

"Will you say a few words over Jack Pendarvis's grave

tomorrow?"

"Of course. We'll see him buried in the kirkyard after Sunday service."

They reached the shore and pulled the launch onto the beach. Declan wanted a drink. He wanted to eat. He wanted to sleep. Most of all, he wanted Caya, to lay beside her, feel her skin against his, listen to her breathe.

Hamish and Fergus, God bless them, were waiting on shore to help carry up the last of the whisky. Tired as they were from the strain of the night, they offered to take Jack's body to the undertaker and drive the wagon of casks to the Pentland Warehouse. The whisky would be safe there until Declan could find a better place to hide it.

Gullfaxi and Goliath waited where he and Alex had left them the night before. They climbed into their saddles, stiff-limbed and grunting with effort, and let the horses find their own way home in the twilight while they closed their eyes and swayed in their saddles. They didn't speak the whole way home. He had never known Alex to remain quiet for that long. When they parted company at the juncture to his house, Alex made a guttural sound that Declan took as goodbye.

Back home at Taldale Farm, his stomach ground out a protest when he filled Gullfaxi's feed bin. He slapped the horse on the neck. "You're a good friend, mate."

Stumbling through the kitchen door, he wondered idly who could have left a lamp burning so late at night. When he found supper laid out on the bunker before him, he almost collapsed with gratitude. Bread, a pint of ale, and a covered plate of warm ham and neeps. Beside it, a glass containing a fistful of gowans.

Caya.

Caya had left him supper. No doubt she was just as exhausted as he, but she had gone to the effort of seeing to his comfort. She loved him. His beautiful wife loved him.

Happy tears rolled down his cheeks. He swiped them away and pulled off his boots. She'd left him water and a towel to wash his face and neck. Having no chair, he sat on the floor in front of the hearth and ate. The food tasted like love.

When he finished, he wasn't certain he had the strength to climb the stairs. The fire had been banked for the night. He considered curling up in front of the kitchen hearth. But he knew he wouldn't like waking on the cold kitchen floor, nor would his sister like finding him there tomorrow morning.

He got to his feet, collected the oil lamp and, with eyes half closed, he shuffled through the dining and drawing rooms. When he reached the stairs and grasped the bannister, he paused. Something was different. Someone had left a cloak hanging on the newel post. Had Caya forgotten her clo—

Declan turned his gaze upward and climbed the stairs to the second floor in a dreamlike state. The door to his room was ajar. He pushed it all the way open, his heart thumping hard in his chest. The oil lamp's soft yellow light shone on an angel asleep in his bed.

He set the lamp on the bedside table and watched her for a long while. She stirred, sighed, and opened her eyes. When she saw him, she sat up and patted the pillow. He still wasn't certain if she was real or just a trick the fairy people had played on him.

"Come to bed."

She *was* real. Declan eased himself down on the edge of the mattress, and said, "Will you forgive me?"

"Forgive you for what?"

"I've been stupid about the dream, a right ass. I love you, Caya. Even if I never dreamed you, I would still love you. How could I not?"

She kissed him then. Set her sweet lips upon his. Swiped her delicate tongue across his bottom lip and let out a soft sigh when he trailed kisses down her neck.

Caya reclined on the pillow and pulled back the bedclothes. "Come. Lay your head on my heart."

He crawled into bed next to her. She smelled of soap and clean linen. He draped an arm and a leg over her soft body, then settled his head on her bosom.

Caya hummed a tune, the sweet sound making a soft vibration against his cheek. Words formed, ruffled his hair, and wafted through his consciousness.

And I would love you all the day,
Every night would kiss and play,
If with me you'd fondly stray
Over the hills and far away.

He closed his eyes and sank into the warmth of her body.

• • •

Caya woke with the skylark's song. Cool rays of predawn light spilled across their bed. Declan lay next to her on his back, his lips slightly parted, thick black lashes resting on his cheeks, and his dark beard stubble making the chiseled lines of his face stand out. He was beautiful to her.

Sometime during the night, he had risen and removed his clothes. She admired his bare chest. Dark fur spread out across his muscles like the wings of an eagle, then trailed in a line down the middle of his belly and disappeared under the bedlinens. He was fast asleep. She could lift the bedclothes and peek...

Declan stirred, and she jerked her hand back. He rolled to his side without waking, presenting her with a tantalizing view of his smooth, muscled back and the very top of his... For goodness sake, it was Sunday.

She slid out of bed and tiptoed to her gown hanging on the door. She needed to wash and dress for church. Inside the adjoining room—the room Declan had made for her—she cleaned her teeth and washed her face in the basin.

Caya had just finished tying the garters around her stockings when she heard Declan call out.

"Caya!"

She ran to the open door connecting their rooms. Declan sat up in bed, his hair in tangles around his shoulders. He rubbed his eyes once and stared back at her.

"I thought I dreamed you," he said in a sleepy voice. He let his eyes roam up and down her body. She wore only her shift. He'd never looked at her like that, with such hunger, and though she knew it was sinful, she liked it.

"I was getting dressed for church."

"I'll take you back to Balforss." He threw off his covers and leaped out of bed, remembering too late that he was naked and bobbing about.

She stifled a nervous laugh at having glimpsed his parts in a condition similar to the last time she'd seen them.

"Och, sorry." He grabbed a corner of the bedclothes and pulled it across his hips to cover himself.

"You need to shave first. I'll heat some water." She returned to her room and bent to poke up the fire.

By the heavy thump of his bare heels on the floorboards, she knew he must be dressing. The pace increased to a rapid *fump-fump-fump-fump.* Was he hopping up and down? The floor shook with what sounded like a horse hitting the ground.

"Och!"

"Declan?"

"I'm all right." He thundered into her room, still buttoning the fall of his britches, hands shaking, eyes wild with panic. "Does anyone know you're here? I need to get you back before they find you missing."

She stood and held up her palms to calm him. "There's

no need."

"Jesus, hurry and get dressed. I have to get you back."

"I'm not going back."

Declan froze. "What?"

She smiled. "I live here now. I'm your wife."

His mouth hung open. Did he not believe her? Did he not understand her? Or had he changed his mind? "You do still want me to be your wife, don't you?"

An odd look appeared on Declan's face. One she couldn't interpret. "Well now," he said. "That all depends."

"Depends on what?" Oh God. Was he changing his mind? Did he wake up and realize she was a fool for trying to save her brother?

"I ken you love me, but I need a wife who will trust me," he said and took a step closer. "I ken it's a hard thing for you to trust given all the lies your brother had told you. And me, I was wrong to take you from him the way I did. I gave more thought to my daft dreams than I did for your happiness and I'm sorry for that, but…"

"But what?" Hot tears pricked at the corners of her eyes.

"When I thought you were lost to me, when I thought I'd never see you again, I knew that I loved you more than my own life. I was ready to toss my life away to save you. That's how much I want you, need you, love you." He held out his hand just like that fateful morning in front of the Crown Tavern. "So, I'm asking you, do you trust me?"

Caya swallowed back her tears and slipped her hand into his. "Yes. I trust you with my life. And if you'll have me, I gladly give you my heart, my body, and my soul. Your love is all that I want in this world. All I shall ever need."

Declan moved so fast she had no time to prepare. Her feet left the floor, and she was in his arms, her body crushed to his hard chest, his lips covering hers, kissing her, kissing her until she nearly fainted from his passionate embrace.

When at last he broke their kiss, she gasped. He nuzzled her face, and his breath roared in her ear.

"I feared this day would never come." His voice was light and trembly. In fact, his whole body shook. He slowly released her and let her slide down his body until her feet met the floor. When she was steady on her feet, he held her by the shoulders and asked, "How?"

She cupped his handsome face in her hands. "Shave and finish dressing. I'll tell you on our way to church."

• • •

Declan listened to Caya's story, enjoying the sound of her voice and the feel of her warm body bumping against his in the saddle. He had positioned her in front of him, her soft bum tucked snug between his legs. Occasionally—often—his thoughts strayed from her account to her round bottom.

"Declan?"

"Huh?"

"Are you still listening?"

"Oh, aye. What did my uncle do after he gave you his blessing?"

"He drove me to your house in the carriage."

"*Our* house," he stressed. Taldale was their house, together.

The closer they got to kirk, the more he became aware of the indecent condition of his body. He stopped Gullfaxi and dismounted.

"But, the church is still half a mile away," she said.

He adjusted the front of his trousers as discreetly as possible. "I'm having trouble controlling my need for you when you're so close, ken?"

She blushed a pretty pink.

They continued down the road, Declan holding the reins,

Caya perched on Gullfaxi's broad back.

"Are we really married?" she asked him.

He squinted up at her. "We're handfast. That's the same as marriage."

Her eyebrows, so blond they were barely visible, drew together and her head tilted slightly. "That's odd."

"What?"

"I don't *feel* like I'm married."

He liked the playful tone in her voice.

"That's because I havenae made you my wife, yet."

"I thought I was your wife already. You said handfasting was the same as—"

He reached up and pulled her down from the saddle. He needed to kiss her, and he didn't care how aroused he got. He had to tilt his head sideways to reach her mouth, as her foolish bonnet was in the way. *Why do women wear these?*

When he kissed her, she responded, opening to him like a flower. Oh God. He thought his heart might burst from her kisses. Would he expire altogether when they actually made love?

"I mean, I'm going to bed you."

Her lips formed a pretty *O* and he kissed them quick.

"After kirk, I'm going to steal you, take you home, and make you my wife. Did you forget about that part?"

Her eyes lowered, and her color rose. "No." She bit her bottom lip, trying not to smile.

He growled in her ear. "Good. Because I havenae stopped thinking aboot what you'd look like naked since I first laid eyes on ye."

She drew her head back, eyes wide and gape-jawed. "Is *that* what you were thinking when you looked at me that night in the tavern?" She sounded scandalized, and it made Declan laugh.

"Oh, aye."

"Shame on you."

"I caught a glimpse of that fine ass of yours yesterday when they pulled us out of the drink, your shift all wet and clinging to those plump round—"

"Declan Sinclair, it's Sunday, for heaven's sake," she scolded.

"I think aboot you naked when I'm in kirk, too."

Caya burst out laughing and clapped both hands over her mouth.

"I'll probably go straight to hell for it, but I'll go gladly. There's no man on earth luckier than me today."

She took her hands from her mouth, and he saw her face change like quicksilver. Her chin dimpled, and her eyes welled with tears.

Alarmed, he said, "Caya, I was teasing you."

She sniffed and shook her head. "I know. I just love you so much, is all."

• • •

They waved to his uncle John, walking into kirk with a line of six women trailing him, looking like a covey of quail. When he cast a look over his shoulder at Declan, he lifted the dreaded eyebrow and then shook his head with resignation. This was perhaps the one and only time he had triumphed over Laird John's will. The man looked tired. When did his uncle get so old? He had never noticed until now.

Declan spotted Margaret and Hamish, as well as his oldest sister, Lizzie, and her husband, Connor. He had completely forgotten he'd asked them to come to kirk when he visited them on Friday. Shite! He slapped a hand to his coat pocket. Amazing. His mam's wedding ring was still there. It was a miracle he hadn't lost it in all the chaos of the last two days.

He stood back when his family approached, allowing

Margaret to introduce Caya to Lizzie and Connor. Caya greeted them all and then thanked Hamish, whom she'd met yesterday on the beach, for his role in her rescue.

Margaret whispered in Declan's ear, "I wish Mam was here. She would love Caya." A mixture of pride and profound sadness threatened to undo him. Margaret was right. His mother would have loved to be here, embrace his new wife, welcome her to his little family.

"Are you watching, Mam?" he whispered. "Do you see how lovely she is?"

They slid into the pew next to Alex. His cousin heaved a deep sigh of relief when Caya took Jemma from his arms.

"Where's Magnus?" he asked.

"Doctor had to shave him to stitch his face. Said he wasnae going out in public until his beard grew back."

Their shoulders bounced with silent laughter.

"Ian and Peter still aboard *The Tigress*?"

"I assume so. Lucy and I are taking the young girl, Morag, back to her family in Wick after services. Sorry we cannae stay for Jack's funeral."

"No mind."

"I'll hire a captain and crew while I'm in Wick and bring them back to *The Tigress*."

"We're really doing this, then?"

"Oh, aye. Da, Fergus, and Hamish want no part of it, but we've got their approval—the four of us and wee Peter. I ken we're sea merchants now." Alex glanced at the crucifix hanging above the altar and crossed himself. "God willing."

Vicar James expressed his sorrow for the loss of Caya's brother. "The body of John Michael Pendarvis will be entered into the ground immediately following services, after which the congregation is invited to the home of Laird and Lady Sinclair of Balforss to mark his passing."

Caya's head whipped around in Declan's direction,

the question in her eyes, *Did you do this?* He shrugged his denial. Then they both looked to Uncle John seated in the pew in front of them. The laird turned and blinked a slow acknowledgment. Caya reached out and put a loving hand of thanks on his uncle's shoulder.

The vicar continued with, "On a happier note, it is with joy I publish the banns of marriage between Declan Sinclair and Caya Pendarvis." James Oswald smiled at them, warm and sincere without any trace of regret. "This is the first time of asking. If any of you know cause or just impediment why these two persons should not be joined together in Holy Matrimony, ye are to declare it."

After services, a stream of people alternately offered them condolences and congratulations. He hadn't expected this outpouring of sentiment from his neighbors. Something the size of his fist had lodged in his throat, making it impossible to talk. Caya squeezed his hand and expressed thanks on his behalf, just like a wife. The reminder of what would happen when he took her home tonight spread through him like a swallow of good whisky.

Caya left his side once to say a tearful goodbye to Morag Sinkler.

"We'll see each other again," Morag called to her. "We're sisters of the heart now." The lass threw kisses and waved as the carriage rolled away.

With any luck, Morag would forget the trauma of the last two weeks and live a happy life. He wasn't as sure about the other three, as their ordeal had lasted longer aboard *The Tigress.* Caya, thank the Lord, had spent less than a day in captivity. She had been shaken, saddened, and angered by the ordeal, but he was confident he could erase her bad memories with his love.

Jack's burial was attended by few. Either people knew about Jack's misdeeds and wanted to steer clear, or they were

eager to get to Balforss for Mrs. Swenson's victuals and Laird
John's ample supply of whisky. Either way, he was glad for the
privacy. Again, Vicar James showed his kindness by offering
prayers and words of comfort at Jack's graveside. Caya cried
only a little for Jack, and Declan was glad he could put his
arm around her, comfort her, hold her. He would hold her
forever if she would let him.

What started as a post-funeral reception devolved quickly
into a celebration of Declan's engagement to Caya. Balforss
halls echoed with laughter. The women gathered around
the dining table havering and serving up plates of food as
fast as Mrs. Swenson and her kitchen staff could produce it.
Their chatter took on a soothing musical quality that made
Declan's heart ache with joy. How odd, he thought, to feel so
happy and contented it hurt.

Men crowded the laird's study, telling jokes, repeating
war stories, shouting friendly challenges. Laird John shone
with happiness, not even minding that the guests had drained
seven bottles of whisky and the last of his brandy. By late
afternoon, Niall Ramsay had won a considerable amount
of money arm wrestling anyone fool enough to take him
on. Ramsay wouldn't have stood a chance against Magnus.
Magnus had arms the size of tree trunks. Why the devil
wasn't his cousin here? Ah, yes. Something about hiding his
shaved face. What a numpty.

Declan and Caya spent most of the day in the middle
of the two groups. They huddled together seated on the
staircase in the grand entry hall of Balforss where they could
see all the comings and goings of their family and guests.
They shared a plate of food and sipped from the same glass
of whisky for hours, as Caya didn't like spirits, and he had no

intention of putting on a poor showing on his wedding night due to over-imbibing.

Around ten o'clock in the evening, Caya excused herself and went above stairs to say good night to the remaining three women they'd rescued from *The Tigress*. When she returned, she took her place beside him, slumped against his side, and yawned.

"Time to go?" he asked.

She lifted her sleepy face and nodded.

"Nephew," boomed a voice from the study. His uncle appeared at the door.

"Yes, Uncle."

"Have ye said the words?"

"The words?" What the hell did Uncle John mean? Declan had been talking all day long. He'd run out of words.

"You have to make your vows in front of witnesses to handfast properly." Uncle John crooked an impatient finger at them. "Come here, you two."

He and Caya stood and crossed the entry floor to his uncle. The other guests, having heard Laird John, squeezed out of the study and dining room to crowd around them in the entry.

"Everyone," Laird John started, "Declan and Caya would like to handfast with you, their friends and family, as witness. Declan, Caya, make your vows to each other now so that your union will be recognized by all and blessed by God."

He hadn't expected this to happen. He'd assumed handfastings were private things between lovers. But his laird had just given him what sounded like an order and everyone was watching.

He took both of Caya's hands in his and gazed into her wide blue eyes. "Caya, I will give you the church wedding you deserve, but until then, I take you as my wife and promise to love you in this life and the next."

Caya continued to smile at him until Uncle John leaned over and said, "Now you, lass."

"Oh yes," she said and dashed away a tear. "Declan, my love, I cherish the day you found me and claimed me for your own. I take you as my husband and promise to love you in this life and the next."

Uncle John took the tartan sash from his shoulder and wrapped it around their wrists. "Now you are bound one to the other with a tie not easy to break. May you grow in wisdom and love, may your marriage be strong, and may your love last forever."

For a few seconds, no one spoke, no one breathed. Then Laird John said, "I ken it's safe for you to kiss your wife now, nephew." The room erupted with chatter. Amid the din of cheers, well-wishes, and toasts to the newly bound couple, Declan noticed a curious smile on Caya's face.

"What is it?" he asked.

"I just realized something," she said dreamily. "You *are* the last man in the world I will ever marry."

• • •

Caya dozed in the saddle, cradled against Declan's chest, for most of the ride back to Taldale. While he put away Gullfaxi for the night, she lit two candles, left one behind for her husband, and made her way above stairs to their bedchamber. Tonight was her wedding night, and, to her surprise, she wasn't nervous at all.

Maybe it was too much of Laird John's good whisky, or maybe it was simple exhaustion, but she was looking forward to the feel of Declan's rough hands on her skin. She smiled to herself while she washed and undressed. Which part of her would he touch first? At the sound of his footsteps on the stairs, she slipped beneath the coverlet and blew out her candle.

"Caya?"

"Yes."

"Are you in bed?"

"Yes."

"Are you asleep?"

She stopped herself from laughing. He might be nervous, and she wouldn't want to make it worse. "No."

"Oh." He exhaled. "Good."

He glided through the bedchamber door, holding the candlestick aloft. Damp ringlets clung to his forehead. He'd washed in the kitchen before he'd come to her, lovely man.

Passing the candle in front of the bed for a closer look, he asked hesitantly, "Are you naked under there?"

She pulled the sheet tighter to her chin. "Yes." *Am I being too bold?*

He swallowed. "Good."

He set down the candle, and in one rapid, yet surprisingly graceful motion, he dropped his trousers, flung off his shirt, then stood for a moment—naked, aroused, chest heaving—before lifting the bedclothes and sliding underneath.

They met full-on like two magnets—lips to lips, chest to chest, and hips to hips. The shocking heat of his body made it difficult to sort one sensation from another. Chest hair prickling her nipples. Slippery tongue swiping at her lips. Rough hands cupping her bottom. The long, hard length of him pressing into her thigh, demanding attention. She wanted to touch him there. Is that what he wanted?

She slid her right hand down his muscled flank. He seemed to know her intent for he rolled onto his back, opening himself to her. It jumped into her palm and Declan groaned with the contact. He wrapped his own hand around hers, closing her fingers tight around his stiff girth, and gently pumped. The flickering wick illuminated his face, brow wrinkled with intensity, mouth open and panting lightly between moans and what sounded suspiciously like Gaelic curses.

He raised his head and tossed away the bedclothes, exposing their bodies to candlelight. An ecstatic gasp escaped, and she clamped her lips together. Only in her wildest erotic fantasies had she ever imagined giving Declan pleasure in this way.

"Oh Jesus God, I love you, but you have to stop." He pulled her hand away and collapsed back against the pillow.

"Did I hurt you?"

He kept his eyes closed and laughed. "No, love. It felt so good I almost came undone." He brought her hand to his lips and kissed it, took a deep breath, rolled to his side and aimed his large brown eyes at hers.

She grabbed a handful of coverlet to pull over her body. Without breaking his gaze, he stayed her hand and pushed the coverlet away. After a moment, he sat up for a better look, letting his eyes roam the length of her nakedness. He leaned his weight on one hand, and with the other traced a long finger around her nipples.

"I have the most beautiful wife in all of Christendom."

Like Declan, she closed her eyes and concentrated on her own pleasure. His cool wet lips captured her right nipple and sucked.

"Oh." She slapped a hand over her mouth.

Declan released her nipple with a kiss and rumbled in her ear. "Dinnae quiet yerself, love. There's only me and the chickens to hear you. The chickens willnae mind, and I want to hear the sounds ye make when I love you." He tugged her hand away from her mouth.

Through shallow breaths, she said, "Blow out the candle."

"Nae. You're too beautiful. I want to look at you. Just like this. Wanting me like I want you." He nudged her legs apart with his knee. A big, warm hand slid between her thighs, covering her most private parts, and her back arched up off the mattress. Then, she lost all reason.

She had no words to describe what he did next. Only that it was exactly what she wanted, what she desperately needed. She groaned and laughed and said a few French words. She remembered shamelessly spreading her legs wider and begging for more. When she came apart in his hand, she called out his name. Many times. Loud and clear.

Once she'd recovered, Declan settled over her, his legs between hers, and guided the center of his pleasure inside her with slow, careful pushes. It was, as Lucy had once mentioned, uncomfortable at first. His progress met with resistance, and he pushed until she yelped at the popping, tearing sensation.

Declan stopped and whispered in her ear, "Now, you're truly mine, *mo chridhe*."

His pace, his heartbeat, and his breathing picked up. Like her, he made sounds of pleasure. She distinctly heard the words *tight* and *slippery* among other Gaelic phrases. Her own pleasure soared, although not nearly like it had when he'd touched her. At the last, his whole body stiffened and jerked. He panted, "I love you, love you, love you," repeating his declaration over and over until he had at last recovered.

She wiped the sheen of sweat from his forehead and held his face in her hands. "And now, *you* are truly mine, my heart."

Caya woke the next morning buried under mounds of blankets and sheets. Declan's bed smelled deliciously of him and their lovemaking. She smiled and stretched, expecting to roll to her side and snuggle against his warm, naked body. But the furrow in the mattress where he had slumbered was empty and cool. Where was he?

She sat up quick and hissed. Declan's attentions had left her feeling a little raw this morning. She hadn't minded at all last night. He'd been so tender, so gentle, and then, in the end, so ardent, how could she have refused when he'd asked to do it a third time?

Truth be told, she'd enjoyed their union more than she'd expected. At first, when her body had tingled and trembled in his hands, she thought she might be making too much noise. But Declan reassured her between his kisses she could cry out as loud as she liked. Even now, her nipples tightened remembering the assortment of words he'd called out just when he... She stifled a wicked giggle.

Wood creaked as bare feet thudded up the staircase. He was trying not to wake her, tiptoeing around in the next room—her room. What on earth was he doing in there? Then a long splash of water and the clunk of a bucket.

"Declan?"

He appeared at the doorway bare legged, bare chested, wearing only a kilt, and grinning like he'd just done something naughty. "Morning, love."

"What are you wearing?"

He crossed his arms and leaned against the doorjamb, trying to look casual. "My philibeg."

"I beg your pardon."

"My uniform kilt from when I was in the army. Margaret collected the laundry this morning. All my trousers are in the wash."

A jolt of alarm sang through her body. *Margaret? Doing the laundry?*

"But I'm your wife now. I should take care of things. What time is it?" She clutched the sheet to her breast and scanned the floor. Pointing to a pile of linen, she said, "Quick, hand me my shift. I need to get dressed."

Her husband launched himself from the doorway, took two long strides, and leaped onto the bed like a cat. She squeaked and scooted backward against the headboard.

"Declan Sinclair, you can't possibly want to do it again. It's broad daylight."

"Oh, aye." He kissed her forehead. "I'd take you at any hour anywhere." He hooked a finger around the sheet and tugged it away for a peek. "Because if I *wanted* you before last night, I burn for you now." He cupped a hand under her breast and kissed her until she moaned and arched into his palm.

When he released her, he tossed away the bedclothes in one sweep of his long arm. She yelped and pulled her knees up to her chin to cover herself reflexively.

Laughing, he scooped her into his arms and lifted her off the bed.

She felt weightless for a moment, and then she panicked. "What are you doing?" Had she driven her husband mad with lust? He said he would take her anywhere. Would he carry her outside and have her in the garden?

"Relax, love. I have a surprise for you."

He carried her into her special room and set her on her feet in front of her French bathing tub. Steam rose from the water's surface. A sacrifice of several dozen decapitated daisies floated on top.

Declan was suddenly bashful. "Margaret said every bride needs a good soak after…after…"

She kissed him. Her darling husband had no trouble making love to her. But for some reason he couldn't find words to talk about it. He quickly shed his reserve and let his hands slide down to cup her bottom and pull her against his aroused…

"What do you call your private parts?" Her hand traveled to the stiff bulge pressing into her middle to make it clear what she meant.

He took a sharp intake of breath, closed his eyes, and went still. "Erm...that's my cock," he said with effort.

"I love you, husband. And I'm very fond of your cock."

Declan's eyes flew open. She chuckled, pleased to shock him. Caya stepped over the edge of the tub and lowered herself into the water with a sigh. "Oh, thank you. This is wonderful."

He knelt on the floor beside the tub, cupping water, drizzling handfuls on her shoulders and down her arms. After a long while she opened her eyes. He was staring at her, adoring her. He plucked a daisy from the water and caressed her puckered nipple with the soft petals.

"I'll be riding into town to see the chair-maker today. This house needs furniture."

"Do you want me to come with you?"

"A'course. We'll have him make whatever you like."

"We need a dining room table with at least two chairs. Maybe four," she said absently.

"We'll need seven."

She stroked his cheek. "I think four will do."

He shook his head as if she hadn't understood him. "Nae. We'll need seven." He reached into the water and placed his palm on her belly, never breaking his gaze.

Caya gasped. "Declan, did you have another dream?"

He lifted his left hand out of the water and spread his fingers wide. "Five," he said, and then he smiled. One of his irresistible smiles. The kind that made her smile back.

Epilogue

Caya entered the kitchen just as dawn streaked through the crack in the shutters. She flipped the latch and swung them open, bathing the room in a pale light. She shrieked when a tartan heap the size of a sleeping cow shifted and rolled over on the floor to her left.

"Magnus, you scared the life out of me," she rasped, clutching a hand to her heaving chest.

A thunder of footsteps from above signaled her cry had roused her slumbering husband.

"Caya!"

"It's all right. It's only Magnus," she called and turned back to Declan's massive cousin. "What are you doing sleeping on my kitchen floor?"

Declan burst into the room with dirk in hand and not a stitch of clothing. "What's amiss?" He gave the impression of a lunatic, with eyes wild and snarled hair sticking out every which-way.

"It's just Magnus." She tossed Declan a kitchen towel and he clutched it to his privates.

"Why's he here?"

"I'm sure he'll tell us over breakfast, but you need to get dressed first."

Deeming the threat neutralized, Declan nodded, turned, and casually strolled away. She took a moment to admire his slim backside. His smooth white bum looked so vulnerable when he was naked.

A few mild oaths rumbled behind her—Magnus using the center workbench to pull himself to his feet. To watch him, one might think Atlas had the easier of the two tasks. But what really gave her pause was when he pushed his own sleep-tousled hair from his face.

"You...you shaved," she stammered, and recalled the set-to he'd had with Dr. Farquhar after the battle on board *The Tigress*. The doctor had insisted he needed to shave Magnus in order to stitch his wound, and Magnus had insisted the doctor soak his head in turpentine. Dr. Farquhar had obviously won. That was only a few days ago. "I've never seen you without your beard. You look so different."

The big-but-no-longer-burly man closed his eyes and deflated. "Oh God. Not you, too."

"I'm sorry. It just takes some getting used to, is all." She shook off the initial shock of the dramatic change in a man she thought she knew well. "The cut on your face is handsome—I, uh—I mean—" She took a breath. "The cut is healing nicely."

Magnus scowled at her. "Thanks." His gaze flicked to something above her head.

She swung around to find her husband, now dressed in trousers and a rumpled shirt from yesterday. She hadn't heard him approach in his stockinged feet.

Like her, Declan was taken aback by the change in Magnus. "What happened to you?" he asked.

Caya dragged over the milking stool and the upturned

wooden box they'd been using in lieu of furniture until their new chairs arrived. "Sit. I'll have tea ready in no time." She hung the kettle over the flame, poked up the fire, and set the cast-iron girdle in the embers to heat. By the time she finished grinding the beans, the two cousins had settled in.

"I heard you wouldnae leave your cot until your whiskers returned." There was a teasing tone in Declan's voice, a dangerous thing to poke fun at Magnus in his irritable condition.

Magnus shifted, and the stool groaned under his weight.

"I came to congratulate you. I hear you two handfasted three days ago." Magnus smiled up at her. "You see? Did I not tell you his dreams always come true?"

"That doesnae explain why you slept on my kitchen floor last night," Declan said, his voice flat and demanding.

Magnus launched himself off the stool on a growl and paced the room, his size making the kitchen look tiny by comparison. Caya judged his agitated state may have been triggered by something embarrassing, something he was reluctant to share. Since Magnus didn't look like he was ready to talk anytime soon, she handed Declan the egg basket.

"Would you go, dear?"

"Me?"

"Yes, please." She poured boiling water over the tea leaves in the pot.

"But I cannae find my boots."

"They're right outside the door where you left them."

He grumbled something in Gaelic and dragged himself outside.

As soon as he'd gone, she set the kettle down and gave Magnus a stern look. "If you won't talk to Declan, talk to me. What's going on?"

He stopped pacing and folded his tree-trunk arms across his chest. "They willnae leave me be."

"Who won't leave you be?"

He pointed in the general direction of Balforss and leaned forward. "Those women," he said, as though speaking of monsters.

"The women you rescued from the pirate ship?"

"Aye." He folded his arms again and thrust out a belligerent chin.

"Do you mean Miss Mary and Lady Charlotte are bothering you?"

"Aye," he said with more force.

"What are they doing to vex you?"

"They keep bringing me *food*." He might have said they kept bringing him snakes, he was that appalled.

"Really?"

"Aye, they do."

Odd. She'd never known Magnus to complain about *too much* food.

He further reported his torture included idle chat, as well. "They stand at my door and ask, 'Are ye well, Mr. Sinclair?' and, 'You were so brave to save us, Mr. Sinclair,' and, 'How can we ever thank you, Mr. Sinclair?' Three times a day for the last three days. I couldnae take it any longer. So, I came here to find some peace."

"Miss Virginia brought you food, too?" She didn't doubt Mary and Charlotte would chase after Magnus, but Virginia?

He shifted his weight to the other foot and spoke to the floor in a volume she could barely register. "She's the only one who hasnae dogged me." As embarrassment spread across his face, Caya glimpsed a moment of unguarded affection for the willowy English woman.

"I see." She poured them tea and pointed to his stool. He sat without protest, waiting while she retrieved the cream and joined him. "Do you *want* Miss Virginia to dog you?" she asked and put a dollop of cream in his cup.

"She would never. She's too dignified."

He was right about that. Of all the rescued women, Virginia was the most levelheaded, the one who held the respect of the others.

"Have you spoken to her?"

"Once. Twice actually. But the first time was on board *The Tigress* in the middle of the stramash, so that hardly counts." His mood lightened as he warmed to the subject of Virginia Whitebridge.

"Tell me about the second time," she pressed.

He leaned forward and rested his elbows on his knees. He gently rocked side to side, smiling at the fire as if revisiting a pleasant memory. "She um…she held my hand while the doctor stitched me up."

"Were you that afraid?"

"Dinnae be daft," he said, offended.

"Then why did she hold your hand?"

"Auntie Flora made her hold my hand and talk to me, distract me so I wouldnae dunt Dr. Farquhar on the head." He turned and complained, "Did ye ken that bastard scalped me while I wasnae looking?"

"You mean, while you were looking at Miss Virginia," she teased. Pink patches bloomed on his naked cheeks. How often had his blush gone unnoticed before having his beard removed? She sipped her tea and motioned for Magnus to try his. "You know, maybe Miss Virginia is waiting for you to call on her."

"I cannae."

"Why?"

Magnus rolled his eyes and pointed to his face.

"I don't understand."

"I need to wait until it grows. I look better with it."

Caya sat back in her chair. Why on earth would he want to hide his handsome face behind—?

"When was the last time you shaved?"

He shrugged. "I cannae say as I've ever scraped my face."

"Have you seen your reflection recently?"

He squinted a suspicious eye at her as if she had it in mind to lay some sort of trap.

Caya grabbed his hand, yanked him to his feet, and dragged him out of the kitchen.

"Cousin, where are you taking me?" he asked, stumbling through the house after her. When she got to the staircase, he resisted. "I've seen the second floor."

"Follow me," she commanded.

After much tugging and cajoling up the stairs, she shoved the monolith into her room and positioned him directly in front of her mirror.

"There now. Look at yourself."

Magnus stood transfixed, staring at the stranger in the glass. He must not have seen himself in years.

"Do you still think you look better with your beard?"

He turned his head to one side, then the other. "I'll be damned."

"You'll be dead if you dinnae take yourself oot of my wife's boudoir." Declan stood in the doorway, legs spread wide and arms akimbo, looking both angry and dumbfounded. "I love you, well, cousin, but Caya is *my* wife. I'm no' sharing her. You'll have to find your own woman."

Magnus tore himself away from his reflection and lurched toward Declan. "I came to ask you, have you had any dreams about me, man?"

Declan relaxed his stance but made no response.

"I ken you had the dream about Alex and Lucy having a bairnie, and then you dreamed Caya was your wife…" He swallowed audibly. "So, I was wondering, did you dream anything of me?"

Magnus waited, hope-filled eyes fixed on Declan. But her

husband didn't blink or flinch. He didn't move a muscle.

At last, Declan swallowed and shook his head. "No. Sorry. Nae dreams."

The big man gave him a faint smile and nodded. "I see. Nae worries," he said, his voice clipped and low. "I'll be off." He slipped out of the room and barreled down the staircase.

"Husband?" Declan wouldn't meet her gaze. "Why did you lie to Magnus?"

Author's Note

Balforss is a fictional place based on a real country home hotel. Forss House Hotel is located at the Bridge of Forss approximately four miles west of Thurso in Caithness. I had the pleasure of staying there twice and highly recommend it to anyone visiting the northernmost reaches of Scotland. This magical place gives the Balforss novels their texture and, I think, their soul.

Acknowledgments

My sincere thanks to Red Oak Writing Studio, Wisconsin Romance Writers, Editor, Erin Molta at Entangled Publishing, and my agent, Cassie Hanjian at DeFiore and Company. To our friends and family, my husband and I express our deepest thanks for their love and gentle support.

About the Author

Jennifer Trethewey is an actor-turned-writer who has moved her performances from the stage to the page. In 2013, she traveled to Scotland for the first time, where she instantly fell in love with the language, humor, intense sense of pride, and breathtaking landscape. Her love for Scotland has been translated into her first series of historical romance novels, The Highlanders of Balforss.

Trethewey's primary experience in bringing the imaginary to life was working for one of the most successful women's theater companies in the nation, where she was the co-founder and co-artistic director. Today she continues to act, but writes contemporary and historical fiction full-time. She lives in Milwaukee with her husband. Her other loves include dogs, movies, music, good wine, and good friends.

Don't miss the **Highlanders of Balforss** *series…*

TYING THE SCOT

Discover more Amara titles...

LADY EVELYN'S HIGHLAND PROTECTOR
a *Highland Hearts* novel by Tara Kingston

Playing bodyguard is not in Gerard MacMasters's plan but Lady Evelyn Hunt is in danger, and it's up to him to keep her alive. After a crushing betrayal at the altar, Evelyn wants nothing to do with love. Kissing a gorgeous rogue is one thing, but surrendering her heart is another. When she stumbles upon a mysterious crime, nothing prepares her for the dashing Highlander who may be her hero—or her undoing.

WHEN A LADY DESIRES A WICKED LORD
a *Her Majesty's Most Secret Service* novel by Tara Kingston

Alexandra Quinn is stunned when the man who'd shattered her young heart rescues her from an intruder at the last minute. Forced to work with the rakish viscount, Alex knows better than to trust Benedict, but the wicked promise in his kiss tempts her. Lord Marlsbrook never wanted to be a hero but a killer has targeted the only woman he's ever loved. He'll do whatever it takes to protect Alex—even from himself.

The Pursuit of Mrs. Pennyworth
a novel by Callie Hutton

Sparks smolder between a PI and his widowed client but neither is looking to form an attachment. Elliot thinks Charlotte is hiding something. Charlotte has no desire to marry again, no matter how handsome and kind he is. The risk to his life and her heart is too great. But more dangerous than a menacing stalker is secrets and if Charlotte's come to light, the passion between them might not douse the flames of Elliot's distrust.

My Scot, My Surrender
a *Lords of Essex* novel by Amalie Howard and Angie Morgan

Brandt Montgomery Pierce is a bastard—and proud of it. Despite the mystery surrounding his birth, he has wealth and opportunity, and wants nothing more. Especially not a wife. Lady Sorcha Maclaren is desperate to avoid marriage to a loathsome marquess, even if it means kissing a handsome stranger. But after the kiss turns into a public embrace, Sorcha and Brandt get more than they bargained for—a swift trip to the altar.

Made in United States
North Haven, CT
26 April 2022

18581820R00217